the house with no rooms

LESLEY THOMSON was born in 1958 and grew up in London. She is the author of several novels, including *A Kind of Vanishing*, which won the People's Book Prize in 2010, and *The Detective's Daughter*, which was published in 2013 and sold over 300,000 copies.

STELLA DARNELL runs a successful cleaning company in west London. Her father was a senior detective in the Metropolitan police. Like him, Stella roots into shadowy places and restores order.

JACK HARMON works the night shifts as a London Underground train driver. Where Stella is rational and practical, Jack is governed by intuition. Their different skills make them a successful detective partnership.

'A gripping, haunting novel about loss and
reconciliation, driven by a simple but clever plot.'
Sunday Times

'The strength of the writing and the
author's brilliant evocation of how a child's
mind works combine to terrifying effect.
A novel one cannot forget.'
Shots Magazine

'Skilfully evokes the era and the slow-moving
quality of childhood summers, suggesting the
menace lurking just beyond... A study of
memory and guilt with several twists.'
Guardian

'This emotionally charged thriller grips
from the first paragraph, and a nail-biting
level of suspense is maintained throughout.
A great novel.'
She Magazine

By Lesley Thomson

Seven Miles from Sydney

A Kind of Vanishing

The Detective's Daughter Series

The Detective's Daughter

Ghost Girl

The Detective's Secret

The House With No Rooms

The Dog Walker

The Death Chamber

The Runaway (A Detective's Daughter Short Story)

Lesley
THOMSON

the house with
no rooms

HEAD
ZEUS

First published in the UK in 2016 by Head of Zeus Ltd

This paperback edition first published in the UK in 2018 by Head of Zeus Ltd

9 7 5 3 2 4 6 8

A catalogue record for this book is available from the British Library.

Paperback ISBN 9781788544740
Ebook ISBN 9781784972202

Typeset by Adrian McLaughlin

Printed and bound by CPI Group (UK) Ltd, Croydon, CR0 4YY

Head of Zeus Ltd
First Floor East
5–8 Hardwick Street
London EC1R 4RG

WWW.HEADOFZEUS.COM

For Mel,
for that walk in Kew Gardens.

And in memory of my mum, May Walker,
for many childhood walks in Kew Gardens.

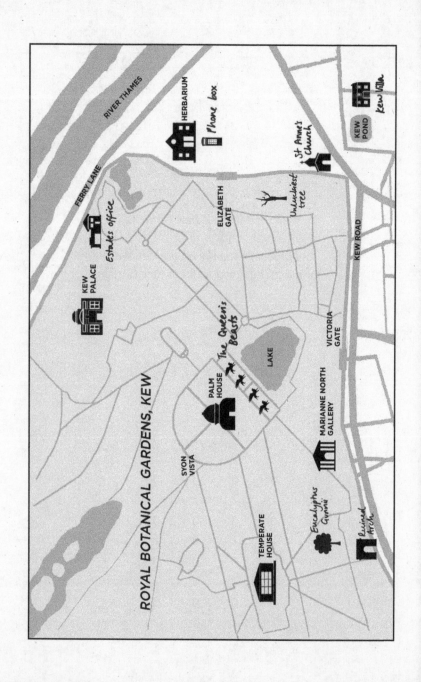

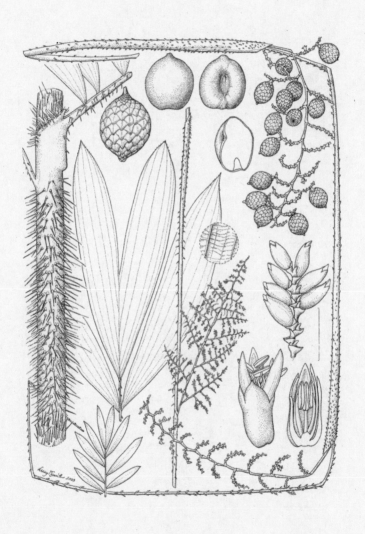

... visitors may, however, be glad to be reminded, that very many of the views here brought together represent vividly and truthfully scenes of astonishing interest and singularity, and objects that are amongst the wonders of the vegetable kingdom; and that these, though now accessible to travellers and familiar to readers of travels, are already disappearing or are doomed shortly to disappear before the axe and the forest fires, the plough and the flock, of the ever advancing settler or colonist. Such scenes can never be renewed by nature, nor when once effaced can they be pictured to the mind's eye, except by means of such records as this ... we have to be grateful for her fortitude as a traveller, her talent and industry as an artist and her liberality and public spirit.

J. D. HOOKER, DIRECTOR
ROYAL GARDENS, KEW,
JUNE 1, 1882.
(*Preface to the first edition of the catalogue for the Marianne North exhibitions of paintings in the Marianne North Gallery, Kew*)

In a world driven by digital content, it must seem strange that botanical illustration is every bit as important now as it was before the age of photography. But an illustration is so much more than a photo – it is a distillation of the most critical features of a plant, selected to help the user understand the species and isolated on a page without the distracting clutter of the surrounding environment. A close collaboration between the artist and the botanist gets the best results ...

DECEMBER 2014
DR WILLIAM BAKER,
Assistant Head of Comparative Plant and Fungal Biology,
the Royal Botanic Gardens, Kew
(From blog on Kew Gardens website: *http://www.kew.org/ discover/blogs/library-art-and-archives/gallery-talk-botanical-artist-lucy-t-smith*)

Chapter One

March 1956

The iron ball suspended from the crane, black against the night sky, was a reverse of the moon. To a nocturnal wanderer, wisping cloud above a chimney could be smoke from a hearth. A laburnum twisted around the windows of one house and a magnolia tree flourished in front of another.

Rounding the corner of the L-shaped street, this rambler might stop short. The windows had no glass and the door of number 21 hung askew. Curtains at number 25 billowed like flitting phantoms. The houses were so many gap-toothed skulls.

Behind façades, walls had been pulverized, the guts clawed out. Against a heap of rubble some wit had propped a door – number 17 – suggesting that our visitor could enter, hear a kettle whistling and smell dinner on the stove.

Foot-scrapers, doormats and clipped hedges indicated a lost existence. A plaster gnome gazed balefully from beneath a laurel bush. Many front doors in the abandoned street were locked. Unable to absorb the uprooting from their homes, residents had secured against intruders and pocketed the key. Useless when intruders came armed with much more than a jemmy.

Rose Gardens, once lively with children kicking balls, playing hopscotch and kiss chase, neighbours chatting, was a 'ghost street'. Only eight houses were occupied, huddled behind a hoarding that offered no protection against swirls of brick dust and the insistent boom of demolition that shook walls, rattled windows and frayed nerves.

The swathe of destruction stretched west towards Hounslow

and east to Hammersmith Broadway as if a warring enemy, oblivious to civilian collateral, had bombed all in its path. Weltje Road, Riverside Gardens, Black Lion Lane, Rose Gardens: street after street had been cut in two or wiped from the map.

This wholesale destruction of urban fabric wasn't military: the 'enemy' was municipal. Leafy Victorian and Edwardian suburbia that had obliterated meadows and orchards were, in their turn, being erased for the extension to the Great West Road.

At number 25, light flickered through plaster-matted curtains. The parlour, once reserved for special occasions and respectable visitors like the vicar or the rent collector, was choked with dust and its waxed floorboards splintered. Two figures, their shadows grotesque in the light of a rubber torch, hunched by a gas fire as if warming themselves at the cold grey elements.

'This is silver. It'll fetch a few bob.' A boy, stocky, bull-like, bit on the casing. 'We've had a good night.' He grinned at no one in particular.

'You'll break it.' His companion ducked out of the light. 'There's someone out there! I said we shouldn't of come.'

'It's my mum's house. We can come when we like.' The stocky boy swung the torch and revealed a zigzagging line of a missing staircase on the wall. There was no ceiling. Above, as if suspended, was a bedroom grate. It was a house with no rooms.

Dangling the trinket from its chain, the boy with the torch crept with feline ease across smashed wood and plaster to the front window. The walls were papered with a pattern of daisies, his mum's favourite flower. With slicked hair, denim jacket and jeans, his chiselled good looks were more James Dean than Cliff Richard. He twitched the curtain as his mum had done every night, waiting for her husband even after he was dead. He scanned the rubble-strewn street with the unblinking eyes of a psychopath for whom even rage is calculated.

'Sweet sixteen, ready with a cheeky grin', Smiler was the apple of his nan's eye, and the bane of his mum's life, 'never here when I need him'.

'You're cray-zee!' He shone the torch into the other boy's face and giggled, a strangely girlish sound given his bulk.

'There!' The other boy pointed across the room. Tall and streaky-bacon thin, he made dipping motions as if he might hit his head on the ceiling that wasn't there.

There was a scuffle and groans. Smiler focused light on an old man with a grey beard and straggling hair. He lay collapsed on boards where there had once been a bed-settee on which the cat would preen itself. Closer inspection showed that his lined face betrayed experience, not years. He was in his forties, dressed in an ill-fitting single-breasted suit, rheumy eyes flicking about him. His body, although wasted, was taut. He was ready for action, if incapable of taking it. The demob suit and boots with gaping soles identified him as a soldier who, back on Civvy Street, had missed out on the spoils of victory.

'I seen everything. I know the bloke you robbed. He fought at the Somme and at Dunkirk, not like you toe-rags,' he spluttered. 'I'll set the law on you and you'll hand that stuff back.' Energy spent, he sagged against the wall.

'Let's go.' The taller boy tugged at the curtain, peering out.

'You heard, he'll tell the police.' Smiler giggled at the word 'police' as if it were rude.

'Give him that silver thing. It's got initials – it'll be hard to fence.' The reedy boy added plaintively, 'I said we shouldn't have gone and we shouldn't be here.'

'That'll get at least a guinea,' Smiler murmured.

'I'll see you get nothing.' The soldier pointed at the thin boy grasping the curtain. 'I know your dad.'

'You better shut up!' the thin boy jabbered, his fear palpable.

The soldier was scrambling to his feet. 'You're a disgrace to your old man. A snivelling coward. That learning's taught you nothing.' He swayed towards the boy and grabbed his arms. In the crude light, they appeared engaged in a weird and ugly dance before the man crumpled to the floor.

The boy stood above him. Something in his hand glittered in

the torchlight.

'You stabbed me.' The soldier sounded astonished.

'What you gone and done?' Smiler played the torch over the man.

'I tapped him!' His voice reedy, the boy clung to the curtain as if to his mother's skirts, eyes blinking, face chalk-white.

'Help!' The soldier's voice rang out, surprisingly strong. A dark patch spread through his shirt front.

'You did an' all!' Smiler sniggered through fingers clamped over his mouth. He took the knife off the taller boy and, with an easy action, stooped and severed the man's windpipe, stepping away to avoid gouts of blood, black as oil, flooding from his neck. Gurgles carried into the rafters as air bubbled through blood and life ebbed.

The silence was interrupted by a sound that both boys had known all their lives: a flock of geese honking as they flew towards the River Thames.

'He's dead.' The taller boy's own windpipe contracted, his voice reedier still.

Smiler wiped the knife clean on the man's trousers; the fabric was stiffened with dirt. He sucked on his teeth, making a kissing sound. 'He was vermin. A nobody.' He giggled as if the joke were a good one.

'He fought for his country.' The taller boy was shaking. 'I tapped him,' he said again.

'Fought, my eye!' Smiler kicked the dead man's boot. 'State of him. Couldn't fight Hitler's cat!' He sniggered. A tinkling sound.

The dead man's eyes glinted through half-closed lids.

'He's alive!' The taller boy tottered backwards, knocking the torch from the other boy's hand. The light went out.

'Get a grip!' From somewhere in the dark, words swallowed in a gale of merriment.

'We could've talked him out of it.' The bleating boy scrambled in the rubble for the torch.

Smiler found the torch and aimed it at his friend. 'Stop whining.

4

You'll get us strung up. You killed him.' Serious now.

'I didn't mean it!'

'This is *your* knife and, like he said – you heard him – you stabbed him. I put him out of his misery. You're a murderer and a thief. You *perpetrated* two crimes. There's a long word to stick up your jacksy with your highfalutin baloney!' He held the light under his chin, which made him look more of a cadaver than the body at his feet.

'I'll explain to the police,' the taller boy said.

'Listen Swatty-Boy, you're eighteen. You'll hang by the neck until you're dead. I'll get Borstal and walk free.' Smiler pushed the knife into a canvas air raid warden's bag slung across his chest. 'You did right. He was a liability and at this rate so are you. Come 'ere!'

'We could implicate him,' the eighteen-year-old stuttered.

'*Imp-li-cate*? What a whopper!' Smiler jammed the torch against his crutch and did a thrusting motion.

'Leave something we robbed so the police think it was him.' The reedy boy was urgent.

'Like what?' Smiler yawned, bored.

'That watch.'

'Where he's gone, he don't need to tell the time!'

'Like you said, he's vermin. The police won't put themselves out looking for his murderer.' The older boy blanched as if, despite everything, he hadn't realized that it was murder.

'It's a bleeding Rolex!' Smiler protested.

'We've got the cash and the ring. And that silver thing. The watch is worth more as a decoy.'

'OK.' Smiler seemed to see the sense in this. 'We'll use the ring. It comes from your share.' He fished in his bag and eventually found a gold signet ring. He thrust it at his friend. 'You do it, since you're so clever.'

'Do what?'

The other boy giggled, a whinnying. 'Stick it on him!'

Perhaps to get it over with, the older boy quickly grabbed one of the man's hands. It was bony and wasted so the ring slipped easily on to his second finger.

'Get his feet.' Smiler was coldly efficient. 'We need to shift him.'

With trembling repugnance, his friend took hold of the corpse's ankles. A boot slipped off revealing a foot netted in a threadbare sock.

They hauled the man across the floor. The older boy dry-retched as a diabolical stench filled the air.

'You shat your pants!' Smiler laughed gaily.

'It's him!'

'Get a move on, or the watchman will catch you!'

The taller boy faltered. 'When they level out the ground, they'll find him.'

'So you're a road-builder now?' Smiler snarled. 'There'll be nothing left of him. Like you said, if they find him, he's got the ring so they'll think he did the house.'

Neither boy could know that Smiler was right and that it would be twenty years before the body of the soldier was discovered, one summer's afternoon in a very different world.

Much in the scullery was unchanged from when the house had been lived in. A length of fabric was slung in front of the sink. Curtains – decorated with more daisies – framed a window in which there was still glass. Below a geyser was a scouring brush and a packet of Tide. A streak of lime ran from taps in a butler sink. Worn flagstones beat a path to a privy in the yard.

'Be a laugh if Mum was here, cooking up tripe and onions, singing to *Music While You Work*!' Sniggering, Smiler opened a door to cellar steps blocked at the bottom by masonry. The boys heaved the corpse into the cavity. Streams of mortar dust trickled out of cracks in the wall when they trod on loose joists. Shovelling with bare hands, they heaped bricks and wood over the body.

They heard footsteps in the street.

'The watchman!' The older boy was paralysed with panic.

'This way.' Smiler shut the cellar door and went out to the yard. He had often entered and left his mum's house by the back gardens;

his knowledge came in handy now.

They kept in the shadows past the Bemax factory and along the towpath. They climbed the steps to Hammersmith Bridge and, halfway along, stopped by the plaque for the dead soldier. Not out of respect or even irony, but because it was their meeting place.

'Throw the knife in.' The eighteen-year-old pointed at the river below. 'Throw *everything* in. It's evidence.'

Smiler's shoulders shook with laughter. Then he sobered and, eyes glittering, said, 'If I have to tidy up your mess, you pay. I'll hold on to the knife. Call it an investment. We'll stick close, like brothers, yeah? I'm in charge. Agreed?' When the other boy didn't reply, '*Agreed?*'

'Agreed.'

Around the corner from Rose Gardens the St Peter's Church clock chimed three times. Sonorous notes, as if tolling for the murdered dead.

On the ink-black river, a police barge chugged up from Barnes. Lapping from the wash carried on the night air. An officer on the deck scoured Hammersmith Bridge for some lost soul who might, in the blue hours before dawn, leap into the unforgiving waters. He saw no one.

Chapter Two

October 2014

> '...The river, on from mill to mill,
> Flows past our childhood's garden still;
> But ah! We children never more
> Shall watch it from the water-door!

Jack stopped chanting as he was deafened by a piercing whoop-whoop, rising and dipping and rising again. Coupled with a beep, it hurt his ears. A passenger had set off the emergency alarm. It was the soundtrack to Jack's recurring nightmare in which he was driving an empty train through tunnels, thinking: Who pulled the emergency handle? But now he was awake and his train – the last one of the night – had been standing room only to Earl's Court.

He went into textbook mode. He didn't brake – when the P.E.A. sounded, a driver should never stop between stations – but continued 'down road' to Kew Gardens. His watch read '11.43'. One, one, four and three. Numbers were signs. His head throbbed from the noise so that he couldn't make sense of the meaning.

Ninety per cent of emergency alarms, as Jack, a District line driver and trainer for London Underground, would explain to novice drivers, were due to accident or 'malicious intent'. His last two had been a hen party dressed as meerkats who activated it outside Richmond station and an electrical fault at Barking. However, he instructed his students to 'follow the drill because one day the emergency will be real'.

The monitoring system flashed up that the alarm had been set off in the sixth car. This was in the middle section of the train, where regular commuters for Kew Gardens station tended to sit so as to alight by the exit. Pressing the talkback button, Jack spoke into the handset, talking only to those in the sixth car.

'Hello, I am your driver. The passenger emergency alarm has been activated. Please could someone tell me what is happening there?'

Quiet.

'Can anyone hear me?' The clatter of the train came through the handset. Possibly a fault or a lone passenger had pressed the alarm and passed out. In his ear, so close that he looked to see if someone was in his cab, was a whisper:

'*A woman is unconscious.*'

As the train slowed to berth at Kew Gardens station, Jack slammed his palm on the whistle-button and sounded a blast to alert station staff. Addressing all the passengers he told them that there would be a delay. His tone was warm because, as he reminded his trainees, 'if you frighten passengers, you risk them becoming ill too'. He asked for any doctor on board to make their way to the sixth car. Jack was comfortable with emergencies.

At the headwall telephone he updated the signaller at Richmond, the voice from the sixth car replaying in his head: '*A woman is unconscious.*' Someone had used that phrase when his mother died. But he had been a toddler then so couldn't trust his recollections.

Most passengers had left at Gunnersbury. There was no one in his car; only three in the second; one man in the fourth had slept through his announcement. In time to his steps, Jack continued the rhyme in his head. The voice was his mother's, as ethereal as the wind.

'Below the yew – it still is there –
Our phantom voices haunt the air
As we were still at play—'

'What's happening?' A man fell into step with him.

'I'm about to find out, sir.'

'Jack bloody Harmon! What are you doing here?' the man exclaimed and, looking at him properly, Jack's heart sank. Martin Cashman was the last man he wanted to see.

A senior detective in the Met, Cashman had worked with Jack's friend Stella's father, Terry Darnell, and frequently declared that 'Tel was my best mate'. Since Darnell's death three years ago, Cashman seemed to think that it was up to him to look out for Stella. She didn't need looking out for. Cashman made no bones about his dislike of Jack. The feeling was mutual, but when Stella was there, they kept it under wraps. She wasn't here now. The two men bristled.

'This is *my* train.' Jack was the little boy who, some thirty years ago, had built railway tracks in the garden at his school using lolly sticks for struts and dampened earth for mortar. A boy called Simon had scoffed at him. *'There's nowhere for the passengers to get out.'*

'I've left the doors open; they can leave if they want,' Jack snapped at Cashman.

'What?' Whisky-breath.

'The Underground is the jurisdiction of the transport police.' *Go away.*

'I was on my way home. I'm a copper; we're never off the clock. What's occurring?' Cashman's hair was short with a flick at the front and thick with product. He wore a sleek grey suit and pointy lace-ups. Jack had never seen the officer, who must be approaching fifty, looking so smart. His habitual style was the unstudied negligence of creased suits and unkempt hair.

'Shouldn't you be cleaning for Stella?' Cashman kept pace with Jack.

Cashman was a detective, nothing escaped him, so he'd remember that Jack sometimes worked for Clean Slate when he wasn't driving trains. He was putting Jack in his place.

'It would be helpful to have you along until the transport police arrive,' Jack conceded. Cashman would stay regardless of his permission.

A woman in a hi-vis jacket raced up the stairs and through the barriers. It was the station supervisor.

'Hey, Jack!' She greeted him like an old friend. Jack liked her, but, irked by Cashman, couldn't think of her name.

Before he could speak, Cashman gave her one of his winning smiles. 'Detective Chief Superintendent Cashman. Met!'

Jack hoped that the supervisor would tell Cashman her name, but she merely nodded as they stepped into the sixth car. Jack reset the alarm handle and took in the scene.

A middle-aged woman in a beige mac and knee-high boots was crouched beside another woman who was sprawled across the aisle. The woman on the floor wore one black soft-leather loafer; the other shoe wasn't on her stockinged foot. A blue wool skirt had ridden up her legs. Jack shrugged off his fleece jacket and laid it over them.

The supervisor, trained in first aid, was checking the woman's neck for a pulse.

At the end of the car, a man sat behind a glass partition. He held a sheaf of papers, but stared ahead as if considering what he was reading. He appeared oblivious to the emergency. Jack was used to the blank expressions on the faces of people waiting as he brought his train into a station: the immobile, dull-eyed stare, like the sightless gaze of a corpse, detached from the dread reality of rush hour. This was different.

'She's gone,' the supervisor said quietly.

Jack was surprised to see that the detective appeared upset. He too took off his jacket and, exhibiting more tenderness than Jack would have given him credit for, laid it over her face. Gently, he addressed the woman in the mac now hunched on a nearby seat.

'What exactly happened?' Cashman had a notebook and pencil poised.

'Gosh, it was quick. This lady was reading her book. Oh, where is it? There!' She got up to retrieve a paperback lying spine up on the rubber flooring.

'You can leave it there.' Cashman was firm, but kindly. 'Until we know cause of death, it will help if we don't touch anything.'

'Of course.' She folded her arms as if to prevent herself touching anything at all.

Cashman was the good cop, warm and coaxing.

'The doors were closing at Stamford Brook and she jumped on. She asked if the train was going to Richmond or Ealing. I said Richmond. She said, "Thank you so much." I'd had a rotten day in the office and that quite cheered me up. In that way trivial exchanges can.' The woman gave a sudden smile and then pulled at the collar of her mac. 'She said she had a stiff neck,' she added in the whisper that Jack had heard through the handset. 'She said, "My neck is stiff."'

Cashman was jotting busily.

'She dropped her book. We were just outside Gunnersbury. I thought at first that she'd fallen asleep. Idiotic, but I was drowsy myself. Then she slid off her seat. I asked if she was all right, when clearly she wasn't. That floor's hard: it must have hurt.' Tucking a strand of hair behind her ear, she lapsed into pensive silence.

Jack was distracted by the paramedics hefting equipment along the car. Someone gave him back his jacket.

'What time did the alarm go off?' Cashman was pulling on his own jacket.

'Eleven forty-three.' Jack remembered the passenger at the end of the carriage. 'Best talk to that man too.'

'What man?

The seat was empty.

'He's gone.' Jack was uncertain. The glass partition reflected the paramedics. Had there been anyone?

'Stella said you see ghosts,' Cashman remarked in the tone of someone sympathizing that a person got migraines.

Jack caught up with the woman passenger as she was being escorted out of the car by the 'nameless' station supervisor. 'Did you notice a man over there?' He pointed back into the car.

'No! I'm sorry. But, like I say, I nearly nodded off. I've had a horrible day!'

'Leave it.' Cashman was by his side. 'No talk of headless horsemen, OK?'

Had Stella said that he believed in ghosts? Jack was exasperated with Cashman, yet rather pleased that Stella took it seriously enough to have told the detective. A knot of passengers was milling around by the barriers. Jack told them that the train would be going out of service because someone had been taken ill. He waited as they dispersed.

'Speaking of Stella, how is she?' Jack had hoped that Cashman had gone while aware that this hope was absurd.

'Fine.'

'Tucked up in bed asleep, let's hope.' Cashman rocked on his heels.

'Hmm.' Jack doubted it; Stella worked into the small hours, but he wasn't going to say this.

The paramedics carried the woman on a stretcher shrouded with a blanket to the ambulance on the street. A shadow crossed a pool of light on the pavement.

'Hey!' Jack called. But by the time he had got through the barriers, there was no one there. The shadow had been the man from the train. Not a ghost.

The foot tunnel stretched ahead bleak and empty. Jack ran the length of it, his rubber-soled brogues making no sound, and up the other side. Outside the station entrance three of the passengers from his train were getting into a taxi. There was no sign of the man from the sixth car.

Jack returned to the westbound platform.

'Chasing rainbows, Jack Harmon?' Cashman rattled change in his pocket.

Jack had a caustic response, but resisted it. Stella liked Cashman. As Jackie, Stella's PA and one of Jack's favourite people, said, it wouldn't help Stella if he and Cashman sparred with each other. Not that Cashman had such qualms.

'... thinking it's an aneurism. A time bomb that goes off without warning. The End.' Cashman drifted to the barrier. 'Tell Stella hello.' He stopped by a newspaper vendor's box and read the headline. He aimed a kick at the box. The metallic clang rang along the platforms. He hurried down the steps to the footbridge.

There were two ways to cross the platforms at Kew Gardens station: a tunnel and a bridge. Although he loved bridges, Jack always chose the tunnel. Like Stella, Cashman chose the air and the light of the bridge.

'That fellow from the Met stepped up to the plate!' The station supervisor joined him. *Polly*. That was her name. With the name came some key facts. Polly liked dogs and took her holidays in Norfolk where she was doing up a barge.

Jack agreed that Cashman's professionalism couldn't be faulted. Jackie said it was one reason why Stella liked him.

'According to her driving licence, the casualty was fifty-six, same as my mum.' Polly puffed out her cheeks. 'No age at all. Scary, how easy it is to die.'

Jack, whose mother had died in her early twenties, thought fifty-six some kind of age. Had his mother lived to fifty-six, he would remember her. He didn't say that he already knew how easy it was to die. One day you're there and then you're gone.

'Jennifer Day,' Polly said as he was getting into his cab. 'That was her name. I pity the poor sod sent to tell her partner. Have a safe one, Jack. There's a hot milk for you anytime you're passing.'

Picking up speed at Gunnersbury Jack drove through darkened stations to the Lillie Road depot where he stabled the train.

At three in the morning, he was walking along the Fulham Palace Road. Somewhere an engine accelerated; closer a door slammed and a dog barked. A fox slunk across the street and vanished behind dustbins outside a kebab shop. When he reached the bins, Jack couldn't see the animal, yet it must be there. Ahead were the lights of Hammersmith Broadway.

The passenger had worried that the floor was hard. Someone had cared for Jennifer Day in her last moments. There had been no one for his mother. Jack hadn't been there.

When Stella had been told that her dad was dead, Jackie said shock had made her super-efficient. She had taken notes and asked pertinent questions. 'You know our Stella, all over the practicalities!'

A psychotherapist had used dolls to explain to the three-year-old Jack that his mummy wasn't coming back and to encourage him to talk. The Mummy doll had the wrong hair so he knew it wasn't true. She would come back. In his thirties he still found himself hoping this. He saw her in the street, in a passing car and on station platforms. Hers was the figure walking away on the driver's monitor or alighting from the last car. She was always walking away.

Jack wove between the stanchions supporting Hammersmith flyover, avoiding cracks on the bird-shit-encrusted pavement. He caught the headline on a newspaper in the gutter outside Hammersmith station: *Copkiller Walks Free!*

On Black Lion Lane he paused by the sculpture of the Leaning Woman before going into the subway tunnel under the Great West Road.

As he brought his train into stations, Jack made up stories about the people on the platforms. The woman whose ruddy complexion suggested she drank to manage her days; the elderly man with the seventies-style hair who wore shorts regardless of the season. The man whose delicate features were riven by a scar from his scalp to his chin giving him simultaneous expressions: placid and surprised. He didn't need to make up a story about the man in the sixth car. He knew who – or rather what – he was. *He was a True Host.*

A True Host was Jack's term for a man or a woman who will murder or has murdered. He had first seen a True Host when he was a child and the qualities had burnt into his soul. Cold penetrating eyes, neat and tidy, ruthless and a chameleon, a True Host gained trust and murdered with methodical care. A psychopath who felt nothing. Jack's mother's death had equipped him to recognize a True Host in any guise. Unable to stop her dying, he would save others. He couldn't rest. Without the True Hosts' knowledge, he used to hide himself in their homes and be their guest. These days, for Stella's sake – the daughter of a police officer, she was a stickler for the law – he was no longer a guest. He had to find other ways to enter their minds, second-guess their actions and merge with their darkness.

He had once saved a woman from a controlling partner by removing the claw hammer that would have split her skull, but mostly True Hosts already had blood on their hands. He had to prevent more. He might yearn to belong in the light with Stella and Cashman, but his fate was in tunnels not on bridges. Jack's home was the subterranean land of Death. Murder was always on his mind.

In the foot tunnel, his mother sang in his head, soft and melodic:

'How many miles to Babylon?
Threescore miles and ten.
Can I get there by candle-light?
Yes, and back again.
If your heels are nimble and light,
You may get there by candle-light.'

Chapter Three

October 2014

A gust of wind whipped a lock of hair into Stella's eye, making it water. Blinking, she slid open the side door of the van and unclipped the dog's seat belt. Instead of jumping down, Stanley clambered on to her shoulder. Bending to avoid banging his head on the door frame, she banged her own head. At the same time her phone buzzed and beeped from her anorak pocket.

Stella had parked the van in a visitor bay outside Thamesbank Heights. The rectangular block of steel and glass sat atop a grassy slope at the end of a winding drive. The developers had gone bust before the marble steps to the foyer of the 'gated community' and the 'Meditation Garden' on the river side of the building could be constructed. When it rained, water collected in the pit beneath the foyer door. Instead of a seated Buddha in a pond, there was a cumbersome old Sony Trinitron television with wires spilling out, and a fridge without a door colonized by wild flowers: nettles, groundsel, clover and creeping ivy. The wasteland was scattered with drinks cans, food wrappers and other rubbish that had somehow crossed the undulating lawns from the road below.

Stella put Stanley down and he trotted beside her to the back of the van. She mouthed, 'Sit!' and was gratified to see him obey promptly. Last week's obedience class had covered silent commands and Stanley was progressing. She lifted out the cleaning cart and heaved her rucksack on to her back. Miming for Stanley to 'heel', she wheeled the cart along a salmon-pink path of compacted rubber (*non-slip, no weeds,* boasted the brochure) to the glass-plated lobby.

Stanley lifted his leg with a balletic swing against a chunk of granite into which 'Thamesbank Heights' was carved. Jack said it was a tombstone for the defunct company, but he saw death everywhere. Jackie said this was because he had lost his mother so young.

Thinking of this, Stella considered that she hadn't heard from Jack for weeks. She tended to hold him responsible for the patches of 'radio silence' but, as Jackie had carefully pointed out, Stella could contact him. Jack saw signs in everything, about which Stella was sceptical, but his going to ground – aside from going literally underground – couldn't be a good sign. She would offer him a cleaning shift. Stella had firm faith that cleaning was a cure-all.

She would have suggested that Jack do this job, but Tina Banks had specifically requested Stella and, besides, she suspected that Jack didn't much like Tina. Not that he would let it affect the quality of his work. She keyed in the entry code and, commanding Stanley to jump over the pit at the foot of the door – his agility training paying off – she heaved the cart in after him.

Stella was familiar with Tina Banks's corner apartment on the fourth of five floors in Thamesbank Heights (*offering stunning vistas of the River Thames and beyond*), because months ago it had belonged to her. Banks had bought it from Stella. Stanley had peed on the 'headstone' just as he had when he lived there. Tina Banks had taken a liking to him and insisted that Stella bring him when she cleaned the flat. He could 'be himself and visit his old haunts'. Stella hadn't asked what Tina thought Stanley 'being himself' meant. She found bringing him an unsatisfactory arrangement because, despite rigorous training, Stanley was apt to snaffle dusters, chew dustpan brushes and growl at the vacuum cleaner. But Stella tried to comply with clients' requests.

She trundled the cart across the sweep of marble to a row of lifts clad in stainless steel that reflected her approach as a series of warped images like a Hall of Mirrors.

When she had shown her father the brochure for Thamesbank Heights – Stella had purchased her flat off plan – Terry Darnell had commented that the entrance was better suited to an international bank than a place where real people lived. Waiting for a lift, Stella contemplated the sleek décor with the objectivity of absence and saw his point. Few 'real people' lived in Thamesbank Heights. Years after the consortium had gone bust, fewer than half of the apartments were occupied. The emptiness had suited Stella, who didn't want neighbours.

As she got into the lift she remembered that the phone had tweeted when she was in the car park.

It was her mother. Or rather it was a notification from Instagram telling her that Suzie Darnell had added to her 'Down Under' album. Suzie was visiting Stella's older brother, who lived in Sydney. Technically adept, Suzie had embraced Instagram. In the two weeks she had been away Stella had received a stream of images, mostly of her mum – in some disguise or other, she could never be sure if it was her mum – taken against an iconic Sydney backdrop. As the lift ascended, she regarded the latest photograph. Her mum was silhouetted against the white Opera House, arms in the air in line with one of the sails. Stella thought she looked in pain. From the angle, Stella could see it was another 'selfie'. Her mum had acquired a telescopic selfie stick at Heathrow airport. Dale wasn't in the shot, although Stella knew he had taken time off from his restaurant to accompany Suzie on what she called her 'jaunts' around the city. Examining the picture, she saw another shadow in the foreground. So Dale was there. Typical of her mum to take a selfie, but leave out the other person.

The photograph was tinted sepia with high contrast. But for

the tip of the sails on the building, everything – including Suzie – was rendered soft focus. The effect was to propel her mum into the past. This, coupled with the geographical distance from London, made Stella uneasy. Since her dad's death she dreaded anything happening to her mum.

Yesterday's photo, taken in the botanic gardens overlooking Sydney, had been given the Warhol treatment: Suzie Darnell, in Marilyn Monroe technicolour, beneath a tree bright with orange flowers. It was too far away for a selfie stick so Dale must have taken it.

The first time her mum had gone to Australia, Stella had grumbled that Suzie only sent a couple of postcards about feeding plants. As the lift doors opened and she stepped out on to the fourth floor of the apartment block, Stella pondered that postcards were preferable. The photographs depicted a woman who was a stranger to her.

Stanley padded beside her along a carpeted corridor with doors recessed either side giving the impression from a distance that there was no break in the walls. Outside her old flat, Stella scratched keys into two mortice locks, the jangling disproportionately loud in the hermetically sealed space. For security, Terry had advised his daughter fit an extra mortice and a London bar. A velvet 'sausage' draught excluder hampered her opening the door. Stella wouldn't have tolerated it; her staff manual advised that *no action must require another action to be completed.* The draught excluder was an extraneous precaution because with triple glazing and snugly fitting doors, there were no draughts.

She was in another long corridor with more doors. Although she didn't miss the flat, Stella liked coming back to it. She gave a few short sniffs. Nose in the air, Stanley did the same. When she had lived here, she had been greeted by reviving wafts of plug-in lavender air fresheners; now she smelled Tina's perfume.

Stella had a preternatural sense of smell that was on a par with her dog's. She could identify a scent or an odour and recall the times she had smelled it. Tina's scent was Yves Saint Laurent's unisex Eau Libre, popular in the 1970s when Stella's father had bought it for her mum, presuming erroneously that it was her favourite. Suzie often declared that this mistake had hammered a further nail into the coffin of their marriage.

Eau Libre had been discontinued, so Tina sourced it at great expense from eBay, calling it her 'one extravagance'. Although Tina was at her office when Stella cleaned the flat, her scent lingered in the conditioned air.

Stella observed that it was stronger today, but, concentrating on Stanley avoiding the wheels of the cart and plotting how to distract him from 'helping', she hardly registered this. She was also distracted by another issue. Today they would hear if Clean Slate had won the contract to clean buildings in the Royal Botanic Gardens at Kew. It was her company's biggest-ever bid and would take it to another level.

Absently Stella led Stanley to heel along to the front room. The room vibrated with music. Stella was prey to a nightmare in which she was scrubbing at a stain that, no matter what she did or what solutions she applied, grew until the room was one big stain. All around a sea of beige and white was blotched with stains. She blinked. The carpet was clean. But gone were the dining table and the chairs.

The music was 'Rebel Rebel' by David Bowie. Stella, who had never been a rebel, knew the track because it was Jackie's favourite.

Slowly Stella absorbed a fact more dreadful than battling with an ever-spreading stain. Feet bare, hair flying, Tina Banks was dancing around the room clutching a long-handled squeegee mop. Stella didn't dance, but if she did, she wouldn't want anyone to see her doing it. She made to leave before Tina noticed her but saw with dizzying horror that it was too late. On his hind legs like a circus dog, Stanley was prancing about with Tina, keeping pace with her steps. Just when Stella couldn't imagine it could get worse, Tina began to sing in a raucous voice. Eyes shut, she sashayed around the room, Stanley beside her.

Stella gesticulated at him, miming silent commands, but his

21

eyes were on Tina. If Tina Banks realized that Stella was watching her dance she would never speak to her again. In a flash Stella – not given to reflection – saw that she minded less that she would lose a client than that she would lose a friend.

Tina opened her eyes and let out a whoop. She grabbed Stanley's outstretched paws and danced with him. Tina Banks was a short woman – barely over five feet – and the dog, stretching up on his hind legs, reached above her knees. Her back to Stella, she called out, 'Hey, Stell, come and dance!'

Stella scrambled behind her for the door. 'I need to clean,' she objected lamely.

'I'm learning to foxtrot. I need your help.' Tina waved her smart phone at a Bluetooth speaker on the window sill and the music stopped. Stanley stopped too. He sat, pert and at the ready for a new command from Tina. Stella had turned down the opportunity to attend her trainer's dancing classes for dogs. Hazily she suspected now that, as Jackie had suggested, Stanley might have liked them.

'I promised Vaughan I'd be step perfect!' Tina was doing stretches, arms to the ceiling, dipping her head to the floor. 'Now you're here, it will be better.'

Stella couldn't see why it would be better. She stalled for time. 'Who's Vaughan?'

'My dancing teacher. He's drop-dead gorgeous!'

'You're learning to dance?' Stella was incredulous. Tina worked as hard as she did; Stella had no time – or inclination – to dance.

'No choice and nor have you. We're with the big players now, Stell. It's not about breaking up huddles in washrooms or sealing a deal on the golf course, we've got to beat these guys on the dance floor. Knock 'em dead in all senses!'

Stella restored and maintained order, stain by stain. She avoided fiction because it wasn't about real life; she faced reality head on. After leaving school she consigned pop music – she and her friend Liz had liked Duran Duran – to her teenaged years. She didn't dance because it served no practical purpose. And like today meant that the furniture wasn't where it belonged. She couldn't see how dancing would help her business and nor did she want to knock anyone dead.

'I'm going to a ball next week. There'll be judges, all manner of wigged-up high and mightys. I have to show them who's in charge. I must be the best, but I won't be with two right feet!'

Tina was best at all she did. The most sought-after criminal lawyer in London, she already had power and influence. Jackie said it was in Tina's nature to be always striving. Stella was unsure that an ability to foxtrot would help.

'Is it the right music?' she asked doubtfully. 'Shouldn't it be Frank Sinatra or . . . ?' She tailed off.

'I can't stand that romantic blather. Bowie is in four-four time, he works a dream.'

Stella's chapter on client relations in the staff manual stipulated that unless *unreasonable, unsafe or illegal, operatives should agree to go outside the cleaning remit* if requested by the client. Stella had been assuming mundane tasks like bringing her dog to sessions or doing extra cleaning. Jack had once had to read a bedtime story to a geranium and Stella's mother Suzie had gone through a phase of insisting that Stella and Jack rake through her rubbish bin searching for items lost years ago that couldn't be there. No client had asked an operative to foxtrot. Stella hadn't defined *unreasonable.* Besides, a lawyer, Tina would drive a truck through any argument. Ruefully Stella admitted that she had broken her key rule, *Never cross the line between client and friend.* Foxtrotting was her penalty.

Last year, Jackie had gone to the ball at the British Cleaning Council's annual conference, dragging along a reluctant Graham, her husband. Stella had refused to go. She hated making small talk – even about cleaning – but the dancing had clinched it. Would she lose the contract with Kew Gardens because she refused to dance?

Tina returned from the kitchen with the brush with extra tough bristles. Stella felt a spark of relief. Tina had been joking, Stella could get on with cleaning.

'Take your boots off – we have to be light on our feet.' She handed the brush to Stella. 'Meet your partner – Basil Brush, if you need a name – rest one hand on his "shoulder" and imagine he has you clasped around the waist.'

As if going to the scaffold, Stella took off her boots and placed them together by the door, as a promise of escape. She took the brush and restrained herself from sweeping up crumbs and fluff from the carpet. Clasping 'Basil' she was thankful that Jackie and Beverly couldn't see her. Or Jack. Except that were Jack here, Stella suspected that he'd be eager to join in.

Tina pressed a button on her phone and the guitar riff began again. 'Do what I do,' Tina shouted over the music.

Perhaps Stella's precise approach, her commitment to systems and her 'stain by stain' methodology had honed her motor skills. Perhaps it was her ability to manoeuvre equipment in tight spaces. Whatever the reason, within two plays of the track she had mastered the box step. She could integrate left and right turns and, with Basil held close, promenaded sideways from the kitchen to the end wall and back. The form and boundary that the dance demanded suited her. It didn't involve – positively discouraged – the extraneous dips and twirls that horrified her about modern dancing. Predictable, reliant on corners and straight lines, if Stella had to dance, then the foxtrot was right for her. Imitating Stella, Tina's steps improved. With David Bowie on repeat, the two women danced on, unaware of the small poodle cavorting at their heels in hectic counterpoint to the regular drumbeat.

Abruptly Tina Banks silenced the music and flopped on to the sofa, panting for breath. Stella could have done another few rounds. Standing in the middle of the carpet, grasping the brush like a shepherd's crook, she was faintly surprised to see Tina so pale and shattered. Tina worked out at a gym every morning, she was a Pilates and hot yoga fanatic and the foxtrot wasn't physically demanding. Stanley sat at Tina's feet, ears cocked, eyes pinned on her.

'You are a natural!' Tina swiped at perspiration glistening on her forehead with her sleeve. She rested her head on a cushion behind her and shut her eyes. 'Vaughan would love you!' she panted. 'Coffee?'

'No thanks. I need to get started.' Stella returned the brush and mop to the kitchen and fetched the cleaning cart from the hall. She laced her boots back on.

It wasn't unusual to have to remind a client why she was there. But Tina wasn't just a client. Stella had started by meeting her for coffee and recently they had graduated to curries at a place on King Street. Tina was exacting, a reason she had given for requesting that Stella did the work. The women were well suited.

'I ought to head off.' Tina struggled out of the sofa, lost balance and fell back; annoyance clouded her face. She didn't like to be seen to fail at anything and so, perhaps to counteract this, did twist stretches as she left the room.

When Stella had told Jackie that she would be cleaning Tina's flat, Jackie had warned Stella that returning to her old home might feel strange. 'What if you hate the changes she's made?'

When she had come to do the estimate, Tina's white sofa – still in its protective plastic – was identical to her own and was positioned under the picture window overlooking the river as hers had been. The walls were still brilliant white. Tina had asked that Stella include her glass-topped dining table and matching coffee table in the sale. When she had lived there Stella had left the walls bare because art attracted dirt and created clutter. After Tina had gone to work, Stella cleaned in earnest; she took down two pictures from the wall by the kitchen door, another change. One was of a tree with orange flowers. Stella paused. It looked like the one in her mum's photo. Stella noticed the legend: '*Study of the West Australian Flame Tree or Fire Tree*, Marianne North, Royal Botanic Gardens, Kew'. Kew Gardens was on her mind; Jack would definitely call this a sign.

On her first visit, Tina had been voluble as she explained that North's paintings were frowned on by botanists because the tree was depicted in context which confused identification. Surprised that Tina was aerated by a tree, Stella had got the point about context confusing an issue. She hadn't questioned Tina further. Her staff manual was strict about not asking the client personal questions.

Over the months, Stella saw that, as she so often was, Jackie had been right: cleaning the flat did make her feel strange. Not because she minded that someone else was living there: Stella was of a logical bent; she believed that if she minded then she shouldn't have moved. But when she was vacuuming corners and buffing windows she was back to when she had done these tasks for herself as if the intervening months hadn't happened. While Jack Harmon would have relished the sensation of time reversing, Stella found it unsettling.

The dancing had delayed her. Stella texted Jackie that she couldn't make their meeting about finding new premises. She didn't mention the foxtrotting. She put back the furniture. After polishing the window she placed a framed photograph precisely where it had been on the sill. This was an action she repeated every week, but today, ruffled by dancing and anxious about Kew Gardens, Stella looked at it.

It was a black-and-white photograph of a man grinning at the camera. He was crouched, one hand resting on a football between his knees, his thick-set figure outlined against a white sky. Stella had assumed he was a film star from the 1950s.

'My dad is the star of his own life!' Tina had corrected her. 'Give the old man a dusting-down, it'll do him good.' She had dropped her businesslike guard, fingers trailing over the frame and murmured, 'My dad was my hero.'

At one of their meetings in the café on Hammersmith Broadway Stella and Tina had discovered that they had the same birthday: 12 August 1966. Tina instantly dubbed them twins and set about proving how much they had in common. They both ran successful businesses, hadn't yet found Mr Right – Tina said he didn't exist; Stella hadn't thought about it one way or the other – and they were 'Daddy's girls'. Stella hadn't said this to Tina. She had told her that when she was seven she had wanted to be a detective like Terry.

Now, scrutinizing the picture of the young man she could see why Tina had drawn a parallel. Terry had had the same good looks as Cliff Banks. Both men had loved dancing and had met their wives at the Hammersmith Palais. A key difference between them was that Cliff Banks was alive and Chief Superintendent Terry Darnell had died of a heart attack in January 2011.

Tina was sure that, as a police officer and a taxi driver, their paths must have crossed. But if she ever asked her dad, he hadn't confirmed this. Stella was certain that Terry had never taken a taxi in his life.

In their family, Terry had the camera. Unlike her mum, he hadn't been one for timed pictures (latter-day selfies). She had no portrait of him. Mostly the photos featuring Terry were team shots of him graduating from police training courses at Hendon College, and there was a picture in the *West London Observer* of Terry as a constable taking part in a fingertip search of Wormwood Scrubs common after the Braybrook Street Shooting. Stella wouldn't have thought of putting these on show in her front room.

She heard a ping. Jackie had acknowledged her text. Stella had cancelled such meetings many times, but Jackie gave no hint of being frustrated. Nearly ten years older than Stella, Jackie Makepeace was something of a mentor to her. She couldn't know that Jackie would have been unsurprised about Stella doing the foxtrot. It would have confirmed Jackie's opinion, shared with her dancer son, that Stella would be a natural. Jackie knew Stella Darnell better than she knew herself. She had kept the office meeting slot free, but hadn't expected it to take place.

Bowling along in her van, Stella passed Rose Gardens North, a short terrace of houses left when the rest were razed for the Great West Road extension. She had lived in the street with her mum and dad until she was seven, when her parents separated. Her dad had continued to live there. She had inherited the house when Terry died and forty years on was living in there again.

Accelerating around Hammersmith Broadway Stella raised her voice above the hum of traffic and belted out 'Rebel Rebel' note-perfect.

Chapter Four

October 2014

George Watson made his way across Kew Gardens. A goose had defecated on the path. Although it was cold, two boys were rampaging about on the grass by the Queen's Beasts. He cast a disapproving look; he wouldn't let a child tear about making all that noise, scaring the birds. Their mother watched from a bench. Actually, no: he realized she was watching him. Since Jimmy Savile, everyone was alert for paedophiles. Savile had done it for any man walking on his own. You needed a dog or a kid to pass as normal. He had his briefcase, but he suspected that increased her suspicion. A mac and a case were not the usual garb for a man in Kew Gardens.

He wasn't aggrieved by her blatant mistrust. His grievances were deeper. Still, he glared at the woman clutching her cigarette as if for dear life. She could have no idea how uninterested in her children he was.

He had seen her before. Not her, but the scene. The mother, the children. Generation after generation in Kew Gardens, like a field of sheep.

One of these times he must have been with Rosamond because he remembered her saying that the mother should be 'interacting with her children'. That would have been when Rosamond paid notice to children. When the problem wasn't being mistaken for a pervert, but trying unsuccessfully to divert Rosamond from wishing she was the mother shivering on the bench. Not smoking – she considered the habit disgusting – but, like this mother, she would be fiercely protecting her brood while they played their idiotic games. The younger boy was bossing the older one, pushing and shoving him. He was tempted to go over and make him stop. The mother had guessed this and through plumes of smoke she was keeping her eye on him.

George Watson hurried out of the gate, past the Herbarium and over to the pond. Minutes later he was pushing open the gate to his house. He looked up. A light was on in the drawing room. A sign that Rosamond was there. He had lived in the substantial villa for over forty years, a continuity that enabled him to chart his infirmities. It took longer to walk up the path, to fit the key in the lock and to climb the stairs to his studio. To get over slights.

With the front door open he called out, 'I'm home.' He sniffed her perfume. Her coat was slung over the banister as if she had dumped it and rushed up the stairs in a hurry to tell him about her day. He felt bad for coming home late, it had thrown everything out. He shut the door and crossed to the drawing room.

Rosamond's knitting was on the table by the sofa. He had put it there; left on the sofa, he might have accidentally sat on it. Knitting and a half-drunk cup of tea – he felt the mug, it was cold – were signs that she had been there.

In the kitchen there was no supper on the go. He liked to prepare their meals and, as he joked to her, one thing he could do with consummate skill was slice and dice.

He smelled cigarette smoke. Not Rosamond, he could be sure of that. Ayrton smoked. He had been in the Herbarium all day making his life a misery. Still, diligence and respect reaped rewards. His own was on the horizon.

He saw the stub as soon as he opened the back door. It had been crushed, the ash made a curving mark on the stone. He prised it off the step and, holding it between his thumb and forefinger, threw it in the downstairs lavatory and pulled the chain. Another slight. It flayed him raw.

Gripping the banister as if it were a climbing rope to aid his ascent up a mountain, Watson laboured up to his attic studio.

Submitting to the pain, he forced himself to look along the shelves where his books were ranged in alphabetical order. The study of an eminent botanist; he pictured telling the journalist about his life, his principles for a revised taxonomy. He would be bluff and hearty: *It's all about DNA these days.*

He sat down at his board and regarded the grey pencil lines. An early sketch, the basic form of structure traced with the camera lucida. Ayrton had called it the doodles of an old man. George had smiled. The trick was to smile. Ayrton was jealous, he couldn't do his own drawings. The best botanists could. George knew he was good. Better than the blowsy young woman Ayrton fussed over. Ayrton had promised that the specimen George was drawing would be named after him. They needed each other.

His eye was caught by a sticky note above his sketch. In block capitals were the words, 'USE OYSTER CARD'.

The last time he had gone on the District line he had forgotten to take it. He ripped the sticky note from the board and, scrunching it up, tossed it in his waste bin.

Several hours later, there was a knock on the door. A far-off thud. He picked up a scalpel. The short sliver of metal could do much damage.

Another knock.

Rosamond didn't approve of uninvited callers. Certainly not at past four in the morning. These days George slept little. Unable to ignore it, grimacing at his tight tendons, George laboured his way down the stairs, calling in a reedy voice, 'I'm coming.' Like a child on the count of ten.

The elderly man in the shadow of the porch was a mirror of himself. Except he wore an absurd cap. George couldn't think of its name. Perhaps the man knew what he was thinking because he snatched his cap off, rolling it up between his hands.

'Howdy do, George!' Palms together at his chest, he did a theatrical bow. George thrilled with revulsion. He tried to shut the door, but the man was already in the hall.

'Do I know you?' George did know him. The revulsion had taken root decades ago. Then, as now, the man reeked of alcohol.

'We're too old for grudges, aren't we?' The man patted him on the shoulder and strolled about the hall scanning left and right, as if looking for something. *Someone.*

'I thought you were dead.' George fingered the scalpel in his pocket and felt the sharp sting of a cut.

'So did I, mate! Where is she?' The man yelled up the stair-well: 'Rosy!'

'She's popped out.' The coat was gone from the banister. He heard how absurd he sounded. 'She's asleep.'

'Wake her up man!'

'She's unwell.' George lowered his voice.

'Poor baby.' The man sauntered into the sitting room. Behaving as if the house was his. His mind racing, George pictured the papers covered in dense print from his solicitor.

With no other living relatives, the house belongs to your wife. Should she predecease you then it is in trust to you...

'Jesus, I'm famished,' the man exclaimed. 'Midnight munchies!'

'It's four in the morning!'

The man ignored him. 'What you got?'

'Rosy made a cake.'

'More than my life's worth to say no to Rosy's homemade!'

When George returned to the sitting room, a slice of chocolate cake coated with hundreds and thousands on a plate, his visitor was sprawled on the sofa asleep. In the kitchen he had managed to convince himself that his visitor was a dreadful trick of the imagination. But, mouth open, snoring loudly, he was real enough.

In the hall the longcase clock struck five. George placed the plate on the coffee table with a crash.

'What in hell...?' Barely awake, the man instinctively put out a defensive hand. He caught the plate and sent it skittering to the floor. Cake scattered all over the carpet. 'Ah look at that.' He marvelled, his rheumy eyes wandering over the lumps of cake without focus.

'I'll call a taxi.' George went to the alcove by the fireplace and dialled a number on the phone.

Fifteen minutes later there was a loud knock on the door.

'The taxi's here.' George hurried into the hall.

The driver, in shirt sleeves despite the cold, was grinning broadly. The elderly man swayed on his feet, tottering on the doorstep.

'This both of you, sir?' the driver asked.

'No. Or actually yes. It's both of us.' George grabbed the man's arm and guided him down the path to the black cab.

George had left the cake on the carpet. As the taxi passed Kew Green, he remembered that the cleaner was coming in the morning. He let others tidy up his mess. He would leave it for her.

Chapter Five

October 2014

'How's business. Good?' Dariusz Adomek, the Polish owner of the mini-mart beneath the Clean Slate office, swiped a litre carton of milk over the sensor and passed it to Stella. He tossed the right money into the till drawer and tore off the receipt. Reaching across the counter to Stanley on Stella's shoulder, he ruffled his head and murmured endearments to him in Polish.

'Good, yes.' Stella paused. 'We're waiting to hear if we've got a big contract.' It was rare for Adomek or Stella to stray from their morning script except to consult on staffing or business issues. Adomek referred Polish friends and relations to Stella's team of operatives. Stella and Jackie checked over his letters and advised on tax forms. The symbiotic relationship was a decade old. It was even rarer for Stella to talk about a potential contract with anyone outside Clean Slate, but Adomek wouldn't tell a soul.

'I'm crossing fingers for you.' Adomek popped a treat from a bowl by a charity box for the local hospice between Stanley's lips.

'Thank you. How are you?'

'We're opening another shop!' Adomek ripped the cellophane off a carton of Benson and Hedges and keeping the packets stacked in a tower slotted them into a gap on the shelf behind the till. 'Adomek's is a chain. Eat your heart out Tesco!' He scrunched up the wrapping and stuffed it into a bin beside his stool. 'OK, so two shops is *not* a chain.'

'It is nearly.' Jackie had once said that Adomek was like Stella, prudent and cautious. If Clean Slate got the Kew contract they would have to move to larger offices and recruit more staff.

Adomek, perhaps guessing her thoughts, said, 'You get this business, you'll need more people. I'm lining them up.'

'Thanks.' Stella picked up the milk carton.

'I got a snap from Suzanne.' He reached under the counter and produced his phone. Quickly he moved his finger over it as if stirring something and slid the handset over to her.

Suzanne was standing in a shop holding a newspaper in front of her chest. Both hands were visible so Stella's brother must have taken it. The paper was *Fakt*, a Polish tabloid that Adomek sold in the shop. Stella couldn't understand the headline. Inset was a picture of two women in leotards, hands clasped as if dancing. She was reminded of the morning with Tina.

'Suzie says she understands every word in the paper. I text her: *Good so can you tell me!*' Laughing, Adomek put his phone back under the counter.

Adomek was teaching Suzie Darnell Polish. Her mum said it was respectful to converse with Adomek in his own language.

Unlike the photographs that she had sent to Stella, this was untouched by any filter or tool. The picture depicted her mother as she knew her. Stella quelled a pang. She hadn't let herself miss her.

Beside the fruit-and-veg display was a door; the murky brown paint was scored with scratches. The door shifted as Stella fitted her key into the lock. She tutted. Despite memos, emails and a laminated notice, staff in the insurance company above Clean Slate left the door on the latch. One reason to move.

Stanley, straining on his lead, forged ahead up the stairs, claws clicking on the frayed linoleum. On the landing, Stella stopped at a door, the wired-glass window blocked by a notice that declared: 'Clean Slate – For a Fresh Start'.

'It's the last straw!' Stella said, mostly to herself, as she pushed on the handle and barged in.

'We guessed you wouldn't like it.' Jackie Makepeace had been Stella's personal assistant for nearly as many years as Clean Slate had been in business. With practised fluidity, she took Stanley's lead from Stella, swapping it for tea in a mug emblazoned with the company logo.

Stella stepped around Beverly the office assistant, who was taking up much of the cramped floor space extracting springy bunches of paper from the shredder bin and cramming them into a plastic sack. Strands of paper had escaped and were all over the carpet. Stanley snatched a bundle of shreds from the sack and, before Jackie could stop him, was tossing them about. Not for the first time Stella considered how wise it was that clients were discouraged from visiting the office.

Jackie had put down a bowl of water for Stanley. He made for it and drank noisily. Stella took a gulp of tea; it was exactly as she liked it. She dropped her rucksack outside a door marked 'Stella Darnell, Managing Director'. This was an initiative of Beverly's. Jackie had stopped Stella from pointing out that the notice was extraneous since everyone – Jackie and Beverly herself – knew this anyway.

'People can change.' The voice came from her office. Looking round, Stella saw a tall man, locks of dark hair falling over the collar of a black overcoat that accentuated his pale features and deep brown eyes. Jack Harmon, driver on the District line, the best cleaning operative she had ever had, began to pet Stanley. The dog, furry chin decorated with paper shreds and dripping with water, set about licking Jack's face. Stella looked away; she drew the line at licking.

Beverly tamped down the paper in the bag and gathered another armful from the bin. 'Life should mean life!' she snorted.

'Beverly!' Jackie shot her a look.

'It's not about condoning, but finding a way to forgive the perpetrator.' Jack sat down in Suzie Darnell's chair. Stella's mum came in three days a week to run the client database. For the next few weeks she was doing this from Sydney.

'I'm done with forgiving.' Stella nursed her mug of tea. 'That company is processing burglary claims and at the same time putting us at risk from "off-street intruders".' She pursed her lips. 'I'll speak to their MD and underline how leaving the front door open puts them at risk too. Anyone could walk in.'

'*Anyone* just did walk in,' Jack said. 'I did and I'm anybody.'

'No you're not, you're *somebody*!' Beverly knotted the neck of the plastic bag.

Stella's first meeting with Jack had been early one morning three years ago. He had found his way into the office because the door had been left open.

'We're talking at cross-purposes.' Jackie placed a mug of hot milk on the desk in front of Jack. 'Sit down, Stell. Like some sugar stirred in?' She waved a spoon at Stella's mug.

'I don't take—' The last time Jackie had put sugar in Stella's tea was when a policeman told her that Terry was dead. 'Is it Mum?' Stella went numb. 'She just sent me a picture.' Not 'just' – it was over two hours ago. A lot could happen in that time.

'Suzie's fine. We thought you'd have seen the news.' Jackie pushed Beverly's vacated chair towards Stella. Jack jumped up and indicated her mother's chair.

'What news?' Mechanically Stella sat down at Suzie's desk.

'They're releasing that man who killed the policemen on the day you were born!' Beverly's voice was muffled by the desk under which she had crawled in pursuit of fronds of shredded paper.

'Bev,' Jackie said nicely. 'Why don't you nip down to Dariusz and get us some milk.'

'Stella's just bought—' Beverly began.

'Take that to the recycling bin while you're at it, there's a love.' Jackie nodded at the overstuffed bag.

36

Hint taken, Beverly stomped from the room. Jackie pulled her chair to face Stella across the desk. Jack, now in Beverly's chair, clutched Stanley to his chest. The dog, sensing a change in atmosphere, cocked his head.

Some children grow up fearing the White Witch in Narnia or the wolf in 'Little Red Riding Hood'; Stella Darnell, the daughter of a detective, was brought up believing that villainy was encapsulated in one name. *Harry Roberts*. She had retained the smallest facts about the events of 12 August 1966. The story of that day was in her DNA. When she returned to the house in Rose Gardens North for access weekends with Terry the house no longer felt like her home. She had lain awake at night, imagining that she heard Roberts's footsteps on the stairs. He would shoot her dad and kidnap her. That he was locked up in prison didn't lessen this fear.

The story was as vivid to her as if she had been a witness to events that day. Terry Darnell was leaving the police station on Uxbridge Road in Shepherd's Bush for the Hammersmith Hospital on Du Cane Road to see his newly born daughter when he was recalled to duty. He joined in the search for an armed gang who had shot dead three police officers in Braybrook Street in the shadow of Wormwood Scrubs prison. Two of the gang were quickly caught, but Harry Roberts was on the run for nearly a hundred days. According to his wife, Terry hadn't seen the baby Stella for days: the number of days varied in the retelling over the years from three days to a week.

'Harry Roberts has been released,' Jack said.

Stella gripped the arms of her mother's chair. 'The judge at the trial sent him to prison for life.' She spoke in a monotone.

Jackie's voice was gentle, reasonable: 'Roberts isn't considered a danger to the public. He's done, um, quite a few years.'

'Forty-eight. The same as my age,' Stella snapped.

Jackie handed Stella the *Daily Mirror*. *Triple Police Killer Freed*. Jackie stirred a spoonful of sugar into Stella's tea. 'Drink.'

They sipped in silence. Outside the rush hour had got into

swing. A double-decker bus inched past; the bright interior sent light along the back wall of the office passing over the staff rota and blue and green box files.

'Since when did life not mean life?' Stella echoed Beverly's words. She watched undissolved sugar granules spin around on the surface of her tea.

'It's inhumane to keep a person in prison indefinitely,' Jack declared.

'Not now, Jack.' Jackie shook her head, but Stella gave no impression she had heard. She drank the sweetened tea.

The office door flew wide and crashed against a filing cabinet. A man stood on the threshold, brandishing a weapon. With the swiftness of bodyguards, Jack and Jackie stepped in front of Stella. Stanley let off a volley of shrill barking.

'I'll call the police!' Stella jumped up. *Harry Roberts.*

'It *is* the police!' Beverly stepped around the man, calm and poised.

'For goodness' sake!' Jackie slumped back in her chair. Jack stood down. Stanley got into his bed by the photocopier where he kept up a low grumble.

The 'weapon' was a rolled-up copy of the *Sun* newspaper. *Fury at Cop-killer's Release.* It was Detective Chief Superintendent Martin Cashman.

'Have you seen this?' He circled the office, waving the paper.

'Yes.' Stella returned to Suzie's chair.

'How mad is it to have to say that it's good Terry isn't here!' Cashman exclaimed.

Jack noticed that Cashman had on the same suit as the previous night at Kew Gardens station. It was crumpled and his chin was shadowed with stubble.

The office phone was ringing. Beverly answered, 'Clean Slate fora fresh start, Beverly speaking, how can I help?' She spoke in a cheery sing-song voice and, frowning with the effort of using her newly acquired customer-service skills, she swept up a pad, Clean Slate branded pen hovering.

'Thank you for informing us.' Beverly was starchy, her face a mask. She slammed down the receiver and leapt up, punching the air. 'Yes!' she roared.

'What?' Stella and Jackie said together.

'That was the Facilities Manager.' Beverly recovered her poise. 'He asked me to pass on a message for Stella Darnell and Jackie Makepeace.'

'That's us, Bev.' Jackie was patient.

'He said to say that Clean Slate has won the cleaning contract for Kew Gardens!'

Chapter Six

June 1976

Chrissie had no interest in art or plants. She didn't want to go to Mr Watson's house after school. Her dad's friend was going to teach her how to do 'botanical illustration', whatever that was. She wanted to get out of it, but whenever her dad told her and her sister, Michelle, to do something that was that.

'Be nice to them; they haven't got kids of their own. You're doing them a big favour. You never know where it could lead,' he had instructed her.

Chrissie felt vaguely sorry for the Watsons not having any children, although, since she didn't know any particularly nice ones, she didn't want them herself. And she tried not to think about 'where it might lead'. Did her dad mean she might have to live with Mr and Mrs Watson?

She arrived punctually at 4.30 p.m. A tall thin lady answered the door. She said she was called Mrs Watson. She was in her late thirties, but to Chrissie seemed very old indeed because her hair was in a tight bun and she had a strict look on her face. She showed Chrissie into a 'drawing room' and told her to sit on a settee that had been left in the middle of the floor. She instructed her to eat a slice of cake and gave her a glass of milk. Chrissie hated milk.

Mrs Watson laughed when Chrissie assumed – given the name – that she was doing her drawing in this room, and said, 'I have to pop out. George – Mr Watson – is up in his studio. When you've finished your tea, take your plate and cup through to the kitchen. Wash your hands. Don't dawdle and go straight up to him.'

Mrs Watson had gone before Chrissie could tell her that she never dawdled, not like her sister Michelle who was always late. When she had gone Chrissie got off the settee and, clutching the plate to catch crumbs, wandered around the room munching the cake.

Lace curtains shrouded three tall windows, including French doors. A side window overlooked Kew Pond. Light from this window cast a sickly subterranean glow over an austere oak tallboy and sideboard on which were arranged silver salvers and bowls. Glass-fronted bookcases entombed leather-bound volumes that, no longer consulted or pored over, were dried and cracked effigies.

The general sense was of gloom. The room offered no respite from the engulfing heat outside; the inert air was warm and Chrissie prickled with perspiration. She rubbed her aching forehead with the flapping cuff of her school uniform shirt. Lacklustre light was absorbed by the sombre Victorian furnishings: faded tapestry and heavy brocade. Perhaps because it provided the only colour, the girl gravitated to a print of a painting that hung above the marble fireplace.

It was of a tree with orange flowers. That a tree should have flowers was a new idea to her. Munching her cake – it was dry and she had trouble swallowing it – she peered at branches blossoming with bright petals.

A clock ticked somewhere. It whirred and struck the quarter to.

The child couldn't know that little in the house had altered over a hundred years. Mrs Watson's family had lived in Kew Villa since Joseph Hooker was Director of the Botanic Gardens on the other side of Kew Green. Perhaps she sensed the weight of ancestors because, although she knew that she was alone, she felt she was being watched.

Cowed by the sepulchral hush, Chrissie retreated to the settee and washed down the rest of the cake with gulps of warm milk. The tea had been billed as a treat by her mum, who was as doubtful as Chrissie that drawing lessons would give her the social advantage that her dad claimed they would. 'She'd be better off learning the piano,' she had hazarded with even less conviction. 'Where are we going to get a piano from?' her dad had demanded crossly and then said to Chrissie: 'George moves in high circles. So could you.' Chrissie didn't point out that a circle led round to where you started from, which could make you dizzy.

In a straight line, Chrissie gingerly made her way along a corridor and down some stone steps. The kitchen was three times the size of the one in her parents' flat, with a table big enough for ten people. Beyond the sink, which, being short for her age, she could hardly reach, she glimpsed a garden. Wilting ivy fringed the window, the leaves dried and shrivelled.

Chrissie reached up to the tap and, although she hadn't been asked to, sluiced the plate and the mug under a torrent of water. She carried on after the crockery was clean because the water, although tepid, was still refreshing. She didn't feel guilty at wasting water during a drought.

She slotted the plate and glass into a rack by the sink, every action methodical, because it was a quality that she possessed and because she was staving off meeting the mysterious Mr Watson.

Treading lightly, she returned to the hall where a thin light filtered through glazed panels in the front door. On her right was the drawing room which was not for drawing. On her left was another door. It was open. Inquisitive, Chrissie went in. She saw a table and high-backed chairs; in the half-light they looked like people sitting upright and well behaved.

'What are you doing?'

Chrissie whisked around. Mrs Watson was at the bottom of the staircase. She had a strange smile that showed all her teeth and her eyes were like gobstoppers.

'I got lost,' Chrissie said, quick as a flash.

'I see.' She came towards her. 'Please go up.'

The little girl scurried up the staircase. There was a thump. She stopped on the landing and peered through the spindles down into the hall. Mrs Watson had shut the front door. She had gone. With only mild relief, Chrissie continued up the next flight of stairs.

A person was coming towards her. Chrissie grabbed the banister. Then she saw that it was a mirror and the person was her reflection.

Made braver by the knowledge that Mrs Watson had left and unwilling to reach the studio, on the second landing Chrissie crept into a room on her right.

She was in a bedroom. The bed stretched away and the air smelled of something nice that raised her spirits. Beside the window, shaded by curtains of damask, was a walnut dressing table. It reminded her of the dashboard of her dad's taxi. Three drawers were ranged either side of the knee space with an oval mirror webbed with silver. Catching herself in the speckled glass, Chrissie shivered. Even to herself, she looked like a ghost.

The silver locket was the first thing she saw when she opened the top drawer. She lifted it out, awed by its cold weightiness. It was heart-shaped with a silver lid. She prised it open and found a compartment covered with glass. A picture was inset, necessarily heart-shaped, of two people. She supposed it was Mr and Mrs Watson when they were young. They were kissing. Yuk! She shut the lid, shutting them in. Then she saw marks on the casing. Not marks, letters. A 'G' and an 'R' were engraved in the silver. The 'G' must stand for 'George' which was what her dad called Mr Watson. She didn't know Mrs Watson's first name. She was so stern that it seemed impossible that she had one.

Hearing a noise, she whizzed to the door and flattened herself behind it. If Mr Watson looked in, he wouldn't see her. If he came right in he would see her straight away. She held her breath. He didn't come in. After a while she risked going outside. There was no one on the landing.

She ran nimbly up the staircase and tapped on a door marked 'Studio'. A voice called, 'Come.'

In contrast to the bedroom, the room blazed with light. Hot sun lit up motes of dust.

'Today we're drawing a daisy. Family Compositae.' With abrupt sweeps of his scalpel, Mr Watson was sharpening a pencil to a fine point. Without looking at her, he gave it to Chrissie. He indicated a chair the other side of the window for her to sit on. Laid out on a table was a sketch pad and a rubber and something nasty that was brown and shrivelled.

His voice dropped down deep. 'Unlike some dead material this specimen has a name. It exists. Now it's your job to bring it to life,' he instructed her.

Looking about for a daisy, Chrissie realized he meant the shrivelled brown thing. How could she bring it to life? She wasn't convinced that it had ever been a daisy.

'Use this magnifying glass to examine the structure of the specimen. Think of a skeleton without flesh. Before you touch the paper with your pencil, I want you to consider carefully what you see.' Although he had given her the pencil, he didn't seem to be talking to her. He looked across the room and waved his hands as if trying to get someone's attention.

Chrissie could see nothing worth drawing. It wasn't a proper daisy. Her instinct was to draw the kind of daisy she knew. She would put the yellow sun in the middle and then white petals around it. Then she would say that she had to go. She stuffed her hands into her pockets so that she wouldn't be tempted to start drawing before she had looked at the brown thing properly. She felt something cold and hard. *The locket.* She had forgotten to return it to the drawer. As from far away, Mr Watson's voice droned on, but in her horror she couldn't concentrate.

'Examine the shape and number of the ray florets... tiny

teeth... tubes with lobes... Look for hairs and bristles on the stems... Count everything. You are not an artist, you are a recorder of reality. You are in service to the plant. I want the truth.' Mr Watson put down his scalpel and looked properly at Chrissie. She sat bolt upright on her chair and stared back.

'Can you give me the truth?' he asked her.

'Yes,' Chrissie lied.

Chapter Seven

October 2014

'It's all I need on top of everything else.'

Stella and Cashman were in a café near the office. Stella had never been there before, although, passing by, had decided that the irritating name – The Waiting Room – hardly instilled confidence in a fast service. But it was the closest place and she had no intention of being out for long. It was designed on the theme of a station waiting room anywhere between the thirties and the fifties: shelves were stacked with leather suitcases, travelling trunks and carpet bags. The walls were lined with old timetables and posters advertising destinations on the London Underground: Golders Green and Wood Lane (for dog racing at White City) and, she saw with a flush of pride, the Royal Botanic Gardens at Kew, showing a stylized version of the Palm House. She doubted that the butcher's block on which stood wine crates filled with condiments and cutlery was free of germs.

The seating was wooden chairs and benches from railway carriages arranged to imply a buffet car. The suspension on Stella's seat was weak and had sagged as she sank into it, making the table inconveniently high.

Cashman had insisted on buying the drinks, which came in white china mugs with the British Rail logo. Stella was mildly surprised to find that she liked the tea. In their 'compartment' was a timetable for the London Victoria to Brighton line, including arrival and departure times for the Brighton Belle. It was dated 1966, the year of her birth. Along with the Kew Gardens poster, the timetable could be one of Jack's signs. It reminded her that he had refused to come for coffee. She wished he was here.

Cashman propped his newspaper between a giant plastic tomato and a glass sugar dispenser. The dispassionate features of Harry Roberts in his arrest photo gazed out at them. A face that, like the Queen's, Stella had known all her life. Aged seven, set to write a story by her teacher that started with 'One summer's day...' she had penned a factual account of the shooting of the officers in the summer sunshine of 1966. 'My daddy did a search on his hands and knees in the grass and there were sniffer dogs.' Her teacher, a crabby woman 'suffering with her legs' and on the verge of retirement, had discounted the piece because it wasn't made up.

On the way to the café, she had found herself scanning passers-by for Harry Roberts, nervous that he might be looking for her. Stupid, because for a start he wouldn't look the same now and secondly he had no reason to come looking for her. Terry hadn't caught him. Jack had said that he would be a harmless old man now.

'You have to question why you're in this job. Roberts is out and those guys are dead. How does that work? After Karen this caps it off!' Cashman stared moodily down at his coffee.

'After Karen?' Stella clattered her spoon against her cup, furious with herself. Aside from her staff manual's rule to avoid talking about a client's personal life, she believed that a couple's business was theirs alone. If Cashman ever talked about his wife, she stalled him, but what with the Kew Gardens contract and Harry Roberts, he had caught her off guard.

'Karen's kicked me out.' He took a slug of coffee and glared at Roberts.

'Kicked you out?' Stella had met Cashman's wife Karen a few times, at Terry's retirement party, at his funeral and when cleaning Cashman's office at the police station, and found her sensible and calm. Not the sort to kick anyone anywhere.

'As good as. The marriage hasn't been working since the kids left home and I got the transfer to Richmond. We've nothing in common. It's an "amicable split".' He was still talking to Harry Roberts. 'She says it's run out of steam.'

Stella had hoped that they would deal with Roberts and she could get back to the office. This was a conversation for which she wasn't equipped. Jack would be better at it, but he and Cashman wound each other up.

'We were running on empty.' Cashman added a stream of sugar from the dispenser to what was left of his coffee and the paper flopped forward, giving Roberts a warped expression. Unable to bear it, Stella laid the paper flat. She eyed Roberts and he stared back at her.

Cashman huffed: 'She's sitting pretty in the house.'

It occurred to Stella that twice when she arrived to clean Cashman's office at Richmond police station she had found him feet up on a chair, jacket off, as if he'd just woken up. She wondered now if he had spent the night there.

'You know the one, after twenty years we've drifted apart.'

Stella didn't know 'the one'. Her relationships didn't start off with much steam and the thought of one lasting twenty years was like contemplating outer space. Twenty weeks was her average.

She opened the newspaper and, in a double spread, found a more recent picture of Roberts. The caption was dated 2009, the year when he had last been seen in public. Handcuffed to a prison officer, his blue prison-issue shirt tucked unfashionably into jeans with no belt, he did indeed look like an old man. Older than Terry when he died. Harry Roberts – like Myra Hindley – had stayed in her mind at the age he was when he was sentenced. Below the snap were black-and-white photographs of the three murdered police officers. Unlike them, Roberts was alive, he had grown old and he was free. Like Beverly had said, 'Life should mean life.' She shut the paper and covered Roberts's face with the tomato-sauce container.

'Till death us do part, we said when we got hitched.' Cashman was stirring his coffee. It seemed he had forgotten about Roberts. 'Karen says I only talk about work. I told her at the get-go: the force is family. You know that from Terry. Karen used to be proud of me, but she says I never talk. Is that true, Stell?' He rounded on her. 'Do I talk?'

Stella was startled. Clearly he was talking now and she didn't rate talking as a positive. Her mum had taught her to believe that 'actions speak louder than words'. When she found him in his office at Richmond station, she had wished Cashman would talk less so she could finish cleaning on schedule. The last time he had delayed her by seven and a half minutes.

'What outcome do you want?' This was Jack's question to clients who insisted on talking about their problems. They didn't welcome solutions, he said, they wanted to be listened to. Jack cleaned while he listened and they talked. Listening was Stella's only option because Cashman was still talking.

'"They think it's all over, it is now!" You're too young to remember that. The football commentator said it at the end of the England v Germany game when we won the World Cup. The thirtieth of July 1966. The nation was on top of the world. Thirteen days later Harry Roberts and his gang smashed our dreams. On the twelfth of August the sun went out.'

'You were a baby too.' Cashman wasn't much older than her.

'I called Karen about Roberts coming out.' Cashman mimed a telephone receiver. 'She said it wasn't me that caught him so why wasn't I stressing about splitting up instead of going on about him?' He scratched his stubbly chin. 'She said it's inhumane to keep a prisoner locked up indefinitely and rob them of hope. Can you credit that?'

Two wrongs don't make a right. Terry's voice echoed from far off. Perhaps Karen Cashman had a point.

'Where are you living?' Stella flushed. He might take the question to mean she would put him up. She did have a spare room.

'On Alan Fry's living-room floor, a guy I trained with at Hendon. In Barons Court – isn't that where Mrs D. lives?'

'Yes.' Stella and her mother had moved to a flat by Barons Court Underground station when her parents split up. A few weeks ago, vacuuming the stair carpet of what was her dad's old house and was now hers, she had recalled the day they separated in detail. Sitting on the top stair, winded by the memory, she had seen the little girl lugging a pink suitcase out of the front door. Not that she believed in ghosts. Cashman's voice roused her.

'...higher up you go the less detection you do.'

Stella nodded, although thinking he was talking about altitude, she didn't know what he meant.

'...the penalty of promotion.' Cashman got up. Detectives wore plain clothes but, unlike Stella whose Clean Slate fleece with the company name embroidered on her shoulder – as on a police polo shirt – stated she was a cleaner, Cashman didn't need a uniform for his job to be identifiable. Suzie Darnell said that if Terry had been a stick of rock, 'the Met' would run right through him.

Perhaps because Cashman had brought Terry to mind, Stella was unwilling to say goodbye. Jackie had once said that if he weren't spoken for, he would be Stella's Mr Right. Whatever: she could talk to him, or rather she didn't have to talk, which suited her fine.

Outside on the Broadway, raising his voice above the traffic, Cashman said, 'Fancy a drink one night?' He beat his palm with the rolled-up newspaper.

About to say yes, Stella checked herself. Jackie would say Cashman was on the rebound and, Mr Right or not, would advise her to 'steer clear'.

'This Kew contract means long hours,' she mumbled.

He smiled stiffly. 'You're with the big players now!' The phrase that Tina had used that morning.

'I won't dance.' Stella had won the Kew job without doing the foxtrot.

50

'Not dancing, just a drink.' Cashman looked puzzled. 'Another time maybe.'

It was wrong to deny a person hope. 'Maybe.' Stella's reply was lost as a lorry roared past.

On her way back to the office, Stella popped into the mini-mart to get her supper. Dariusz was unloading ready meals into a chiller cabinet. Seeing her, he called, 'Jackie told me Kew Gardens is yours! Congratulations, Stella Darnell! Have this on the house!' He handed her a bottle of champagne and a microwavable shepherd's pie.

Chapter Eight

June 1976

'*The Cat in the Hat* is for babies!' Bella Markham slit the stem of a daisy with her thumbnail and threaded another daisy stem through the slender gap. The chain was a metre long, owing less to Bella's tenacity than to her ennui. In the searing heat of the late-afternoon sun, all three girls were as limp as the flowers. They had come to Kew Gardens after school and had flopped out on the parched grass in front of the Palm House. Behind them, ethereal in sunlight, the sheets of curving glass seemed as if fashioned from ice. The dark blue skirts of their uniform absorbed the heat and their white shirts, sticky and crumpled, were untucked. Their ties hung loose around their necks. Bella and Chrissie sat cross-legged facing each other. Only Emily was at home in the heat; she sprawled on her back, her denim hat, Brownie badges sewn around the brim, tipped over her face to protect her from the sun's blistering rays.

'Anyone can read it,' Chrissie maintained while privately agreeing. Bella had asked them to name their favourite story. Emily's had been something called *Jane Air*. Chrissie didn't read books, but had come up with one that her dad was reading her at bedtime. She was struggling with how to tell him she was too old for the story and too old to be read to. Her triumph at having a ready answer for Bella vanished.

'*The Cat in the Hat* is for kids who can't read,' Bella insisted.

'I loved it.' Emily's voice was muffled under the denim hat. ''Specially the Things.'

'Yeah, well, they were all right,' Bella conceded. She nipped another stem with her teeth.

'Would you lie to your mum?' Emily sat up and flapped her hat in front of her face in a futile attempt to cool herself. 'The children in the story have to decide what to tell their mum when she comes home. She won't believe that a cat with a hat called. If a cat had called on you, what would you tell your mum?' She was looking at Bella.

'My mum never believes what I tell her.' Bella was gruff.

'My mum would believe me if I said a cat had visited.' As she said this, Chrissie realized it was true. Her mum believed anything she was told. 'I would tell her the truth,' she decided.

'What's your dad's job?' Bella changed tack. Her question like a punch in the stomach because Chrissie had no planned answer.

Since Chrissie had started at the prep school for 'young ladies' in Kew, her dad kept telling her, 'That school costs a fortune, so don't go saying your mum's a cleaner or I'm a cabbie – you won't get friends.'

'He draws flowers.' It was Thursday and her drawing lesson with Mr Watson was in less than an hour. She looked at Bella's daisy chain and observed to herself that Mr Watson must have made a mistake: the brown shrivelled thing he had made her draw wasn't a proper daisy. Could she take one of these daisies along and explain that to him? Like telling her dad she was too old for stories about a cat wearing a hat, this wasn't feasible.

'No one draws flowers for a living!' Bella held up her daisy chain, frowning.

'My dad does,' Chrissie asserted. Then, because her dad was always saying that the best form of defence was attack: 'Are you allowed to pick flowers in Kew Gardens?'

One afternoon Chrissie had spotted Bella leaving school in a taxi. Her dad drove a taxi! Chrissie had found something they could share. The next day she told Bella that her dad looked nice and was about to say about her dad having a new taxi when Bella had exclaimed, 'He wasn't my dad! My father's a *barrister*. Sometimes I'm fetched in a cab to save taking buses.' Emily Hurst's father went off to wars in foreign places and sent back writing for newspapers which to Chrissie was as strange as drawing flowers, although Bella didn't seem to think so.

Despite her slip about Bella's father, after that Bella had insisted Chrissie 'go round' with her and Emily. Chrissie told her dad that she had made friends.

'There're lots more daisies.' Bella pulled up several more as if to make her point. She asked carelessly, 'Does he sell his pictures? Your dad.'

'He makes them for botanists.' Chrissie called on her one botany illustration lesson. She hadn't expected to go into detail, supposing that Bella would be impressed and that would be that.

'That's stupid.' Bella examined her daisy chain. The entwined flowers were limp and dead.

'It's nice that he gives his pictures away.' Emily was back under her hat. A stick-thin girl with blonde hair, her floaty manner led Chrissie to vest her with the power of mind reading. Emily would know she was lying. She sought to change the subject and rounded on Bella:

'It's stupid that your dad wears a wig to work if he has his own hair.'

'That shows how much you know.' But Bella frowned as if this notion was new to her.

'I have to go.' Dumbfounded by heat and the effort to maintain an ever-growing fiction, Chrissie hadn't kept an eye on the time. Her lesson with Mr Watson was in twenty minutes. Hopes that she could escape the other two were dashed when Bella and Emily said they would walk with her.

Ranged outside the Palm House were the Queen's Beasts:

a series of mythical animals carved in stone. Chrissie liked one called the White Greyhound. The size of a telephone box, he sat on his haunches like Chrissie's family Sealyham – Smash – begging for a biscuit. Without thinking she said, 'If he were real he would tear us to smithereens.'

'Shreds.' Bella's daisy chain hung around her neck. 'You rip *things* to shreds, not smithereens; that's glass.'

'I know,' Chrissie said, although she hadn't known.

The girls toiled around the lake, across browned grass, crispy and springy under their feet, and out of the Elizabeth Gate on to Kew Green.

The sun was baking; Chrissie's legs were so heavy that they didn't work properly and her head was thumping. It was twenty-five minutes past four. She had to be there at half past. Her dad would kill her for being late. He said Mr Watson's time was precious. He might have a meter that made time into money like the one in her dad's taxi.

'Why does your dad draw pictures for botanists? Can't they do them for themselves?' Bella persisted.

'He's good at it and they're not.' Chrissie was dismayed that the girls were still with her. She had expected them to go off in taxis. She wished she hadn't agreed to go to Kew Gardens after school. She only had to please her dad. Now she was trapped.

'Fancy drawing flowers!' Bella snorted.

Chrissie was frustrated. Echoing something she had overheard her dad say to her mum, she blurted out, 'His wife has more money than she knows what to do with.'

'His wife?' Bella was looking at Chrissie with gimlet eyes. 'You mean your mother?'

Chrissie felt herself grow hotter. 'Yes. We live in a big house,' she plunged on irrelevantly. 'Only some people can do drawings.' Her lie was out of control.

'He should take a photograph. That's what my dad would do,' Bella said.

This had struck Chrissie when Mr Watson was explaining

drawing, but she couldn't agree with Bella. 'There are particular reasons for not doing that and they are secret,' she announced.

'How does he draw them? The plants?' Bella asked airily.

'It's too complicated to explain now.' Dimly Chrissie sensed that Bella, fingering the daisies around her neck, actually wanted to know.

'I'm hot.' Emily was fanning her face with her hat.

Mired in untruths, Chrissie didn't see that Emily was trying to defuse the situation. Snatching at a fragment from Mr Watson's lesson she said, 'My dad draws all the different parts of a plant. The parts are' – she counted them on her fingers – 'roots, stems, scales, the calyx and the corolla. The fruit and the seed… and there's more. I don't have time to say them all.' Ahead, the railings around Kew Pond shimmered in the heat as if they too were made up.

'How does that help a botanist?' Bella hid that she was impressed.

'A photograph would only show one plant and not all of it.' Chrissie dredged up what Mr Watson had said. 'Mr Wat— My dad has to draw a plant's character, that's what you call it, and then the botanist decides which family the plant belongs to. He needs the drawing to give a plant a name or the plant doesn't exist.'

'That's ridiculous.' Bella rallied. 'The plant must exist or he couldn't draw it.'

'If something doesn't have a name you don't know what to call it.' Emily was tightrope-walking along the kerb, her hat low over her face.

'If you don't have a name, you can't exist.' Chrissie was stead-fast. 'Not properly,' she added. The railings got no nearer.

'I didn't have a name when I was born, but I was still there,' Bella said.

'How do you know?' Chrissie demanded.

'There're photographs.'

'Of you being born?' Emily tilted her head to look at Bella under the brim of her hat.

'No! That's disgusting.'

'So how do you know that you existed?' Emily pursued.

'This is mad.' Bella hugged her satchel to her chest and then she rounded on Chrissie. 'What do you need for drawing plants?'

Chrissie had to think fast. She conjured up Mr Watson's studio. Her mind was fuzzed by the image of a large piece of chocolate cake scattered with hundreds and thousands. She grimaced. 'A pencil that must be sharpened. A pen with ink, but not the sort you write with. Um, a knife. Not like a knife and fork. It's called something else that I've forgotten.'

Bella appeared to be listening. Behind them, on the other side of the road, St Anne's Church clock struck half past. The children, enervated by the broiling heat, straggled up to Kew Pond.

'This is where I live.' Chrissie stopped by the Watsons' double-fronted villa and, for good measure, placed a proprietorial hand on the gate. 'Goodbye then.'

'Where's your key?' Hands on hips, Bella didn't move.

'I don't have one.' Chrissie didn't have a key to her parents' flat so this much was true.

'It's a massive house!' Emily exclaimed.

'Not once you're in it.' Chrissie's blithe manner hid fear. Lying had unexpected ramifications. Like the creeping tendrils of an octopus, lies crept everywhere. 'I'm not allowed a key until I go to the big school,' she spluttered out the truth.

'What is a "big school"?' Bella was spiteful, her eyes glittering.

'It's a secondary school,' Emily explained cheerfully. 'I call it that too. Let's hope we all go to the same big school.'

'I'm going to Cambridge and I'll row in the boat race,' Bella snapped.

'You have to go to a big school first,' Emily said kindly.

'I might not get a key even then because my sister lost hers and my dad won't let her have another.' Chrissie was learning to lace her lies with truth for added plausibility.

'I've got a key!' Bella flourished a copper-coloured Yale from which dangled a troll with purple eyes and two-toned pink frenetic hair. 'I'm allowed to make a cup of tea with no one in the house and I can cut bread with the bread knife and make soup out of a tin.' She stamped her foot. Neither of the other two guessed that she was lying: Emily because she supposed that everyone told the truth, while Chrissie was bound like a fly in her web of deceit and couldn't think straight.

'I can do what I like when I'm inside there.' Chrissie gestured at the black front door. She was three minutes late for her lesson.

'Prove it.' Bella drummed a beat on the iron gate.

'Stop it, Bella,' Emily said.

'She has to prove that her mum and dad live here. We don't know anything about her; she could be anyone.' Bella sounded reasonable.

'Chrissie, there's your mummy.' Emily tugged at Chrissie's arm. 'There we are!' She rounded on Bella.

A woman was coming down the path. Her mauve trouser suit sparkled in the sunshine. Chrissie clutched the gate. Blood roared in her ears.

'Yes,' she managed to say and, with clumsy fingers, fiddled with the latch. She rushed through and slammed it shut before Bella could follow. She blundered up the path. At all costs Mrs Watson must not get to the gate. Then Bella would find out that she wasn't her mum and that Chrissie didn't live in the big house and that her father didn't do botanical illustrations. Then, like the dead material that had no name, Chrissie would not exist.

'Christina, we were beginning to wonder if you'd fallen into the crater on the Great West Road! I've made a chocolate cake with hundreds and thousands.' Mrs Watson ushered her inside.

Chrissie had no idea what crater Mrs Watson was talking about. When they were in the dark hallway, she looked back. Emily was hopscotching away, her figure blurred in the heat haze. By the gate the White Greyhound stood on its haunches, stony eyes watching her. Despite the searing temperatures, Chrissie shivered and her teeth began to chatter. The White Greyhound was saying something. Two words carried on the still air:

Prove it.

Chapter Nine

October 2014

Stella emerged from the lift into the carpeted corridor and wheeled out her cleaning cart with Stanley beside it. If Tina was in her flat, Stella would say that there wasn't time to dance. Yet dimly she found the possibility of a foxtrot appealing.

She shut the flat door and, stooping, unclipped Stanley's lead. The little poodle pottered along, snuffling at skirting boards, wending his way back and forth across the path of the cart.

'Walk on,' she commanded. She was vaguely uneasy that Stanley hadn't made straight for the living room where Tina had laid a square of fake lamb's wool on his old place by the sofa. Her unease grew as she became aware that she couldn't smell the lingering scent of Tina's perfume and that instead the hallway was tainted with the stale smell of cigarette smoke. She didn't have to be a detective to work out that this meant that Tina, after months of giving up, was smoking again. This was extraordinary, because Stella had grown to trust that when Tina made her mind up to do something, she never failed to do it. This was a quality that the two women had agreed they shared.

Stella strode around the flat and, despite the cold outside, flung open every window to dispel the smell.

Tina had stopped smoking for sufficient time to become revolted by the habit in others – the cloying odour of smoke on the clothes and breath of a smoker even if they weren't smoking at that moment. She complained at the smell clients left in her office and how it made a person appear dirty and unattractive regardless of their looks or hygiene habits. Now Tina was a smoker again.

Quelling her disappointment, Stella set to with a bottle of environmentally friendly disinfectant, spraying it on to the stainless steel splashback behind the kitchen sink, the counter top, the sink itself, vigorously wiping every surface until it gleamed. Again she had the odd sensation that she still lived here and that the last eight months – during which she had met Tina – had not happened.

From the living room Stanley started to growl. In the time she had owned him – over a year – Stella had been learning how to decipher his variety of noises. Short shrill barks meant he wanted her attention, if he was stuck in the garden or wanted to be fed. Mewing meant someone he liked was nearby. Jackie said he did it when Stella was coming up the stairs at the office. Frantic barking was guarding, whether from a cyclist, someone on a skateboard or in a mobility buggy – he objected to people on wheels – or footsteps passing the house after dark. He took exception to the refuse collectors and the recycling float and more recently to the relief postwoman.

The low guttural growl, steady and unremitting, was a warning. A preamble to guard-dog barking, but in a flat with CCTV, a coded key pad at the entrance, three deadlocks and a London bar, there was nothing for Stanley to guard.

A scourer in her rubber-gloved hands, Stella peeped into the living room to signal silently to him to be quiet. Stanley was standing on a sofa arm, tail down, eyes black as pitch. Stella dropped the scourer. A man stood by the dining table, fingers splayed on the polished glass. Looking at Stanley, he addressed her: 'I don't think he likes me.' His tone was pleasant, his eyes merry, apparently oblivious to what Stanley might do to him. The odour of stale smoke caught her nostrils.

'Who are you?' Stanley's growls gained momentum. Heart

thumping, Stella tipped her hand. He went quiet. All she had to do was mouth 'Go!' and the fluffy apricot poodle, the size of an average family cat, would launch off the sofa and rip the man's throat out. She hoped.

'We used to have a dog, bigger than him, but not half as fierce. Useless if my girls got in any trouble – he'd run a mile if he heard a car door slam!'

'Who are you?' Her mobile was on the table within reach of the man. She would never get to it before he did. Stella drew herself up to her full six feet, several centimetres taller than the man. She put him in his late fifties. He looked strong; she could see his muscles flexing through the fabric of his shirt as he tapped the table. She had no chance. The tapping was a steady beat.

He smoothed a hand over his thinning scalp and began rolling up his sleeves. 'You missed a bit.' He jabbed a finger at a faint mark on the carpet.

Taken aback at his change of tack, Stella looked at where he was pointing. She hadn't missed the stain; it dated from her time in the flat when one night – or early morning – she and Jack were having a case meeting and she had knocked over his mug of milk. So far no remover – and she had tried many – had erased it. Jack said that the stain was a reminder of the beauty of life's imperfections.

Never antagonize a criminal if your escape route is blocked. Terry's dictum came back to her.

She looked up and the man winked at her. 'My idea of a joke – not very good. I hear you're the best.' Grinning, he stepped towards her. At that moment, the hall door swished across the thick pile. *An accomplice.* Stanley began to mew. He shot off the sofa and seemed to literally fly across the room.

A short woman in a grey pin-striped skirt suit, holding a leather attaché case, stood in the doorway. Dropping the case, she reached down and gathered Stanley up, shutting her eyes.

'Is you my ickle bitsy bubsa boo, is you, is you?' She mumbled like a ventriloquist to avoid the dog's clacking tongue.

Stella was astonished. Tina Banks, the hot-shot lawyer who

took no prisoners because she got them off, was babbling baby talk at Stanley.

'Hey, I wanted to be here when you two met!' She tilted her face out of reach of the dog. He nestled into her neck. 'Stella, this is my *dad*!' Tina Banks shunted Stanley higher on to her shoulder.

Her legs as weak as jelly, Stella croaked, 'Oh, great. Er, hi, I've finished, so I'll be—' The stain on the carpet was darker. It was spreading. Stella saw Tina's dad glance at it and felt herself grow hot.

'I gave her a turn. You didn't say I was coming? Stella had me for a burglar and was about to set the dog on me!' Mr Banks rocked with laughter, his arms folded.

'I expected to be here when you arrived,' Tina snapped.

Stella was suddenly reminded of interchanges with her own dad. Tetchiness, impatience and – something that until now she had forgotten – that taking for granted, the knowledge that whatever happened, her dad would be there. Until one day he wasn't. Tina had said their dads were alike; now Stella saw what she meant. She felt strange. The sensation was envy, a rare experience for Stella: she made the best of what she had. She wished now that she could be irritated with Terry because he had alarmed the cleaner.

'Cliff Banks. It's good to meet you, Stell. I know you already. My girl tells me you're following in your dad's footsteps and catching the bad people. She says you're the cleanest detective in town!'

'That's not what I said, Dad.' Tina Banks remonstrated, her voice muffled in Stanley's woolly coat. She didn't say what she had said.

'We was having a laugh about that mark.' He scuffed at the stain with polished loafers. He laughed and Stella saw the younger man in the photo on the window sill. His face was used to laughing. Banks must be older than fifties: given Tina's age and that she had an older sister, he'd have to be late sixties.

Tina was dismissive. 'I asked Stella to leave it, she was in danger of going through to the floor.' Tina put Stanley down and kicked off her heels, padding past Stella in stockinged feet to the kitchen. Stella heard her put on the kettle. 'I've wanted you two to meet for ages.' She lounged in the doorway. 'Stella's dad passed, sadly.

It would have been perfect if you two could have met. I'm sure you'd have known each other.'

'Had a few coppers in my cab. Good tippers!' Mr Banks grinned at Stella.

'My dad never took taxis.' Too late she saw that the comment might be seen as impolite. She followed Tina into the kitchen.

'If you're lost, ask a policeman or a cabbie, my ma used to say.' Banks didn't seem offended.

'My dad has the Knowledge; he's a living compass. He never gets lost. Leave on left King Street, Right Weltje Road, Left Great West Road, Right Hammersmith Bridge Road, Forward Hammersmith Bridge...'

'Will you listen to that?' Banks beamed with pride. 'She used to call over my runs. She's the best!'

'Stella's dad was high up in the Met.' Frowning, Tina was setting out mugs in the kitchen. Stella wiped away a splash of milk after Tina had sploshed some in the mugs, mildly surprised at Tina's clumsiness.

'Better than being high up a tree!' Mr Banks wandered into the kitchen and gave his daughter a peck on the cheek. 'Saw your picture in the paper. My daughter, the star! Teach them to mess with you. Mind you, that bloke you got off looked well dodgy to me.'

'It's not my job to judge clients, Dad, you know that. Someone gets in your cab, you take them where they wanna go.' Stella noticed that Tina's London accent was stronger, like Cliff Banks's. Like Terry's. Tina seemed embarrassed by her dad's affection. Terry wasn't like that. Or was he? There was so much she didn't remember.

'See, Stella? My girl's got all the answers. Smart as you like. I'd have had forty fits if she'd followed me on the cabs! We sent her to the best school – I knackered meself keeping her there – but she didn't let me down.'

'Did you knacker yourself, Dad?' Tina handed him a coffee.

'You know I did, darling.' He pinched Tina's cheek. A red mark bloomed on her skin and then faded. He grasped her hard as if she was a little girl.

63

It was as if Tina hadn't known the sacrifice that her dad had made for her. Yet she had told Stella that, unlike her sister, she had been sent to private schools and graduated from law school. Who did she think paid? Stella was grateful that Terry hadn't worked hard to get her to a posh school. You owed your parents enough as it was. Then again, his ambitions for her were modest compared to Banks's intentions for his daughter.

Stella drank down her coffee and snatched up her rucksack from the sofa. 'I've got a recruitment meeting. It was nice to meet you.' She nodded at Mr Banks and again he grinned at her. 'I have heard all about you.' She had heard that he was like Terry; it made her think he was Terry.

'All *bad*, I hope!' They stood with the stain on the carpet between them. 'If your dad was a patch on me, he's all right! Bet he'd be chuffed at you now.'

Suzie said that he'd been disappointed when she became a cleaner. He'd wanted her to join the police. That Terry would be proud of her now was incomprehensible.

Banks got up and kissed her on the cheek. 'Watch yourself, doll.' He squeezed her arm. With Terry uppermost in her mind, Stella was flustered.

'Give Stella a break, Dad,' Tina warned. Dimly Stella saw that Tina had put her mug on the glass table; she had forgotten the coasters to protect the glass. 'Terry Darnell was a top detective. People are always telling me. Catch you soon, babes.' She ruffled Stanley's ears. 'You too, Stell.' She air-kissed Stella and gave her one of her father's winks.

In the lift, dazed, Stella watched the floor numbers illuminate as it descended: *three, two, one*. The doors slid aside revealing the glass-walled foyer. As she headed across the marble she was struck by three thoughts.

One, she hadn't held her dad's hand since she was seven.

Two, Terry had never visited her flat; he had never dropped in for coffee like Cliff Banks.

And three, she was still wearing the Marigolds.

Chapter Ten

June 1976

'You lied!'

The two girls were standing at the top of a flight of stone steps; their shadows, elongated in the afternoon sun, fell across a girl on the grass below. Behind them the Palm House, a palace of glass, shimmered.

'I did not.' Chrissie tossed her hair. The sun in her eyes and the others above her put her at a disadvantage. And she *had* lied.

It was Saturday. The uneasy trio had come to Kew Gardens with a picnic and set up camp by the Queen's Beasts. This series of twelve grotesque statues carved in Portland stone stood on guard outside the Palm House, commemorating the reign of Queen Elizabeth II. The girls were sitting near the Yale of Beaufort who Emily said could swivel his horns different ways at once. They had summarily dispatched their packed lunches. Bella had called Chrissie's Scotch egg a 'pig's eyeball'. This had put Chrissie off it so Emily had exchanged it for one of her Marmite sandwiches, a haphazard affair that she had made herself, with one end of the bread thin and crumbling and the other too thick to bite. It had too much Marmite, but Chrissie had eaten it because it was nice of Emily to swap.

Emily had cut her finger slicing the loaf. Bella said that she was lucky not to have died; her dad defended lots of criminals who had 'killed with knives'. She warned Chrissie to look out for blood on the sandwich. Her own lunch, cheese and ham rolls, had been prepared by something she called an 'oh pear', which Chrissie gathered was a servant. She couldn't ask directly because she had declared that her 'oh pear' was on holiday and her mother had had to make her lunch.

After this, they had explored the Palm House. Bella had chased off along metal grilles that led between the greenery. Shouting 'Boo!' she appeared suddenly from behind huge leaves. Above them towering palm trees were lost in a thick mist. Steam clogged Chrissie's nose. Soon they were all hot and sweaty and relieved to escape to the drier, if no less hot, air of the gardens.

Now they were at the top of an avenue Emily called the Syon Vista. Weeks of drought had turned the lush green sward stretching to the Thames to a brown frazzled strip, bordered by beds of concrete-grey soil in which the plants and shrubs had dried up and died.

Chrissie had dressed up. Or rather her mum had insisted she did. She sported a pink blouse with green Oxford bags and brand-new pink flip-flops. To her dismay Bella's flip-flops were the same, but in blue, and she wore South Sea Bubble stone-washed jeans with front pockets like the ones Chrissie's elder sister Michelle was still saving up for. Emily was clad in baggy patched denim, topped with her Brownie-badged hat.

No one could remember when it had last rained. Only at night was there relief from the burning sun, if not from the relentless heat. Bewildered by the stifling humidity of the Palm House, the children were unsure what to do next. Into this vacuum, Bella had flung her accusation that Chrissie had lied about her mum and dad.

'My daddy could send you to prison,' she followed through.

'Your dad's a barrister, Bella, not a judge,' Emily said. 'They don't send people to prison and anyway why would he? I don't think Chrissie lied about living in that huge house.'

Chrissie wanted to hit Bella, but no one at her new school picked fights. This was a pity, because she would definitely win a fight with Bella.

'She has to prove it. We need "co-oberated evidence".'

'They *are* my mum and dad!' Dizzied by the heat, Chrissie felt she might pass out at the horror of being found out.

It was two days since Chrissie's lie about Mr and Mrs Watson's. All of Friday, Bella had said nothing and by today, when nothing was said while they ate, Chrissie had begun to relax. She was learning to accommodate her parallel life. In one life she was the daughter of a taxi driver and a cleaner with a sister called Michelle who was in love with David Essex and in the other she lived with Mr and Mrs Watson in Kew Villa with a bedroom of her own and a garden as big as a park.

'You told Miss Sharp that you could say every street in London.' Bella advanced down the steps and began pacing around on the grass, her hands clasped behind her. 'That's impossible! She didn't believe you.'

'Actually it could be possible.' Emily was picking at a fraying thread on her skirt. 'Actors learn parts for plays that have miles more words than streets in London.' She pulled at the thread and it came away, loosening a panel of denim. Winding the thread around her finger, she added in a dreamy voice, 'No one should lie.'

Chrissie could have hugged Emily. What she had told Miss Sharp, their form teacher, was true. Although she hadn't told the whole truth. Chrissie was her dad's 'Calling Partner', although he already possessed the Green Badge qualifying him as a London taxi driver. He liked to refresh the Knowledge with her. He recited the 320 runs and, although Chrissie kept the book by her, she could correct him without it, because, keen to make him happy, she had learnt the routes off by heart. He had to know over twenty-five thousand streets as well as thousands of places like Kew Gardens. Most of these streets and landmarks Chrissie knew too. She was 'street-perfect'.

Chrissie would have liked to be a taxi driver, but her dad

insisted that the point of her going to an expensive school and having drawing lessons was so that she could do better for herself. Chrissie thought that driving a taxi was better than drawing dead plants or wearing a wig on top of your own hair. If she was a taxi driver she could go where she liked and no one would know. Then, while he was reading her *The Cat in the Hat*, her dad had told her that a taxi driver had to be of good character and never have committed a crime. A lie was a crime. Chrissie knew then that she could never be a cabbie.

She raised her voice as an aeroplane flew overhead and began to chant, 'Leave on left Putney Hill, Right Lytton Grove, Left West Hill, Right Sutherland Grove—'

'Stop!' Bella shouted. 'Who cares since you're not a stupid taxi driver!'

'If we get lost, Chrissie could find the way home.' Emily snapped a length of cotton hanging off her hem with her teeth. The hem came down.

'Your mum's going to be cross,' Bella commented without malice.

'She won't notice,' Emily piped confidently. 'She's out a lot.'

'How could she miss it?' Bella asked.

'She won't notice,' Emily said again.

'We won't get lost because we know where we are,' Bella returned to Emily's comment, adding superfluously: 'I'm in charge!' She blinked rapidly and tossed her hair.

'Who says you're in charge?' Chrissie asked.

'I did just then.'

'We could all be in charge.' Bending, Emily pulled at another thread. Her hat fell off and tumbled down the steps to Chrissie's feet.

'Only one person can be in charge.' Chrissie forgot that she wanted to keep Emily on her side. Emily helped her with questions that confounded her. *What sort of mount do you prefer? What's your favourite, Paris or Berlin?*

'I saw your mum shopping by Kew Gardens station this morning.' Bella's voice was pleasant. Chrissie assumed she meant Emily's mum but then saw with a jolt that she was looking at her.

'No you didn't.' Chrissie breathed rapidly. It was as if the sun had sapped the atmosphere of oxygen. 'My mum was at home, she made my packed lunch.' Sweat trickled into one eye; she rubbed at it with a fist.

'She must have sneaked out without you knowing.' Bella balanced on one leg, a foot resting on her calf. She was always doing ballet poses. She cupped her chin in a pose of genuine puzzlement although Chrissie wasn't fooled. She was confident about sticking to her story but, feeling a twinge of doubt, began to rake over the morning's activities. She and Michelle had helped her mum clean the flat. Her mum had been supervisor. She hadn't gone to the shops. And she wouldn't go on a train to Kew because the shops were in King Street, around the corner.

With a terrible whoosh Chrissie guessed the truth. Bella meant Mrs Watson. She stalled for time. 'This morning?'

'Yes, cloth ears.' Sniffing victory, Bella did a cartwheel.

'My mum went shopping this morning,' Emily said helpfully. 'It could have been her, except it was Oxford Street.' She came down the stone steps and picked up her hat.

'I wonder if you lied?' Bella speculated. She did another cartwheel. 'You don't look like her one bit.'

'I do.' A shutter of red came down over Chrissie's eyes. She curled her fists.

She landed Bella a high kick and sent her flying. She kicked her until she stopped moving and speaking and was nothing but a brown sprig. Dead material.

'I don't look like my mum or my dad. Everyone says that. They call me the Cuckoo in the Nest.' Sitting on the top step, Emily twisted thread around her index finger. 'She must be Chrissie's mum; we saw her.'

The red mist cleared. Chrissie regarded Emily; she was surrounded by wisps of torn cotton. She had stretched her blouse over her knees so it looked like she had huge bosoms. Chrissie would have laughed at this with her friends from her old school, but at the prep school even the jokes were different.

Bella turned on Chrissie. 'Prove that the lady in that house is your mother.'

'I don't mind if we don't have proof.' Emily brightened. 'Although you could bring a photograph of your mum. Let's all do that.' She was perched on the bottom step.

'Why do we need to know what our mums look like?' Chrissie was dismayed. Emily had deserted her.

'Because we do.' Bella was icy.

The sun was a big metal plate pressing down on her. *Chrissie had proof.* She reached into her pocket and then held out her hand, palm uppermost. The silver caught the sunlight. 'I happen to have this.' She was nonchalant.

'What's that?' Hands on hips, Bella didn't move.

'That's gorgeous!' Emily got to her feet and peered at the locket. 'You should wear it round your neck; it would look beautiful on you.'

'It's not all.' Chrissie prised open the case with clumsy fingers. She held it up for Emily to see. She didn't look at Bella.

'That's your mum!' Emily exclaimed with delight. 'How clever to make it so tiny. Is that your dad? Golly, they're kissing!' She gave a mew of delight.

'That's revolting.' Bella hugged herself. 'Parents shouldn't do that. Mine don't.' She frowned.

'Do what?' Emily looked at her.

'Kiss and all that.'

'Yes they should.' Chrissie sensed a chink in the armour. 'It's how we exist. Our mums and dads go to bed and—'

'Shut up,' Bella spat.

'Don't you think it would suit Chrissie if she wore it?' Emily, apparently oblivious to the prevailing aggression, appealed to Bella.

'I might lose it.' Chrissie couldn't say that if she wore it she might be sent to prison and then there was no chance of being a taxi driver. 'Anyway, it's not mine.' She knew to add in a sprinkling of truth.

'Give it to me.' Bella strode over and put out a hand.

'No.' Chrissie closed her fingers around the locket. 'I'm not to give it to anyone. My mum said I could show you, but I must bring it back.'

'Is it a family heirloom?' Emily enquired. 'My dad says Mum's sold all our ones. They argue about it.' Her brow puckered briefly.

'Yes.' Not knowing what an 'air loom' might be, Chrissie gave herself a 50 per cent chance that this was the correct answer. 'Anyway, that's all the proof I'm giving you,' she told Bella.

Her dad said she was a winner, but even winners needed back-up. *'Your new friends will help when you're older. It's how it works. Tell George – Mr Watson – I'm right behind you. That'll impress him.'* Chrissie felt a pall of gloom descend at the idea of still knowing Bella when she was grown up. Nor could she tell Mr Watson that her dad was behind her. He would look over her shoulder and see she was lying.

Blinded by the glare of the sun, pinpricks of light danced before her eyes. Another aeroplane roared across the sky. As the sound died, Chrissie announced, 'I have to go.'

'We'll come with you.' Bella gave a sly smile. 'I want to ask your dad about drawing plants.'

'Race you.' Chrissie snatched off her flip-flops and, her ruck-sack bouncing against her back, pelted up Syon Vista. The short dry grass stung the soles of her feet. Emily shouted that she was going the wrong way, but Chrissie ran faster. She veered off the avenue and plunged through a shrubbery.

She was deep in the hinterland of the Botanic Gardens. With temperatures a record high, visitors were sheltering in the cafés, but even on normal days this area was rarely frequented. She pushed on between rhododendron bushes, tripping on tree roots, inhaling eucalyptus and the scents of other exotic oils released by the searing heat from the bark of trees brought from far-off lands. She was oblivious to cuts flecking her skin from grasses razor sharp through lack of rain.

At last certain that she had shaken off Bella, Chrissie stopped.

Getting her breath, she put on her flip-flops and, depleted by the heat, plodded on. Mesmerized by the crunch of tinder-dry brushwood beneath her feet, she wandered along a meandering track of compacted soil slippery with pine needles, and pushed through thickets of foliage.

She was a winner. She told Bella out loud, 'I'm in charge.'

Triumphant, it didn't occur to Chrissie that she was lost. Or that if she shouted for help, in this remote part of Kew Gardens, no one would hear.

Chapter Eleven

October 2014

Jack placed his London Underground pass on to the barrier sensor at Kew Gardens station. A train had just left so there was no one on the eastbound platform. It was eleven forty. He strolled to the 'head end' and regarded the two screens on the driver's console. They displayed two angles of the dark empty platform. He flicked a glance at the top of the console: there was nothing there. Since the 'One Under' case last year, he'd been looking out for objects left there and once had seen a tin of mandarins. The case had involved a child's toy left on top of consoles on the Wimbledon line and a man hit by a train at Stamford Brook station. It was the first case brought to Stella by a client. The first two investigations that he and Stella had worked on had been cold cases. Stella had found the files in her father's house after his death.

The tin of mandarins had gone when Jack made the down-road journey and no more tins of fruit – or anything else –had appeared since. Probably left accidentally by a driver. Most explanations for strange occurrences were boring. The One Under case was only last year, but it felt longer ago since he and Stella had worked as a team. He missed it.

In that time the 'Grime and Crime Agency', as Lucie May – reporter and erstwhile friend of Terry Darnell – had, not altogether kindly, dubbed it, had solved two cases. They had reunited a cat with its owner and found a missing person. Both 'jobs' were done free of charge. The missing person case wasn't in theory minor. Suzie Darnell had noticed newspaper deliveries for an elderly woman on her corridor mounting up. A few 'door-to-door inquiries' (two doors) established that the neighbour was staying with her niece in Brighton and had forgotten to cancel the papers. Jack suspected Suzie had rustled up the mystery to keep their hand in. It hadn't required teamwork; Stella had done it by herself.

On the other line, a Richmond train was approaching. The driver waved at Jack and he returned the gesture automatically – one driver to another; then the driver switched on his cab lights and Jack realized that he knew him. Darryl Clark had got the One Under at Stamford Brook. Jack was pleased that Clark was back at work. One man had beaten his demons.

The doors shut and the train gathered speed, clattering off down the track, lights absorbed into the darkness. Jack had two days off. He had spent that day and the evening walking the streets of West London. He had crossed the river four times, the final time over the bridge at Kew, and ended up at Kew Gardens station. He hadn't made a conscious decision to take a train, he was rarely a passenger, but now that he was on the platform he understood why he was here. Jennifer Day, the woman who had died on his train, had been at the back of his mind all day. With a shock he remembered how her life had ended here. Strictly speaking she had died a few metres up the track, but it wasn't necessary to be precise. Eleven forty-three. The time that the P.E.A. alarm had been sounded on his train. It was a sign that tonight's driver was Darryl Clark; everything was connected. Coincidences are non-existent.

There was something tied to the fence on the other platform. Jack stepped to the edge of the platform and saw that it was a bouquet of flowers. The flowers were dead and limp. They must have been left for Jennifer Day. Something was attached to the wrapping. A card, perhaps left by her family, flapped listlessly in the damp breeze. At the inquest her two grown-up children, a man and a woman, had kept close to the husband as if he might crumple to the floor. The term 'looked like he'd been hit by a truck' was apt. The man's face was alabaster-white and blasted by shock. Jack had read somewhere that most people want to die in their own homes. Jennifer Day wouldn't have wished to die on *the floor of a late-night train amongst strangers* as Lucie May, unafraid of raw truth, had phrased it in the *Chronicle*.

There was someone on the platform. He must have been in the last car of the Richmond train. Jack retreated into the shadows of the canopy. The man was strolling towards the barrier, swinging a golfing umbrella; it tapped as it touched the platform. Tap. Tap. Tap. He was passing the flowers. He stopped. Tap.

The man approached the railing and, with a deft movement, ripped off the card. He gave it a cursory glance and let it drop. It floated to the ground a metre from the railing.

Abruptly he swivelled on his heel and looked across to where Jack was standing, shrouded in darkness. Adept at invisibility, Jack had learnt to close down. He had told Stella that people sense when they are being watched, even from behind. He concentrated on the bundled cables beneath the platform lip: even thoughts could attract attention. He dressed in black to blend with the night. The man's gaze paused at the spot where he stood. *He knew he was there.*

There was a clatter. A boy had pushed through the turnstile and dropped his skateboard on the platform. He was scooting towards the man and the flowers. The man resumed his stroll up the platform with what Jack took to be an Oyster card held lightly between his fingers.

Keeping in the darkness of the canopy, Jack glided swiftly to the barrier and slipped behind a pillar. The man passed beneath the bleak lamplight and as he turned to the barrier, Jack saw his face properly. A ripple of shock passed through him. It was the man from the sixth car. *The True Host.*

Jack forced himself to stay by the pillar. The man was aware of Jack. His only option was to outthink him.

The man left the station and went into the tunnel. *Like Jack, he hadn't chosen the bridge.* Moments later, he came up the steps close to Jack's pillar. Had he not been acutely aware of him, Jack might have missed him. He was holding his umbrella across his chest like a rifle. Treading like a cat, the man slipped through the ticket office and out on to the concourse.

Jack pushed back through the barrier and, staying in the ticket office, looked out through the window. The man was out of his sightline, yet he forced himself to remain where he was. The True Host couldn't know what he was made of. Not yet. If Jack showed no sign of following him, he might be put off the scent. He couldn't know that Jack had a mind like his own.

Jack stared at the Lloyds chemist on Station Approach. To keep his mind free he listed the items that were sold. *Moisturizer, plasters, cotton wool, prescription drugs, sun-tan cream...*

The man was caught in the reflection of the chemist's window walking towards Kew Gardens Road. Spectral: although he was alive, there was no sign of life. He dealt in death.

'What you doing?' The boy was balanced on his skateboard, jiggling to music in his headphones; the wheels rolled back and forth.

Jack felt a frisson of alarm. It was the innocent who gave the game away.

'Waiting for someone.' He looked stern. The boy was no more than fifteen, he should be at home in bed.

'No one's coming,' the boy said with a confidence that was uncanny – as if he *knew*. He pivoted his riding foot and pushed off. When Jack came out of the station, the scrawl of the wheels on the pavement was fading. He had lost the True Host. Jack didn't panic. He would find him.

Most people assume that they will not be chosen from a crowd. No one will follow them and learn their habits. Most consider themselves invisible. The majority of commuters ignore station warnings to stand back from the yellow line at the platform's edge. Not just to avoid the train's slipstream, but because a True Host might be waiting to push them beneath the wheels. CCTV doesn't pick up intention. Few people expect the unexpected. Sometimes someone fell on to the rails and died beneath the wheels of the train. Verdict: accidental death. When Jack pulled into stations, his gaze travelled across faces searching for the killer. He forced them to see that he *knew* them. He had to stop them committing a terrible act. How many lives had he saved in that way?

People leave windows open at night, a door on the latch while they take their dog for a last walk and secrete keys under the mat. They rely on experience. It didn't happen yesterday so it won't happen today. If it does happen, it happens to other people. A True Host infiltrated existence and rendered it void.

Jack had learnt early that adults weren't to be trusted. He had developed an antenna for those who carry death in their hearts. It was months since he had found a True Host. He had forgotten the effect that it had on him. He felt barely alive.

There were no cars outside the station to provide cover. Jack walked as if he had a destination, blotting out the True Host. If he checked his watch and began to hurry it would appear contrived. He submitted to the deadness. Yet if the man was a True Host he would recognize Jack. A man with a mind like his own.

Jack passed the health-food shop, the flower shop and an optician's. At the end of the road he used the zebra crossing although there were no cars coming.

He found him on Leyborne Park, walking with purpose. Jack risked staying on the same pavement as if he didn't care if he was seen. The man crossed the South Circular and went down Forest Road and into Priory Road. Tap. Tap. Tap. The sound echoed in the empty streets.

Jack tried to keep in the shadows, but the street lighting was effective so if the man looked round he would see him. At the end of Priory Road the man stopped. Jack ducked behind the trunk of an oak tree.

The man remained still, a hand resting on one of two iron gates. The words 'Kew' and 'Villa' were wrought into the top of each. The man unlatched the gate. He shot a cuff and consulted his watch. He closed the gate and continued on his way, walking faster now. Swinging the umbrella higher. Tap. Tap.

On Kew Road the boundary wall of the Botanic Gardens stretched off into the distance. It wavered slightly as if the bricklayers had lacked a plumb line when they built it. More likely the centuries had caused the wall to shift out of true. The gardens were Stella's latest client. It was also one of his favourite places. Since he was a boy he had nurtured a dream of going to the Herbarium and seeing the centuries-old collection of plant specimens, many of them unidentified. His mother had promised to take him when he was grown up. Or had she? Whatever, it was surely another sign. Jack roused himself. The man was walking fast now.

Jack stepped into the doorway of the Maids of Honour tea shop. He would be out of sight. He glanced into the shop. He had gone there with his mother. It was when she had promised to take him to the Herbarium, he was sure now. He could see the table at which they had sat. Or had they? Like most things to do with her, he might have made it up.

The pavement beneath the Kew Gardens wall was empty. The pagoda peeped above the dark bulk of the trees. Even a True Host couldn't scale the high wall. Heedless of being seen Jack checked under and between parked cars on the opposite side of the road. Nothing.

If Stella were here, she would insist that there was a logical explanation. Unlike him, she didn't believe that people disappeared – drifting between time zones or into other lives – she would examine the bricks and mortar. Keeping to the boundary wall, Jack went in the direction that man had been going.

He had played a game in the car with his mother. Singing to music on the radio when they were about to enter a tunnel she told him to keep singing. *'Hold the tune, keep the beat.'* When the car came out of the tunnel and radio reception was restored, their singing was in synch with the song. It was 'Endless Love', the duet between Diana Ross and Lionel Ritchie. Yet the song was released three days after his mother's death so that couldn't be true. 'It's true for you,' Jackie had said. Jack hummed it now and, as if coming out of a tunnel and picking up the song again, he saw where the man had gone.

No ghosts, no magic. The explanation was as prosaic as Stella would have expected. There was a door in the wall. *Bricks and mortar.* The True Host had gone into Kew Gardens.

Jack had walked along here – night and day – and hadn't noticed the door. He tried the handle, knowing that it would be locked.

He retraced his steps. By the time he arrived at the Victoria Gate it had started raining. Large drops that in moments would soak him. A car was coming down Kew Road towards the bridge. A lamp at the front came on, the orange light blurred by rain. A taxi. Jack put up a hand and flagged it down. The driver's offside window slid down. A silhouetted figure in the darkness.

Jack gave an address – not his own, he never divulged that – and heard the click of the passenger door unlocking. Inside he did up his seat belt and settled back. He hoped the driver wouldn't chat and noted that the glass partition was closed. The driver remained silent.

Jennifer Day had died amongst strangers. One of the 'strangers' had been a True Host. In her report of the inquest, Lucie May had said Day's death had been 'accidental'. Cashman's layman's diagnosis had been correct. She had died of a cerebral aneurism. A blood vessel had ballooned and burst, flooding her brain with blood. She had died instantly, and the coroner had assured her family that, apart from the stiff neck she had mentioned to her fellow passenger, she had felt no pain. Yet it had happened in the presence of a man who made it his business to extinguish life.

Jack started to text Stella that they might have another case. Stella would ask for proof. He put away his phone as the taxi pulled up beside the statue of the Leaning Woman.

Chapter Twelve

June 1976

Chrissie blundered out from a tunnel of pines and japonica bushes into sunshine. She stepped on to an asphalt path swollen and blistering in the heat and cracked where weeds had forced their way through. The weeds were dead and tangled. Her flip-flops stuck to the tacky bitumen and she tripped. One flip-flop came off and she yelped when the ground burned her foot.

A shiver went down Chrissie's spine. She was lost. Then she felt relief. There was a house. Shattered by running away from Bella and by the heat, mechanically she counted the windows. She did it twice before she decided upon seven.

She would ask the people who lived in the house to tell her the way home. Trusting, Chrissie pattered across the grass. She grabbed a metal handrail to drag herself up steps to a veranda; the metal was scorching and she snatched her hand away.

She was outside a grand porch with two front doors. The house was bigger than Kew Villa where Mr and Mrs Watson lived. Chrissie faltered. If a person like Mrs Watson answered, she would be cross that she had left her friends and wouldn't tell her the way home.

Her dad had told her not to be frightened of anything. Chrissie knocked on one of the doors. No one came. Undaunted, the little girl took off her flip-flops and, putting them by the door, went inside. Almost immediately she saw a woman's face. A ghost!

'He-hello.' The woman stared at her as if she was blind and calming down she saw that it was a statue. If she had been with Bella and Emily they might have made a joke out of it. Even though it wasn't funny.

Two more doors led into the house itself. One was ajar and a strange smell drifted out. Without knocking again, Chrissie crept inside.

Light spilled down from the dirt-encrusted windows high above. There was no ceiling. It wasn't a real house, there were no doors or rooms. Above her she saw a railing protecting a ledge that ran around all the walls of the house, but there were no stairs to reach it. Chrissie felt uncertain and thought of running out, but the tiles on the floor felt wonderfully cool on the soles of her feet so she stayed.

'Hello?' No one replied. Chrissie ventured further in, trying not to breathe in the strange smell that made her think of gravestones and dead spiders.

The walls were completely covered in pictures with no spaces in between. Chrissie felt a pressing on her chest at the sight of them all squashed up together. She peered up at one. It was of a tree with orange petals. It was the same picture as in Mr and Mrs Watson's drawing room. For some reason, instead of reassuring her, this made her feel faintly afraid. A house with no rooms and vast expanses of wall entirely filled with paintings. She gulped for breath.

Chrissie heard something. A cough or a sneeze: she couldn't tell. About to call out, she remembered that she was in someone's house without permission. Keeping close to the wall, thinking of her dad's instruction about winning, she took little steps and came to a break in the wall. She was in the entrance to what she could see was a proper room. It had a lower ceiling and four walls and a door opposite. Taking another step she saw a cupboard. There were pictures all over the walls here too. Her mum would have a fit: it would be hard to clean properly.

A lady lay on the floor. White teeth, white eyes, white hair. Chrissie clamped a hand to her mouth to stop herself yelling at the top of her voice.

Eventually she asked, 'Are you all right?' The lady wore a skirt and her legs were bare. Chrissie kicked something and, jumping back, saw that it was a shoe. Black with a silver buckle.

She heard something beyond the door on the other side of the room. She flung open the cupboard, pushed in and shoved herself to the back. Instantly she saw her mistake. This was the first place that Bella would look. Her dad told her off for acting without thinking. She should have left the way she came in. She shouldn't be in someone else's house. It didn't occur to Chrissie that the sound – definitely footsteps – might not be Bella.

She stuck her finger in a knot hole and managed to draw one door shut. But Bella might see her finger poking through. She jolted with shock. Through the gap between the doors the lady was looking right at her. Gobstopper eyes staring. Chrissie stared back.

She shut her eyes. *Bella was coming.* When Chrissie opened her eyes, it wasn't Bella that she saw.

The Cat in the Hat was balancing an umbrella on his paw. Chrissie snatched her finger out of the knot hole. The door shifted outward and the crack widened. The Cat in the Hat swooped down and flapped open a big bag. He began to put the lady into it. Chrissie screwed up her eyes, but still she saw the cat as he leapt and bounded about, his long tail twirling in his hand, holding his umbrella as if it were a gun. Silently Chrissie chanted Run 82 to make him stop.

'Leave by left Gloucester Road, Right Elvaston Place, Left Queen's Gate, Right Kensington Gore...'

When she risked looking again there was no one there. The pattern made by a mix of octagonal and rectangular tiles was uninterrupted. Her head was thumping in earnest.

She clambered out of the cupboard and raced across the dimly lit gallery out on to the veranda. A bluff of heat enveloped her and the sunlight pierced her eyes. She had no idea which way she had come. Parched lawns stretched away before her.

She ran along the veranda and leapt down the steps on to the grass. Her ankles shooting with pain, she ran beside the bitumen path until, crippled by a stitch, she could run no more.

On the veranda of the red-bricked house with no rooms, a shadow fell across a pair of child's flip-flops. The shadow, stark in the sunlight, might have been mistaken for a creature in a stove-pipe hat.

Chapter Thirteen

November 2014

'You are not owed a penny. My company has reimbursed you for everything. This is about truth and lies. It always has been.' A pause. 'It's a bloody name. It means nothing.' Pause. 'Time is not a luxury at our disposal.' Tina Banks rolled her eyes. 'Twat!' She flung down the receiver, startling Stanley, snoozing in the basket Tina had bought for him.

Stella was cleaning the electrochromic glass partition. It was now frosted but at the press of a button could clear, giving Tina a panoramic view of her staff in the sprawling office beyond. Stella had never heard Tina swear before.

It was six o'clock in the morning. As usual when Stella had arrived to clean Tina's law offices in Brentford, she found her already at her desk and on the phone. She had beckoned Stella in when she had attempted to leave. She had begun cleaning reluctantly, because Tina, who said that she and Stella were morning people, appeared to be in an uncharacteristically angry mood.

Tina snatched up the pen and underlined something on her pad, scoring the paper.

'I… er—' Stella sprayed a cloud of Mr Muscle all-purpose cleaner on to her cloth and rubbed at the glass vigorously.

'If you press any harder you'll frost it permanently.' Tina scowled. 'Get down, you'll rip my tights!' Stanley, distressed by her fury, was pawing at her, behaviour that, against Stella's advice, Tina usually encouraged.

Stella wondered if the Ball hadn't gone to plan and foxtrotting hadn't opened the doors that Tina had intended that it should. Stella mouthed to Stanley to return to his bed, realizing too late that he had stolen an anti-static cloth.

'We'll have to review him coming if he's going to be naughty.' Tina glared at the dog.

'Yes.' Stella lured Stanley out again with a chicken treat. She tossed it across the room for him to 'find' and retrieved the cloth.

'That's rewarding him for bad behaviour.'

'The trainer advises that I "pick my battles". That wasn't worth a head-to-head.' Stella confirmed to herself that the glass was clean.

'Your *trainer!*'

Stella was baffled: Tina knew that she took Stanley to dog classes, both obedience and agility; she often said that 'more people should take trouble with their animals'.

'Either he's being naughty or he's not. If the law went along those lines, people would get off for some crimes and not others.' Tina was icy.

'Isn't that what happens sometimes?' Stella was furious with herself for arguing. She set about packing up the cart. Tina's office was the last on her job sheet. Tina would usually have the coffee on and insist Stella stay for a cup. Today the percolator was empty and cold.

'None of us is blameless. It's not wrong if you get away with it. He will be getting up to all sorts of stuff that you don't know about.' Tina tilted back in her leather armchair, twiddling the pen between her two forefingers and thumbs.

'I dare say.' Astonished at Tina's character change – or rather the advent of a side of Tina that Stella had supposed was reserved for bitter legal disputes – Stella wheeled the cart to the door and gestured for Stanley to follow. He set off towards her and then detoured to Tina's desk.

'This way, Stanley!' Stella dispensed with the silent command. He was making for something under the desk. She swooped down and got there before him. It was a silver pendant on a chain. 'Is this yours?' She placed it on Tina's desk, noticing that it wasn't a pendant, but a heart-shaped locket.

'No.' Tina's face clouded over. 'Where was that?'

'Under your desk.'

'A client must have dropped it.'

'I've just vacuumed – it wasn't there then.' Stella was puzzled.

Tina rounded on her. 'Are you accusing me of lying? No chance that you missed a bit, I suppose?'

Stella was used to clients being peremptory, even rude. Mrs Ramsay, an elderly woman, had been erratic and demanding and Stella had taken her moods in her stride. If clients were rude to her staff she sacked the client. Clean Slate operatives must be treated with respect. But it wasn't possible to sack Tina Banks – she was a friend; and besides, Stella could take it. The dancing had been out of character, but this was different again: Stella didn't recognize Tina. She was being angry with her for a quality that Stella had supposed they shared. A commitment to perfection. Dumbfounded Stella agreed: 'I must have missed it.'

'Ignore me.' Tina swept the locket off the desk into an open drawer and slammed it shut. Swivelling away from Stella, her back to her, she asked, 'Found any detective cases lately?'

'We don't go looking. Clients come to us.' Tina knew this. Stella clipped on Stanley's lead. In the early morning, Tina kept her office door open and the glass clear so that she could greet her staff as they arrived. Now the glass was frosted and Tina's door was shut.

'*Do* they come to you?'

'We've had a couple of things.' Stella hoped Tina wouldn't ask her about her mum's missing neighbour who wasn't missing and the cat who had been lured to the house two doors down by morsels of fresh fish and a bed in the porch.

'If you were proactive re new business, you'd sweep up!' If Tina intended a pun, she gave no sign. 'I ran into that ancient hack from the *Chronicle*, Lucie May, at the coroner's court last week, snouting for pickings like the carrion crow she is. She was singing your praises as a private eye.'

Lucie May never disclosed her age, and Stella and Tina had agreed that, with her immaculate make-up, short skirts and high heels, she could be anything from fifty to seventy. Stella and Lucie May had an uneasy relationship. Close to Terry, Lucie May had resented his daughter, as she had put it to Jack, 'playing detective'. Since the One Under case, May had changed her tune, though surely not to the extent, Stella thought, of praising Stella to others.

'She told me I'd lost weight. I said, "At least I'm not a head on a stick!"' Tina scooted her mouse around the mat like a toy car. This *was* in character, Stella had seen that: impatient with intractable objects, Tina broke them. Tina joked that her capital asset costs were sky high. Stella respected equipment: she kept her carpet cleaners, duo-speed floor scrubbers, even plastic warning signs spick and span.

'I was thinking of hiring you.' Tina bashed the mouse down on the mat.

Stella was already cleaning Tina's office and flat. The only hiring she could do was to increase the number and length of the sessions. 'To be honest, it's not necessary to—'

Music interrupted her. Stella was transported to 1973 when, aged seven, she had been given David Cassidy's 'Daydreamer' by her dad on the first access weekend after his separation from her mum. He had given her a present each weekend until her mum told him that it was too late to be 'Super-Dad'. The music was Tina's ringtone. She cut Cassidy off mid-croon.

'The cleaner's here. Hold on.' The handset clamped to her ear, Tina Banks edged around her desk and left the office. As Tina stalked through the open-plan office Stella caught the words,

'Everything must come out…' Then Tina was gone. Stella heard the boom of the staircase door slamming.

Tina never referred to Stella as 'the cleaner'. Stella didn't mind, it was what she was and clean environments were vital. Tina often said that cleaners made the world go around as much as criminal lawyers and that her mum had been a cleaner.

Stella gave the office a last scan. At the carpet where she had found the locket there were suction marks on the pile. She *had* vacuumed there.

She guided the cart along a gangway between baffle screens. Tina was returning.

'You're done for the day.' In high heels Tina was still shorter than Stella.

Puzzled by Tina's personality change, Stella broke a cardinal Clean Slate rule and asked, 'You OK?'

'I will be.' Tina went into her office and as she turned to shut the door she added, 'I'm a winner.' She shut the door. Through the frosted-glass partition Stella saw a smudged shadow. Tina appeared to hesitate. Was she coming back? Stella waited. Tina returned to her desk and sat down.

In the lift, squeezed in with Stanley and the cart, Stella was bewildered by their exchange. Seldom offended or hurt, she didn't take Tina Banks's manner personally; she stuck to facts. Tina was adamant that she hadn't dropped the locket. No one had come into the office while Stella was there. While able to admit a mistake, Stella knew that the locket had not been on the carpet when she had vacuumed.

Reluctantly Stella faced the most likely explanation. Although she had denied it, Tina had dropped the locket. In other words, she had lied.

Chapter Fourteen

June 1976

Chrissie shrank into the shadow of the porch to avoid the sun. Her head thumped; the heat had created a dislocation from reality so she felt as if she was floating above herself.

Bella and Emily were not at the gate. She had given them the slip after school, but didn't put it past Bella to sneak along to the house by Kew Pond to meet her 'mum'. Since last weekend's picnic in Kew Gardens, Bella hadn't spoken to her. In a snatched exchange in the girls' toilets, Emily had imparted the unsurprising news to Chrissie that Bella had 'broken' with her.

'If you say sorry, I'm sure she'll be fine. She was hurt that you ran away. Bella's actually quite nice,' Emily had advised as they washed their hands at the sink.

'I'm not sorry,' Chrissie had pointed out.

'You mustn't lie,' Emily had said solemnly. 'That would be wrong.'

Since lying was what Chrissie did all the time, she had nothing to say. She was about to tell Emily about seeing the lady with the gobstopper eyes on the floor in a house with no rooms in Kew Gardens, but Bella had come into the toilets so Chrissie left.

Huddled in the Watsons' porch, Chrissie considered going

home. She could pretend that she had gone to the drawing class and use the time to go to Ravenscourt Park and play with her old friends under the railway arches. Except she would have no drawing to show her mum and dad. And Mr and Mrs Watson would tell her dad she hadn't come and he would be cross. He would also be cross that she was a 'broken friend'. Besides, she had learned the parts of a flower off by heart and wanted to display her knowledge to Mr Watson.

Petals (easy). Sepals, ray florets, perianth, stamens...

Five days had passed since Chrissie had hidden in the cupboard in the house with no rooms. Over that time she had come to believe that what she had seen was a dream. Steeped in heat, colours bleached and sound muted, she had gone to bed with what her mum called sunstroke; her mum had said that her 'brain was addled'. Her dad told her off for not wearing a hat. Lying in her bedroom with the curtains drawn, she had watched the cat wearing a tall red hat, his umbrella tapping on the tiles. The lady with the gobstopper eyes was talking, *I've made chocolate cake... hundreds and thousands...* Drifting in and out of nausea Chrissie had told herself that cats couldn't carry umbrellas. Perhaps it wasn't an umbrella...

Chrissie knocked on the Watsons' front door. She was taken aback when Mr Watson himself answered.

'Ah, Christina, it's you.' He sounded as if he wasn't expecting her. 'Mrs Watson has popped out to the shops. She's baked you a chocolate cake. It's in the drawing room. *As usual.*' Maybe he was as fed up by the regular appearance of the cake as Chrissie was.

'When will she be back?' Chrissie peered past him into the dim hall. 'Mrs Watson, I mean.' *Who's 'she', the cat's mother?* Bella whispered in her ear.

'She didn't say. Eat your tea and come to the studio.' Mr Watson was climbing the stairs.

Chrissie hovered in the doorway of the drawing room. A plate with a wedge of chocolate cake smothered with hundreds and thousands was on the table by the settee next to a glass of milk.

She plumped down on the settee, knees together, and nibbled

at the cake. It was the nicest so far, sticky and sweet, not dry and needing the horrid warm milk to wash it down. Mrs Watson hadn't put out a serviette for her chocolatey fingers so Chrissie held the plate up to her chin to stop chocolate getting on the sofa.

Chrissie ate fast. If she could finish before Mrs Watson got back, she could return the locket without her knowing. This was risky because Mr Watson might change his mind and fetch her. He hadn't done so before, but Chrissie had long ago worked out that because a thing hadn't happened before it didn't mean it wouldn't happen. He had never answered the front door before. She gulped the milk and was surprised to find it was cold.

Bang!

Cheeks bulging with cake, Chrissie looked wildly about her.

Bang! It was the door. Maybe Mrs Watson didn't have her own key either. Chrissie was dismayed; she wouldn't be able to return the locket.

Mr Watson wasn't coming to answer. Chrissie wiped at her mouth with the back of her hand and, putting down the empty plate, trotted out to the hall.

A man was going down the path. When he heard the door open, he came back. He grinned down at her. 'I thought there was no one home!'

'I'm here,' Chrissie informed him.

'Is your daddy here? Or your mummy?'

The man was wearing a dark blue suit with a blue tie. He fiddled with the tie. Chrissie's dad never wore a tie. Mr Watson did. The man was waiting for her to speak. She answered truthfully. 'She's popped out.' Chrissie was intrigued that a person believed that she lived here. It made her believe it too.

'OK.' The man frowned. 'What about your daddy?'

'Can I help?' Mr Watson was behind her. To make room, Chrissie stepped on to the path, blinking in the sunshine.

'Detective Inspector Darnell, Met Police. Mr Watson?'

'Yes, that is me.' Mr Watson was patient. 'It is I.' He corrected himself primly.

'I have a couple of questions.' The police detective ran a hand through his hair, like her real dad did. He smelled like her real dad; Chrissie guessed he must have the same after-shave.

'Is it about my wife?' Mr Watson asked. 'Is she all right?'

'If we could speak privately?' The detective flashed a smile at Chrissie and for a second she thought he wanted to speak to her.

'Is my wife ... is she hurt?' Mr Watson clutched the door frame. He thumped the wood.

'Not that I've heard, sir. It might be best if I came in. If your daughter—'

'She's not my daughter. She's come for a lesson.' He looked at Chrissie. 'Go up to the studio. Do not touch anything!' Mr Watson sounded even crosser than before. *He knew about the locket.*

Starting up the stairs, Chrissie remembered that she hadn't put the plate and her glass in the kitchen like Mrs Watson asked. *'As usual.'* She crept into the room to get them.

'...nothing to worry about, but we are bound to follow it up,' the policeman was saying. His voice made her think of the chocolate, rich and brown.

'Who called you?' George Watson had a higher voice – higher than usual.

'As I say, it was an expression of concern...' The detective was walking around the room looking at things. *He was looking for the locket.*

'...when are you expecting Mrs Watson?' The man sounded as if Mrs Watson was a friend and he was sorry to miss her.

If the policeman searched her, he would find the locket. Chrissie couldn't move. The locket was heavy in the pocket of her pleated skirt. If he found the locket he would put her in prison. A bad character, she would never be able to drive a taxi and drive away for ever.

'She went to the shops. I know she was going to the Marks in Chiswick High Road. This is preposterous – *who* expressed concern?' Mr Watson demanded.

'I regret that I'm not at liberty to say, sir. Have you any idea who might initiate such a call? It was made from the telephone box outside the Elizabeth Gate. It's near to the Herbarium. I understand that's your place of work, sir.'

'I can assure you that my wife is fine. She gave Christina her tea and then popped out to the shops.' Mr Watson went towards the door.

Chrissie got out of his way. 'I came to get my tea things.' It was true, but it felt like a lie.

'What lesson are you having?' the policeman asked her.

'Botanical drawing.' She fingered the locket; the silver was warm.

'With Mrs Watson?' The policeman had his hand on the front door and his X-ray eyes on her pocket. The locket became molten.

'Mrs Watson gives me tea then I do dead plants with Mr Watson.'

'Did Mrs Watson give you your tea today?'

'Is it legal to be interviewing a minor without her parents present, officer?' Mr Watson intervened.

'As I said, sir, it's an informal inquiry about your wife. I'm sure this young lady can help me.'

'Yes, she did give it me.' The man reminded Chrissie of her dad and she knew how to make her dad happy. 'Mrs Watson gave me chocolate cake and this glass had milk in it. It was especially cold today which was nice and her cake was delicious. Then she popped out. She told me to take the plate and glass through to the kitchen. I wash them up, although she didn't ask me to.'

'Mrs Watson gave you cake?' Detective Inspector Darnell was looking at her the way Bella Markham had, as if he didn't believe her. Chrissie was fed up with people questioning what she said.

'Mrs Watson bakes cakes.' She glared at him. 'With hundreds and thousands.'

'She'd forgotten to get chops for tonight's supper. The heat is getting to us all—' Mr Watson began.

'I understand, sir. Your pupil has been helpful. Could I take her name please? In case we have further questions. A formality.'

'My name is Christina Banks and I was born on the twelfth of

August 1966.' Chrissie stood next to Mr Watson. She held the locket tight.

The policeman stared at her. 'Well, Christina, you've been very helpful.' He went on looking at her. At last he said, 'My little girl was born on the same day as you.'

'Will that be all, officer?' Mr Watson interjected.

'Darnell, Detective Inspector Terry Darnell.' The officer stepped into the sunshine. He was stocky with features used to smiling. 'Give my regards to your wife. I'm sorry to have bothered you.' He was looking at Chrissie.

George Watson began to close the door.

'One thing.' He was back. 'What was your wife wearing when she left the house? In case we should see her out and about in Chiswick High Road.'

With the barest hesitation, George Watson said, 'A light blue dress with a cross-hatched pattern and black shoes with silver buckles. You'll have to forgive me, Detective Inspector, I'm not great on ladies' wear. My wife always looks nice, is all I can say.'

'She had a silver locket round her neck,' Chrissie offered. 'She showed it to me when she gave me the cake. It's got a picture of Mr Watson and Mrs Watson inside. It was a present from Mr Watson and she loves it more than anything in the world.'

The policeman frowned as if he didn't understand English. 'For an occasion, sir?'

'No occasion,' Mr Watson replied diffidently.

'Should it come to you who might have made the call, we'd appreciate you getting in touch, sir. Thank you again, Christina.'

Mr Watson closed the front door and the hall went dark. Chrissie heard a car start up and drive away.

'Go to the kitchen and wipe your face, you've got chocolate on it,' Mr Watson said.

Smarting with embarrassment because the policeman must have seen the chocolate too, Chrissie strained over the sink. She turned the tap full on and, with a shriek and a clunk, water spattered down. She dampened a tissue and rubbed at her cheeks and mouth. Lifting the lid of a pedal bin she tossed in the damp tissue. It landed on a box lying amongst tea leaves, apple peelings and foil milk-bottle tops. She read the writing on the box: 'Exceedingly good cakes!'

The picture on the packaging showed a chocolate cake decorated with hundreds and thousands.

Chapter Fifteen

November 2014

Jack flung himself down on Stella's white sofa. It was one of the few items that she hadn't sold to the lawyer when she left her flat.

For the first two years after her dad died Stella put off selling his house. She commuted between it and her flat in Brentford. Jack had worried that she expected Terry Darnell to return from the dead and claim his home because she had behaved like a custodian rather than the owner. But suddenly, after the One Under case, Stella had given her brother a share of Terry's house and moved in.

The sitting room had been pale before – beige had been Terry's favourite colour – and was now white. Stella's changes were minimal. The walls remained bare. 'The Hay Wain' went with Suzie when they separated and, like his daughter, Terry hadn't hung up any other pictures. Yet to Jack, the uninterrupted straight lines and clear surfaces in the air-freshened rooms were as homely as Jackie's warmly decorated home wreathed with delicious smells of cooking and scented candles and filled with the paraphernalia of a contented family life.

When Stella's brother had visited from Sydney, he accidentally countermanded Terry's frugal habits, maintained by Stella. He had turned on the central heating, switched on lights everywhere and cooked rather than reheated food in the kitchen. Since he had returned to Sydney, Stella had kept some changes. The gas fire was blazing in the front room and lights were lit. But she wasn't a cook. The smell of a ready meal wafted out from the kitchen.

Jack uncrossed his legs at the ankles and, no more comfortable, recrossed them. He was engaged in an internal struggle. Although she had invited him and he had refused, he was piqued that Stella had gone to the café with Cashman. So when he arrived he had gone into the living room, knowing that Stella expected him to follow her to the kitchen. So intent was he in proving – to Stella, as well as himself – that he was at home in her house, he found himself on her sofa when he would have preferred his chair in the kitchen.

Oblivious to his moody machinations, Stella had offered him shepherd's pie and hot milk. Jack had refused the food and agreed to the drink although he hadn't had supper and was hungry. By the time Stella handed him his hot milk and honey he was ashamed that he had been mean-spirited. This made him no nicer.

'No pictures on the walls yet,' he sniped.

'Pictures collect dust.' Seemingly oblivious to his jibe, Stella was matter-of-fact. Jack felt shame. Stanley stood beside her like the faithful hound he was. It seemed to Jack that his eyes were reproachful.

'Art gives a place character,' he persisted despite himself. 'It proves that you live here; it shows what you like.' A minute earlier he been thinking how he found the house homely because it reflected Stella. Had Jackie not been due soon to celebrate the Kew Gardens contract, he would leave; he was being rotten company.

'I don't need to prove that I live here.' Stella looked puzzled. 'I *know* I live here. So do you or you wouldn't have known where to come. And I have utility bills.' She was perched on the edge of the armchair opposite him. Stella liked upright wooden chairs that meant business. She would prefer the kitchen, he reflected ruefully. The kitchen was the one room she had kept unchanged from Terry's time. Generally he did anything to avoid hurting Stella. What was the matter with him?

'We could go into the kitchen if you like,' he said.

'It's OK.' Stella rarely took out her moods on people. While her practical, no-nonsense attitude could be frustrating, she was largely consistent. You knew where you were with Stella.

'Well done about Kew Gardens.' He blew a cloud of steam off the surface of the milk.

'Jackie's a dab-hand at tenders. They're like an exam. It was a team effort and I guess we ticked all the boxes.'

'It's not just "ticking boxes", Clean Slate lives and breathes those policies. You have staff development, you pay above the living wage and you encourage innovation. You operate environmental management and comply with that ISO thingy.'

'ISO, fourteen thousand and one,' Stella murmured peaceably.

Jack considered telling Stella about Jennifer Day, the woman who had died on his train. Despite lack of proof, he wanted to share his suspicion that her death might be murder. But he barely believed it himself. Stella was speaking,

'...choose what areas you want to clean in Kew.'

'Sorry?'

'You might have a preference of zones.' Stella decided where her staff cleaned. She was making an exception for him. She continued, 'I think there's one you'd like. A building outside the grounds called the Herbarium. No herbs: it's got old cupboards packed with plants. They are all withered and dead. Most of them are over a hundred years old.' Stella could well be thinking that cupboards crammed with dead plants needed a clear-out but, never one to judge, wouldn't say so.

The Herbarium would have been Jack's first choice. Enthused that Stella knew him well, he blurted out, 'William Hooker started his collection in the nineteenth century and passed it to his son Joseph who succeeded him as Director of Kew Gardens. Darwin has handled at least one of those specimens; there's a sheet with his signature.' Stella had made his dream possible. His mother had kept her promise. 'I wanted to be a botanist once,' he confided to her.

'I thought you wanted to be an engineer.' Stella gathered up a file bulging with papers and balanced it on her lap. It was labelled 'The Royal Botanic Gardens, Kew'. She pulled out a hefty stapled document and ran her finger down the text.

'I did. But it started with botany. Most things do. Joseph Paxton based his design of the Crystal Palace on the structure of a lily leaf.'

Stella had remembered that he had wanted to build tunnels and bridges. He had settled for driving a train through tunnels and over bridges. Not a compromise, because he loved driving. Just as he loved cleaning for Stella.

'Kew Gardens is divided into six zones. The zones furthest from the Estates Office are reached by bicycle. You won't need a bike because the Herbarium is by the Elizabeth Gate. I'll do the galleries on the south side. The Shirley Sherwood and a weird place that looks like a house called the Marianne North Gallery. The walls are crammed with paintings. I guess they ran out of space because there's not a centimetre between them.'

'The Victorians favoured cheek-by-jowl hanging. Although by the time North designed her gallery, it was an outmoded—'

'They're a specialist job so we're not to touch them. I have to mop the floor with clean cold water, no detergents.' Stella underlined something on the document.

'Cold water wouldn't do in the Herbarium,' Jack mused. 'Moisture would damage the collection.'

'Exactly!' Stella looked pleased. 'You vacuum only. Don't open cupboards in case the plants get sucked up.' She checked her watch. 'Jackie'll be here soon.'

Jack's mood lifted. An evening with Stella and Jackie was just what he needed.

Jackie had insisted they mark significant milestones. Winning Kew Gardens was significant. A sign. Jennifer Day dying on his train in the presence of a True Host was a sign. Cashman had been on his train too. Did that mean anything?

There was a heavy thump on the front door. Stanley sat up and let out a rumbling growl. Jackie always gave a cheery rat-tat-ter-tat-tat.

Something was wrong.

Chapter Sixteen

June 1976

A throng of visitors filed through turnstiles into Kew Gardens at the Victoria Gate. In the white-blue sky, the rumble of one aeroplane after another mingled with the drone of rush-hour traffic. The sounds were punctuated by an irregular beat of a loose drain cover clanking as cars and lorries drove over it

Blinkered by the heat, no one noticed a girl keeping up with an erudite-looking man. Had they done so, perhaps they would have assumed they were father and daughter and been charmed by the sight of them hand in hand. The man's thinning hair straggled to his collar and his pale linen suit was creased by wear and hot weather. His plastic sunshades, clipped to rimless spectacles, were off kilter. He carried a scuffed briefcase. In contrast, the girl's school uniform, although a little too big for her, was pristine. Her progress beside the man's purposeful stride was hampered by a bulging canvas satchel. The pair were not father and daughter, but teacher and pupil. Chrissie's uniform was second-hand, but she was not to tell anyone.

A week had passed since the policeman had visited Mr Watson and, ever since, Chrissie was frightened that he would come to her mum and dad's flat with a search warrant for the locket. Whenever she passed a police officer in the street – and it seemed that every day she did – she expected to be clamped in handcuffs. But by Thursday, the day of her next drawing lesson, she was still free.

When she had arrived at the villa by the pond for her lesson, Mr Watson had again opened the door. He had informed her that they were going on a field trip.

Chrissie's topsy-turvy blend of fact with fiction skewed her logic. She had told the policeman that Mrs Watson had given her tea so it must be true. The dreadful fear that Mrs Watson would know she had stolen the locket fuelled the unwitting lie. Chrissie quelled the fact that she hadn't seen Mrs Watson. Indeed, it was no longer fact.

Since they were on a field trip she couldn't carry out her plan. Chrissie had given up on returning the locket to the bedroom upstairs. She would hide it in the drawing room and make Mrs Watson suppose that she herself had dropped it there. Relieved by this solution, Chrissie had considered her plan as good as executed so had been aghast when Mr Watson led her across Kew Green, through St Anne's churchyard to Kew Gardens. The locket still tucked in her blazer pocket was like a boulder. She would have to keep it another week.

The gardens were crowded with visitors eating ice creams, poring over maps and peering at notices that showed the names of trees and plants. Stupefied by the sun, they drifted like ghosts across the browned lawns. Mr Watson's voice came from far away, '...have you been to the Marianne North Gallery?' *Have you got my wife's locket?*

Her mouth dry, her legs weak. Christina said, '*No!* I have not.'

'Then this will be a treat.' Mr Watson was going down a track between bushes. Overarching branches let in scraps of sunshine and the bright shards of light confused the eye. Looking behind her – she hadn't given up on the policeman – Chrissie realized that they were alone. No one else was going to the gallery.

'Botanists don't approve of Marianne North's paintings.'

Mr Watson was talking with his studio voice. 'They don't help to identify a species. Can you remember why not?' Belatedly Chrissie grasped that he was talking to her. Dizzy with mounting apprehension as they went further down the shaded track, she fumbled for the answer.

'A drawing shows just the plant's structure so that the bottomist can see what it is more easier.' Sweat trickled down her face.

'Botanist!' he corrected her. 'And "easily" not "more easier".' He increased his pace, forcing Chrissie to do the same. 'That is true and not true.'

This sent Chrissie into a greater flap because she couldn't see how something was true and a lie. She trotted beside him.

'The location in which a plant is found growing tells us about the environment that it needs in order to flourish. Nearly a century since North was painting, her trees have been chopped down, water has reclaimed land and many plants she captured in her paintings are extinct. So today her work has new value: it depicts vanished flora. I am taking you to a shrine!'

Chrissie didn't know what a shrine was, but found the word unsettling because Mr Watson was obviously very excited about it. They rounded a bend in the track and she nearly cried out loud. There was the house with no rooms. She *had* been here before. She had lied. As they mounted the steps to the porch, her heart tumbled in her chest.

In the porch Mr Watson showed Chrissie the lady she had thought was real when she came before. He said it was a 'marble bust of Marianne': a rude word that ordinarily Chrissie would have sniggered at, but with the locket heavy in her blazer pocket, she did not feel like laughing. The huge room was lighter than it had been on Chrissie's first visit. Globes suspended from the ceiling spread a gentle illumination over the hundreds of pictures on every wall.

'This is my favourite.' Mr Watson led her to a corner to the right of the door. 'Marianne painted this in Australia. Look at that orange. It could be burning! You can see why it's called the flame tree.'

Christina had known which picture he was going to point out before he did. The tree with orange flowers. She agreed that it looked like proper fire. He didn't say that it was the one he had in his drawing room. Far from feeling heat, she had goose pimples.

'Marianne has given us the shape of the tree, the flowers, leaves, the colour of the bark. If a botanist wants more, then he goes to painting number 766. See?'

Chrissie was interested to discover that all the pictures had numbers. The tree picture was 764. It saved counting.

'*Flowers of the Flame Tree*. Marianne is exceptional,' Mr Watson whispered. He let go of Chrissie's hand and reached towards the painting. He stopped and took her hand again, gripping it tighter.

Versed in the dramas of her sister's copies of *Jackie* magazine, Chrissie hazily considered that Mr Watson loved the lady with the bust. This was why Mrs Watson seemed cross. No. Mrs Watson was cross because Chrissie had stolen her locket.

In the glass of the frame she caught a flash of red and white and whipped around. She and Mr Watson were opposite the doorway where she had had Addled Brain and seen the lady with the white gobstopper eyes and the cat with the umbrella. Perhaps sensing that he had lost her attention, Mr Watson demanded, 'What's the matter?'

'I thought I saw something.'

'We are alone. No one comes. No one appreciates Marianne's work.' He pulled a strange face and Chrissie noticed that one of his front teeth was grey. She felt sorry for him. There was no point in being in love with a dead person.

'My dad says I could be a bottom… a botanist. He says I'm to watch what you do.' Chrissie wanted to cheer Mr Watson up.

'You should always listen to your father.' Mr Watson didn't look cheered up. Letting go of her hand he sat down on the high-backed bench facing the flame tree. Patting the seat, he bid her join him. 'Marianne expressed life. She deserves her place in botanical history.' He dipped his hand into his case and eased out a sheet of paper.

'This is for you,' he said, his voice suddenly quiet as if he did after all think someone could hear him. Instinctively Chrissie peered around the bench to the room where she had seen the lady on the floor. Or thought she had.

'*Eucalyptus gunnii*. You will find an example of this up the path from here. I don't want you to forget this. Ever.' He eyed her sternly. Chrissie looked at the drawing. Like the daisy weeks before, it didn't look like a tree. It was bits of a tree, she now understood this. There was a leaf and there was the trunk.

'Is it to do with guns?' she ventured at last.

'A gun? Certainly not! The species is named after the renowned collector, Ronald Gunn. In the nineteenth century he sent hundreds of specimens from Tasmania to Kew. Gunn, so therefore *gunnii*.'

'Did Marianne— er, Mrs North have a plant called after her?'

'She did. *Northia* was the genus.' He led her across the gallery. Chrissie gaped at a picture showing brightly coloured trumpets. '*Nepenthes northiana*. The pitcher plant. Marianne painted this in the mountains of Borneo.' He breathed.

'Do you have a plant named after you?' If Chrissie had failed to cheer Mr Watson up earlier, it seemed that her question achieved her aim. He became animated.

'Not yet. But I will. *Watsonii*. Yes, most definitely. But one must wait. You must never ask a botanist to name something after you or you put back the possibility by years. Softly softly… yes.' His nose made a snuffling sound.

'Will I be able to draw like you?'

'Almost certainly not.'

Chrissie nodded sagely. The news was a relief.

'This drawing is a map that will lead you to the truth. It's our secret; keep it safe.' Abruptly Mr Watson stood up and went through to the smaller chamber. She followed him. There was no one on the floor. She breathed more freely. The strap on Chrissie's satchel dragged on her shoulder. Gingerly she drifted to the spot on the tiles where, in what had definitely been a dream, the gob-stopper lady with white eyes had lain.

'What are you doing?' Mr Watson was sharp.

'I like these tiles.' Chrissie did like them so it was true. There was a mix of ones with eight sides – octagons, she had learnt at her old school – and squares and oblongs fitted together.

'It's time to go. Your father will be waiting.' A fleck of white appeared on Mr Watson's lip.

'The meter is ticking.' On a reflex, Chrissie echoed one of her dad's favourite phrases.

'Everything has a price.' Mr Watson pushed open the porch door and stepped out into the heat.

Chrissie's satchel caught in the closing door and she lost her balance. Something flew in the air and landed with a jingling on the veranda. Too late she understood the sound.

'You dropped this.' With a grey-toothed smile, Mr Watson held out his hand. In his palm lay the silver locket.

Chapter Seventeen

November 2014

Jackie Makepeace was toting a bottle of Sainsbury's champagne in a chiller sleeve branded with the Clean Slate logo. Despite this prop of celebration, she had a serious expression and didn't look, Jack thought with concern, in the mood to celebrate. Stella shut the Kew Gardens file and announced breezily, 'I'll get glasses.'

'Wait a minute, Stella, love.' Jackie placed the bottle on the coffee table, hovering her hand above it as if to stay it. The polished glass table top gave the impression that the bottle was suspended in mid-air.

'We can go through the finer points in the office,' Stella objected mildly. Jack guessed that it wouldn't take much to encourage her to look at the finer points there and then.

'Sit down, Stell.' Jackie indicated the armchair and joined Jack on the sofa. She unwound her scarf and slipped off her quilted Barbour jacket, folding it on the sofa arm. Jack's foreboding grew; Jackie always hung up her coat in the hall. 'Has Tina Banks called you?' she asked Stella, who remained standing.

Her question seemed to galvanize Stella. 'I knew she would cancel the contract. She was cross this morning, I've no idea what

I did wrong.' She pushed back her hair and, for Stella, looked flustered. Jack was surprised. Had they fallen out? It was hard to fall out with Stella because she didn't argue or disagree with people.

'Clients don't need a reason.' Stella did a motion in the air as if wiping Tina away like a stain.

Jackie had the kindly expression that usually reassured Jack. Tonight it did not. Tina Banks came with Stella on dog walks and they met for coffee. Jackie said she was Stella's best friend, not counting the two of them and a girl – woman – she had been at school with. She often urged him to make an effort with Banks: 'For Stella's sake.'

Stella and Banks were born on the same day in 1966 in Hammersmith Hospital. Like Stella and his mother, Banks was a Leo. Stella dismissed astrology, so Jack hadn't suggested that sharing a star sign could be a problem. Leos were loyal, confident and generous – like Stella and, he was sure, his mother – but also vain and domineering like Banks. The flash of satisfaction he felt that he had been right was followed by fierce compassion. Tina Banks cancelling would be a blow to Stella. More than anything, Jack hated Stella to be hurt.

'No, lovey. It's not that.' Jackie indicated the chair again and this time, clutching the Kew papers, Stella sat down. 'She hasn't cancelled,' Jackie said softly.

'What then?' Stella asked.

'She hasn't been in touch, not even a text?'

'No. Was it about the stain in her flat?' Stella asked. 'Her dad said he was joking.'

Jackie said that Stella's not minding things left the space clear for Jack and her to do the minding for her. From Jackie's face, Jack could see that she, like him, was minding now.

'What's happened?' he asked Jackie.

'Tina's sister Michelle called the office asking for Stella.'

Stella cradled the papers. With a forefinger, she traced the 'K' for Kew on the title page.

'There's no easy way to say this. Michelle said that Tina's been diagnosed with ovarian cancer. It's too late to do anything because it's spread to her liver.'

'She was all right yesterday.' Stella's finger went over the 'K' again. It reminded Jack of Suzie, Stella's mother, who, when she was agitated, used to tap on a cushion as if touch-typing her speech.

'The only treatment is palliative. She's been referred to a hospice, but she's in denial. Keeps saying she's a "winner" and she'll beat this. She agreed to go in to let the "meds kick in" and then she claims she'll be "back on her feet".'

Stella stood up. In a toneless voice she said, 'Tina will sort it.' The absurdity of her words hung in the air.

Eventually Jackie said, 'She's known for weeks. She didn't tell anyone because, as I say, she's insisting that she will survive.'

'She hasn't been ill,' Stella stated firmly.

'Ovarian cancer is called the "silent killer". It creeps up with no warning; you get symptoms when it's too late. Michelle said that any symptom she had, Tina ignored. They fell out when Michelle used the word "terminal". Tina's only speaking to her because Michelle avoids saying cancer and listens to her plans for the company.'

'She's with the big players now.' Stella was stern.

Jack wondered if Stella had misheard 'palliative'. She must know what it meant. He was unsurprised by Banks's use of 'kick in'. The mechanistic certainty implied was Banks's trademark. The only grey in Banks's world view was in her logo. Still, he was shocked; like Stella, he did rather think of the short feisty lawyer as able to 'beat' anything.

'Stell, Tina won't get better. She's dying,' Jackie said.

Stella put the papers on the armchair. 'Tina is a survivor.'

Jackie darted a look at Jack and he read her thoughts. Stella was also in denial.

'Michelle says that Tina wants to see you.'

'Since she hasn't cancelled, I'll clean her office in the morning.' Stella went to the door. Subject closed. Jack realized he had stopped breathing.

'Tina's not at the office,' Jackie said. 'Like I said, she's in the hospice, for help with her symptoms. She's asking to see you, love.'

'Why?' Stella was listening now.

'Because you're her friend.' Jackie was taking a firm approach.

'Where is the hospice?' Jack tried to help Jackie.

'By Kew Gardens. I did wonder if you might pop in after your first shift there tomorrow morning?'

When Jack had been in hospital after the One Under case, Stella had sat at his bedside like a wraith, white as a sheet. She had stared at the fluids bag on the rack by his bed unable to speak. Stella operated from the principle that all stains could be eradicated. This news – outside of the binary consideration of dirt and cleaning – would be beyond her comprehension. If he was honest, it was beyond his too.

Stella turned off the gas fire. 'I'll see her when she's back in the office. Her sister is mistaken. Tina went to a ball this week and was the best at dancing. She wouldn't want me seeing her in hospital.'

'It's a hospice, they're for—' Jack got a warning look from Jackie.

'Michelle said that she wasn't well enough to go to the ball.' Jackie picked up the champagne. 'I'll put this in the fridge.'

Jack heard the fridge door open and shut. Stella stood in the hall as rigid as a guard, Stanley at her feet, tail down.

Jackie returned from the kitchen and grabbed her jacket and scarf from the sofa.

'See you after I've been to Kew Gardens,' Stella said.

'No hurry.' Jackie briefly patted Stella's sleeve.

Jack didn't hear if Stella answered their goodnights. The door was closed before they reached the gate. The hall light was off.

'What can we do?' He leant on the still-warm bonnet of Jackie's Nissan Juke outside St Peter's Church.

'Nothing. Stella's in shock; give her time.' Jackie chimed in, she grasped the steering wheel in gloved hands. 'Her world is about to flip upside down; we can only be there for her, keeping everything else normal. Come back to ours?'

'I'm fine.' *Fine*. He wasn't fine. Jack pushed off the bonnet.

The loss of warmth awakened a desire to go with Jackie and sleep in her spare room. For ever.

"Night, Jack.' Jackie leant out of the window and squeezed his arm. 'You've got the Herbarium first thing, that'll be nice.'

Jack watched the tail lights of Jackie's car disappear down Black Lion Lane. He should have gone with her. Jackie belonged to a brighter and cleaner world that he could only look at from the outside. But for one night he might have pretended...

He took out his phone and, before he could stop himself, texted Stella.

An hour later, moving in the shadows, Jack was on the towpath by Kew Bridge. He was alert for the held-breath silence of a True Host.

Chapter Eighteen

July 1976

Chrissie climbed up the steps. In the sweltering heat, her legs were leaden. Spangles of light fell across the walls.

'This is William Hooker,' he called from the landing.

Chrissie supposed William Hooker was the botanist who, when they had come into the Herbarium minutes earlier, Mr Watson told her had a 'short temper' and she must be polite to him. She had been irritated because she was never rude. For the second week in a row they were on a 'field trip' (with no fields – she didn't count Kew Green). Ordinarily Chrissie would have welcomed this; her dad had described her pictures as grey scribble, but wouldn't let her stop having lessons, saying, 'Rome wasn't built in a day.' It was another week when she couldn't return the locket.

Since Mr Watson had handed the locket back to her last week, he had been extra nice to her. Before they went out, he had given her a larger slice of Mrs Watson's cake – Mrs Watson having popped out – and sat with her while she ate it. He asked her lots of questions about school. *'What is your favourite subject?' 'How is your Latin?'* Not having ready answers Chrissie had to lie. All the time the silver heart was boring into her and the cake lay heavy in her stomach.

Chrissie reached the top stair and saw that William Hooker wouldn't notice if she was rude or not. He was a statue.

'Do you know him?'

'I'm not that old, Christina! Hooker has been dead a hundred and eleven years.'

'Oh.' Chrissie was cross with herself. It was best to wait to hear what Mr Watson said and then to answer. Yet he seemed to know 'Marianne'. Her arms hung limply. She was fed up with dead plants and dead people. She wished she was playing on the slide under the railway arch in Ravenscourt Park. She didn't care about getting on in life or moving in circles.

'Hooker was the first Director of Kew Gardens. If you don't count Joseph Banks. Which we must. Especially as he's your name-sake! What was his son's name?'

A test. This always happened in the drawing lessons. They would be going along quite nicely and Chrissie would be copying the brown sprigs when Mr Watson would make her answer something impossible. Fog descended and yet again she was enveloped in panic. 'Cliff Banks?' She named her dad.

'I mean William Hooker's son!' Spit flew out of Mr Watson's mouth. He was pointing at another statue. The face had black pin-pricks in the eyes and curling stone caterpillars for eyebrows. Chrissie read a plaque beneath him.

'Joseph Hooker.'

'Just so. We've talked about him, haven't we? Now follow me.'

They went up another staircase and along a corridor and then another and after a very long time arrived on a balcony. Chrissie looked over the railing and saw another balcony below. Unlike the balcony in the house with no rooms these were connected at each end by two spiral staircases.

'Is this a church?'

Mr Watson tsked. 'No, Christina. This is Joseph Hooker's sanctum. We are in his herbarium!' He began to go down the nearest staircase. Chrissie gingerly took hold of the rail, her hand, damp with fear, slipping on the swooping metal.

There were cupboards everywhere. Chrissie considered hiding in one until Mr Watson got bored of looking and left. But the last time she had hidden in a cupboard she had got Addled Brain and seen the Cat in the Hat and the lady with the white gobstopper eyes. She blotted out this memory.

'See this?' She found Mr Watson by one of the cupboards. Inside there were drawers, too small for toys or even knickers and socks. Certainly no room to hide. Mr Watson took out a folder, identical to the one Chrissie had used at her old school for her project on the moon expeditions. Inside were not pictures of astronauts, as she half expected, but a sheet of paper with brown dead plants like the ones that Mr Watson drew in his studio. Her heart sank.

'Read that to me.' Mr Watson pointed at the inside of the cupboard door. A faded notice, dirty and curling at one corner, was pasted to the wood. Chrissie knew it was wrong to stick things on furniture: Michelle had got in trouble for gluing a photo of David Essex to the headboard of her bed. She tried to read the faint type.

'The words are funny.'

'They're not funny, they're French. The left column is in English.'

Christina read in halting speech.

'"Visitors studying in the Herbarium are requested to observe that the removal of specimens, or any portions of them, from the sheets—"'

'Enough!' Mr Watson interrupted. 'What's the date?'

'June the ninth. One eight eight two.' Chrissie found it hard to say numbers over a hundred. But she guessed why he was showing her: 'That's today!' She guessed wildly, immediately seeing her mistake.

'This is 1976 and it's not June the ninth.' Mr Watson heaved a sigh. 'This was composed by Joseph Hooker.' He pointed at the name at the bottom of the notice. 'It's nearly a hundred years old and it's still true. You must put back anything you use and you can't detach any "fruit, flower, or leaf" without first getting the approval of the Keeper of the Herbarium. What is wrong with this instruction?'

'It's old?' Christina was frightened that a dead man could leave instructions. Was he brown and shrivelled like the specimens?

He raised his eyebrows and Chrissie thought of the stone caterpillars above Hooker's eyes. 'This last line is contradictory. The wording could specify that no portions of the specimen be removed without permission. By listing those three parts, he implies that other parts *can* be removed.'

'But he says it's "absolutely..."' Chrissie took a deep breath and tackled the next word, syllable by syllable, '"Pro. Hid. It. A. Bit. Ed."'

'*Prohibited*. Your dad boasted that you came top at reading!' Mr Watson was querulous. Chrissie wondered why her dad had said that because it wasn't true.

'Hello, George.'

Chrissie couldn't see anyone. Nor, it seemed, could Mr Watson. He slammed shut the cupboard; the sound reverberated around the vast space.

'Who's the little friend, George?' A man was leaning over the rail of the spiral staircase above them.

'A friend's daughter.' Mr Watson gave a cough.

'You have friends!' The man grinned broadly and then became serious. 'There was a man here asking for you. Could that have been the father perhaps?'

'My daddy's working,' Chrissie asserted. Then she remembered she must not say that he drove a taxi and felt herself go red.

'Is he now? So George is minding you, is he? Or are you minding George?' Another grin.

'Wait outside,' Mr Watson hissed at Chrissie.

'I don't—' Christina began to say that she didn't know how to get outside, but Mr Watson jerked his thumb towards a door beyond more cupboards.

'Through there. Wait for me in the hall.'

As Chrissie walked away she heard the man say, 'You've cocked up this plate, George. I wonder if it would be better to start afresh...'

'I did what you wanted,' Mr Watson said and Chrissie paused. He sounded really cross.

'Clearly you did not do as…'

The little girl heard footsteps and hurried along a passageway. She came to a green baize door and burst through it. She was in the hall. In the gloom above she could see William Hooker gazing sightlessly at her with his crawling caterpillar eyebrows. She flung herself at the main door and rushed down the steps and out into the street.

'Chrissie, what are you doing here?' The door of a telephone box opened and someone came out.

Chrissie was so pleased to see a familiar face that she nearly hugged Emily. 'Why weren't you at school today?' She had meant to be casual as if she didn't care that Emily had been absent. But she had cared. She was her only friend even if Emily wasn't allowed to speak to her. 'The teacher said you were ill.' She shielded her eyes from the glare bouncing off the hot pavement.

'My mum tells them that when she wants me to stay with her,' Emily explained.

'Why does she want you at home?' Chrissie's own mum said that she was 'only too glad to get you kids out from under my feet'.

'She doesn't like being on her own when my dad's away. She's asleep now so I sneaked out. I thought I might catch Bella. She would have tried to call me after school.' Emily stirred up a cloud of dust in the gutter with the toe of her sandal. 'Why don't you make it up with Bella? It would be much simpler if you did. Then we could all have fun again.'

'There's nothing to make up.'

'It would be good if Bella said sorry for saying you lied, but she won't. I think if you said you were sorry for running away, she would let you go round with us again. I mean I know you're not sorry, but even so…' Emily wasn't in her uniform; she wore her denim hat crammed down, bending her ears. Chrissie couldn't see her eyes. 'That was her on the phone.' She tipped her head at the bright red box. It appeared to waver in the heat as if it too were imaginary.

Chrissie blinked. 'How could she ring you from in there?'

'She's got the number. We both have it.'

'But how could she know you'd answer? What if someone else was in there?' Chrissie had never heard of getting called while you were in a public phone box.

'We plan the time and I am ready and waiting by the phone. I live near your house by the pond actually, in the next road.' She whipped off her hat and then put it back on, jamming it even further over her face. 'I hold the receiver so as to make people think I'm talking. But you have to keep the metal things down or it won't ring.' Emily flapped her arms about, which reminded Chrissie of Mr Watson explaining about dead plants. 'Bella must have tried to ring me and then gone home. I was thinking of ringing her at home instead. But I just tried and there's no answer.' She blinked rapidly in the bright sunlight.

Chrissie imagined being friends with Bella and Emily again and waiting for the telephone in a call box to ring or ringing either of them from it. If they were friends she wouldn't have to pretend to her dad that she had friends when she didn't. She was sick of pretending – it was all she ever did. Then the reality of what Emily had said sank in. She meant she lived close to Chrissie in Kew, not in Westcroft Square in Hammersmith. She could easily find out that Chrissie didn't truly live there. She batted off the fear. 'She should say she's sorry for making me prove I live in that house.' Taken up with the injustice, Chrissie had forgotten that Bella was right to doubt her honesty.

Emily was scrutinizing the Herbarium. 'I've always wondered who lives here.'

'Joseph Hooker. He's a friend of my dad's.' Too late she saw how stupid the lie was. And pointless since Emily wouldn't care either way. She felt herself go beetroot red and tottered back against the railings as heat engulfed her.

'Isn't Joseph Hooker dead?' Emily was puzzled. 'Do you mean the man who ruled Kew Gardens in the Victorian times?'

'No. Another one. My dad's there now, talking to him about one of his pictures.'

Emily snatched off her hat again, gave it a bash inside and this time screwed it up in her hands. 'Chrissie, can I tell you a secret?'

Chrissie nodded. Then, seeing that Emily wasn't looking at her, said, 'Yes, OK.' She weighed up the pros and cons of keeping someone else's secrets. Would it get her into trouble? Would it make her important if she had a person's secret to keep?

'My mum drinks.'

'Right.' Chrissie didn't think this much of a secret. 'Everyone drinks. We'd be dead if we didn't. That's why all the plants are dead. There's been no rain for ages—'

'I don't mean water. Cinzano. She drinks a bottle every day. When she drinks Cinzano she cries about my dad. I have to stay at home with her to make up for him being abroad.'

'You're not at home now.' Chrissie latched on to a certainty.

'I sneaked out to talk to Bella. She rings to see if I'm OK. Dad's reporting on the Lebanese civil war.' She twisted her hat in her hands. 'I thought of running away from home. What do you think?'

'Where to?' Chrissie was amazed. The idea had never occurred to her. Now that it had, it seemed a good thing to do. No more drawing lessons; no more school where she had to pretend things.

'Anywhere. I'm not sure where. Actually I can't, it's too hot to go anywhere.' Emily flapped the hat in front of her face. 'The North Pole!' She laughed and then made a funny sobbing sound.

'Best wait until it's colder,' Chrissie advised. 'And you need to take food with you.'

'Don't tell Bella I said that,' Emily said.

'I don't think she'd want to come, she isn't brave like you.' Chrissie hadn't thought this until now. Emily was the bravest of all of them.

'About my mum.'

'Doesn't she know?'

'She said my mum was an alcoholic. I said she wasn't. I lied. That was wrong. I tell her that Mum gets tummy bugs because of the heat. You can, you know.' She had her wise face on.

'Yes, it was wrong to lie, but—' Chrissie was about to tell Emily about her own lies when a voice made her jump.

'There you are!' Mr Watson was coming down the Herbarium steps. 'You should have waited in the shade. You could get sunstroke.'

'This is Emily.' But there was no one there, just scuff marks in the dust. The sun pressed down on her head.

The high temperatures were set to continue. People – young and old – were dying. In the blasting heat, nothing was real. Nothing was true.

Mr Watson led Chrissie back across Kew Green to his house by the pond. In the hall he called, 'We're home, darling.' Mrs Watson's coat was draped over the banister. Shaking his head, he hung it on a peg.

Mrs Watson's reply was drowned out by the chugging of a diesel engine. Chrissie looked down the path and saw her dad's taxi at the gate.

Chapter Nineteen

October 2014

Stella had forgotten that at 6 a.m., when she came to clean the Marianne North Gallery and the Shirley Sherwood Gallery next door, it would be dark. When she and Jackie had 'walked' the cleaning zones, it was daytime and Kew Gardens was busy with visitors. Trevor, the Facilities Manager, had brought them to the galleries in a buggy. The galleries were half a mile from the Estates Office. For the first weeks, until she handed it to another operative, Stella would do the job, reaching the cleaning zone on a bike with a cart attached. The bicycle lamp, powered by a dynamo, dimmed whenever she slowed. The wind was against her and when she pushed on the pedals the cart swayed, further hampering her progress.

A grey band of mist hung over the lawns. The gardens were unlit and the boundary wall was too high for street lights to penetrate. Stella had memorized the location of the gallery on the map, but at the Palm House, she took a wrong turning. She peered into the darkness; the mist made shapes like figures queuing in silence before the glasshouse. Stella was furious with herself for thinking this.

The galleries must be to the left, but if she cut across the grass the wheels would damage the lawn. Clumsily she led the whole contraption around, aware all the time of the silence. She was metres from the South Circular, but it seemed to Stella that the quiet was absolute.

Cycling had warmed her, but the creeping fog chilled her again. Jackie had suggested Jack come with her, but apart from the fact that Stella had allocated one operative to the galleries, she knew he wanted to clean the Herbarium. If Jack was here, he would have got them straight to the gallery.

Starting again from the Elizabeth Gate she wiped moisture from her eyes. Now she could hear blood pounding in her ears and her rapid breathing. She was fit but, rattled by the darkness and the odd quiet, was already exhausted.

It wasn't silent any more. She heard a swish of leaves and rustles in the undergrowth either side of the path. Bushes thickened to form a tunnel. The figures in the mist were crossing and recrossing in front of her. She pedalled faster. The lamp brightened and the external sounds increased. Ridiculous. Jack believed in ghosts and insisted that 'we are never alone'. She *was* alone.

At last, at a bend in the path, she came upon the Shirley Sherwood Gallery, a modern single-storey building that she had looked forward to cleaning. Beyond was the Marianne North Gallery. She was starting there first.

In the daylight the generously proportioned house, with its closed-in porch and canopied veranda, had appeared attractive. Stella had seen a photo of it on the Kew Gardens website. In the photo, the terracotta bricks and the green lawns in the foreground were steeped in sunshine and Stella had likened it to houses that she cleaned in Chiswick and Richmond. Now, outlined against the orange-mauve sky, clouds racing past the chimney pots, it belonged in *Psycho*.

Behind her was yawning darkness. Again Stella told herself that she wasn't in the middle of nowhere, but close to a busy road.

A crunch on gravel. *Footsteps*. Stella jumped off the bike and kicked the stand down. She fumbled in her anorak for her phone. Staff were given an emergency code to call. Her finger hovered over the keys. It wasn't a footstep, it was beating wings. Geese rose out of the darkness and flew upwards. Terry had explained about their 'v' formation, but she couldn't remember what he had said. It wouldn't help her now.

Birds featured in another of Hitchcock's films. She forced herself to breathe long and deep. *Two in, two out. Two in, two out.* The gravel sound happened again. It wasn't the geese. Nor could it be gravel: there was no gravel. Trevor had said that Kew Gardens was hard to break into, that was the point of the wall. Security was tight.

She was definitely alone.

She unhitched the trolley from the bike and lugged it up the two flights of steps to the veranda. Twenty-five minutes already, way over the allocated ten to get there. When she got to know the route, ten minutes should do it.

Inside the tiled vestibule, following instructions on the sheet, Stella deactivated the alarm. Wheeling in the cart, she yelped and then controlled herself. It was the bust of Marianne North. Thinking statues were real was Jack's thing.

MISS MARIANNE NORTH.

THE ACCOMPLISHED ARTIST AND TRAVELLER IN
MANY LANDS WHO PAINTED ALL THE PICTURES
IN THIS UNIQUE COLLECTION AND PRESENTED
THEM TO THE NATION.

BORN 1830. DIED 1890.

Dipping into the cart, Stella found the duster and flapped it around the stony features. The task wasn't on her sheet, but it grounded her.

The air inside the gallery was like a tomb, not that she cleaned any tombs. Dead leaves, rotting vegetation, stale smoke. *Stale smoke?* The detectors would pick up a smoker. In the glow of the 'night light', it was, as Jack had said, like a church. He had talked about a votive silence. Stella, who deplored playing music while she cleaned, wanted a radio on now. 'Rebel Rebel' would break the silence, votive or otherwise.

In the sickly green of the security lighting, the black-framed paintings, hung so close together, resembled a giant grid. When she had first seen them, she had decided that this arrangement – it covered the walls entirely – would discourage dust from accumulating. However, a devotee of deep cleaning, she relished jobs that required her to get behind the visible – bath panels and skirting boards – and would love to give this place a proper going-over. She had been disappointed that 'Kew experts' would clean the paintings. Now, on this dark and misty morning, Stella was grateful that her task was only to mop the floor with cold water. It was challenge enough.

She turned on the gallery lights and was dismayed to find that the two globes slung from the high ceiling made little difference to the vast space. Jack would like it: he was happier in the dark.

Used to negotiating furniture, filing cabinets, sofas, a plethora of occasional tables and knick-knacks, Stella had looked forward to mopping the stretch of tiled floor with only two high-backed double-sided benches on it. She hurried through to an antechamber lined with more paintings, furnished only with a cupboard, and out to the yard where she filled the bucket. Here she could hear traffic. She was relieved to hear the familiar sound of a diesel engine pulling away, a delivery van or a taxi.

In the antechamber, she squeezed the mop out on the bucket ringer. No water must be left on the tiles when the public arrived. Methodically, she swished her way across the floor and then out into the main gallery. It was satisfying to see the tiles and iron-fretted grilles along the base of the walls glisten in her wake. Picking up speed, she'd soon covered the entire area.

Preoccupied with getting to grips with the job, it was only on

Stella's third trip to the yard that she thought about Tina. Her good mood plummeted. As water thundered into the bucket, she went over what Jackie had said and reassured herself again that the sister would be fussing. Tina wouldn't want Stella turning up at her sick bed. Then again she had supposed Tina wouldn't want Stella to see her dancing when instead she had asked her to join in.

The bucket made a hollow clank on the tiles. The noise unnerved her. She wished again that Jack were here. No: if he were, he would see ghosts everywhere and fray her nerves to a rag.

The mop in one hand and bucket in the other, careful not to spill water, she passed through the main gallery and into a central chamber. Two minutes and she would be done.

The names of the countries where North had painted were lettered in gilt on wooden panels above her head. This little chamber depicted the Seychelles, Tenerife, South Africa and India. Illuminated by a solitary low-wattage lamp, it was to Stella's mind dark. Here, the smell of stale smoke was stronger. Shame Kew Gardens didn't sanction plug-in deodorizers.

She dipped the mop into the water, twirled it about, lifted it out and leant on the bucket, her feet either side to stabilise it. She squeezed out the excess. She lowered the mop to the floor and began her scything motion, back and forth, her movements fluid. She worked from the rear of the chamber towards the doorway.

Her boot caught something. She peered down and made out a hand, palm outstretched. Absurd. The job had got to her. She switched on her phone's torch app. In the bright light she saw another hand, two legs, lace-ups. An elderly man, white hair around his head like a halo, was asleep in the corner. Trevor had said it was nigh on impossible to get locked into the gallery. *Not true.*

'I'm sorry, but I need to clean here.' Her line for when she found offices or rooms occupied. The man didn't stir so she raised her voice: 'Excuse me, but I have to do this floor.' She heard how haughty she sounded. Concerned not to frighten the man, she bent and touched his shoulder. She met with solidity. Like wood. Hard and unyielding.

The man lying beneath painting number 521, *Mr Smith's Garden*, on the unmopped tiles wasn't asleep. He was dead.

Stella had seen few bodies. The first had been her father at the Royal Sussex County Hospital where he was brought after he had collapsed and died in the street. However, the daughter of a police officer whose bedtime stories for his little girl had featured sniffer dogs and bloodied fingerprints, Stella was versed in the stages a corpse goes through after death. She didn't need a pathologist to understand that the man was dead.

The bike ride in the foggy dark, strange sounds in the gallery and the silence of the gardens had made her jittery. But now, with a corpse at her feet, Stella switched into action. Calmly, she dialled a number on her phone. Not the emergency services or the Kew code, but the first person who came to mind. A number that, without memorizing it, she knew by heart.

'All right, Stell?' Martin Cashman asked.

Chapter Twenty

July 1976

'Are you OK?'

Chrissie was startled. Since Bella had forbidden girls to talk to her, she was unused to anyone who wasn't a teacher speaking to her. She was sitting on the patch of grass in Kew Gardens where the girls had had their picnic, in what seemed another life. Close by was the White Greyhound: her favourite of the Queen's Beasts. Warm air wrapped around her like a woolly blanket.

Emily stood in front of her, a hankie balled in her hand. She rubbed vigorously at her nose with the flat of her palm, rubbing so hard that Chrissie thought she must flatten her nose into her face. Her eyes were red as if she had been crying. But one thing Chrissie had gathered about Emily was that, whatever happened, she never cried. She had hay fever.

She looked about her, but couldn't see Bella. Nevertheless, she whispered: 'You're not meant to talk to me.' Suddenly she didn't want Emily to be in trouble.

'I don't care. I like you.' Emily blew her nose, making a squeaky sound like a dog's toy. 'I think she likes you really.'

'I don't care.' This was true. When you were in charge you

126

didn't care if people liked you, only that they did what you told them to do.

'We can go on being friends, if you like,' Emily said.

'You'll get in trouble.'

'I won't. Bella's quite nice really,' Emily said. 'She doesn't mean to be mean to me,' she added without apparent rancour.

Chrissie had never supposed a person could do something they wanted because they liked someone. She had never paused to consider whom she liked. She suddenly wanted to reward Emily for being braver than she could be. Not counting the locket, she had nothing to give her. Then she considered that this wasn't true. 'Emily, shall I tell you a secret?'

'I'm good with secrets,' Emily remarked.

'Come with me.' Chrissie jumped up and set off past the Queen's Beasts, unconsciously counting them off, like a colonel inspecting the rank and file. The Yale of Beaufort, the Red Dragon of Wales... the Griffin of Edward III fixed her with a diabolical expression that made her realize she was going the wrong way. Instead of retracing her steps – she didn't want Emily to spot her mistake – she led them around the lake.

Perhaps Emily guessed anyway because she asked, 'Where are we going? Is this the way?' Nevertheless she jogged gamely beside her.

'You'll see.' Chrissie was going at a clip for fear of changing her mind. 'Yes, it is the way.' Glancing across the lake – a spread of bright steel in the remorseless light – she fancied the Griffin was still watching her.

Mr Watson wasn't in the Marianne North Gallery. Nor the gobstopper lady. Or the Cat in the Hat. Chrissie checked the middle chamber and the end one with the cupboard. Finally sure that they were alone she hissed at Emily, 'I saw a murder!'

'What do you mean?' Emily gaped at her, hankie clamped to her nose.

'I saw a *murder*!' Chrissie said it again, struck that she had truly seen a murder. It hadn't been Addled Brain. She tugged at her skirt and smoothed the fabric.

'I don't think you can have done, Chrissie.' Emily embarked on a fit of sneezing.

'I did,' Chrissie said more to herself. She went to the middle of the room. The tiles where the lady had been lying were no different to the others. There was no red for blood.

'Did you tell the police?' Emily's voice was muffled in the hankie.

'I don't know any.' Chrissie reflected that she did know a policeman. There was the one who had a daughter who was exactly the same age as her who had come looking for Mrs Watson. 'It was right here.' She pointed at the tiles and then shrank back and banged against the cupboard. The gobstopper lady was back on the floor. She was staring at her with the Griffin's eyes.

'If you saw a murder you should have told the police.' Emily didn't believe her.

For a flash of a second, Chrissie hated her. Then the feeling went away and she felt exhausted.

'Are you sure you saw one? What exactly did you see?'

'A lady and a cat,' Chrissie said slowly. The lady was Mrs Watson. Chrissie clamped her hand over her mouth to stop herself shouting out the words.

'A cat?' Emily's eyes were streaming. 'What colour cat?'

'Black. It had on a red bow tie and a tall hat striped red and white.' The words tumbled out. 'There was a fish that was cross because it had come out of its bowl and an umbrella. It had a tail – the cat, I mean.' *Mrs Watson had gobstoppers for eyes.*

'That's *The Cat in the Hat*!' Emily was jubilant. 'You said about it at the picnic. I worried that the cat would visit me and my brother when my mum left us alone. Now when she goes out, it's better because I don't believe that the cat will turn up. But someone else could—'

'*The Cat in the Hat*'s not real, stupid!' Chrissie hadn't meant to be unkind.

'Did you dream about the murder with the cat? I think my dreams are real and my mum sees things. Daddy can't take her out in case she sees them. But he's mostly at a war so it doesn't matter.'

'It must have been a dream.' Chrissie had tested her secret on Emily and she had said that it was a dream. *The Cat in the Hat* was a story. The cat wasn't real. The tiles were clean. If there had been a murder there would be blood. She had told the policeman that Mrs Watson had given her tea. She *had* given her tea.

Still, if Mrs Watson were dead she couldn't hand Chrissie in to the police for stealing her locket. Chrissie let herself relax.

Then another thought cancelled the moment of relief. Had she murdered Mrs Watson but, like Emily's mum, she couldn't remember murdering her?

Chapter Twenty-One

October 2014

'Joseph Peter Hooker. Date of birth, seventh of November 1944. He was about to be seventy. Might mean something. Couldn't face growing old, decided to end it here. I can think of worse places.' Through the plastic evidence bag, Martin Cashman was peering at the dead man's driving licence. In protective gloves – his own, although Stella had offered him a pair of hers – Cashman flicked at the bag with a forefinger. 'Comes from Sydney. In Australia,' he added as if those grouped around him in the Marianne North Gallery wouldn't know where Sydney was.

'Hooker! Could he be a relation?' asked one of the two WPCs who had arrived moments before Cashman and had 'preserved the scene'.

The name rang a bell, but presuming it must be a client, Stella said nothing.

'A relation of who?' Cashman frowned. 'Whom.'

'Joseph Hooker, Director of Kew Gardens, sir.' The woman, perhaps guessing it was unwise to outsmart a senior officer – especially CID – looked as if this information was a surprise to her too.

'Good work, Hoxton. Give him a call.' Cashman handed the

bag to a young man in a suit, pointy lace-ups and a haircut slick with product who was a younger version of himself. 'Tread lightly, our man here could be his dad.' He told her.

'Joseph Hooker died in 1911, sir.' The WPC studied the tiles at her feet.

Stella saw why she knew the name. Jack had said Joseph Hooker had collected plants for the Herbarium.

'Still, there could be a link.' Cashman laid the licence on the bench and, picking up another evidence bag, scrutinized a collection of plastic cards from the man's wallet. 'He's called Hooker and he's lying dead in Kew Gardens.' Cashman jabbed a thumb at the antechamber where, under an arc lamp, the pathologist was crouched over the body. He snatched up a bag containing a deerstalker hat found next to the body. 'Should be called Sherlock!'

He moved on to a soft packet of cigarettes branded Winfield Blue. This explained the smell of the stale smoke.

Cashman put the evidence bag next to a pocket London Underground map and some loose strips of Juicy Fruit chewing gum in their respective bags. 'No suicide note.'

'Martin.' The pathologist, a woman space-suited in forensic overalls, beckoned to him from within the blaze of the arc lamp. She was as tall as Stella, which, although they were surrounded by police officers, made them the tallest in the room.

Stella considered taking the opportunity to slip away, but Cashman indicated for her to follow him.

The pathologist had turned the man over so that he lay face down. One trouser leg had twisted when the body was moved revealing a lizard-skin calf. Stella recoiled. There was a stain on the tiles. It was all she could do not to grab her mop and wash it off. There was another stain on the man's jacket. Stella didn't need to be any sort of detective to see what had happened to Joseph Hooker.

Cashman had undergone a transformation. No longer tired or irritable, he looked little older than his boyish sidekick in the winkle-pickers. He turned to the PR woman from Kew Gardens who stood beside Trevor the Facilities Manager near the door of the gallery. 'The Marianne North Gallery won't be opening today.'

'Will you cordon it off from visitors?' Trevor asked.

'There will be no visitors. Kew Gardens is shut until further notice.'

'We only close on Christmas Day!' the woman objected.

'We can't have the public hoofing about destroying evidence.' Cashman was frowning at the body.

Stella recognized Cashman's quiet excitement: she had seen it in her dad. Her mum still grumbled that Terry had loved the fuss of a high-profile crime. But her mum was wrong; Terry hadn't courted publicity, he was a detective who wanted just to do his job.

Cashman looked up. 'This is murder.'

'Are you sure?' The PR woman must be seeing the headline pinging around the world. *Murder in Kew Gardens!*

'I *am* sure.' Cashman rocked on his heels. 'Although we do it to each other all the time, it's actually impossible for a man to stab himself in the back.'

The outer doors banged and a woman who looked every inch CID swept into the gallery. Shoes encased in protective plastic, she stood in the doorway to the antechamber. 'Sir, the SIO's broken his leg.'

Stella was no stranger to acronyms. In her world, 'S' stood for stain, 'I' for intensive and 'O' for odour, but in police jargon, it meant 'Senior Investigating Officer'. Terry had been one early in his career. His first case was the Rokesmith murder in Hammersmith.

Cashman groaned. 'How'd he do that?'

'He fell off a horse.'

'Crowd control?'

'Dressage.' Her face was blank.

'A detective on crutches. Perfect.' Cashman made a sucking sound through his teeth.

'It's a bad break, sir, he's not mobile. He's not available.' She paused. 'And nor is anyone else.'

Stella made sense of this exchange. In a rare conversation about his work, Terry had told her that senior investigating officers were appointed from a central pool. The SIO built a team from detectives in the locality of the crime. This would be Richmond station where Cashman had just been transferred. As Chief Superintendent, he was too senior to lead an inquiry. He was here now because she had called him.

'What about you?' Cashman was asking. 'Have you done the training?'

Stella started to shake her head but then realized that he was talking to the officer in the suit.

'Not yet, sir,' the woman said.

No one spoke. Then Cashman cleared his throat. 'Listen up. The press will be all over this. Kew Gardens is an iconic site in the UK. It's a key tourist attraction and has international botanical renown.' He adjusted the knot of his tie. 'A murder could jeopardize public confidence, causing economic and reputational damage. This case needs a detective with considerable experience and expertise.' He twitched the lapels of his suit. 'I'm the Senior Investigating Officer.' He raised his voice. 'I'm in charge.'

Chapter Twenty-Two

July 1976

Chrissie clutched at the wire on the sagging link fence. She was outside her old school. It was after home time so everyone had gone. She looked at the little garden which the children planted to give them a feel for living things. Sweet peas, nasturtiums, straggling honeysuckle and sunflowers were drooping and shrivelled in the heat.

After a bit, she trailed across Glenthorne Road into Ravenscourt Park. In the shadow of the viaduct for the Piccadilly and District lines, the path was gloomy and barely cooler than in the sun.

That morning at breakfast she had broached the possibility of stopping the drawing lessons. She began with her mum, a sensible way in to get her dad to change his mind about anything.

'...since I don't want to do drawing when I'm grown up.' She had been the last one at the table; Michelle had left to get the bus to the big school.

Washing up, Jenny Banks had been singing the chorus of 'Never Going to Fall in Love Again' to the radio. 'Ask your dad,' she had said at last.

'Ask him what?' Clifford Banks had come in and, tossing his

car keys on to the table, reached around his wife and poured himself a glass of water. He drank half and threw the rest away, splashing the draining board. 'That man gets on my wick!' He indicated the transistor on the worktop, from which Noel Edmonds's voice was bantering.

'Nothing.' Chrissie was gruff.

'Don't give me cheek, girl.'

'Don't mind him, sweetie.' Jenny Banks had spoken in a stage whisper to Chrissie. 'Your dad's been in a mood since that the crater opened up in the Great West Road.'

'So would you be if you had to go out of your way for airport runs in this heat. I'm a broiled lobster in that cab.'

Pushing the dishcloth into a plastic grab suctioned to the wall, Mrs Banks said under her breath: 'Poor man, no place to die.'

'What man?' Chrissie had piped up. Surely her dad wouldn't die in his taxi?

'Now you're *not* to get nightmares—' her mum began.

'They found a dead man in a hole a week ago. The heat melted the tar and the road gave way. Rumour is that he was a burglar and he'd been there since the houses there were demolished.' Her dad had no compunction about telling his daughter how it was.

'Don't matter what he did, no one should die like that. Under all those bricks – it doesn't bear thinking about.' Suddenly aware that her nine-year-old daughter was all ears, Mrs Banks turned up the volume on the radio.

'Ask me what?' To Chrissie's dismay her dad returned to what he had overheard when he came in.

Dorothy Moore was singing about her world being turned 'misty blue'. Chrissie felt her own world fog over. To distract him, she blurted out, 'I love this song,' although she didn't know it.

'She's wanting to stop those classes. She might as well since she's not getting on with them.' Her mum swayed to the music. 'Face it, Cliff, she's not Leonardo da Vinci!'

'Not if she doesn't stick to it.' Clifford Banks swung around to his daughter. 'D'you want to end up cleaning like your mum?'

'What's wrong with cleaning?' His wife flicked the washing-up brush at him, spraying him with water.

'There's everything wrong. Or being a cabbie. What's she at this expensive school for otherwise?'

'Since it's George paying—' At a look from her husband Mrs Banks had stopped and joined in with Dorothy Moore.

'I like cleaning,' Chrissie had muttered. And she longed to drive a taxi. Except, since the locket, she wasn't of good character.

'I can't see you up at five scrubbing fifty toilets, my girl,' Jenny Banks interrupted her singing to retort.

'It's good for Watson you being there. Good for his wife too.' Clifford Banks leant over the sink and switched off the radio. His wife, seemingly unaware, continued with the song.

Chrissie couldn't say about the locket or the Cat in the Hat. Nor could she say about the policeman because he gave her a bad feeling. In confusion she had scooted her spoon around the empty Shredded Wheat bowl and crammed it in her mouth.

'It's not up to Chrissie to make up for them not having kids. Besides, that Rosamond Watson doesn't help herself. Last time I saw her in the street, she couldn't crack as much as a smile. No wonder she's got no friends.'

'Has she got no friends?' Chrissie was intrigued. Mrs Watson lived in a big house and owned jewellery. Maybe having friends wasn't as important to getting on as her dad said.

'She keeps herself to herself, that's all.' Her mum wiped her hands on a towel and hung it from the grill handle. 'Come on, Cliff, like Chrissie says, she won't be drawing flowers for a living. She'll need something decent.' Her mum had snatched up the packets of Cornflakes and Shredded Wheat and put them back in the cupboard.

'A botanical artist *is* a decent job. Watson started out in a council flat and now he's got a bloody palace in Kew!'

'Thought you said that was his wife's? You said he's a bad botanist.'

'He's *not* a botanist. And, poor sod, that Rosamond never lets him forget that he's a just a pen man. She expected more of him for her money. He just does drawings.'

'Well, we work as hard as him,' his wife said, seemingly irrelevantly.

'Course we do – he's not up all hours driving. Plants don't complain and give low tips.' Chrissie's dad had giggled at his joke.

'Plants have tips on their leaves,' Chrissie commented.

'They do, sweetheart! Listen, you stick going there, keep on Mr Watson's right side.' Cliff Banks grabbed his car keys. 'Get your skates on, I'll give you a lift to the school.'

Toiling now beside the railway arches Chrissie clutched the locket – unable to hide it in the bedroom she shared with Michelle in case her sister or her mum found it, she was condemned to carry it with her all the time. Yet unconsciously the little girl had come to need it. She fingered it in class, avoiding Bella's fierce glare; like a talisman it made her feel protected.

Fretting about how to keep on Mr Watson's 'right side', she resolved to return the locket tomorrow if there wasn't another field trip. She was startled by shouts and whoops of laughter echoing from one of the arches under the viaduct. These were drowned out by the clatter of a Piccadilly line train on the tracks above.

Chrissie ran up to the arch and looked into the gloom. There was a tower, so tall it almost touched the curving brick roof. At the top was a fairy-tale cottage with doors and windows. Out of one door came a chute and from the back an iron ladder. Several faces were crammed in one window. Chrissie recognized friends from her old class. Boys and girls were pushing and jostling for a turn on the slide, as she had when she had gone to the school around the corner. Chrissie grabbed the sides of the metal chute and began to climb.

'Chrissie, be careful!' a girl shouted from the top of the chute and then yelled with undisguised glee, 'She's back!'

Chrissie kept going, confident that with her feet wedged against the sides of the slide she wouldn't slip.

'You could fall,' another girl warned, her voice thrilling at the possibility.

'I'll make her fall!' Chrissie recognized Geoff Lyons, a boy who had won the high-jump championship for Hammersmith. He pushed the first girl aside and took up the space in the doorway. 'It's my turn. Out of the way!' There was no conviction in his voice.

As she got higher, the pull of gravity was stronger. One slip and she would tip over the side and crash on to the concrete below. Geoff Lyons drummed the metal with his shoes, making the frame vibrate. She pushed on up.

'You're not in charge now.' But Geoff Lyons shuffled out of the way.

'Yes I am.' Chrissie threw herself on to the platform and, sitting down, arranged her skirt over her bare legs, feet sticking out over the chute. She looked around at Geoff and said, as a concession, 'You're after me.'

The boy bit his lower lip to stop a self-conscious grin. Behind him the other children on the platform surged forward.

It was a potent rumour amongst the children – a grisly tale – that long ago a boy had pitched off the slide and split his head on the concrete. Stains on the ground around the iron supports were his blood and brains. His ghost haunted the arches, making a 'whoo-whoo' like a train whistle. Michelle said that the boy had died on King Street outside the park ten years ago and the blood had been cleaned up.

At her old school, Chrissie could scale the chute or zoom down the ladder like a fireman holding on to the handrails. This was just one reason that she was in charge. At the prep school where she was now, badges of honour were won for obscure attainments to do with Latin and composition. Now she was back in a world with rules that she understood.

She shuffled on her bottom to the edge of the slide and swivelled round so that her back was to the chute. To cries of incredulity, she flung herself backwards and shot downwards. Halfway she lost her balance and tried to break her speed by grabbing at the sides of the chute, but, propelled by momentum, she tumbled head over heels and crashed over the side on to the ground. Inches from her nose were the stains. Time stopped. Chrissie was gazing at her own brains.

Everything righted itself. She wasn't dead. She clambered to her feet, brushing down her skirt and hazily noting a tear in one of the pleats; she pushed back her hair and did a jig. Everyone was clapping and cheering. The sensation was one of pure joy.

Knowing when to leave a scene, Chrissie went back to the path, but instead of going to the park gate, she continued past the arch with the ponderous roundabout that took two kids to push it. She passed the sandpit where her dad had made her castles, patting the top of the bucket like a magic trick and lifting it to reveal the firmest castle she had ever seen. He had been cross when she had tapped it with her spade and it had collapsed.

A bird or an animal, a fox maybe, was snuffling in the bushes. She parted the branches, but couldn't see anything. She heard a sniff. One of the kids from the sandpit was hiding. She had done that when she was little.

'This is a stupid place – anyone will find you.' She spoke to the leaves. 'I just have.' Although she couldn't see anyone, Chrissie pushed her way in, smashing tinder-dry branches.

Huddled in a ragged spot of sunlight, not blinking, not moving, was a girl. Chrissie had seen eyes like that before: staring gobstoppers. Then the eyes blinked.

'Bella!' Chrissie touched Bella's arm. The girl flinched.

'Ouch!' she hissed.

'I didn't press hard.' Chrissie squinted down at Bella's arm. She was astonished: she had only brushed the girl's skin, but where her fingers had been there were marks.

Bella Markham had broken friends with her.

Broken. Chrissie found herself wondering what she could do to Bella if she had meant to hurt her. If Bella Markham weren't there then Chrissie would be in charge. Without Bella and Mrs Watson everything would be happy ever after.

In the shadow of the railway arches, above the crash and bang of the trains, no one would hear Bella's screams. No one would know.

Chapter Twenty-Three

October 2014

'Police confirmed that a body found by cleaners in Kew Gardens in the early hours of the morning died in suspicious circumstances.' Cashman's voice came out of the four speakers in her van, so clear he might have been in the van with her. The information he gave was brief. He appealed to anyone who might know Joseph Hooker to come forward. Cashman had been right – the murder in Kew Gardens was the top news item, beating the fighting in Syria and a bomb blast in Afghanistan that had killed seven people.

Stella was relieved that the BBC hadn't named 'the cleaner'. But still, barely two hours since she had found the dead man, Lucie May knew the cleaner was Stella. She had left messages and texts demanding an exclusive. 'You owe me, Officer Darnell.' Stella hadn't replied. Yet it would only be a matter of time before the reporter caught up with her. Jackie would field any other approaches. Jack had texted; she would reply later.

As she was getting into the van parked in the Kew Gardens Estates car park, another Instagram picture had winged in from her mum. Suzie was on an underground train. Through the window behind her, a station sign said 'Bondi Junction'. Suzie was apparently absorbed in a copy of the *Sydney Morning Herald*. The caption below the picture read *Commuting in Sydney – driver not patch on Jack*. Stella wondered how her mum could judge this. Her hands were visible, so Stella supposed that her brother had taken it, but it was as likely that Suzie had inveigled a real commuter into photographing her.

Cashman was refusing to give a date for when Kew Gardens would reopen. Stella knew that the galleries would be shut for several days while they gathered evidence. She turned off the radio. Tina would advise her how to handle the media.

She had driven to the hospice on autopilot and had been sitting outside for twenty minutes.

She frowned at the substantial Edwardian house wrapped in a flourishing Virginia creeper, the only colour on a day that had dawned grey. The mist lingered over the Thames off to her left. Stella didn't think that she would be allowed to see Tina. She had been in a room with a dead body; it must compromise infection-control rules. Not that murder was an infection from which Tina needed protection.

Stella returned to her first belief that Tina wouldn't want to be seen unwell. She tapped the steering wheel. She should have rung before coming. She could ring now. She took her phone off the dashboard cradle and found Tina's mobile number. She hesitated. Surely they didn't allow mobile phones in a hospice? She didn't have the landline number. She could find it on Google. When she tried, she found she had no signal. She had passed a sign at the entrance – perhaps the number was on there.

Stella leant on the driving wheel. A woman and a man were making their way up a ramp to the entrance; the woman was helping the man although he didn't look old enough to need help. Tina would have a fit if Stella held her arm. Stella started the engine. Jack said that families knew less about relatives than friends and partners. Stella didn't know much about her brother, or either of her parents. Michelle Banks was wrong; if Tina wanted to talk to her then she would call herself.

Decision made, Stella started the engine and drove slowly back down the drive. At the gate she pulled over to let a taxi pass. The cab had privacy windows, so she couldn't tell if the driver had thanked her. After it had gone, she wondered if it was Tina's father. Tina would be pleased if it was her dad.

In his text, Jack had said he might have found them a case. If he meant the murder in the Marianne North Gallery, she would have to emphasize that it was a police matter. Cashman wouldn't appreciate them treading on his toes.

Passing Kew Gardens, she glimpsed the Marianne North Gallery through the gates. She saw a flash of police tape, blue and white against the grey of the day. She hoped Jack had found something. Tina had advised they go and get detective business. Stella shuddered. They would only take cases brought to them. Whatever, she did want to work on a case with Jack again: they made a good team.

She parked up behind the Clean Slate office on Shepherd's Bush Green and saw that her mum had sent another photo. Two in one day. This time Suzie was sporting crazy headgear. A logo to her right indicated that she was in David Jones. Her brother had said that their mum was practically living in the department store. Suzie claimed that it was due to the air-conditioning. But, having spent her childhood with Suzie trailing around Derry & Toms in Kensington and Peter Jones in Sloane Square, Stella was unconvinced. Tweaking the image, she enlarged it.

The caption was: *Elementary, my dear Watson.*

It was the second time in as many hours that Stella had seen the hat. She was astounded, less at the coincidence than at the fact that Suzie Darnell was wearing a deerstalker.

Chapter Twenty-Four

July 1976

Bella, jammed between the branches of a bush, her head in her hands, made Chrissie think of a Guy Fawkes waiting to go on a bonfire.

'You OK?' Chrissie managed. 'I didn't mean to hurt you.' It was true.

Perhaps because Chrissie sounded sympathetic, Bella's shoulders shook with great sobs. When she finally looked up, Chrissie saw that her skin was blotched red. One of the blotches was dark. It was a bruise.

'I didn't do that.' Chrissie had an edge to her voice. She expected that Bella would say she had beaten her up. She would be expelled. She wouldn't mind, but her dad would go mad.

'It wasn't you.' Bella struggled between sobs. 'They said I was a rich prig.'

'Who did?' In the fantasy where Bella Markham was dead, 'a rich prig' was one of the names Chrissie had called her.

'Horrid children. They laughed at my uniform and said I talked funny. They pushed me off the slide. I said I thought I was better than them, which I am. Did you send them?' She looked at Chrissie with watery eyes.

'Send them where?'

'To kill me.'

'I don't know who they are.' But she did. The 'horrid children' must be her friends. Chrissie remarked, 'If I was going to kill you I'd do it myself.'

'They said if I told anyone in the whole wide world they'd kill me properly.'

'They didn't push you off the slide. You must have fallen.' Chrissie looked stern. Not even Geoff Lyons would do that.

'Yeah, well.' Bella shrugged. 'They could have done.'

'Get up.' Chrissie held out her hand and was remotely surprised when Bella scrambled to her feet and took it. Her fingers were hot and Chrissie nearly snatched away her hand. She brought her out of the bushes on to the path.

At the roundabout arch she commanded, 'Sit there.' She stomped back to the arch with the slide.

Her timing was perfect. Janice Maynard had whooshed to a stop at the bottom of the chute. When she saw Chrissie she broke into a smile. 'Did you see that?' she asked brightly.

'Yes.' Chrissie grabbed her arm as she was about to head back to the ladder for another go. 'Stop.'

Looking up at the rusting cottage on top of the slide, she signalled to the children huddled there. Geoff Lyons was about to come down.

'Get down here.' Her voice boomed in the vaulted space. She waited until the children – six in all, her old gang – were clustered around her. Without waiting to see if they were following, Chrissie marched out back to where she had left Bella.

Bella Markham was hunched on the roundabout; she gripped one of the iron handrails as if it were moving and she might pitch off. When she saw Chrissie with the children, she pushed herself towards the middle of the roundabout. Seeing that there was no escape, she drew her legs up under her and folded her arms over her chest. The blotches on her cheeks were livid and her uniform was in disarray.

'OK, so this is Bella. She's at my new school. She can't help being rich or a prig and often she isn't nice. So you'd all better leave her alone or I'll smash your faces in. OK?' Chrissie drew herself up, but was still shorter than all the other children apart from Geoff Lyons.

'She said I smelled,' Janice Maynard pointed out.

'She's like that.' Chrissie shook her head. 'You have to ignore her. It's cos her dad wears a wig to work.' Her forbidding look quelled a snort of laughter.

Chrissie put an arm around Janice. 'No one hurts my friends. If she touches you, I want to know.' She cocked her head, waiting for an answer.

'I wasn't there,' Geoff Lyons said at last. 'I came at the end.'

'What did you do?' Chrissie demanded.

'What do you mean?' He shuffled about on the cracked concrete.

'Did you stop it?'

'No, I ... er—'

'It's worse to do nothing than to do something,' Chrissie said. 'Bella fell off the slide. Did anyone help her?' No one spoke. She jutted a thumb at Bella. 'Come here.' Bella didn't move. 'Now!'

Bella scrabbled off the roundabout and limped over.

'She said we pushed her,' Kathy Haynes said.

Chrissie nodded. 'She's always saying stuff like that.' She rounded on Bella. 'Tell them you're sorry you lied.'

'I'm not sorry. They smell.' Bella flinched at her temerity. 'Well, they do,' she muttered.

'We all smell. I'll tear your arms off if I have to,' Chrissie said.

'They could have pushed me off.'

'No one here would do that.' Chrissie pulled a face. 'Except maybe you.'

'Sorry then,' Bella said.

'It's wrong to lie,' Chrissie echoed Emily all the while she clutched the locket. 'Next time you see Bella, remember she's my

146

friend. She's in my gang at the new school. So is my friend Emily, but she's not here. Everyone there smells.'

Janice Maynard played her last card. 'She said you was a liar, Chrissie.'

'She's still my friend. Go!' She flapped her hand and, like a flock of birds, the children scattered out of the arch.

'They'll kill me if they see me again and you're not here,' Bella said when they were alone by the roundabout.

'Yeah, they might,' Chrissie agreed. 'What're you doing round here anyway? You live by Kew Gardens.'

Bella reddened. 'We've moved. We live here now.'

'Where?' Chrissie probed.

'Goldhawk Road. My mum's found a flat. We were in Kew, but she owed on the rent and we left without paying.' The words tumbled out. 'We left the washing up. And Bruce the Bear.' Her lip wobbled.

'What about your dad with the wig?'

'He lives with his "mistress". He doesn't pay bills. My mum says he has his cake and he eats it.'

'Who made it? Is it chocolate?' They were walking under the arch to King Street.

'Made what, the wig?' Bella was chewing the side of her thumb. The blotches on her face had faded.

'The cake your dad eats.'

'I don't know,' Bella replied miserably. 'I don't think she meant a real cake.'

'I see.' Chrissie didn't see. Bella hadn't asked why she was in Hammersmith when she lived in Kew. 'See you tomorrow then,' she said before Bella could do so.

'You can be leader if you want.' Bella undid the band fastening her hair, retwisted the hank and pulled it tight.

'No thank you.' Chrissie shook her head. She had a fine sense of how to wield power. Bella Markham would have to ask her more than once.

King Street shimmered in the haze. Melting tar fumes cut the air.

'You're better at leading.' Bella gave a crooked smile; the braces on her teeth glittered in the sunlight. '*Pleeease*, Chrissie.'

'OK.' Chrissie sighed reluctantly. ''Cept you have to say it.'

'Say what?' Bella looked anxious.

'Say I'm in charge.'

'You're in charge!'

Chapter Twenty-Five

October 2014

As he moved along Priory Road, Jack sang a rhyme from his babyhood:

'There were two birds sat on a stone,
Fa, la, la, la, lal, de;
One flew away, and then there was one,
Fa, la, la, la, lal de.'

He stopped at the house by the pond in Kew where he had seen the True Host briefly stop. He must establish whether he lived there. All but the attic window was in darkness.

For years Jack had tracked True Hosts through London and found his way into their sanctums. The risk wasn't being arrested for breaking and entering (he never broke in order to enter), but falling victim to his Host.

A detective's daughter, Stella played by the book – the law and her staff manual – and last year he had promised her to stop going out at night. But that left the innocent – and the guilty – to the mercy of a True Host free to own the night-time lanes and byways, to lounge in alleyways and meander across wasteland. After the One Under case, Stella had said Jack must be unfettered by the demands of others. Not that she had put it like that, but he had taken the gist to mean that she accepted that he walked at night. Yet, tonight, every bone in his body screamed that he shouldn't be here.

So, keeping in the shadow of a plane tree, Jack nearly shouted out loud when a man stepped into the lamplight.

'Are you OK, sir?' A police officer.

'Yes thank you.' Little over a century ago, Jack's nocturnal outings would have made him a criminal, but not any more. He stood his ground.

'Would you mind telling me what you are doing, sir?' the officer persisted.

'It's a time when you can be on your own. No one bothers you.' A bad start. Jack's mouth was dry. He should have seen the policeman before the policeman saw him. He drew his coat closer around him and affected nonchalance. 'It helps me wind down.'

'I see.' The officer did not see. He got out a notebook and flipped it to a fresh page. 'Perhaps you'd tell me what you were doing in the early hours of yesterday morning, sir?'

Jack got it. Since Stella had found the body in the Marianne North Gallery, police would be patrolling the area near Kew Gardens in case the murderer returned. They would be looking for anyone acting untowardly; in the eyes of most people, Jack acted untowardly on a daily basis.

He explained what he did for a living and that after a shift in the cab he needed to stretch his legs. He admitted that he had been walking the night before. He had been on the other side of the river, in Richmond Park. There might be shots of him on CCTV.

Perhaps because he could make sense of a train driver behaving in such a way, the young man seemed convinced. But since Jack lacked an alibi – he had been in the vicinity of the murder at the time – he made a big thing of taking down his details.

Jack regretted not going to Jackie's when she had invited him, then she could have vouched for him, although not of course for the whole of the night. He considered saying that he knew the detective in charge of the Kew Gardens murder. No point, because Cashman would be happy to have him as the prime suspect.

Allowed at last to continue on his way, Jack walked around the pond, hands behind his back, aware that the constable was watching him. When he reached the far side of the pond the young man turned and went off down Priory Road, his footsteps echoing in the silent street. Jack waited until they had died away and strolled back to the tree.

He hadn't heard back from Stella about his having found a case. He regretted the text, sent on a whim, because his evidence was flimsy. A woman dead on his train and a True Host who had left the scene without identifying himself amounted to little. Jack had come now in the hope of gathering more facts.

There was a light at the top of the house. Was someone reading in bed? Was the light in a bedroom? The encounter with the constable had shaken him. He shouldn't have been seen and, worse, the policeman had recorded his name and where he lived and worked. Jack had as good as put himself in the frame for a murder. He would resume his investigations at home. Pulling up his coat collar, Jack set off briskly towards Hammersmith.

Google Street View had introduced a new feature which Jack dubbed 'the Time Slider'. By sliding a marker along a bar he could explore a street, a path or lane in other time zones, back to 2008. Jack would have liked the Time Slider to take him back decades and show his mother strolling around St Peter's Square, clasping his hand – fuzzy figures caught on camera as they examined beetles crawling up walls and blackbirds perched on branches – but six years would have to do. He was used to 'walking' London on Street View in a parallel existence, now he could go back in time.

The embers of a fire in the grate sent faint orange flickers across the ceiling. As the heat died, the chill reasserted itself. Jack was in his room at the top of his house. His eyrie was next to what had been his parents' bedroom; it had been his mother's private space and he felt her presence most strongly here.

Unwilling to risk another encounter with the Met, Jack was now restricting his initial detective work to online. Cloaked in invisibility, he 'journeyed' along Priory Road in August 2010, the time zone a random choice. Kew Pond looked dry, a basin of mud. He zoomed in and saw that the surface was green with algae. He returned to Priory Road and focused on the house where he had seen the True Host. It was daytime and he could read a name fashioned in the wrought-iron gates: Kew Villa. The curtains were open. He paused the cursor by the tree where the constable had accosted him.

There was someone at the front window. His heart thumping, Jack peered at the screen. Like all figures captured on Street View the face was fuzzed out. A phantom hovered behind glass that reflected wispy cirrus clouds in the sky. It could be a man or a woman. A man, he thought. Regardless, Jack was certain that the person was not the True Host.

He stopped in his virtual tracks. The mouse jerked in his hand. He didn't need to see the marque on the car's radiator grille to identify it. The Toyota Yaris Verso was parked by the gates to the house. Jack directed the cursor closer to the car. He was dexterous, aware that a clumsy dab could propel him up the road or into a tree. He went a little to the right and enlarged the image.

Like faces, the number plate was fuzzy. But this didn't extend to the rest of the vehicle. The sun had shone brightly on the day in summer 2010 when Google photographed Priory Road. The image was so sharp it showed a dent on the driver's side wing and flecks of metal where the paint had been scratched. There was a shadow behind the steering wheel. Jack pressed the magnifying tool. He had only met him twice and then only for minutes, but he was familiar from newspaper photographs. The man in the

Toyota Yaris Verso was Detective Chief Superintendent Terry Darnell, Stella's father.

Jack hadn't noticed that the fire had gone out. The room was as cold as a fridge. He huddled in his coat. The only light was from his computer's screen. To ward off demons that were never far away, he soothed himself, singing softly:

'The other flew after, and then there was none,
Fa, la, la, la, lal de.'

'Why was Terry outside Kew Villa in August 2010?' Grabbing a pencil Jack jotted down the question on a slip of paper by the keyboard. By the angle of the sun, it was morning. Inconveniently, Google didn't provide times of day.

The position of Terry's shadow suggested that he was reading, perhaps a newspaper. It could be that Terry had been waiting for a friend. Jack didn't think so. Like Cashman had said at Kew Gardens station, police officers were never off the clock.

There were few reasons why someone sat for long periods in a car. Terry had the typical stance of a detective on a stakeout. 'Who was he watching?' Determined to be methodical – Stella would approve – Jack wrote down the question. He had respect for the Met detective in whose footsteps he and Stella were tentatively treading. The newspaper wasn't a clumsy prop; Terry was hiding in plain sight, a trick at which Jack was proficient.

Jack couldn't know how long Terry had been in the Toyota. He could have parked moments before the Google car captured him and only glanced at the newspaper. Or he could have been there hours. He had retired in 2009 and by August 2010 had only months to live.

Jack sat in the darkness, the gentle glow of the screen making hulking creatures out of the desk and the cupboard, and faced the truth. He wasn't an armchair detective, he would have to go and see for himself.

Outside he stopped to stroke the door knocker, a short-eared owl who was his friend, and, without a backward glance, he hurried down the steps into the night.

There was no sign of the policeman. Nor were there cars of any colour outside Kew Villa. The camber where the Toyota had been was cross-hatched by shadows of branches. Terry's absence was palpable. On his night walks through the empty streets of London, Jack felt not just the absence of those in bed asleep, but of the dead. Avoiding cracks in the pavements, he sensed his own mortality.

He was certain that Kew Villa had been the focus of Terry's interest. He looked up at the house. The window where he had seen the face was blank, the curtains drawn. The light was still on in the topmost window. A child's bedroom perhaps; more likely a study. No child would be awake now.

Not true. As a child he had lain awake watching the hands on the clock drag around.

Jack continued around the pond into Bushwood Road and behind the house found a door in the garden wall. It was unlocked and swung open on oiled hinges. He took a step back. That shouldn't have happened. It was like an invitation. The True Host was expecting him. He went numb. There was no garage and the bins were by the front steps, yet someone used the back door regularly.

Through the opening, instead of the Palm House, was an overgrown lawn. In the shadow of the wall, he checked his watch. He was due at the Herbarium at a quarter to six. Being situated outside Kew Gardens, it was open as normal. He pulled the door closed. He felt the same unease as it moved too easily and shut with the minutest click.

Jack told himself it had been a good night's work. Google Street View had given him evidence for Stella. Apart from Jennifer Day's death on his train, a man acting suspiciously at the scene had gone to a house that four years ago her father had staked out. Not a lot to go on, but no less than for their other cases.

The Kew Gardens Estates Office was at the end of Ferry Lane. As Jack trudged along the long single-track road, he glimpsed the river, a black ribbon through the trees. On his left was the wall of the Herbarium and then Kew Gardens. He didn't look behind to confirm that he was alone as he sang. His voice lilted on the dawn breeze:

'And so the poor stone was left all alone.
Fa, la, la, la, lal, de.'

Chapter Twenty-Six

July 1976

'How are you liking your school?' Cliff Banks called through the open glass partition in his taxi. He watched his daughter in his rear-view mirror.

'It's nice.' Chrissie slid along the seat to avoid her dad's eyes. She leant on the armrest and gazed despondently out of the window at the dusty streets. She would like to be walking home on the path by the viaduct with Janice and Geoff sharing penny snakes and sherbet fountains. She didn't want to be pretending to go home in a taxi driven by a man who wasn't supposed to be her dad. The bit about going home in a taxi was true, a notion that didn't raise her spirits. The locket, secreted in her skirt pocket, weighed her down like a boulder.

Her dad echoed her thoughts. 'You'll go up a notch after this! Bet most of the girls don't go home in a taxi cab!'

Chrissie was on the verge of retorting that she wasn't the only girl collected in a taxi, but that would upset him. Recently Bella had started to take the train and Emily always walked. Since Bella had moved to Goldhawk Road, Chrissie had to go right down the platform and get in another carriage to avoid her. When

Bella had confessed that she lived in a rented flat and that her dad didn't live with her, Chrissie sniffed an advantage that confessing the truth about her own life would nullify. So far as Bella knew, Chrissie lived in a huge house and rode about in a taxi. Chrissie felt uncomfortable, because if she could tell the truth Bella could have come in the taxi too. Her thoughts went on in this way as her dad's taxi wended through the sun-drenched streets of West London, the open windows making no difference to the static heat in the cab.

'Who were those girls you was with?' Her dad was chatty, but Chrissie wasn't fooled. Her mum said he was anxious for her to get on and not have his sort of life. Chrissie couldn't see what was wrong with it. Her dad had more fun than Mr Watson, who only smiled when he was doing his drawings and hardly even then.

'My friends. I'm in charge,' she reassured him. They were passing Kew Gardens. She would rather be in there making a daisy chain. Through the bars of a gate she glimpsed a chimney. *The house with no rooms.* She shivered.

'You all right, sweetie?' Her dad was watching her in the mirror.

'I've been there.' She pinched herself. Mr Watson hadn't said that the field trips were a secret, only his drawing of the eucalyptus tree. She guessed her dad wouldn't think looking at other people's pictures was proper work. She fixed on the notice with her dad's cab number fixed between the jump seats opposite: '34425'. She knew it off by heart. One day she could have a taxi number of her own.

'Where?' her dad was asking. He didn't sound at all cross.

'There's a house in there with paintings all hung up next to each other. They were done by a lady in the Victorian times. Mr Watson took me.'

'Was it useful?' His eyes were twinkling.

'Yes.' Useful? She didn't know what that meant. 'Mr Watson told me not to do them like that though. He says botanists don't want pretty pictures, they want drawings that make them decide the name of dead plants. But he loves her.' She considered telling her dad about her visit there by herself, but that would mean explaining about running away from her friends and worse about

157

Mrs Watson on the floor. Last Thursday Mrs Watson had made country cake with raisins. Chrissie didn't like raisins, but with Mrs Watson having just popped out, she hadn't had to eat them.

'Loves her? His wife better watch out then!' He laughed.

Before she had time to consider the wisdom of it, she said, 'Mrs Watson was with us.'

A cyclist cut across the taxi's path. Cliff Banks braked. Something slid out from under the seat. 'Try going in a straight line, mate! What was that, sweetheart?'

'Mrs Watson came too.' Chrissie wriggled around on the seat. It was too hot to breathe in the cab.

'She keeps a weather eye on him.' Cliff Banks slowed to let a car come out of a driveway on to the road.

Chrissie hunched into the corner of the cab. The visit hadn't been useful because it meant that she couldn't drop the locket behind the settee. She reached into her pocket and touched it. She had come to like the locket and didn't want to give it back. If her dad asked Mr Watson about the field trip he would find out that she was lying. It seemed she couldn't stop herself lying.

Her dad drove over Chiswick Bridge. Waiting in traffic Chrissie saw a boat with men rowing on the river. A man on a bicycle was shouting at them from the towpath through a megaphone. The men must be glad to be on the water where he couldn't reach them. She wished that she was there, floating down the river in the sunshine.

On the Great West Road, traffic had slowed to walking pace. Chrissie peered out of the window at a line of wooden barriers protecting a hole so deep that she couldn't see to the bottom.

'Have they found more dead men?' she said, trying to forget the locket.

'Just that robber. He was buried under the demolished houses long before you was born.'

'Were you born then?'

'Yes, I think so. It was in the fifties.'

'I feel sorry for him being crushed by bricks.' Chrissie was telling the truth; she did feel sad for the man. She would hate her flat to fall on top of her.

'Don't. Some of us do an honest day's graft for a living, we don't steal off of others.' He strained over the luggage space to see into the hole. 'Would you credit it, the man was wearing a ring from the robbery, bold as brass! Anyway, that's not how he died. He was murdered.'

'How was he murdered?' Forgetting the locket, Chrissie pictured the Cat in the Hat pointing his umbrella like a gun.

'His throat was slit. Don't be telling your mum what I said, she'll accuse me of giving you nightmares. You can bet that the robbers argued over the loot.'

Chrissie shuffled along the seat and out of view of the mirror. Her foot caught something plastic. It had come from under the seat when her dad braked. She grabbed it. Inside were two bright pink flip-flops. Despite the stifling heat, Chrissie shivered. The flip-flops were the ones that she had lost on the day of the Addled Brain.

'What's that, Chrissie?' her dad asked.

'My flip-flops.' She stared at the bright pink plastic.

'I've been driving round with them for days.' He slapped his forehead. 'George, Mr Watson, says you left them at his. Didn't you say you lost them when you was playing with your friends?' He was watching her in the mirror.

Goose pimples came up on her arms. 'I can't remember.' Saying about Mrs Watson had happened without warning, she wouldn't lie again.

'I goes to George, didn't she notice she had bare feet? He told me you took them to school and after the lesson you left them at his. What a chump, Crystal!' At the sound of her special name, Chrissie felt heat return. 'Remember now?'

'Ye-es.' Why had she taken them to school? They weren't allowed to wear flip-flops there. The bag came from Boots the chemist. She had gone shopping there with her mum and Michelle. Maybe Mrs Watson had got it on one of her shopping trips.

Chrissie laid the flip-flops on her lap. She had taken her flip-flops to school by accident and left them at Mr and Mrs Watson's house and now here they were. The taxi picked up speed.

'Put them on. They'll be cooler.' Her dad winked at her in the mirror.

Chrissie undid her sandals and swapped them for the flip-flops.

'That better, Crystal?'

'Yes.' If she had left the flip-flops at Mr Watson's, it meant that she hadn't gone to the house with no rooms and hadn't seen the lady with gobstopper eyes or the Cat in the Hat. 'Dad?' she began.

'Yes, lovey?' Cliff Banks swung off Hammersmith Broadway and into King Street.

She had left the flip-flops outside the house with no rooms.

'Nothing.' Chrissie gripped the seat as if she was in an aeroplane doing a loop the loop. The only way her flip-flops could have been at Mr and Mrs Watson's house was if Mr Watson had put them there. It meant that he had been at the house with no rooms. That meant that he knew she had been there too.

Chapter Twenty-Seven

October 2014

Stella was sitting in what she still caught herself thinking of as her dad's kitchen although it was some years since Terry Darnell had died and had left the house to his only daughter. She was populating the Kew Gardens rota, adding in new recruits to work alongside her long-term operatives. She couldn't afford for anything to go wrong. She pulled a face; things had gone wrong on her first morning: she had discovered the body of a murdered man.

She usually worked in what, when she was a child, had been her bedroom, but tonight after supper – a cottage pie because Jackie said she ate too many shepherd's pies – she had stayed downstairs. She rested her elbows on Terry's pine table and regarded the spreadsheet with little comprehension. Beside her was a cooling mug of tea. Although she had had four showers over the last two days, she could still smell the stale smoke from in the Marianne North Gallery. When she tried to sleep she saw the dead man's face, lips drawn back from his teeth, eyes staring into the far distance.

An email pinged on to her screen. Subject heading, *A good day for bad news!* Lucie May. *Howdy Agent Darnell, 'Detective finds body and solves the case'. Call!*

Lucie May was ringing hourly on both her phones. She had put a note through the door. Stella kept the hall light off to discourage May and other press hounds from doorstepping her. It wouldn't stop May.

No word from Tina. Stella hadn't told anyone she had gone to the hospice although she suspected that Jackie knew because when she had returned to the office, she had given her a mug of sugary tea and asked if she was OK. Stella had insisted she was fine. She told herself that she had to be fine because detectives couldn't be squeamish and that if she was squeamish about anything, it was that the police had dirtied her clean floor. Stella blinked away the image of the staring old man. Cashman had said the victim must have known his assailant, for he had been trusting enough to turn his back on his killer. Haunted by the image, Stella turned the thermostat up to twenty-two degrees.

'Wendy said that the Facilities Manager at Kew gave Clean Slate a ninety-eight per cent rating for your first morning. But for the small business of there being a corpse in the Marianne North Gallery, he'd be a happy man!' Jackie had said.

'What was the two per cent?' Stella had asked.

'That'll be his margin for improvement. In the circs that's impressive.'

Stella had spent the day in her office deep in spreadsheets and emails. She decided again that when Cashman gave the all-clear for the galleries, she would continue cleaning them. It wasn't fair to ask anyone else, at least until the murderer was caught. Why would someone want to kill an old man? Who was he? The murderer must be caught. She imagined Beverly's cry in the office, *'Life should mean life!'*

Stella's eye fell on what nowadays she thought of as Jack's chair. Long ago it had been her mum's. Her tea was cold. Putting it in the microwave she noticed Terry's coaster stuck to the bottom. She prised it off and set the timer for twenty seconds.

Drinking the tea, she flipped the coaster between her fingers and the words 'Botanic Gardens' caught her attention. '"The Fire

Tree" No. 764. Marianne North Collection.' Out of nowhere she remembered that after Terry's death she'd had to cancel his Friend of Kew membership. She had considered it odd that he was a friend – of any organization other than the police – but certainly of Kew. Her dad had liked trees – he had once bought her a book about British trees – but she couldn't see him strolling around the Palm House. Or the Marianne North Gallery, come to that. At the time, she had supposed he was preparing for retirement. Now she doubted this. Whatever had made Terry buy a pass for Kew Gardens and a coaster of a Marianne North painting, it hadn't been because he was winding down.

Stella sat back in her chair. He had just renewed the membership when he died. Jackie had urged her to transfer the pass into her name, wander in the gardens in the spring evenings after work, but she never had. Now that Clean Slate had the cleaning contract, to go there would feel like work.

Terry had been a detective until the last day of his life. She held the coaster to the light. Why had he bought it?

There was a huff from the floor by the fridge. Stella looked down. Unlike Jack, she didn't believe in ghosts, but the back of her neck tingled as if she was being watched. She had only recently lost the sensation that Terry had just left the room. It wasn't a ghost, of her dad or anyone else. It was Stanley stretching in his bed. He was fast asleep on his back; paws poking up to the ceiling, he looked in rigor mortis. Stella banished the association. She was getting like Jack.

There was a bang on the door. Stanley flew out of his bed and, claws skittering, hurtled along the passage giving ear-splitting barks.

'Sssh!' Dogs were a giveaway. Lucie May would know she was here. Stella hoped that despite the noise, she could pretend to be out. She peeped around the door jamb at the front door. Stanley was leaping about under the letter box, barking shrilly.

Jackie had said that Stanley might put off intruders. Looking at his small furry form she doubted that he would put off anyone. Except Lucie May, who had no time for pets.

A shadow filled the glazed panels in the door.

Her phone signalled a text, the loud beep another giveaway. She snatched it from her trouser pocket. Jack.

Are you there?

The old man's murder had made her jittery. Only one person visited so late; she kept milk in the fridge ready.

'Woo-woo-woo!' Stanley kept up his clamour. Jack was his best friend.

Stella headed down the hall. Jack's brand of topsy-turvy would get them both back on track. As she opened the door, it struck Stella that Stanley never usually barked when Jack called.

Chapter Twenty-Eight

July 1976

'What are you doing in here?'

Chrissie whirled around. Mr Watson was in the doorway. Her mind raced as she tried to think of an explanation for why she was in his bedroom and said the first words that came to mind: 'Mrs Watson asked me to fetch her...' Her eye fell on the chair tucked into the dressing table over which was slung a cardigan or a shawl, she couldn't tell. 'This!' She snatched it up. 'She's cold.'

Chrissie clutched it and began to edge to the door. Mr Watson didn't move out of the way.

'How can she be cold in this heat?' he asked with apparent curiosity. 'What did she say exactly?'

'I don't know,' Chrissie replied miserably, covering both his questions. She herself was boiling hot.

'Then you must take it to her.' He stood aside. 'We don't want her catching her death,' he said. 'Christina.'

The girl stopped on the stairs.

'Do ask Mrs Watson not to keep you too long. We have lots to do today.'

Chrissie nodded dumbly and continued down the stairs.

'Christina.' He was on the landing above her.

'Yes.' The locket was like a lump of stone in her pocket.

'Tell Mrs Watson that...' His voice was faint.

'Pardon?'

'On second thoughts, leave your tea and come up now.'

'Mrs Watson will be cross if I don't finish her cake,' the girl said with no conviction. She returned to the landing clutching the scarf.

Mr Watson giggled. It made Chrissie think of a girl at her new school. He put a hand on her shoulder and guided her ahead of him up to the studio. Inside he picked up his scalpel and began sharpening a pencil. He spoke so softly that Chrissie only just caught the words:

'We both know that Mrs Watson won't be cross, don't we, Christina?'

Chapter Twenty-Nine

October 2014

A dark shape loomed on the path. Stella was about to slam the door shut when the faulty lamp-post opposite flickered to life and in the watery glow she recognized Martin Cashman. She nearly hugged him with relief.

'It's very late!' Adrenaline flooded her system. As a child – in this house – she had been told never to answer the door or the telephone without an adult beside her. Grown-up, she had modified the rule to: 'Never answer the door after dark'. In winter this was after four o'clock. The exception was Jack who might appear at all hours.

'Sorry!' Cashman put up his hands.

'Come in.' Stella left the door for Cashman to close and returned to the kitchen. Stanley hung back, his eye on the detective as he took off his coat, shook it and hung it with care on one of the hooks. He kept close company with Cashman's trouser bottoms along the passage. Back in the kitchen he jumped into his bed, but remained alert and, his chin resting on the cushioned rim, fixed Cashman with a wary stare.

'Tea, coffee, hot milk?'

'Hot milk?' Cashman pulled a face.

'It's just some people like—'

'Coffee'd be grand.' He rubbed his hands with apparent relish and grabbed 'Jack's chair', swinging it around and sitting astride it.

Cashman, like Jack, had chosen the position that gave him a view of both exits, through the house and out to the garden.

She hadn't replied to Jack's text. She would wait until Cashman had gone. She hoped that Jack wouldn't turn up now with Cashman here; she didn't want to deal with them sparring with each other. She flicked the switch on the kettle.

'I want to run stuff by you, chew the cud,' Cashman said.

'What stuff?' Unpractised at entertaining, she didn't have biscuits.

'Our body in the Marianne North Gallery.' Cashman spoke as if she should know. 'I wondered if anything had come to mind. However small?'

Our body. She opened a jar of instant coffee and, digging into the solidified mass, loosened some granules. She felt a flicker of relief that the 'cud' wasn't his failed marriage. Perhaps he'd sorted it by now. Her parents were always breaking up and making up. Until they broke up and got a divorce.

'Nothing has.' She wouldn't mention the figures in the mist, the crunch of non-existent gravel or the geese; she put them down to her state of mind. 'Isn't stuff on the case confidential?' She shouldn't have pointed out an error of judgement.

'It *is* confidential.' He flashed her a look. 'But you're Terry's girl. Family!' He tipped the chair forward as if urging a horse forward.

Shrugging off the implication that she was anyone's girl, Stella got down a mug from the cupboard and, opening the fridge, frowned at the three milk cartons in the door shelf. Jack hadn't been round for a while.

Not true. Jack had been round very recently. She had given him hot milk and he had left without finishing it. *Tina.* Stella told herself that Tina's illness was a glitch which she would sort and move on.

Stella ripped the tab off a milk carton with her teeth and sniffed it. OK, but another day and she would have to throw it away.

'When you cycled to the gallery did you notice anything unusual, even inconsequential?' Cashman asked in his detective's voice.

'Everything was unusual.' Stella handed him his coffee. 'It was the first time I'd been in Kew Gardens at half five in the morning.' She poured hot water on to a Brooke Bond teabag and mashed it against the side of the cup. Sloshing in milk she returned the carton to the fridge and joined him at the table. 'I told that woman detective all I know.'

When he joined the force, Martin Cashman had been mentored by Terry. Now in his forties, he had until recently resembled him, but with a new trendy haircut and swish suit he had lost about five years. Stella had seen this happen with men who split up from their partners. Since her dad's death, Martin Cashman had always said he was 'there for her'. She hadn't thought he meant so late at night. Whatever, he had 'been there' more than once and she wouldn't forget.

Cashman had taken his jacket off and rolled up his shirt sleeves. When she had first met him, after Terry's death, Stella blamed him for his part in shortening Terry's life. Her mum said Terry spent more time with his mates in the force than with his family. Jack had pointed out that Stella spent most of her waking hours at work. But with three solved cases under her belt, Stella had begun to tentatively think of herself as a detective. Since he was prepared to share information about his case with her, perhaps Cashman did too.

'Nice coffee, Stell.' He raised the mug in a toast and took a gulp. It would be scalding, but Cashman was the kind of man – as Terry had been – who treated the smallest domestic action as a danger faced down. He had called her 'Stell'. Only Jackie and her family did that. And Jack.

Cashman was speaking. '...creepy in the dark by yourself. You should clean in pairs.'

'It's not economical and anyway Kew Gardens is safe.' She bristled at his advice, although she had decided this herself.

'Someone's been murdered there!'

'The police patrol the streets by themselves.'

'They're trained in self-defence; they carry truncheons and radios. You can't combat a mugger with a mop and bucket.'

Stella considered listing the chemical sprays in her armoury, but saw a flaw in her defence. Kew Gardens required compliance with environmentally sustainable cleaning materials; nothing she used for the Marianne North Gallery would incapacitate an assailant. Nevertheless, she settled back in her chair, unconsciously comforted by Cashman's concerns.

She returned to the murder. 'Did the staff who locked up the gallery the night before see anything?'

'The woman in charge said she couldn't have missed the body. She checks all the rooms.'

'Did she look down?'

'What do you mean?'

'She'd be checking for punters looking at pictures, not men sprawled on the floor.'

'Good point.' Cashman nodded approvingly. 'Thinking like your dad!' He looked about him. 'Please could I have sugar? One advantage to single life.' He chortled. 'I can eat what I like!'

'Married or not, your teeth will rot!' Stella regretted the admonishment; it wasn't her business. She said hastily, 'You can do what you like.' It sounded like permission granted. She rummaged in the cupboard and found a packet of sugar behind a tin of beans. It dated from Terry's time and, like the coffee, was rock solid. She bashed it on the counter and loosened some crystals.

'My teeth are a medical wonder. No fillings, see?' He bared his lips. Stella agreed; his teeth were brilliant white. Probably because he hadn't had sugar for years. Handing the packet to Cashman with a spoon, she sat down again.

Cashman heaped a teaspoon into his tea, then another. 'We have the time of death: it's a narrow window between four and six a.m.' Drinking his coffee, he sighed appreciatively.

'It was someone with access to the gardens and to the gallery after hours,' Stella surmised.

'Right, but the gallery staff have alibis. Most were in bed – luckily for them not alone and also lucky that they were with their partners, except for a young man, hardly out of the playpen. He was on the phone from five ten to five forty. We triangulated his mobile, and he was, as he claimed, at his parents' home in Palmers Green. That's a schlep from Kew so he's out of the frame.'

'He could have been giving the murderer directions,' Stella said.

'Great minds!' Cashman licked his spoon. 'He *said* he was listening to the cricket scores. But Pam, my DC, is a cricket fan and she questioned what cricket scores he could be picking up. Turned out it was a sex chat line. Jeez! Terry said we see the seamier side of life. He envied your job.'

On her eighteenth birthday Terry had left a police application form on the kitchen table. He hadn't wanted her to be a cleaner. 'No way,' she muttered.

'He said if you offered him work, he'd snap it up!' He swung his leg over the chair and swivelled to face her. 'You know where you are with a duster. Karen said this job gives us a skewed view of life. No wonder she wants out.'

'I thought you wanted out too.' Stella blew across her tea although it was no longer hot.

'It's run its course, but the force helped it along. Terry warned me: Don't take your eye off your marriage, Marty, or it'll take its eye off you. I followed most of his advice to the letter. That was one gem I ignored.'

Marty. There was much about her dad that Stella didn't know. 'Mum says their marriage was a "wrong turning" in her life, it didn't *go* wrong.'

'She didn't mean it.' Cashman was dismissive. 'She loved your dad.'

Jack maintained that Suzie leaving Terry – on a cold day in November 1973 – was her wrong turning, not the day she had met him. She talked about Terry all the time; Jack reckoned that Terry was the love of her life. Stella stuck to facts; if her parents had loved

171

each other – whatever love *was* – they'd have stayed married. Jack hadn't heard their rows.

'Not all the keyholders have alibis.' Cashman beamed at Stella. 'You don't!'

'I was here. Asleep.' Not funny.

'With only that dog to back up your story.'

'I don't let him into the bedroom…' Too much information.

Cashman pulled a face at Stanley. The dog watched him with inscrutable eyes, his body tensed. Jackie said that any 'Mr Right' must pass the 'Stanley test'.

Marty. What had Cashman called Terry?

'I set off for Kew Gardens at about a quarter past five. It takes fifteen minutes to get to Kew from here with no traffic. And I'm not a keyholder; we're given new codes by the Facilities Manager. I arrived at the gallery at six.'

'It seems unlikely you'd have called it in if you had murdered him.'

'It's good cover,' Stella objected.

'Are you trying to be my prime suspect?' His eyes twinkled.

'Just saying.' She shrugged. 'I take it Trevor has an alibi?' She liked Trevor, but the nicest people were murderers.

'The manager has an alibi, his wife. Not my favourite kind of corroboration, but no reason to doubt it, as with the others. All the staff we've interviewed so far have more to lose than gain by killing someone. Job, reputation, freedom. No one has a connection with Hooker or has Australian relatives.'

'My brother's in Australia,' Stella said.

'There you go again. At this rate I'll have to arrest you!'

'Mum's there now. Look at this.' She showed him the photo of Suzie in the deerstalker. 'Actually, it might be worth checking out David Jones; it's a department store in Sydney. A long shot, but Joseph Hooker could have bought his deerstalker hat there.'

'Cool look for a detective!' Cashman whistled. 'It's afternoon there, I'll ring them.' Stella looked up the number on her laptop and he called the store.

Fifteen minutes later, once Cashman had established his credentials, the woman at David Jones told him that they had one account holder called Joseph Hooker and that the address matched the one on the New South Wales driving licence found on the body. 'The man purchased a deerstalker three years ago. She went into a sales pitch. She tried to sell a deerstalker to a detective!' He roared with laughter but then grew serious. 'She told me that Hooker's account's been "dormant" for over a year. That could mean he may have been in the UK some time.'

'With that suntan, I'd bet he just got here,' Stella remarked.

'We already knew that the address on his licence isn't current. It's a house in a district called Crows Nest. The man and woman renting haven't heard of Hooker. The letting agency said their client is one Jane Church and she's gone walkabout in the bush.'

'You mean she's lost?' Stella felt a lurch of dread. This was a new potential disaster to befall her mum in Australia. Suzie was highly likely to put on a stupid hat and send an Instagram picture of herself lost in the outback.

'She'll surface for food and fuel, but we need her to surface now and confirm if she knows Hooker.'

'Since he was killed on site, Hooker must have gone willingly with his killer to the North Gallery.'

'You said in your statement that you went out to the yard to fill your bucket with water. Could anyone have been in the building when you arrived and taken that chance to leave?'

'Yes. I didn't go into the room with the body and I left the front doors unlocked.' She wouldn't do that again.

'Lucky or the killer might have attacked you to get out.' Cashman pivoted the chair on its back legs. 'Pathology report says Hooker was suffering from advanced heart disease. He was stabbed with a short-bladed knife, possibly a scalpel. Anyone of medium strength could have overpowered him.'

'He was stabbed from behind so she, or he, didn't need to overpower him.' Stella tried to ignore Cashman's rocking on the chair; it would make the legs give way. He was acting as if he felt at home. 'A scalpel would have taken strength because the blade is short.'

'Or someone with dexterity. It was an upward thrust into the lungs: the killer knew what he or she was doing.'

'There was a smell.' Stella was racking her brains; apart from the fog and the geese there had been something.

'What sort of smell?'

'Stale smoke, but he was a smoker so that's explained. It made me think of my friend who used to smoke.' There was something else, but it eluded her.

'What friend?' Cashman spread his hands out on the table. 'Driver Dan the Underground Man?' After the One Under case, Cashman had been tougher on Jack than on her for not telling the police. He had warned him to 'lay off playing detective and stick to the day job'. Jack had pointed out that detection *was* his day job, he drove trains at night. Since then Martin referred to him by names such as 'Thomas the Tank Engine' or 'Driver Dan'.

'Someone called Tina.'

'You think your mate was there?' Martin looked incredulous.

'Tina has an alibi, she's in a hospi— She's ill.'

'Wait a sec, is this Tina Banks? The lawyer?'

'Yes.' Stella didn't divulge clients, but Tina had put a testimonial from Banks Associates on the Clean Slate website so it was no secret.

'She's your friend? I'm sorry!' Martin stopped tilting his chair. 'What a bloody waste.'

'She'll be OK.'

'I heard she's riddled with cancer. Terry had a lot of time for her.'

'Dad knew Tina?' Tina had never said. She had never said she was ill either.

'We all groan if Banks is defending our villain; we know it's a lost cause. It's hard enough to get them behind bars, then they get to walk free – look at Harry Roberts.'

Stella had been frightened to come downstairs to get herself a glass of water in the night in case Harry Roberts was lying in wait for her. She saw with sudden clarity that Martin must have dropped in late at night when Terry was alive. They had sat here drinking coffee – or something stronger – 'chewing the cud'. Martin laughed mirthlessly and scratched the shadow of stubble on his face. Then as if to underline that he felt at home, he got up and refilled the kettle. He was putting in too much water, it would waste electricity, but Stella stopped herself saying so. Stanley was sitting up, wild-eyed, and she mouthed to him to lie down.

She caught a whiff of Martin's after-shave. Gillette. Stella used to buy her dad the same after-shave every Christmas and birthday. 'Where was the surprise?' Jack had asked. But Terry, like Stella, hated surprises. She still caught herself hovering over a bottle of Gillette in Boots.

'What was that?' Cashman went to the back door. His breath clouded the glass as, palms cupped around his face, he peered out into the night.

Jack. Stella never knew which door he would arrive or leave by. To use the back door he had to scale two garden walls in St Peter's Square. If Cashman caught Jack out there, he would arrest him.

'It'll be a cat. Or a fox, it's their mating season.' She had no idea about the habits of foxes.

'Foxes mate earlier in the year; by October their cubs are dispersing.'

Martin would be an amateur naturalist. She had to hope that Jack had seen him there and gone. Yet she didn't want Jack to go. She must answer his text.

Martin gave himself three spoonfuls of sugar. During one of her early-morning cleaning shifts, he had let slip that he had started working-out at the gym. Now she supposed it was the effect of his marriage break-up. Terry's divorce had done nothing for his health.

Always consider the unlikely. She heard Terry and then heard her own voice: 'What if the man isn't Hooker?'

Cashman pulled his chair up to the table and his knee touched hers. She didn't move her leg. 'Meaning?'

It was a hunch. She could hardly say it was Terry's idea. It was the sort of thing Jack would say. She snatched at the idea as it evaporated. 'The address on the licence is out of date or it might be false. The wallet mightn't have been his. He might have stolen it. Or the murderer might have planted it on him.' She expected Cashman to scoff, but he said:

'Good thought. We need to talk to the woman in the bush.' He scratched his chin. 'Given where and how he was murdered, it's looking like an inside job. Scalpels are two a penny in Kew Gardens.'

'I guess that simplifies it.'

'It still means hundreds of people.' Cashman lifted his cup and saw the coaster. He read the label. 'This is in the Marianne North Gallery, where the body was found!'

'Terry bought it.'

'Why?' Cashman was incredulous.

The obvious explanation was that Terry had needed a coaster. It was typical that he had bought only one – he had rarely entertained. Actually that wasn't true. There had been Lucie May and 'Marty'.

'No idea. What was this "we" business? You've established that Joseph Hooker was Australian. But what if the man in the Marianne North Gallery isn't really Joseph Hooker?'

'Until we prove otherwise, we assume so.' Cashman dangled a desultory hand to Stanley. The dog gave a low growl.

'He doesn't like that,' Stella said quickly.

Cashman kept his hand there a moment longer. With a yawn, he rose and washed up his cup. He put it on the draining rack. 'Time for bed.'

It was nearly 4 a.m. Stella hadn't noticed the time go by. *Time for bed*. Martin was going down the passage to the hall. By the time she caught up with him, he was on the doorstep shrugging into his coat. In the dull lamplight he looked young and fresh-faced.

'Fancy a drink tomorrow?' He put his collar up against the biting cold, reminding her of Jack in his coat. 'Today!'

'Yes.' Stella startled herself.

'See you in the Ram at eight.' He leant in and kissed her cheek.

After Martin Cashman had gone Stella stayed on the doorstep, gazing unseeing into the blackness. Sniffing the night air, she smelled fabric softener. Had she not been distracted, she would have identified the source. Instead she supposed vaguely that it was from washing hanging in a nearby garden.

Shadows of branches moved across the pavements. One shadow didn't move. Because it wasn't the shadow of a branch.

Chapter Thirty

October 2014

We have another case!

Jack chanted the words under his breath as he bowled along Hammersmith Terrace and went left into Black Lion Lane. The Ram pub was in darkness. He paused on the pavement; the pub was where, in 2011, he had first seen Stella. She had been reading in the corner. She had been working on what became their first case.

It was five to four in the morning. He had turned up late at Stella's before, but this was so late it was early. She would be up soon; he would catch her as she left for Kew Gardens. He would have to be sensitive because it would be strange for Stella to see her dad alive in his car on Street View.

He stopped in the subway tunnel, a tiled passage smelling of piss. Above him came the occasional swish of a car or a lorry on the Great West Road.

'Hello,' he said as if talking to someone beside him. His voice was hollow. Sometimes when he was in the tunnel – his favourite subway – he fancied that he could hear the chatter of those who once lived there. Not in the tunnel, but from when there had been houses there before the Great West Road was extended.

He calculated that he was standing in what had been the cellar of number 33 Black Lion Lane. Whole streets, row upon row of Victorian and Georgian houses, had been crushed to make way for the road. Shadows, pools of light, special places, associations and memories smashed by an iron ball. It was up to Jack to hold the facts and dreams of so many lost existences. Tonight he couldn't hear anything because his own mind was busy.

He strode up the ramp. As he had expected there were no lights in the windows of the houses in Rose Gardens that had escaped demolition. He took up position in the bushes opposite Stella's house. There was no light in the street because the only lamp-post – Stella's lamp-post, he called it – was faulty and was off more than on.

The blinds in her bedroom were closed and clouds racing across the sky were reflected in the clean glass. Jack didn't feel good about watching her house. He should go back to his eyrie. He could see her after cleaning in Kew. But if he saw a movement or a light, he would knock on the door.

Everything happened in sequence. Stella's hall light went on. The lamp-post came on and suffused the privet hedge outside her house in orange light and the front door opened. Two people were outlined in the hall light. Stella. And someone else. Jack couldn't believe it. The other person was Cashman.

Why was the detective visiting Stella at four in the morning? Jack didn't have to wait for an answer. Cashman was kissing Stella. On the mouth, long and lingering. Jack made up what he couldn't see. Stella didn't like Cashman. *Did she?*

Cashman was walking out of Rose Gardens North, hands in pockets, sauntering as though he owned the night. He unlocked his car and moments later headlights sliced the dark. Jack knew the cars that parked in Stella's road. He should have seen the black Audi when he arrived. If Cashman was such a good detective, he should have detected that Jack was there. Anyone could have been hiding in the bushes outside Stella's house.

Stella had said that to be an effective team, they must tell each other everything. She hadn't told him about Cashman. Only when the Audi had driven away down St Peter's Square, the engine purring like a cat full of cream, did Stella shut the door. Light drifting through glazed door panels went out.

Jackie had stopped him from going for coffee with Stella and Cashman when the detective had turned up at the office. Jack had supposed that it was because she thought Stella would handle Cashman better on her own. But it must be because they were having an affair and Jackie was giving them space.

Jack drifted into the cone of lamplight, uncaring if Stella saw him. He wanted to shout up to her window that she was making a mistake, but his voice was mute.

We've got a new case!

Stella had a new detective. A proper murder case.

Martin Cashman was a wrong turning. A dead end. Jack took out his phone and dabbed a text. Seconds after he pressed 'send', he received a reply.

Hey Jackanory, get your arse over here!

Stella's lamp-post went out. He was in darkness.

Chapter Thirty-One

October 2014

'A nippety-nip, honey-bee?' Lucie May in a short skirt and a shirt that showed her cleavage sashayed before him into the sitting room. Jack was greeted by a peculiar smell. Since Lucie had given up smoking she had tried all sorts of substitutes from e-cigarettes to raw carrots and twigs of real liquorice. The last two didn't provide nicotine but could be flourished and chewed upon as she worked. Jack hoped she hadn't succumbed to proper smoking, but the odour pricking his nostrils suggested a noxious herbal mix.

'I'd rather have hot milk.' They had this exchange every time he visited.

'Goodness!' Visibly crestfallen Lucie flounced to the kitchen. 'Find a perch in my nest, cuckoo,' she warbled to him.

A nest could probably literally be constructed with the contents of Lucie's sitting room. Large – when she bought the thirties semi in the nineties, she had demolished the dividing wall ('My Shirley Valentine moment') – it was scattered with papers, books and newspapers, discarded cardigans, half-chewed carrots, the pickings of a story written or abandoned. Lucie had an office upstairs, but as far as Jack knew, she worked downstairs. He took up his 'perch' in the corner of the sofa.

Lucie was a reporter on the *Chronicle*, the local newspaper. She covered anything from school fêtes and lost pets to road-traffic accidents and murder. After the One Under case, she had got several stories syndicated globally. For a while it had seemed as if Lucie was headed for brighter lights than the streets of Hammersmith and Fulham. Jack had expected her increase in income to propel her to a condominium in central London. But nothing changed. Despite her constant complaints about her editor – the holders of the post changed, but Lucie spoke as if the personality was the same – she remained in the job. She didn't use the extra money to modernize her house, which, apart from 'the wall', hadn't been touched since the sixties. Nor, although she must be flirting with seventy, had she slowed down. She continued chasing stories and meeting deadlines by a whisker. She continued to grumble that her editor took the best stories and, as far as Jack knew, she hadn't begun the book that had been 'simmering' for decades. After her brief success, Lucie's life had stayed the same.

'Here you are.' She gave Jack his milk and floated to the other end of the room where she concocted her 'nippets'.

'Sure I can't tempt you?' she asked merrily. 'Do you goo-ood? Gin dashed with tonic – horrid stuff, it's packed with iodine – garnish of lemon and chattering with ice. Bob's your uncle and Charlie's your aunt!'

'Quinine,' Jack said involuntarily; Lucie wasn't great on corrections or feedback.

'So what's going on in the dark regions of your subterranean world?' She breezed over, sipping her drink. Lucie never asked how he was unless she was on the sniff for a story. Tonight he knew what she was after.

'I won't ask Stella.' He shook his head. 'You're looking smart.' At this time of night Lucie was usually in slouchy leggings and a baggy jumper, 'legacy of long-divorced hubby'. Smart was perhaps overstating it, but even though it was after four in the morning she was in full make-up.

'A shindig at the town hall. Must impress the biggy-wigs or they think you're dead,' Lucie stated obliquely. Jack doubted anyone supposed her dead since her byline was in the paper each week and she had over a million followers on Twitter.

'You're not here for milk. What's festering?' She grabbed a plastic bottle from the top of the television and rapidly operated the spray lever. Clouds rose into the air and the strange smell got stronger.

'What is that?' Jack coughed.

She read the label on the bottle. '"Placid Pet". Natural calm for your pets.'

The smell wasn't unpleasant, yet not pleasant either. 'Have you got a pet?' He scanned the room. A dog or cat could easily be sleeping amidst the heaps of paper.

'No!' Lucie exclaimed. 'How could I have a pet? I'm never here. They need company and fuss.' Jack thought that described Lucie's needs.

'But the spray—'

'It's to keep *me* calm. I'm at the damn coal-face dawn till dawn. Wreaks havoc with the nerves.' She eyed him beadily. 'I spotted it online when I was researching a story about dogs being poisoned with sausage treats in Ravenscourt Park. It's working – I don't even want a fag. Chillin' is us, man! The thing is, Jackal, you got to live in the present. Be in the "now"!' She mussed up her mane of 'blonde' hair and gave her trademark corncrake cackle.

'There are calming substances for humans. Incense, essential oils…'

'I don't want my house reeking of hocus pocus. With this, you know where you are.'

No wonder Stella found Lucie baffling. Although to the casual observer, Lucie might appear frenetic, Jack did think her calmer. He undid his shoes and settled on the sofa cushions. He was probably Lucie's idea of a pet.

'Did Terry Darnell have a case in Kew?' With Lucie there was no beating around bushes. 'On Kew Green.'

'The Cleaner's Detective! Where is Miss Marple?' Lucie embarked on a hoarse rendition of Betty Wright's soul hit 'Clean-up Woman'. Having Terry Darnell in common made her relationship with Stella prickly at best, although since their last case it had improved.

'Are we moonlighting, Jackaroo?' Lucie dipped into a bag of carrot crudités from Marks and Spencer. She was the only person Jack knew who looked cool nibbling a carrot.

'Stella's busy,' he said gruffly. 'I'm doing preliminary work on a case.'

'What case?' Lucie was businesslike, Stella forgotten.

'I found this.' He brought up Street View on his phone and passed it to her. Carrot between her lips, cheeks drawn in as if she was inhaling from it, accentuating cheekbones of which she was proud, Lucie grimaced at the screen.

'That's Terry's car!' She enlarged the image. 'Where's this?'

'Outside a house by the pond in Kew.' Lucie wouldn't find it odd that out of over a thousand streets in London, Jack had lit upon Terry's car. All the same he wouldn't say he had found it while hunting a True Host.

'August 2010. It was taken not long before Terry died.' She pulled a face. 'Who lives in this house?'

'I don't know.' Stupid not to check. Not least because around Terry Darnell, Lucie lost objectivity. Lucie and Stella were chalk and cheese, but it seemed that both were attracted to men in the CID.

'Did he stay the night, we ask ourselves?' Lucie bit on the carrot.

Jack was quick to reassure her. 'He's not visiting anyone, Terry's *in* the car.' He pointed at the windscreen. 'Could he be watching the house?'

'Creepy!' Lucie fell silent. She patted at her hair as if Terry could see her. Jack realized that he was banking on Lucie knowing the workings of Terry Darnell's mind.

Tentatively Lucie stroked the screen. It scrolled to a picture of a District line train berthed at Earl's Court station. Jack retrieved his phone; Lucie would happily trawl through his gallery in pursuit of a story.

'He never mentioned that house to me.' She tossed the end of her carrot into a wastepaper basket beside her gin station. 'Terry was a dark horse. Like his daughter.'

Terry's daughter. Jack felt a pinpricking. Stella once said that she wouldn't date a married man, she wouldn't collude in the betrayal of a partner, even if she hadn't met them. She *had* met Karen Cashman. Jack was shocked by her volte face. In abandoning her principles, Stella had betrayed herself. She was his benchmark. He was filled with sand; like hitting an air-pocket in an aeroplane, he was falling and falling. Lucie May was ruminating aloud:

'...he did say he was tying up a loose end, correcting something... Can't remember.' Lucie stirred her gin and tonic with a swizzle stick topped with a devil's head, the tongue curling over grinning lips, horns pert. She took a long drink and the level in her glass dropped at an alarming rate. 'I assumed he meant the Rokesmith case...' She trailed off.

Jack had met Stella during the Rokesmith case.

'Sure you don't fancy a nippet?' She patted his leg. Lucie could surprise him with flashes of empathy. Her next question told him that the empathetic moment was brief. Lucie's mind was on Terry. 'He might have guessed he wasn't long for this world and wanted everything done and dusted so he could die in peace?' She ran her tongue along the length of the swizzle stick.

'Maybe.' Not an answer he would have given Stella, but she wouldn't have asked the question. Sticking to facts, she would point out that if Terry had foreseen his death then he would have made a will, eaten better and not spent out on a new boiler. Stella would say her dad had lived as if, like the Louis Armstrong song, he had 'all the time in the world'. Stella lived as if she might die at any moment. Not by appreciating life to the full, but ensuring there was nothing in the pending tray. She would leave no footprint. No stain.

'He could have parked there and gone off moments later.' Lucie hooked out a cube of ice. It glinted like a diamond as big as any hotel. She crunched it up.

'True. Yet I don't think so.' Always avoid the boring explanation.

'Have you asked "Clean-up"? She might know.'

'I only found it a couple of hours ago. I didn't want to wake her.' Jack gulped the milk to hide his expression.

'She might welcome you waking her!' Lucie gave a wheezing cackle. 'So, boychick, one good turn deserves another. Get Stella D. to talk to me.'

'She won't.' Jack spoke with conviction. 'And what good turn? You haven't told me anything.'

'That remains to be seen.' Lucie tapped the side of her nose.

'*Do* you know something?'

'Time will tell.' She regarded her glass with a quizzical expression as if unsure how it came to be empty. 'I'll give thought to it and that's giving a lot, considering how much I have to think about.' She scrambled off the sofa and pattered in stockinged feet to the drinks cabinet. 'You should nab Cashman. He and Terry were best buddies. Get him while he's down – the bloke's at sixes and sevens since his marriage broke up.'

'What?'

'Him and Kaz the Snazz have called it a day. Hasn't Stella told you? They were as thick as thieves in that café on the Broadway the other day.'

'She was talking about Harry Roberts and how did you...' Lucie May got everywhere. Useful if you needed something and not if you wanted a private life. The milk that he had drunk was a solid lump in his stomach.

'Cashman's having a second childhood. Works out, wears skinny-fit suits from River Island and goes to a hairdresser. He scrubs up well. Wouldn't mind a spin around the wheel with him myself! Lah de dah!' She waltzed about the room, brandishing the devil's head swizzle stick. 'Oh hey, here's something! That solicitor – Tina Banks, the one you don't like – she's got cancer. We're not

186

supposed to know, but everyone does.' She tinged her glass with the devil's head.

'I knew.' Jack didn't want Lucie May going on one of her tangents. Especially this tangent. He got up. 'So you think Terry was following up on a failed case.'

'A loose end isn't a failure. He was a good detective, one of the best.' Lucie May squatted at her mini-freezer – kept in the sitting room to save a trip to the kitchen – and drew out an ice tray. She twisted it in her hands; the action put Jack in mind of a chicken's neck being broken. Ice flew across the top of her gin station.

'You said he had to correct something,' Jack reminded her.

'So, we all make mistakes.' She was fractious. 'If we're sensible we keep them close to our chest.' Lucie swept a couple of ice cubes into her glass and jammed the rest back into the tray. 'Not you, darling, we'd know if you piled into the buffers at Ealing Broadway or opened the doors before the train was in the station. Not that you would – we're safe in your lovely hands.'

'It's not possible to open the doors if the… What mistake did Terry make?' With Lucie it paid to be patient. A mine of snippets of fact and fiction, eventually she would retrieve the salient detail.

'There was one time he turned up, late at night.' Lucie arched her eyebrows as if Terry Darnell visiting her in the small hours was exceptional. 'He said something about not following stuff up. No, that wasn't—'

'Lucie! What were his actual words?' Jack forgot to be patient.

Shutting her eyes, Lucie batted the devil's head against her lips. Then she adopted a gruff voice as if she were channelling the dead detective: 'I've let someone get away with murder.'

Chapter Thirty-Two

November 2014

Stella was the first to arrive in the office. This was unsurprising since it was 7 a.m. and the business opened at nine. However, Jackie was often in by half past seven. This morning she had a hygienist appointment so would be later.

Stella planned to stay an hour and then go to Kew Gardens and meet the Herbarium team as they came off shift at nine o'clock. She wanted to see Jack. The rest of the gardens were still closed as the police searched the grounds. She had slept fitfully and before getting up had answered his text asking if she was *there* with another question: *Where is 'there'?* She felt uncomfortable about this now. Jack had probably meant Rose Gardens North, so she could have said yes. Martin's visit had thrown her. The truth was that she wasn't ready to tell Jack that he had called, although she wasn't sure why.

She ran up to the women's toilet and filled the kettle from the tap marked 'Drinking Water'. Despite the notice, she didn't trust it – she had a horror of dead birds in water tanks – but there was no other option. She poured some into Stanley's bowl and, leaving the kettle to boil, went through to her office.

By 8 a.m. she had finished two long quotes for potential commercial clients and emailed them off. Her tea undrunk, she settled to read her mum's customer report. Suzie Darnell continued to update the customer database from Sydney. Every month she provided a breakdown of customers over the domestic, commercial and public sectors. Clean Slate had a mix of clients in all three areas with Kew Gardens the largest. With no debts Clean Slate was, Suzie reassured her, 'economically robust'. Stella gazed at the figures for Banks Associates without absorbing them. It wasn't that Cashman had kissed her and asked her for a drink that had kept her from sleeping. It was what he had said about Tina. *'She's riddled with cancer.'*

She was just preparing to go to Kew Gardens when she heard the outer door open. The tell-tale floorboard by the photocopier creaked. It couldn't be Jackie and Beverly was never in this early. A lost courier. Stella tutted. Someone in the insurance company had left the street door off the latch again; she had locked it on her way up. Stanley let off a volley of shouty barks and rushed into the main room.

'Is anyone here?' A woman's voice. Then in a tone that lacked authority and so would have no effect on the dog: 'Down please!'

Tina!

The woman backed up against the photocopier wasn't Tina. Stella made a fleeting assessment as disappointment sank in. Long hair, quilted jacket, tight jeans and ankle boots.

'Are you Stella Darnell?'

'Speaking.' Then Stella remembered she wasn't on the phone. 'Yes I am.'

'Please could you come with me?'

Stella did a 'down' command with her fist and was faintly gratified to see Stanley obey.

'Where to?'

'To see Tina. I'm Michelle, I'm Tina's sister.'

Michelle Banks was a less-expensive-looking version of Tina: the clothes were smart, but not designer. She was softer somehow.

Stella snatched a duster from a pile of samples on Beverly's desk and began wiping the surface. She caught herself and put it down.

'Tina asked to see you.' The woman spoke without Tina's energy or conviction. 'I told your secretary.'

'I've had a lot...' Even murder wasn't an excuse. 'Is – is she all right?' She heard how lame the question sounded.

'Fine apart from that she's dying.' The woman shook her head in hazy apology.

'I meant...' Stella didn't know what she meant. Tina won her battles; her vocabulary didn't include failure. She said that she and Stella tackled life head on, they focused on solutions. Cancer was another battle that Tina would win.

'She's asking for you.'

Stella retreated towards her office. 'I've got a meeting at nine, I'll go after that.'

'There may not be an "after that".' Michelle Banks looked at Stella. She had Tina's eyes.

Stella parked in the same space as on her first visit to the hospice, facing the exit. Through trees, the Thames glinted silver in the autumn sunshine. When she turned off the engine she was startled by the ping of an incoming text on her phone.

Are you ok? Jackie asked.

Unscheduled mtg. Forgetting how to spell 'unscheduled', Stella made three attempts before it looked right. If she told Jackie she was visiting Tina, it would make it true. She wasn't ready for it to be true.

Less than two miles from the hospice, Jackie was sitting in her husband Graham's car.

'Was I right to tell Michelle Banks where Stella was?' she wondered aloud.

'I doubt it.' Graham Makepeace gestured 'thanks' to a woman

in a Fiat 500 who let him out of their street on to the Chertsey Road.

Jackie smoothed her safety belt, pulling it loose and letting it go. 'But how would Stella feel if – *when* – Tina Banks dies and she hadn't said goodbye?'

'Terrible. But not your business.' Graham took the Great West Road exit off the Hogarth Roundabout. 'Stella will have to live with her mistakes. Look at Nick with Clare: we saw that disaster a mile off, but you warning him made him dig his heels in. The relationship lasted months beyond its expiry date.'

Jackie wasn't convinced. It was her job to protect Stella, not to expose her to her worst fear: death. Stella hadn't been able to say goodbye to her dad; he was dead when she got to the hospital. Jackie didn't want it to happen again. It was a risk because while Stella faced reality head on, around death – not counting detective cases – she faced the other way.

'To be fair, you're always spot on, Jax.' Graham flashed her one of his looks that reminded her why she had married him thirty years ago. 'The net result of your actions is happiness!'

Jackie reached over and fluffed her husband's hair. Then she stroked the disarrayed locks back into place. 'I'll text her.'

'Is that wise?'

'No.' The murder in Kew Gardens had taken the shine off winning the contract, and now this.

Are you ok? Jackie pressed 'send'.

A cacophony of tinny church bells heralded Stella's reply: *Unshedulled meeting.*

'She's spelled "unscheduled" wrong,' Jackie murmured. 'That means she's at the hospice.'

'Mission accomplished.' Graham eased the car around Hammersmith Broadway.

The trouble was, Jackie Makepeace reflected sadly after Graham had dropped her at the office, sending Michelle Banks to find Stella wasn't the issue. What mattered was that Stella didn't make friends easily and she was going to lose a good one.

*

Stella passed colour-coded recycling bins and went up a ramp to a door. Inside she was confronted by the steamy smell of school dinners. The cabbage aroma might have dampened the spirits of some, but Stella inhaled deeply and a calm descended. She had looked forward to lunches at the schools she had attended. Lunch was the time in the day when the little girl had understood what was expected of her. She had appreciated the process of queuing for dinner and receiving fixed portions of food, circles of Spam, mounds of potato, blocks of ice cream and squares of chocolate pudding.

Her mood was further strengthened by a yellow plastic sign: 'Cleaning in Progress'. Rounding a corner, she caught a whiff of stringent disinfectant laced with the powerful air freshener she used to dispel unpalatable smells. Surrounded by the smells and apparatus of her world, Stella picked up pace.

'Can I help you?' A woman with a bundle of files under her arm pushed through double doors.

'No thanks.' Stella made to pass.

'Are you looking for someone?' the woman persisted.

'I've come to visit Tina Banks. She's, um, she's staying here.' Stella looked beyond the woman, hoping that Tina might appear, phone clamped to her ear, and they could leave. *Stell! My sister fusses over nothing. Got time for a cuppa and a bite?* She was kidding herself; this was a hospice. Tina was ill. *'Riddled with cancer.'*

'You've come in by the staff entrance.' The woman smiled kindly. 'Let me take you round to reception and I'll check if Tina can see you.'

'She's expecting me,' Stella countered and, stepping back, kicked over another hazard sign. Was Tina expecting her? Tina disliked the unexpected. 'I should go,' she said.

'Let's find out how she is.' The woman was kindly.

Stella followed her along what seemed a labyrinth of corridors. Keeping her nerve, she focused on the clean floors, coved skirtings, a Sluice Room, and she identified the smells: cleaning agents, polish, disinfectant and washing powder. The woman was speaking.

'I didn't take your name. Mine's Laurel.'

Stella blurted out, 'Stella Darnell,' as if she was an imposter.

'This way, Stella.'

More doors and they were in a reception area, bright with sunlight. Stella was ridiculously relieved to find a rack of confectionery and biscuits. Items from an everyday world. Bounty bars and KitKats, Mars bars and Digestives above boxes crammed with crisp packets, salt and vinegar, cheese and onion. She grabbed a bottle of Buxton's mineral water and fumbled in her pocket for change.

'Drop it in here. Our receptionist isn't in yet.' Laurel indicated a box on the desk beside a post tray and a hospice collecting pot.

Stella shoved in all the coins in her hand, enough for at least six bottles of water. Then for good measure she added two more pound coins.

The woman dialled a number on the phone. 'Hello, Jean, Stella is here to visit Tina.' Stella fixed on a poster advertising a 'Sleep Walk' that began at midnight, assembling on Kew Green. Vaguely she thought it was the sort of thing that would suit Jack.

Laurel paused. 'Oh, I see.'

Sensing a problem, Stella whispered hoarsely. 'I'll come another time.'

Laurel rested the receiver back on its cradle. She exuded an air of calm that Stella found inexplicable given she was working in a place where people were ill and dying.

'She's having her bedding changed. They're nearly finished.' She got up. 'Meanwhile could I get you to sign in? For the fire regs.' There was a visitors' book on a table by the entrance, which had Stella come in through the front entrance she would have seen. Stella was surprised to see that her hand was shaking. She squirted out hand gel from a bottle beside the pad. Out of habit – when she visited companies she checked for possible business rivals – she scanned the visitor list for the day before. Michelle Banks and Cliff Banks. Tina's family was the same size as her own, one parent and a sibling. She blotted out the idea of Dale and her mum visiting her in a place like this.

'Come through.' Laurel led her past a carousel rack of Christmas and greetings cards, a fire extinguisher and a fire assembly point notice. The familiar objects were like stepping stones across turbulent waters.

Laurel stopped outside a door numbered twelve. The next room was fourteen. Many hotels didn't have a number thirteen in case their customers considered it bad luck. Here, it crossed Stella's mind, the precaution was unnecessary. She followed Laurel into the room.

A diffused light trickled through a closed blind; the gentle glow picked out an armchair and a built-in wardrobe. Through a door she saw a toilet 'caged' within a frame of mobility supports.

Michelle Banks was sitting by a bed with bars on the sides like a cot. Beside it was a tall metal stand with a bag of liquid attached. Michelle got up and signalled for Stella to take her place. Stella tried to refuse, but Michelle wasn't looking at her. Stella sat down. Her knees touched the side of the bed and she whipped them back. She tried to shift the chair away, but it wouldn't move and, turning around, she saw the door closing. She was alone.

Not alone. A woman was propped up on a criss-cross arrangement of pillows, hands resting on the sheet. Shrunken, thin, her wrists bony.

'Thanks. For. Coming.' Weak, halting speech.

Tina's eyes had retreated into their sockets, the cheekbones that she had claimed were her best feature jutted out, her skin was translucent, lips cracked and colourless. Black lines outlined her eyes as if she was bruised. Her head was like a skull. There were strange red blotches, like a doll, on the centre of both her cheeks. She had changed drastically in only a couple of days. Her eyelids fluttered shut.

'I meant to come sooner…' Not true. But for Michelle Banks she wouldn't have come. Hazily supposing she must keep the patient conscious, Stella said brightly, 'She seems nice, your sister.'

'She'll do,' Tina murmured. 'Mitch did my make-up in your honour!' She gave a crooked smile. 'Bloody awful: she uses the eyeliner like a crayon. Thinks it's frippery. I told her, when they say you look young for your age, they mean twelve, even a corpse looks better with make-up!'

Stella was sure Michelle had been wearing make-up. She knew that Tina took half an hour to 'put her face on' because she did it in the office while Stella cleaned around her. It seemed to her that Michelle Banks had done a good job: Tina's make-up looked fine. Tina herself did not.

'She's been brilliant. When this rubbish is over I'll treat her to a spa day.' Tina licked her lips slowly as if searching for something with her tongue.

'Over?' Stella echoed, bewildered.

'When I'm out of here.' She moved her head robotically and stared at Stella. 'Going to beat this. You. Get. That.' She heaved a sigh and shut her eyes. She didn't speak for so long that Stella decided she had gone to sleep. Then, her eyes still shut, she whispered, 'Got a job for you.'

One of Tina's hands moved across the sheet, her fingers grabbing at the material as if for purchase, the effort seemingly monumental. 'Stuff. To. Sort.' She succumbed to a cough thick with phlegm that didn't clear her throat. This seemed to rob her of what energy she had mustered.

'It can wait.' Stella's voice was hoarse. She bit her tongue and the pain summoned up saliva, but made no lasting difference.

'It can't.' Tina fixed her with a glare.

'OK, what's the job?' Talking about work returned a vestige of normality to the situation. She patted down Tina's covers until there were no creases. 'Cleaning can wait until... until you're out.'

Tina became agitated. She raked her hair from her forehead and stared wildly at Stella as if she had just seen her and was outraged that she was there. It was exactly as Stella had feared. Tina hated being seen like this.

'No!' Tina's eyes were bright and her voice strong. 'Not cleaning. I need to pay. God. Forgives.' Her tongue clacked against the roof of her mouth. 'Make good.'

'Have a drink.' Stella picked a plastic beaker of water with its straw off a bedside locker and brought it to Tina's mouth. She nudged the straw between her lips.

Liquid climbed the straw and dropped. It rose again as Tina applied every ounce of strength to suck on it. Were it possible, her cheeks became more sunken. At last water reached her mouth and dribbled in. She swallowed with the sound of a drain. Stella was reminded of her nana drinking her morning tea, sitting up in bed.

At last Tina shut her eyes and with fluttering fingers signed that she had had enough.

'Before you leave, please tackle the dishes. They're piling up.' She was fierce. 'Wash them *all* up or that man in the conical hat will have words.'

'I don't think—' Stella looked about the room, but the only things that could be washed up were the beaker and a jug of water. There were no dishes. And surely they had staff to wash up.

'Tell him to go.' Tina Banks stabbed a finger towards the end of her bed. 'Gobstopper…'

Stella looked where she was pointing, but there was no one there. No gobstoppers either. Horrified, she realized that Tina was hallucinating. She was talking gibberish.

'Tina, there's no…' Stella looked desperately at the door. She should call someone. She had heard somewhere that it was better to go with a person's hallucinations or they got anxious. Or was it the other way around and you should put them right?

Tina coughed and spluttered, 'Cat in a hat. Two things. Fork. Bag. Look behind the fire.' She jerked her head and then spoke normally: 'No point calling for nurses, one sniff of smoke and they get out.'

'There isn't a fire.' Stella wasn't going to humour Tina about such a serious thing. 'There would have been an alarm.' She hoped she was right.

'You'll take me with you?' She clutched at Stella. 'Don't leave me here.'

She must bring Tina back to reality. 'I'm due at your office tomorrow, shall I leave your flat until you're back?'

'Dust gathers. Did you get the contract at Kew?' Tina was herself. Talk of cats in hats seemed to have passed.

'Yes.' Stella slumped back in her chair. 'We started this week.'

'Did it go well?'

'Yes. Actually no.' Tina was a lawyer, she dealt with the truth. 'I found a man in the Marianne North Gallery.' She took a breath. 'He was dead.'

Tina raised herself up on her elbows but then collapsed back on her pillows. 'It wasn't a cat!' She began to chant. 'Forward Hammersmith Road, Forward Hammersmith Broadway, Left Butterwick, Right Talgarth Road, Right…' She snatched at the sheet as if trying to pull it off. Then she was still.

For some time there was silence, broken only by a murmur in the passage. Stella checked her phone and was surprised to find she had only been in the room seven minutes. She tidied the top of Tina's bedside cabinet, threw away a scrunched-up tissue and lined up the jug with the beaker and a box of tissues. She moved a copy of *The Cat in the Hat* out of the way of the water. The well-thumbed pages were crinkled as if water had already been spilt on them. It explained Tina's going on about the cat. She supposed that illness had caused Tina to regress. She knew that, aside from client briefs and legal documents, Tina didn't read. She was startled by Tina's voice, loud and clear.

'I want you to catch a murderer!'

Tina started to cough. Stella offered water, but Tina waved the glass away. The coughing got worse. Stella pulled the emergency cord.

Chapter Thirty-Three

November 2014

Over the next days, the weather grew colder as autumn gave way to winter. Biting winds ripped the last of the leaves off the deciduous trees in Kew Gardens and pelting rain reduced them to mulch.

Two days after the discovery of the body of Joseph Hooker in the Marianne North Gallery, Martin Cashman sanctioned the reopening of the gardens. At the end of the week, crime-scene tape was removed from the gallery and the public were allowed in. Stella resumed her cleaning shift.

Contrary to fears, visitor numbers to Kew Gardens and to the gallery rose dramatically. Interest was less in Marianne North's pictures than in the antechamber where Hooker was found. Martin had withheld the cause of death from the press. This created a vacuum that seethed with speculation (the dead man's name was a gift for journalists keen to draw links with his nine-teenth-century namesake): *Was Joseph Hooker murdered by a frustrated botanist?*

Sightseers took surreptitious snaps, although no one knew the exact place where the body was found. One enterprising girl from a local prep school was filmed by a classmate sprawled on the floor. This earned her some notoriety on Instagram and suspension from school for a week.

Armchair sleuths speculated the victim had been poisoned. They researched toxins from rare botanical species such as *Physostigma venenosum* which caused death by asphyxiation and was obtainable at Kew. The elegant Victorian tiles – terracotta being the colour of dried blood – were examined by those steeped in *Dexter* and *Silent Witness* for 'blood spatter' and 'human traces'. Consensus was that the gardens, suffused with history, demanded a fictional detective from the past, Lord Peter Wimsey, Sherlock Holmes or Miss Marple, not the Met's present-day besuited CID.

Two days after the murder, it had emerged that Joseph Hooker was alive and not so well. Jane Church returned from her trip into the bush and said that Hooker was her father. He was living in a care home in Sydney. When the police questioned him, he admitted that he had lost his wallet on a visit to London a year ago. Anxious to disguise suspected dementia, which would disqualify him from a room in the care home, he hadn't reported it.

Stella's hunch that the victim had a false ID was right, but Martin didn't applaud her because now the victim had no name or confirmed nationality. Despite the tan, given the licence was not his, he might not even be Australian. His features, apparently in repose, were issued to Interpol and published in the foreign press, including the Australian media. So far the only people to come forward were those complaining about seeing a dead man's face in their paper. No one had identified him. Stella's mum, keen to help, sent a lengthy text detailing that she had no idea who he was. By the end of the week, other news pushed the murder to the inside pages and Marianne North's marble bust, in the porch of her gallery, was left in comparative peace. An elderly man with a rucksack resumed his daily vigil on a bench in the gallery. He had been hospitalized with pneumonia at the time of the murder so, frustratingly for Martin, had an alibi.

The heavier 'footfall' after the murder had meant that Stella increased her mopping to three times a week. Against the advice of Martin and Jackie, she continued to do this by herself.

'Take Dan the Man, not that he'd be protection.' Martin drained his pint of Fuller's London Pride and rapped the glass down on the table.

Stella suspected that Jack would be the best person to protect her from a murderer, but didn't say so.

Tonight, their third outing to the Ram, they had graduated to food. Cashman was doing long hours on the case and had got into the habit of coming around to Stella's around midnight to update her on progress. Tonight, the case having reached an impasse, he had awarded himself a meal in the pub. His late-night visits had put Stella off inviting Jack over. Since Tina had said the odd thing about a murderer – not to mention the cat in the hat – she hadn't spoken to Jack.

'We think the murder was premeditated. The killer could come back. I'm worried about you.' Martin squeezed her hand. 'You may have seen something incriminating that puts you at risk.'

'I didn't see anything.' Again Stella had the feeling that this wasn't true, but whenever she tried to conjure up that morning, it was a blank. Aware of Martin's hand covering hers, she couldn't think.

The Ram had been her dad's local. Stella didn't believe in ghosts, but in this pub she would catch his shadow on the wood-panelled walls as if he had passed there on his way to the toilet and would come back any minute. Perhaps Cashman had felt this too because he added, 'Terry would say this too.'

This had the effect of steeling Stella's nerve. Terry had never waited up for her when she was a teenager because she had lived with her mum in Barons Court. He had once said that the 'thing about you Stell, is you can handle yourself, no one pulls the wool over your eyes'. She sipped her ginger beer. 'The killer might be anywhere in Kew Gardens. We can't stop cleaning altogether. It's hard to hide in the gallery; there are no rooms. Besides, you don't think the murder was random.'

Cashman had to agree with this.

Each time Cashman left Rose Gardens North, he had kissed her. Not the passionate kiss that Jack thought he had seen, but a peck on the cheek.

Contemplating her hand, still in his, Stella said, 'You don't need to look after me.' She liked the feel of his hand though.

'It's what your dad would have wanted.' He clasped her hand in both of his.

'You're married,' Stella said abruptly. She pulled her hand away.

'We're getting a divorce. I'll have one of your "fresh starts", please, Stell!'

Stella cleaned for many single men who had lost partners through death or divorce. She put them into two groups. There were those who were crushed by the loss, grew beards and lived off takeaways. They left a trail of cartons, cans and bottles around their homes. When a third party recognized crisis point Clean Slate was brought in and restored order while the man's friends and relatives took him to the barbers and made him wash. After a series of blind dates and city breaks he landed a new partner and Stella's job was done. She preferred this type to the other sort, who were bent on substituting the partner ASAP. They saw Clean Slate as a dating agency, there to provide a match who would segue into their routine as if it had never been interrupted. Adept at fending off unwanted attentions, Stella handled these jobs. Once she had broken her rule and had a relationship with 'Type Two'. She wouldn't make the mistake again. Cashman was in this group. She would steer clear.

Since Stella had found the dead man she had seen Martin Cashman every day.

'This case is beating me, Stell.' Martin took her hand again and began counting through fingers, one by one. 'We've interviewed everyone at Kew. Nothing. Someone's hiding something because it *has* to be an inside job. It's virtually impossible to climb that wall and certainly to get into the gallery.'

'They could have hidden until the gardens closed.' Stella had contradicted her earlier argument. Luckily he didn't notice.

Martin ran his hand up her arm, under the sleeve of her jacket. His fingers were warm.

'How are your kids taking the split-up?' she heard herself ask.

Martin let go of her hand and raked through his hair. 'They've got their own lives. It's good for them to see another side of us both. Life's not all discipline and routine. It's messy too.' He teased a lock of hair off her forehead.

Stella preferred life to be about discipline and routine. She waged a war on mess.

Martin pursed his lips. 'Karen's got a new man.'

'How do you know?'

'I was passing the house the other night and saw him going in.' He went to the bar and ordered another round of drinks.

Unwilling to leave Stanley on his own, Stella waited for him to return and then went to the toilet. Shutting herself in the cubicle, she rebuked herself for referring to Martin's kids. It was nothing to do with her.

Someone had written across the door in felt pen: 'We get one go at life – don't piss it away'.

Ripping off toilet paper Stella tried to scrub off the words, but then caught herself. The cleaning contract for the Ram was one that Clean Slate had failed to get. When she flushed the lavatory she heard her phone, a distant ringing over the thunder of the water in the pan. She didn't recognize the number and had no intention of having a conversation in a toilet.

In the passage she made way for a woman to pass. The woman looked like Tina.

We get one go at life…

Stella had been back to the hospice three times since her first visit. The first time Tina was asleep and, after sitting in the room with her for an hour, Stella had left. The second and third times Tina's father arrived and Stella hadn't wanted to intrude. She would go after her shift at Kew Gardens tomorrow morning.

'The stumbling block is the victim.' Cashman was tucking into his lamb burger. Stella felt mild irritation as it occurred to her fleetingly that Jack would have waited – not that she minded. She did mind him giving Stanley a chip; it would encourage him to beg at the table.

'Have you traced where the real Hooker stayed when he was here? Or where he lost the wallet?' She had ordered shepherd's pie. A familiar meal that, unlike Cashman's burger, was easy to dispatch.

'He stayed in a hotel on Sandycombe Road in Kew. He paid by card, so he had his wallet then.' Cashman bit into a chip and, leaning down, gave Stanley the other half. Stanley snapped it out of his fingers and shuffled closer to him, sitting stiffly upright.

'Maybe he was heading for the airport when he lost it,' Stella speculated. 'Which airport did he fly out from?' The shepherd's pie came in an unruly heap. She stabbed unsuccessfully at a pea.

'Heathrow. There's CCTV of him there, but none on the Underground. The hotel owner thinks he took a taxi. We've put out a call to cabbies to see if anyone remembers him or found the wallet. Nothing. But if a driver fancied a larger tip and pocketed the wallet, he's not going to 'fess up.'

'London cabbies work hard to get the Knowledge. No amount of cash from a wallet could compensate for losing their licence.' Stella was hotly defensive, thinking of Tina's dad.

'He could have lost it on an Underground train. When drivers take a train back to the depot, there are items that passengers have left in the carriages. Nothing to stop an operative lifting a wallet; London Underground don't strip search.' Cashman no longer sounded objective.

'They hand in everything they find,' Stella snapped. She knew he was thinking of Jack. 'The victim could have stolen the wallet himself and changed identity.'

'Possibly, but Hooker's name isn't on the flight manifests. If our man came into the UK recently, it was under another name. His own perhaps.' Cashman scowled.

'Maybe Hooker didn't lose the wallet in London. He might have forgotten where he lost it. The victim might have stolen it off him in Sydney.' Stella was working her way through the mound of shepherd's pie. She preferred her ready meals: they were rectangular so she could eat in straight lines.

'The credit card wasn't used after Hooker paid for the hotel in Kew and he requested a replacement when he returned to Sydney. He told Visa he had mislaid it in the house.' Cashman ripped open a sachet of mayo and squirted it over his chips. 'Is it possible that the murderer planted a stolen Australian licence on the victim in London?'

'Maybe the killer collects IDs. He did it to confuse the police. It's worked.' Stella was enjoying herself. Terry had weighed up evidence, drawing and redrawing conclusions.

'The packet of Winfield cigarettes he had on him is Australian,' Cashman said. 'The labels in his clothes have been ripped out.'

'Except the deerstalker.' Stella pictured her mum in the hat. She wished again that Suzie would send her a normal message. It was as if in going to Sydney, her mum had changed character as well as hemisphere. She had lost her in more than one sense.

'Joseph Hooker lost the hat at the same time as his wallet.' Cashman gave Stanley a whole chip.

'Did you show the real Hooker the picture?'

'He didn't know him.'

'Are you checking passengers on flights from Sydney in the last month?' Stella asked.

'Are you looking for a job?' Cashman laughed loudly, startling Stanley. 'Yes, we're on it. People get a message from the police, they don't rush to call back.' He crammed a forkful of chips into his mouth.

Stella froze. Cashman had mayo on his chin. Should she say something? She dabbed at her own chin to give him a hint to do the same. He didn't notice.

'The means of death was unusual. It would have been easier to use a penknife with a longer blade. It's like the murderer wanted us to think it's an inside job.' He munched on a chip. 'Which suggests it's not. Then again it might be.' Martin scratched at his chin, missing the blob of mayonnaise by a centimetre.

Stella scraped her plate clean and laid her knife and fork side by side. Martin's phone rang. 'What you got, Rach?' he demanded. There was a pause, he scribbled something on his napkin with a ballpoint and rang off. He thumped his fist on the table. Stanley bristled, his eyes an impenetrable black.

'The man's underwear was handmade. No way of tracing the cotton. He has no name. It's as if he doesn't exist!'

Stella tried not to look at the mayo. 'The longer the delay before you find out who he really is, the more chance the murderer has of covering his or her tracks.' She lifted out a clean napkin from a dispenser on the table.

'As if I need reminding.' Martin looked glum. 'His shoes were a British company. Crockett and Jones.'

Stella knew the brand: Jack's shoes came from there. She didn't say so.

'They were bought here. The company says they're about forty years old. Not unusual to wear their shoes that long apparently.' He pulled a face. 'I prefer my footwear fresh and up to date. This is a bloody needle in a haystack.'

Although his clothes – crumpled shirts and sleeveless pullovers – were always clean, Jack never looked terribly smart. But his shoes were an exception: he polished them to a shine.

'I forgot to mention the contents of his coat pocket.' Martin nibbled on a chip. The mayo was as bright as neon. Stella looked away. 'Strange.'

'What was strange?' Martin had held up the items in evidence bags in the Marianne North Gallery on the morning that she had found the body. Chewing gum, plastic store cards, the driving licence. Not strange.

'Crumbs and those sprinkles you put on cakes.'

'Hundreds and thousands.' Stella saw a flash image of herself at a table with a slice of cake in front of her. Terry was urging her to 'eat up'. The picture vanished. 'He put cake in his pocket?'

Martin looked disapproving. Stella didn't say that Jack was likely to carry a sandwich or a muffin in his coat. He ate on the move.

'The options are that the victim could be British and he lived in Australia, or he's Australian and forty years ago lived here. Or he was living somewhere else entirely.' She unfolded and refolded the napkin. 'Somewhere hot to get the tan.'

'The Winfield cigarettes suggest the former,' Martin murmured.

'Something's not right about the Winfields.'

'What do you mean?'

'Probably nothing. It's gone now.' Stella's memory had become unreliable. She reached across the table and carefully wiped Martin's chin clean with the napkin.

Stella couldn't work out where she was. It wasn't her bedroom: the slants of light from the lamp-post outside were at the wrong angle. Then she realized she was on the left side of the bed; she usually slept on the right. About to shift across, she saw that she wasn't alone. Lying on his back, his profile outlined in the slatted light through the blinds, was Martin Cashman. Gradually the events of the evening returned.

She became aware of what had woken her. A phone was ringing. It was her mobile. She propped herself up on her elbows. It wasn't in the bedroom. Pulling on a T-shirt and jogging bottoms she raced along the landing. The sound came from the study. She had dumped her bag in there on the way to the bedroom and, what with everything, had forgotten to take out her phone. She fumbled with the zips and buckles on the rucksack and then saw it on the desk by her keyboard.

It was the same caller as when she was in the pub toilet. Or another 'Unknown caller'. *British Woman Lost in the Outback!* She should have answered the first time. Fear made her curt: 'Stella Darnell.'

The phone to her ear, she came out of the room and went down the stairs.

'Stella, is that you?' A woman's voice.

'Yes.' Stella was patient. Her mum always asked if it was her after Stella had given her name and when it couldn't be anyone else.

'It's Michelle.'

Stella couldn't think of a client called Michelle.

'Tina's sister.' The voice sounded faraway.

'Oh yes. Hi.' Stella sat down on the last step in the hall. At the same moment, the faulty lamp-post outside went out. Michelle was speaking.

'I'm sorry, I didn't catch that.' Ludicrously, Stella found it harder to hear in the dark. Then she heard perfectly.

'Tina has died.'

Chapter Thirty-Four

November 2014

Jack shut the garden door at the back of Kew Villa. He was closing off his exit: if he had to leave quickly, opening it would waste valuable seconds. Yet he couldn't risk alerting the True Host. If he left it ajar, it might bang in the wind. It wouldn't creak: as he had noticed the last time he came, the hinges were oiled.

The moon was three-quarters – on the wane – and a monochrome sheen picked out an overgrown lawn bounded by shrubs. Holly, dogwood and juniper created large patches of shadow: his kind of garden. Following the line of the shrubbery, Jack approached the house.

Five storeys including the basement and, as before, there was only a light in the top room. He crept down some steps to the basement door. It was locked. He moved stealthily to the side of the house, careful to avoid twigs or dried leaves, those tell-tale signs of a night intruder.

Kew Villa was detached. It was cut off from the road by a high wall set at right angles and Kew Pond acted like a moat. Jack peered in through grimy glass and saw a kitchen full of clutter: appliances, crockery, empty milk bottles. The wooden cupboards hadn't been updated for decades. The door was also locked. Jack looked about him. He was standing on a mat.

He lifted it up and found a key. This should have pleased him – so far it had been easy. Too easy. Like the oiled hinges. A coil of fear stirred; Jack breathed deeply. *He was expected.*

His back flat against the wall he kept still. The cold of the bricks seeped through his coat and chilled him further. But it wasn't this that made him cold to the core. He had a bad feeling about the house. He should leave.

Turning the key, Jack grimaced as the door opened, expecting a creak, but like the door in the garden wall it made no sound. Nevertheless, he stayed where he was and counted to ten. Then another ten. He ventured inside, ears tuned for footsteps, any change in atmosphere, or for another door that would open on oiled hinges and admit his attacker. Nothing.

He glided across the kitchen and through a door already open, out to a lino-covered passage. His sense of direction told him correctly that this led to the hall.

He stopped in the shadow of the staircase. Straight ahead was the front door. No light penetrated the fanlight. But as his eyes became accustomed to the deep gloom, Jack made out a longcase clock beside the door. It wasn't ticking. His heart skipped a beat. A True Host made time wait. He dared to move closer to it and made out the position of the hands. The clock had stopped at seventeen minutes to twelve: 11.43. The time the passenger emergency alarm had gone off in his train on the night that Jennifer Day died of an aneurism in the sixth car.

He retreated to the shadows and looked up the staircase. The house was silent, but Jack knew that he wasn't alone. Somewhere above, the True Host was waiting. He was pulling Jack towards him as if he was attached by a slender thread. It stopped him turning and running out of the front door. He had no choice but to keep going.

His jaw rigid with tension, Jack kept to the sides of the treads to avoid a creaking stair. He wouldn't abandon his method even if he was exposed.

The first room on the landing was a library. It had windows on three sides including the front. Bookshelves filled the walls; a wooden library ladder had been left next to the door. A desk with a leather swivel chair was placed in the centre of the room. He checked behind it and behind the door. No one there.

On the next landing he had a choice of two doors opposite each other. His fear so great he felt as if he was floating above his body, Jack opened the nearer door and let himself become part of the darkness. After what seemed an interminable length of time, he gathered himself and, hearing no breathing, switched on his torch app. He was in a bedroom, austere and forbidding. It was like his grandmother's bedroom in Twickenham. A satin quilt was spread over a double bed; pillows and cushions were heaped at the head. He half expected to see her there, pale and waxy in death as in life.

A flicker of movement. Jack recoiled from a blurred spectre in a mirror on a dressing table with three drawers. A trick of the dust. He peered into the glass. There was no dust. This was surprising to him, because, despite the opulent furnishings, the room had a dowdy, neglected air. He lifted the back legs of the chair tucked beneath the dressing table. Where they had rested were indentations in the Turkish rug. This was one of Stella's tests. The chair hadn't been moved for a good while, either to sit on or clean beneath. He sniffed the pillow – not one of her tests – but, lacking Stella's keen sense of smell, he was none the wiser. He wished that she was with him. Stella would not enter a building without the owner's permission.

With shifts on the Underground and cleaning at the Herbarium, it was several days since Jack had seen Stella. He felt out of touch with her. He disliked this, but it did make it easier to do something of which she would disapprove.

He slid out one of the drawers and a smell escaped into the room. This one he could identify. It was patchouli. Lucie May dabbed it liberally on herself – now it competed with Placid Pet. The drawer was crammed with jewellery. A pearl bracelet nestled next to a necklace of black glass beads and one of chunky wood.

His mother had worn patchouli. Or had she? Patchouli didn't fit with the sombre wood and brocade that implied that the room hadn't been decorated since Victoria was on the throne.

The second drawer contained a hotchpotch of the sort of useless objects that every owner stored until the day when they might use them. Jack had seen these in many houses: a necklace with a broken hasp, loose beads, single earrings, tooth picks, scraps of sample wool and fabric. He prised open the lid of a velvet ring box; there was nothing on the silk cushion inside.

In the last drawer he found two pairs of John Lennon spectacles, their arms entangled in ocular embrace. He parted them and lifted one pair to his face. The wearer was very short-sighted. When he put them back, he had trouble shutting the drawer. He pulled the drawer further out and found a wad of newspaper stuffed at the back. He extracted it, careful not to tear the paper.

He heard something. He stopped. Silence. He was dizzy with fright. Fear of his own fear. He had often explored the homes of murderers or would-be murderers without a frisson of nerves. What was different now? He was out of practice. Since he had met Stella he seldom visited True Hosts. That must be it.

On the other side of the bed was an oak closet. A Narnian wardrobe. Jack saw them everywhere. They offered promise of another, better place. He unfastened the latch and pulled open a door. A bluff of patchouli and camphor greeted him. A metal rail was bowed with the weight of dresses and skirts, heavy coats and woollens. Jack pinched his nose to ward off a sneeze and, clutching the wad of newspaper, clambered inside as if it was the most natural thing in the world. He pushed to the back and tucked his knees up. If someone looked in, he would be out of sight. He felt calm descend.

Delving through the clothes, he reached out and swung the door to. He couldn't lock it from the inside. A True Host would see that the door was unlatched, but Jack wasn't yet certain that a True Host lived in the house. He needed more evidence. The trinkets and flotsam in the dressing-table drawers were not a True Host's trophies, the keepsakes of their terrible crimes; they were objects of life.

He directed his torch app to the back of the wardrobe to prevent light spilling between cracks or knots in the wood and spread the newspaper across his knees. The article was dated Thursday 8 July 1976.

A4 MAN MAY HAVE BEEN MURDERED

By Lucie May

Workmen mending a crater in the Great West Road got a grisly surprise.

'Found a shoe, didn't think nothing of it, you get all sorts in our line. I goes to pick it up and there was a foot inside. Not what you expect!' a shaken Kevin Manning told the *Chronicle*.

Further digging revealed that the foot was attached to a man's body aged, police estimate, between thirty-five and forty. 'Judging from the state of decay, he had been buried at least twenty years. Probably in 1956 when the A4 was extended west. Had it not been for the damage caused by the unseasonable heat his "grave" might have remained undisturbed,' Detective Inspector Davidson told us. As we reported last week, soaring temperatures melted the road surface opening a crater big enough for a family car.

No one of the man's height and build was reported missing in the 1950s and police believe that the man was a tramp sheltering in a house slated for demolition who was crushed by masonry.

Police ask for anyone with information to contact Hammersmith Police Station.

Jack discovered another cutting stuck to the paper, held by the tight fold. He prised them apart. The print had blurred, but was legible. Also from the *Chronicle*, it was dated 15 July, but wasn't, Jack was surprised to find, by Lucie May.

MURDER ON THE GREAT WEST ROAD

By Malcolm Bennett

A man found buried beneath the Great West Road, uncovered by the hot weather, was murdered, police have confirmed. Home Office pathologist Cornelius Jarvis emphasized that blunt-force injury to the skull was not the cause of death, but probably the result of being crushed during demolition of houses to build the road. Police have refused to reveal the exact cause of death.

D.I. Davidson told a crowded press conference that the theory is that the man was part of a gang of burglars. He was probably killed in an argument over the loot. A gold signet ring found on his finger was engraved with the initials 'GR'. (See inset picture.)

Davidson confirmed that Judge Henry Ramsay reported a burglary at his home in St Peter's Square in February 1956. The items stolen had belonged to Judge Ramsay's late father Gerald. Aside from the ring, they were a Rolex timepiece, a significant sum of money and a silver locket containing a photograph of Gerald Ramsay and his wife Anne. Judge Ramsay confirmed that the watch, an early Rolex, was purchased by his late father in 1921. None of these items has been recovered from the vicinity of the body. The locket is heart-shaped and, like the ring, is engraved with the letters 'G' and 'R'.

Davidson described the deceased as 'too well built' to have got through the Ramsays' rear basement window, the robber's entry point. The front door was double-locked, forcing any intruder to exit the same way. It's likely that the dead man had an accomplice, a boy or boys: he was a 1950s' Fagin. Such a boy would now be in his thirties.

Jewellers have been asked to check records for the purchase of the silver locket and the Rolex watch in the last two decades.

Police ask for anyone with information to contact Hammersmith Police Station.

The print danced before Jack's eyes. He had known the Ramsay family most of his life. Isabel Ramsay, the judge's daughter-in-law and mother of three, had befriended his mother when she 'didn't know what to do with the baby'. Isabel had died days after Terry Darnell. The robbery must have been just before her time. Why had the owners of this house kept cuttings about a burglary that happened several miles away? Who lived here? The articles added to Jack's conviction that he had stumbled on a mystery, a case for Clean Slate.

He became aware of the silence. It was pure: no creaks, no floorboards flexing or firing of a boiler. No external sounds. The fear that had gripped him when he entered the house returned.

The sides of the wardrobe were closing in. He was the man in the road, crushed by smashed beams and collapsed walls until all of life had gone.

Jack reached out a flailing hand and pushed at the door. It swung open soundlessly. Whoever lived in this house had oiled every hinge.

Jack crawled out of the wardrobe on his hands and knees. Locks of hair were saturated in sweat and stuck to his forehead. Again a voice in his head berated him for ignoring his instincts and entering the house.

The atmosphere was dry and dead. More like a charnel house than a home where people lived happily or otherwise. It didn't fit with the home of a True Host. Intent on a mission, True Hosts were nothing if not happy. The man from the sixth car had come here. Why? Was this his home?

Google Street View didn't lie. The images showed that Terry Darnell had watched Kew Villa in August 2010. Could his interest have been related to the robbery and subsequent murder in the fifties?

Preoccupied with so many questions, Jack didn't immediately notice a shaft of light cutting down the stairwell. Someone had come out of the top room. There was no time to hide in the bedroom. He shrank into the shadowy recess of the doorway.

If the person switched on the landing light or wanted to go into the bedroom he was in full view. His body turned to liquid. He summoned up all his will to make himself invisible, to blank his mind.

A man was coming down the stairs. He moved with the confidence of someone familiar with the space. He crossed a beam of moonlight slanting in from the landing window. Something flashed. *A knife.* On the landing, he brushed the wall inches from where Jack stood with his back to him. Jack could have put out a hand and touched him. It wasn't a knife. It was a scalpel.

'Coming.' The man spoke quietly as if not to waken someone. *Who?* Someone must be sleeping in the room opposite.

Jack battled with the horror that was overwhelming him. In the half-light, Jack couldn't tell if the man was the True Host. He should be able to tell. The man continued down the stairs without looking behind him.

Jack ducked back into the bedroom and went to the window. Cautiously he drew aside the curtain. The window overlooked the duck pond with an oblique view on to Priory Road. Parked where Terry's Toyota had been was a taxi, the engine running, the 'For Hire' lamp off.

The man he had seen on the stairs crossed the pavement to the taxi and spoke to the driver through the window. Then he climbed in the back. The taxi did a tight U-turn and chugged off towards Kew Green.

Jack had to prevent himself rushing out of the front door. He made himself leave the way he had come in.

Tonight the statuary in Mortlake Cemetery unnerved him. Angels pointed fingers at him, cherubs and gargoyles fixed him with their stares, laughing and grimacing by turn. He leant on a mausoleum. He had been so close to being discovered. He hadn't seen the man properly, either on the landing or in the shadow of the taxi. He had failed to establish if he was the man from the sixth car.

Jack shrugged into his coat and something rustled in his pocket. He had forgotten to put the newspaper back in the drawer. A stupid mistake. Jack hesitated; then he went down a barely visible track between the gravestones. He couldn't return to the house. He wouldn't be lucky twice.

Chapter Thirty-Five

November 2014

'I've never seen anyone dead before.'

Stella was about to say that nor had she, then remembered that she had seen several dead people, starting with her dad and ending with Joseph Hooker – or whatever his name was – in Kew Gardens. She made a non-committal sound, but Michelle Banks wasn't listening.

They were sitting in what was described as a 'Place of Peace': a bench on a bed of gravel picked out in LED lights beneath the fronds of a willow tree. Opposite the bench, in a pool of water, was a stone sculpture with holes like cheese and a chunk of driftwood. The night was freezing, but Stella was no more willing to go inside the hospice than it seemed was Michelle, since she had been waiting in the car park when she arrived.

Stella felt she was a spare part. When Michelle Banks had rung, she had flung on clothes and driven through the empty streets, Michelle's words repeating in her head.

Tina has died. Tina has died.

The truth dawned. Her friend wasn't there. Tina wasn't anywhere. *Tina has died.*

'How was she?' Stella saw that she shouldn't have believed Tina. She should have listened to Jackie. Even Cashman had known Tina wasn't going to get better. She should have come when Tina first asked for her, when they might have had a meaningful conversation – at the least she would have got to the bottom of the murderer thing. She had let Tina down. The lights washed over the smooth stone sculpture. A slight breeze ruffled the water, making the reflection of the stone bend and warp.

'It wasn't peaceful, if that's what you're asking.' Michelle dug her boot into the gravel, making a dip. She pushed the stones back and then did it again. Unable to watch the futility of the action, Stella looked away.

'Yes.' It wasn't what she had meant. She didn't know what she had meant.

'So much for people turning into saints on their deathbed. Tina was spiteful, she said Dad would be upset that his favourite child was dead, as if that pleased her. True, my father has – had – no eyes for anyone but his beloved "Crystal". He let us think he worked day and night to send her to expensive schools and get her through law school. The state system was good enough for me.' The scuffing intensified, gravel flew up and splashed into the pond. The garden was far from peaceful. 'It was a lie!'

'Tina didn't go to law school?' Involuntarily Stella scuffed the gravel too.

'Yes, of course she did. But – Chrissie told me last week – Dad didn't pay a penny. His friend George covered the lot. What was special about Tina?' She made an odd sound that made Stella think of the way Stanley howled when he had nightmares. 'Ignore me. I know what was special about Tina: she was the best sister I could ever have.' Michelle glared down at the water as if Tina might be there.

'I suppose it was the drugs.' Stella found herself confirming that the pale shape reflected in the water was the sculpture and not a face.

'She kept going on about you. I didn't know you were so close.' It sounded like an accusation.

218

'We worked together.'

'I thought you were her cleaner.' Michelle was seemingly as capable of spite as her sister, but Stella didn't consider it an insult, so didn't notice. 'You can't argue with someone when they're dying,' she murmured more to herself.

'We had coffee sometimes.' Stella didn't mention the foxtrot session. Her foot tapped to David Bowie's 'Rebel Rebel'. Ghost music, Jack would have said.

'I'm overwrought. I haven't slept for weeks. And now Tina's died without seeing Dad. They say you can control when you die so why didn't she wait? He'll be gutted, he's hardly left her side. I'll have to deal with him without her. Ignore me,' she said again.

Whoever 'they' were, they had been wrong about her dad too. Terry wouldn't have chosen to have a heart attack in a street. Stella stood up. 'What did Tina say about me?' She regretted the question. It sounded as if she was only thinking of herself. She shouldn't have come. She had come to see Tina. Stupid, since Tina was dead.

'Like you said, she was high on morphine. Something about cake being from a shop. Oh, and she left these for you.' She reached down beside the bench and produced a plastic bag. 'She made me go to the office for this. Would you believe that it was in the safe! Looks like rubbish to me, feel free to chuck it out.' She passed the bag to Stella.

Stella realized that she had been hoping for a sign of the old Tina. A cleaning instruction or an explanation of a legal technicality. When she had seen her, Tina had rambled on about murder and her last words were about a fork and a cat. Tina had truly gone. She didn't look in the bag because it seemed rude with Michelle Banks complaining that her sister hadn't thought of her. But inwardly Stella felt faintly gratified that after all Tina had left some of herself for her.

'She left instructions for her funeral – seems she wrote them years ago. No flowers and everyone in black.' Michelle's voice cracked.

A distant rumbling grew louder. Spears of light cut through the willow. A taxi was chugging up the drive.

'Shit, it's Dad!' Michelle spun on her heel and, tramping out of the Place of Peace, chased after the taxi.

Stella remained by the pond. This wasn't the time to offer Cliff Banks her condolences. She should leave the Bankses to grieve by themselves. Her phone buzzed with a text. Martin. She had forgotten about him.

Bed's too big. Coming back?

Unable to think of a reply, she closed the app. A breeze rustled the willow. She imagined the feel of Martin's body, his smell, a mix of after-shave – Gillette like Terry – and beer. Last night had been good, but it belonged to a different life. A life where Tina was alive. It was three in the morning and she was sitting in the garden of a hospice. Her routine was in pieces.

By the time she reached the car park, Michelle Banks was walking up to the hospice entrance, her arm through her father's. Mr Banks's taxi was parked next to her van. She waited until they had gone inside before opening the van and climbing in.

There was a '1' next to the message icon on her phone. It should have gone when she opened Cashman's message. She dabbed the envelope icon and nearly dropped the phone. The '1' was beside Tina's name.

Please never shed fruit was sleet, how dear hehe No Kesto Mar.

Chapter Thirty-Six

November 2014

The Herbarium at the Royal Botanic Gardens at Kew was originally in an eighteenth-century mansion outside the Elizabeth Gate. Over two centuries, initially under the auspices of Kew's Director William Hooker and then his son Joseph as the collection of specimens grew, it was extended several times. In 2010 an air- and temperature-controlled building opened. Cylindrical-shaped and clad in wood, it housed the library, botanists and artists with a roof terrace commanding a sweeping view of the Botanic Gardens, the Thames and the misty reaches of West London.

Jack was cleaning in Wing C, the Victorian building. Wendy and the rest of the team had been allocated the modern complex.

He approached the desk, the wood rich and mellow in the light of a lawyers' lamp, at which stood a wooden office chair upholstered in cracked leather. It was empty, although a mug of steaming coffee testified that the occupant couldn't be far away. Given the receptionist was absent today, Jack hesitated over the visitors' book: he preferred to arrive and leave unnoticed. But Stella, Queen of Risk Assessment, stipulated that operatives must sign in. He scribbled his name, noting that, not counting Clean Slate people, he was the first visitor of the day. He was pleased; he wanted to be alone with the specimens.

He wheeled his equipment cart to the lift. It contained only a Henry vacuum. No chemicals for this job, nothing must damage the integrity of the dried plants. Already Jack thought of them as his friends.

He watched the lift light descend and wondered how Stella was doing in the Marianne North Gallery; he had offered to clean it with her, but she had refused. Instead of going home from Kew Villa early that morning, he had stopped at Stella's house in Rose Gardens North.

Cashman's car had been parked outside. Lucie May had said that Cashman had left his wife, but Jack didn't trust him. He hadn't yet told Stella about seeing Terry on Street View. Since seeing her kiss Cashman he feared she would dismiss the idea that he had found a new case. Stella was moving with real detectives now.

He looked again at the lift light: it was still descending; yet he didn't see why it had gone up. Wendy and the others were starting at the ground floor. He was the first visitor. It would be the security guard doing a final round, he decided as, at last, the lift arrived and the door slid aside. Stepping in he was intrigued to find that the interior had been padded with canvas quilting. A notice was stuck to the material: 'Caution Mirror Behind'.

A message for Medusa! Jack imagined telling Stella. Although she might not have got the reference to the gorgon who turned people to stone with a look. Perseus had vanquished Medusa by looking at her in the reflection of his shield. Stella didn't have time for myths, she faced life head on.

'Everything is a myth,' he said as the lift rose upwards.

He entered the old Herbarium on the top floor and stopped by a balcony that ran around the sides of the building. There were two more balconies below. All were linked by spiral staircases at each end of the vast hall. The staircases and railings were painted a cheery post-office red. Jack could sense volition in the twisting metal and imagined the botanists – Joseph Hooker, George

Bentham and Charles Darwin – who, over the centuries, had worked here.

On the other mornings Jack had worked with another operative, a young man called Sam. But Sam had called in sick that morning so Jack was on his own. This gave him time to properly appreciate the place. A vast palace filled with treasures.

Within alcoves on each level were row upon row of cupboards painted an institutional cream gloss. Between these were alcoves. Jack set down the Henry vacuum and went into the nearest alcove. A column radiator beneath a window pumped out heat. On a government-issue table that looked as if it dated from the 1940s was a microscope, a measuring scale, an anglepoise lamp and a 'sharps' box for used scalpel blades. Files and paper were stacked on a table at which stood a wooden stool with a leaf-shaped hand grip cut into the seat and an office chair. The window reflected the alcove; it would be dark for two hours yet. A strip lamp slung from chains cast a bleak light.

Without the other cleaner there, Jack tingled with excitement. The Herbarium was all his. He opened a cupboard labelled 'Lamiaceae'. He knew enough about botany to recognize the genus that included the species lavender and rosemary. An indentation inside the door read 'F Coote VR'; the joiner's mark dated the cabinets to before 1901 when Queen Victoria died. The smell of naphthalene and mercury chloride, the Victorians' noxious choice of preservative, wafted out. He felt a surge of excitement. The shelves were packed with files of specimens stored according to their characteristics. A sheet of yellowing paper was stuck above the joiner's stamp. Jack read the faded type: 'Visitors studying in the Herbarium are requested to observe that the removal of specimens, or any portions of them, from the sheets is absolutely prohibited without the permission of the Keeper. No flower, fruit, or leaf is on any account to be detached for analysis without his approval.' The author was 'Joseph D. Hooker, Director. June 9th 1882'. The notice was itself a specimen, its order still held true. The Herbarium was filled with phantoms, human and botanical.

Jack slid out a file and laid it on the table. Stuck to the sheet was a scrap of brown stuff, shrivelled and nondescript. He read a sepia-stained typed label: 'Flora of the Malay Archipelago'. The label was as illegible as a doctor's prescription: he gleaned that the plant was a 'something triflora'. The specimen had been found by 'Dr King's Collector' in '1881'.

Excitement that he might be the first to look at the delicate brown leaves since the late nineteenth century was dashed when Jack saw a bar code at the top of the sheet. The sheet had been digitized recently. His fingers hovered over the dried plant; he wanted to touch it, to make a connection with 'Dr King's Collector' across time.

The cabinets held specimens waiting to be named and assigned a place in a taxonomic order. Some would be lumped in with existing species as Joseph Hooker had so often done. Hooker might be dead, but his legacy lived on; the Herbarium was alive, ever growing and re-forming. Jack slipped the folder back into the compartment. He felt a tingling on his neck. He looked over the railing. A shadow passed across the parquet floor below. It would be the security guard.

A cardboard strip, like a match book, lay on the floor by the radiator. Jack bent to pick it up and read the words 'Do Not Touch'. Below these was 'Insect Monitor'. Without touching, he peered behind the flap of cardboard and gave a start. A large spider was sitting beneath it. It was surrounded by six small spiders and a beetle. They had been caught on the sticky surface and all of them were dead. Rather like a scene of crime, each insect was circled by coloured dots. Three spiders had red dots; two green; and the large spider, the remaining small one and the beetle had blue dots. Crouching on the floor and twisting his neck, Jack read the back of the flap. The colours corresponded to inspection dates, three so far this year. Insects were the enemy of the specimens. They had to be lured into the trap. The trap monitored the threat level. Stella would approve. Despite his passion for the specimens, his dreams of working with them, Jack shuddered. Insects had their place too.

He set to work. He vacuumed, he got into every corner, nosing the brush along the base of the cupboards. He worked around chairs and tables in the alcoves, taking care to disturb nothing.

He didn't see the man in the last alcove until he bent to untangle the cord from around the table leg. He switched off the vacuum.

'I'm sorry to disturb you.' Surprise made his voice tremble.

The man didn't respond although he must at least have heard the vacuum. Jack tugged the Henry out of the alcove. Slowly, the man looked up from his work and let his gaze rest on Jack. Jack dropped the vacuum brush; it clattered on the parquet. He never forgot a face. The man was smiling; it wasn't the smile of a friend.

'I'll get out of your way,' the man said pleasantly, but he didn't get up.

Jack saw Jennifer Day lying dead on the floor of his train. He saw the ghostly man behind the glass partition. The figure in darkness, inspecting a bouquet of flowers on the station platform.

The murderer returning to the scene of the crime.

It was the man from the sixth car.

'I'll come back later.' Fear sapped him of strength.

'Have we met?' The man's skin was smooth as if life hadn't touched him. Only his hands, worn and wrinkled, put him in his sixties.

Jack wouldn't lie, but he knew how to avoid the truth. 'I've never cleaned here before.'

'I see.' The man was toying with him. True Hosts didn't forget faces. He knew Jack as Jack knew him. He smiled again as he said, 'I never forget faces.' He was strolling through Jack's mind, picking out thoughts and threading them through his fingers.

It was Jack's practice, in the presence of True Hosts, to become invisible. He had been caught out this time; like an insect, he was stuck to the floor, dots all around him, marking his position. He glimpsed his reflection in the window, wraithlike and insubstantial.

'I'll come back.' He moved towards the balcony railing. Then stopped. If he pitched over it, he would die; no one would hear him scream. In a reconstruction of the event, Cashman would presume Jack had been careless. Stella would know better, but would wonder if he had been distracted by botany and lost his balance.

'No, I will go.' The voice might have belonged to a man or a woman. True Hosts defied definition. 'The dead can wait.' He smiled as if it was a joke that Jack would share.

Jack watched the staircase, but the man didn't appear on it. He must have gone out another way.

Jack completed the rest of his shift in a daze. When he returned to the foyer, a woman in her mid-fifties was sitting at the reception desk. She was fitting cards into the plastic holders of visitor tags.

'All done?' she enquired without looking up.

'Yes.' Jack put in the time of his exit in the book. With dismay he saw that the botanist – the True Host – hadn't signed in. He had hoped to learn his name.

'Has anyone arrived since I was here?' He tapped the time of his arrival. 'Since six ten?'

'Your colleagues have finished.' The woman spoke without judgement that Jack was last.

'The botanists…?' Jack waved a hand airily.

'Why do you ask?' She was less friendly now.

'In future I want to avoid getting in their way.'

She relaxed. 'Mr Watson is here.' She tutted. 'He forgets to sign in.'

'Everyone here deals in life and death,' Jack opined, struck by the notion. The woman was looking at him strangely. He grabbed the cart and hurried out to the car park. He shoved the cart into the back of the van.

The lights of the Herbarium windows seemed suspended in the dark. A shadow crossed a window on the top floor. Jack was gratified. He had learnt that the True Host was called Mr Watson and that he was a botanist.

Unbidden a voice whispered: *'The dead can wait.'*

Chapter Thirty-Seven

November 2014

Stella crossed the tiled floor in the Marianne North Gallery through to the back, belatedly noting that she was tiptoeing. In the glare of the lamp in the yard, she filled her bucket with freezing water from the tap. Beyond the wall, she heard a car go by. Traffic on the Kew Road would be picking up. Stella liked it here, closer to 'civilization'. She hadn't admitted it to Martin, or Jackie, but since finding the body she disliked coming here. She wouldn't take Jack off the Herbarium even though he had offered, but she could do with him. Not for protection – she wasn't scared – but Tina's death had given her a jolt and she couldn't get the dead man's face out of her mind. She would like the company. Jack hadn't answered her text asking where *there* was. As the days went by the more her reply struck her as sarcastic. She would catch him at the Herbarium this morning and put things right.

Swishing the mop over the tiles in the main gallery, negotiating a cupboard by the doorway, she considered that Tina had been dead five hours. Soon it would be five days, then five months. She batted the idea away. How long Tina had been dead didn't matter. All that mattered was that she was dead. Clasping the long mop handle, Stella pictured Tina foxtrotting, holding the mop and singing to 'Rebel Rebel' at the top of her voice.

Stella finished. She squeezed out the mop. She looked at the tiles. One patch looked dry, but she had definitely cleaned there. She wouldn't have missed a section.

Stella Darnell never makes mistakes. She did make mistakes. She had kidded herself that Tina would be all right. Not all messes could be cleaned up.

The dry patch on the tiles was shaped like a person. Stella tipped her head and then saw that there were other dry patches. She had barely dampened the mop to ensure quick drying and the method was working. It was Jack who saw the bodies of the dead everywhere. It was lack of sleep. Jackie would say it was because Tina had died, but if anything Stella blamed Cashman. If blame was the word.

She went to the antechamber where she had found a real body. After cleaning the floor, Stella looked to see if the outline of his corpse was there, but the damp sheen on the tiles was unbroken.

She couldn't rid herself of a vision of the man's eyes listlessly regarding her. The 'dead gaze' as Jack had once called it. Stella snatched up the bucket and began mopping the main gallery. She didn't hear the porch doors open or detect a drop in temperature as cold air stole in from outside. She only knew that she wasn't alone in the isolated Victorian building when she felt a hand on her shoulder.

'What the—' she shouted.

Martin stopped her. 'It's me.'

'What are you doing sneaking up like that?' she stormed at him.

'Your phone went to voicemail. You should keep it on when you're here. You never know what might happen. Actually, you do know,' he admonished her. 'I was worried when you went off.' He looked sheepish. 'Are we OK?'

'I *do* keep it on.' She fumbled in her trouser pocket and produced her phone. The battery was dead. She always charged it when she went to bed, but with Cashman there had forgotten to.

It was lucky that the battery had lasted for Michelle Banks's call about Tina.

'We're fine.' Stella breathed in his after-shave. She didn't feel like explaining about Tina so she was relieved when, pacing the gallery, he began to speak.

'Our man was definitely killed in there.' He nodded at the ante-chamber. 'A botanical pathologist has identified pollen and soil samples specific to Kew Gardens. John Doe walked to his death. No signs of a struggle, no defensive marks on his hands, or soil in his nails. Suggests he knew his killer. Stupid place to commit a murder: this locale has its own fingerprint. No other soil like it in London.'

'Since he was found here, you'd have tied it to Kew Gardens anyway,' Stella pointed out crossly.

'Why did you head off like that?' Martin was treading on her clean tiles, his voice echoing in the strange gallery, every wall lined with paintings and samples of wood.

The little light that there was seemed to be sucked into the walls. Stella found she was looking at the picture of the tree with orange flowers, the original of the one in Tina's flat. 'Tina has died.' She used Michelle's words to her on the phone. She sploshed her mop in the water and squeezed it out.

'You're kidding!' Martin stopped his pacing. 'I am *so* sorry!' He made as if to cross the tiles to her, but Stella put up the broom handle and he stopped.

'Want me to come with you to the funeral?'

Stella went blank. 'I… er…'

'Sorry, Stella, it's too soon to be thinking of that. When the time comes, I will be there.' He ran a hand down his face.

'Best I go on my own.' Stella hadn't thought about a funeral. Or that she would go to it.

'Want me to wait for you to finish?' He seemed at a loose end.

Stella did want him to stay, but that would mean she couldn't talk to Jack afterwards. 'I'll be fine. I'll see you later.' She crossed the tiles as if a Rubicon, and kissed him.

When she had finished the Shirley Sherwood Gallery Stella packed the bucket and mop in her equipment cart and mounted the bicycle. She switched on her head torch. The unlit path was black, like a chasm tapering into mutable darkness. She regretted that Martin had gone. Glancing back at the Marianne North Gallery, with its opaque windows and chimneys black against the sky, she felt a surge of terror. A scream pushing up inside her, Stella pushed hard on the pedals and rode away. Past the Temple of Bellona, past the lake with the Palm House duplicated on its mauve-black surface, past the Elizabeth Gate and past the Unluckiest Tree that had twice been struck by lightning and hit by a light aircraft. Not that Stella took in any of this. When she arrived at the Herbarium, her lungs on fire, her eyes stinging with trickles of sweat, it was to find that again she had missed Jack.

Frustrated, Stella ran to the van. She let Stanley out to pee and then clipped him back on his seat and plugged her phone into the dashboard jack. It came to life. No texts. Halfway down Ferry Lane, the Thames on her right, she veered on to the verge and cut the engine.

Where are you? she texted. Jack wouldn't answer for ages, if at all. She let out the handbrake.

Ping!

Here.

She wound down her window. In the thinning darkness a figure stepped away from the river wall. The scent of soap powder and apple shampoo sliced through the cloying odour of river mud.

Chapter Thirty-Eight

November 2014

Jack was paler than his normal pale with dark raccoon circles under his eyes. Early mornings didn't suit him. Unlike Tina and herself, who were larks, he was a night owl.

It was a quarter past nine; the day was pewter grey. Rain clouds hung over the Thames.

Stanley clasped Jack's trouser leg as Jack fussed him. 'He's cuddling me,' he crowed.

'It's because you give him treats,' Stella retorted.

'I don't suppose it's just that.' He scratched the dog's ears; Stanley gave a growl of contentment.

'He's missed you.' Stella looked across the river to the north bank and realized they were opposite Thamesbank Heights; in the dull flat light the block was insubstantial, unreal.

When she had lived there, she had thought that the towpath was too far away for anyone on it to see into the flat, but she could make out Tina's living-room window. A light was on. Tina! *No.* Tina was on a rack in the hospice fridge.

Twigs, rubbish and brown scum raced downstream. Twisted rope patterns on the water betrayed powerful currents.

Stella shuddered – currents that could drag a person under in seconds.

'Jackie told me about Tina.' Jack lifted Stanley on to his shoulder. The dog settled, paws dangling like bagpipes, regarding the river with inscrutable hawk-eyes. Jackie said that Jack was the one man of whom Stanley approved.

'She expected to get better,' Stella said pointlessly.

'Some people can't accept that they are going to die. When the time comes I hope I'll welcome it,' Jack said.

'No one else would welcome you dying.' Stella was sharp. Lucie May had once called Jack her Prince of Darkness and there was a kind of glamour about Jack's gaunt features, but there would be nothing glamorous about him being dead. She stared at the yellow light in the window of Thamesbank Heights and let herself think that Tina was foxtrotting around her living room. 'Tina wanted us to solve a murder.'

'She what?' Jack's face was buried in Stanley's coat, his voice muffled.

'She was hallucinating.' If she had binoculars she could see into the living room. Then she would see that it wasn't Tina in her flat.

'If she meant the Kew Gardens murder, forget it. Cashman is all over it.' Jack jiggled Stanley on his shoulder like a baby.

Stella wasn't ready to tell Jack about Martin. What would she say? She hardly knew what she felt for him herself. She was seeing him later.

'What did Tina say?' Stanley regarded Stella beadily from Jack's shoulder and Stella had the odd notion that, like a ventriloquist's dummy, he might speak for him.

'It was why Tina wanted to see me.' She looked back at Thamesbank Heights. The light had gone out in Tina's window. 'She asked me to catch a murderer.' She batted off the image of the hospice room crowded with the props of illness: grab handles, supports, canisters of wipes and cardboard sick bowl. She breathed in the smell of river mud to block out the olfactory memory of faeces and stale urine and another odour that she now knew signalled death. An odour that, given her preternatural sense of smell, no amount of antiseptic cleansing could dispel.

'Stella?'

Stella couldn't keep her mind on their conversation. It began to rain.

'Don't discount what she said because she was dying.' Jack opened the sliding door of Stella's van and Stanley leapt on to the jump seat. He clipped the dog in. 'When a person's dying they don't waste time playing games. Not once they realize they can't control their death. It seems to have taken Tina some time to see that. Oh no!' he groaned.

'What?'

'Don't look!'

'Why?' Stella's heart missed a beat.

'Stanley's got your job sheet. Pretend you haven't seen him or he'll shred it.'

'I haven't seen him.' Stella caught Stanley's reflection in the wing mirror. Clamped between whiskery jaws was a piece of A4-sized paper. Over the top of it she could see the whites of the dog's eyes. He was waiting for her to notice, then the game could begin. A game that only he could win because taking the sheet off him risked losing a finger. Despite knowing better, Stella darted a look at him and true to form, this precipitated a blood-curdling growl. The paper slipped from his mouth. With a snap he retrieved it and the stakes went up a notch. He wouldn't have been in the van if she hadn't rushed out in the middle of the night.

'He'll drop it if we ignore it.' Jack had been to a couple of dog-training classes with her and was a canine expert.

'Act like we don't care.' She didn't care. Before Tina's death, a ripped-up job sheet would have been a disaster.

'Tell me what Tina said,' Jack said.

'She wanted us to solve a murder. I had to leave because she was unwell. I went back, but couldn't talk to her.'

'That's not what you said the first time.'

'What wasn't?' Stella replied evenly.

233

'What were her exact words?'

Stella often wished Jack would be more precise and not so airy-fairy, but this wasn't the time to start. However, she should encourage him. She tried to conjure up the morning in the hospice when, briefly, Tina had sounded her old self. *'I want you to catch a murderer!'* The rain intensified. Stella took shelter in the van, ignoring Stanley although she had given up on the job sheet. Jack got in beside her.

'Before you said she wanted us to "solve a murder".'

'It was "I want you to catch a murderer." Stella was sure. 'What's the difference?'

Jack rubbed a porthole in condensation on the glass and peered out at the river. 'If Tina had said she wanted us to *solve* a murder, it would imply that she knew of a murder, but not who did it.' He steepled his hands under his nose. 'We win!'

'What?'

'Stanley's dropped the job sheet!' He fished the paper out from the footwell. 'No damage. He wanted our attention, didn't you, Stanislav!'

'Go on.' Stella folded the paper in the glove box out of the way.

'Tina said she wanted you to *catch* a murderer. Meaning that she knew of a murder, or specifically that she knew of a murder*er*.'

'She defended murderers, she would have known loads of them.' Stella didn't know why she was arguing. She wanted Tina to have left them a case.

Jack dismissed it. 'Too obvious.'

'She rambled about a cat wearing a hat. Like I said, it was the drugs.' Perhaps Cliff Banks had gone to the flat. Michelle had said he would be 'gutted'. Stella would never know how Terry would have reacted if she had died. He used to say his own mum – her nana – was in heaven keeping watch over Stella. Who was Tina keeping watch over? She doubted Tina had believed in an afterlife; like Stella, she would think that it defied logic.

'There must be a way of finding out what she meant.' Jack leant his head against the rest, long legs stretched out as far as the van allowed.

'Tina didn't believe in the afterlife.' She must put Jack off any notion of a séance. Thinking of the afterlife she remembered Tina's text. 'I got this from her.' She handed her phone to Jack.

'*Please never shed fruit was sleet, how dear hehe No Kesto Mar.* Was Tina into crosswords?' he asked.

'She didn't have time.' Stella flapped a dismissive hand. 'It's nonsense. Her medication had probably addled her brain.'

'"Hehe" means laughter in text language. Could it be a joke?'

'Tina didn't make jokes.' Stella reread the text. 'Maybe she wanted me to bring her fruit. I nearly took grapes, but she could hardly drink liquids, so it was pointless. "Dear" could mean "expensive". She worried about money.'

'Bring her some fruit and catch her a murderer.' Jack pulled a face. 'Could it be a code? Since she was literally dying, this text must have taken all her strength. I find texting hard enough at the best of times.'

'Tina dictated everything,' Stella said. 'I do it when I'm alone.'

Jack sighed. 'It's like number-nine buses.'

'What is?' Stella rubbed her face, stifling a yawn. Buses. Fruit. Hats. Cats.

'We have no cases, then two come at once.'

'Two?'

'Look at this.' Jack fiddled with his mobile phone and then passed it across to her. Quietly he said, 'It might make you feel a bit strange.'

She looked at a picture of a sunny road on Street View. Without hesitation, she exclaimed, 'That's Terry's car.' She tapped the screen. 'He's in there.'

'Yes, he is.' Jack was rolling one of the cigarettes that he never smoked because he had given up after they solved their first case. 'Did Terry ever mention this house? It's by Kew Pond.'

'Not to me.' Gingerly she reached out and touched the blue of the car. She did feel a bit strange. 'I wonder what my dad was doing there.'

'I suspect that Terry was staking it out.' Jack snapped shut the cigarette case. 'Our job is to find out why!'

Chapter Thirty-Nine

November 2014

Jack was on an 'S Stock' train, the sort with no doors between cars. He was dancing down the aisle, yellow straps, seats, glass partitions stretching into infinity. Cilla Black was singing 'Something Tells Me'. Lucie May was dancing towards him, twirling and spinning to the music. He woke up.

The music continued, swelling in volume. It was his phone. He flailed about in the dark and found it under his pillow.

'Chop, chop, Jacko!' The song was the ringtone that Lucie had programmed in for when she called. Jack scrubbed at his hair.

'Hey, Luce,' he croaked.

'Tell me I didn't wake you up.' She sounded devastated.

'You didn't wake me up.' There was an explosion on the other end of the line. It was followed by more. Lucie was eating a carrot.

'What would you do without me?' she mumbled through a mouthful of carrot.

'I'd be at a loss,' Jack replied. 'Have you remembered what Terry meant when he said he had let someone get away with murder?' Cilla Black was still in his head, singing that tonight something good would be happening. Lucie's mantra.

'Get here in five.' Lucie cut the line.

Lucie lived around the corner. One minute to dress and splash his face. It would take him three minutes and fifteen seconds of smart walking. Five minutes if he went by Rose Gardens North. Jack decided not to torture himself; he didn't need to confirm that the black Audi would be outside Stella's house. He knew it would be.

A taxi was parked in British Grove outside Lucie's house. There was someone in the back. Jack faltered. *The True Host.* He had a name for him now. Mr Watson. But drawing closer, he saw that it was empty. No True Host would be so conspicuous. If he was being watched, he wouldn't know it. But then he didn't know it.

'You're losing your touch, Jack.' Voicing his thoughts, Lucie May was chiding him as she beckoned him in with a finger. 'Where's Detective Darnell?'

'Asleep, I suppose.' Jack's stomach took a dive. He was filled with the urge to tell Lucie. To open his heart to her. He sat down on the sofa and, to stop himself, grabbed a carrot from a bag of Marks and Spencer crudités on the coffee table and crammed it into his mouth.

'Here's what I've got.' Lucie May was in reporter mode. 'When Terry said he'd let someone get away with murder, I supposed he meant it metaphorically. He didn't elaborate and we were – how can I put this? – in a delicate position at the time. I was narked that he didn't have his mind on the job. Except he did have his mind on the job, just not… Oh well, water under the proverbial.' She regarded her carrot as she had once ruminated at a cigarette from within an aureole of smoke. 'It came back to me today while I was in court listening to an interminable case about a man whose cat was run over. I get the big stories these days. Terry said that, and I quote, "Stella opened my eyes. I'll never trust what kids say again."' She snatched up the bottle of Placid Pet and squirted it about in the air.

'Stella lied to him?' Stella never lied. Although thinking of Cashman, it seemed she didn't always tell the truth.

'I was more than happy to believe the prodigal daughter wasn't perfect; it got tedious hearing about his gorgeous girl. Sometimes in the throes of – I won't call it passion – he even called me "Suzie". I bumped into Terry with Stella once in the Wimpy Bar on Hammersmith Broadway when she was a sulky teenager. She was working through an ice-cream sundae and looked like life was a drudge. I said so later and Terry wouldn't have it. Girls Stella's age used energy for growing and she would be a stunner like her mum. That told me. So I was well pleased that any scale had fallen from his eyes!'

Jack tried to steer Lucie back to the point. 'What had Stella lied about?'

'She hadn't lied. I think it was because of her that he'd let some other child pull wool over his eyes. Frankly I wasn't that interested.'

'And?' Jack prompted.

'And nothing. That was it. You want all of me?' Lucie cackled and flew to her gin station where she chopped up a lemon, the blade whizzing so fast it was blurred. Thin slices fell into a heap on the wooden board.

'It's amazing that you've remembered so much,' Jack tried to mollify her.

'It came to me out of the blue. Terry told me on the first of September 2010. I remember it as clear as day because it was my birthday – still is – and he took me to the Ram. A real date, God save us! Anyway, what's the drama, Terry will have documented his inquiry: he was a meticulous policeman.'

'He retired in 2009. There won't be documentation.'

'I know that! But Terry never stopped being a detective. Not until...' She waved the knife in the air. 'But the "Lying Child" happened years earlier, in 1976. Terry said it was during the drought, which makes it around June time. I was covering deaths from the heat, old people and infants, while practically expiring myself. Sure I can't tempt you to a nippet?' She shunted the lemon slices into a dish and began assembling her drink. 'Get your partner in crime to beguile her tame policeman into nosing about HOLMES.' Another throaty cackle. 'All roads lead to the detective's daughter!'

238

'Stella won't do it.' Jack was firm. Stella wouldn't ask Martin to look at the police database. Actually he was unsure what she would not do.

Flourishing her freshly concocted gin and tonic, Lucie May cast herself on to the sofa. 'Had to be when Terry was at Richmond, because that big old house on Street View is in Kew. I'm surprised that Stella doesn't remember because until she went to secondary school and got into make-up and Duran Duran she worshipped her pa. He was a good dad, whatever Suzie Darnell would have us think. Your best bet is for Clean-up Woman to ask her boyfriend.'

'What?' The room tipped.

'Jackanory, we both know that right now Detective Darnell will be lying in the long arms of the law.' Lucie took a slug of her drink. 'Smarty-Marty'll do anything for Terry's girl. Get him to interrogate the HOLMES database and you're skippy lambs.'

'I found a story you did in the seventies.' Jack hadn't planned to show Lucie the articles he had found in the house, but he had to stop her talking about Stella and Cashman. He thrust the newspaper at her.

'Bloody man!' Lucy waved the cuttings in the air, spilling her drink on the sofa. 'Malcolm bloody Bennett, that goat of an editor. He saw the meat on this story and stole it. He went on to the *News of the World*, fast cars, girls and chasing up white lines in the loo. Now he's in the Scrubs for something unpleasant. Fiddle dee dee!' She gave a raucous laugh. 'This was one of my first jobs.'

Lucie claimed many pieces as her 'first job' so that it was hard to pinpoint her actual age. Again Jack marvelled that, considering the quantity of nippets she consumed, her memory was prodigious. However trivial the story, she could summon up apparently irrelevant detail.

'Rose Gardens was Terry's street. Not that he was there in the fifties when the murder happened,' Lucie said.

'Could there be a connection between Terry being outside Kew Villa and that he lived in the street near to where the robbery happened?' Instantly Jack saw his mistake.

'Why should there be?' Lucie narrowed her eyes. She hooked an ice cube out of the glass and slid it off her finger into her mouth. She crunched it up.

Flustered by Stella and Cashman, he had made a slip. The link was that he had found the cuttings in Kew Villa, but he couldn't tell Lucie he had gone into the house illegally. Not because, like Stella, she would disapprove, but because she would insist he took her there now. Any minute she would ask him where he found the cuttings and he couldn't lie.

'Did the police catch the burglars?' he deflected her.

'No. They found a fingerprint on the back window ledge as reported in another article by Convict Bennett. The perp had no record so "didn't exist". And since he was buried in an unmarked grave under the slow lane of the A4, he didn't exist, did he!'

'They suspected that the robbers were boys,' Jack reminded Lucie of what was in her article. She carried on as if she hadn't heard.

'The Ramsays never got their loot back. Those boys are no doubt middle-aged pros by now. That fingerprint's never shown up again. Then again, they could be pushing up the daisies. If they were robbing in the fifties, they'd be into their sixties now.' Her tone implied this made them far older than her. 'The link between the robbery and Kew Villa is what?' Lucie's nippets didn't befuddle her.

'There may not be one,' he hedged.

'Who was living there when Terry was pretending to read a newspaper outside? Did you check?' She was on a roll.

Legwork was more Stella's line. 'No,' he confessed, feeling himself grow hot. Hearing about Tina's death and finding out about Cashman had put it out of his mind.

'Clean-up should wangle her mop in there and snout about.' Lucie tipped her glass back and downed the watery dregs. 'Stella's your woman. By the way, Jacko, where did you find these articles?'

Chapter Forty

November 2014

Lucie May was wrong. At the moment that Lucie was asking Jack about the newspaper cuttings, Stella wasn't with Cashman. She was in her old bedroom in Rose Gardens North scrutinizing the computer screen. Not counting Stanley, outstretched on the mat behind her, she was alone.

At the last minute Cashman had cancelled their meal at the Ram; he needed to stay at work.

She was studying the image on Street View that Jack had showed her that morning. That day in August 2010 had been sunny. But then every day on Street View was sunny.

She zoomed in on the Toyota Yaris. There was the scratch on the driver's door and the dent on the off-side wing from when Terry was broadsided by a car jumping the lights on King Street. It had happened in June 2010. He had gone to Charing Cross Hospital with minor whiplash. Jackie had met him in A and E. She had been there with her younger son who had broken his ankle skateboarding. Stella was down as Terry's next of kin, but he hadn't called her. Jackie had mentioned that Lucie May was there. Stella had assumed May was covering a story, but since supposed that Terry had called her.

There behind the wheel, a phantom, was Terry. She clicked on the zoom. This broke the picture into pixels, but by screwing up her eyes, she restored some clarity. A silver smudge on the dashboard morphed into a flask cup and a slash of red was a KitKat wrapper. She moved the cursor to get a better view, but her hand jerked and the picture swept back to normal size and she was at the rear of the car. Jack was better at this.

This time when she enlarged the windscreen, the flask cup had gone. There was a KitKat wrapper, but it was in the dip behind the steering wheel, not on the dashboard. There was something else; Stella zoomed in. She needed no more focus to recognize a bag from Tesco. Nor did she need to see inside to know there would be a pork pie, likely two.

She glanced at the date. It was still August, but the disappearing flask cup indicated a different day. Frustratingly Street View didn't give the whole date so she couldn't know if it was the next day after the first image or a week later. It did tell her that Jack's hunch was correct: Terry hadn't parked on Priory Road on just one day. He was outside the house on at least two occasions. He had been on a stakeout.

Terry was dead so she could never ask him why he was watching Kew Villa. Wrong. She *could* know. Stella dragged open a drawer in the desk. It was stuffed with receipts; one sprang out and floated to the carpet. It was for patio furniture bought from Homebase in Ealing in 2006. Terry had never been freelance so he didn't need to keep receipts to claim tax, and after he retired from the force, he couldn't claim expenses. But he believed in paper trails, a habit Stella had picked up from him, and he never threw anything away.

In the days after Terry's death Stella had systematically shredded documents of no value for probate or the Inland Revenue. Ancient bank statements and council tax bills. Then, diverted by the Rokesmith case, she had stopped. After she and Jack had solved the case, Stella saw the wisdom in keeping everything. She had stowed Terry's papers and books in the attic, but hadn't got around to emptying his desk.

She emptied the drawer on to the carpet. Sensing a game, Stanley was on his feet, tail wagging. He nosed at a stray paper.

'Leave!' Stanley sloped back to bed.

Stella lifted a wad of receipts from the pile. They had been in Terry's wallet and were held together by the fold. She set about arranging them in date order.

The first receipts were for 2009. She stapled together each month's worth. As the night wore on, she worked methodically: receipts ranged from big-ticket items like the computer on the desk through to a suit from Marks down to a bar of chocolate. That Terry had kept receipts for chocolate had made her impatient in the days after his death, now she was depending on his adherence to detail.

It was nearly five o'clock, she hadn't slept, but she was fizzing with energy. Soon she must leave for Kew. She didn't need to clean the gallery, she had mopped it only yesterday, but Stella found she could not keep away from the strange house on the outskirts of the gardens.

A receipt dated at the end of August 2009 for patchouli oil puzzled her until she remembered that the strong-smelling oil was Lucie May's perfume of choice. She had a vague memory that May's birthday was in September. Suzie used to complain that Terry never remembered her birthday. People change.

Washed-out blue ink swam before her eyes. On Sunday 8 August 2010 at thirteen minutes past eight Terry had bought a *Sunday Mirror*, two KitKats and three cans of Diet Coke from the newsagent in Kew station. Stella had bought a bottle of water from there herself after seeing Jack in Ferry Lane that morning.

Six minutes later, at nineteen minutes past, he was in the Tesco Express metres from the station. The receipt detailed a packet of mini Melton Mowbray pork pies and a cereal bar. Stella guessed that the latter was Terry's nod to healthy eating. The next receipts were replicas of the first two and continued until Wednesday 11th. There was a ticket for three hours' parking on the morning of 12 August for the car park in Ferry Lane, metres from the entrance to the Kew Gardens Estates Office where she was due in an hour. She felt a frisson of surprise that Terry had been there. Before parking he had got a coffee and chocolate croissant from the Starbucks on Station Approach. Why had he relocated from Kew Villa to Ferry Lane car park?

Stella's phone beeped. Jack! Perfect timing because she had something concrete to report, but snatching up her phone she saw it was her alarm to get up for work. Since she was already up, she had fifteen minutes to spare.

The rest of the receipts ran until the middle of August and were for more junk food from the same shops. A taxi receipt was unexpected, because, as she had told Cliff Banks, Terry never took taxis; he had always preferred to drive himself. Next to this was a day ticket to Kew Gardens. She experienced the same astonishment as she had when she found the 'Friend of Kew' membership card and coaster. The Botanical Gardens were the last place she associated with Terry. He had no time or patience to wander in glasshouses. It was dated the same day as the Ferry Lane parking ticket. It seemed that once in Kew he had bought a pot of tea and two slices of cake. If his car was in the car park, why had he taken a taxi? And who was with him?

She clipped the receipts together and tucked them into her Filofax. Knowing precisely when Terry had staked out the house by Kew Pond didn't tell them why he had. Like the murderer that Tina had wanted them to catch, there was no evidence on which to build a theory. No victim. No murderer. Nothing but shadows.

She fed Stanley, let him out in the garden, and left him snoozing in his bed. Jackie would bring him into the office.

On the way to Kew, Stella realized with a shock what Terry had been doing on 12 August. He was with her. That day in 2010 had been the first time since she was little that Terry had treated her on her actual birthday. How could she have forgotten?

He had bought her chocolate cake with hundreds and thousands, thinking it was her favourite, so she hadn't admitted that, along with fizzy drinks, she had never liked chocolate cake.

244

A text arrived as she was carrying her mop and bucket of water into the Marianne North Gallery. Not Jack.

I can come to Banks funeral on 17th with you. Martin. Instinctively Stella glanced towards the doors, thinking Martin might appear. She had locked the door; no one could get in. Stella felt a frisson of annoyance. Another text pinged. Expecting Martin, she saw it was from Michelle. *Funeral 2pm Monday 17th Mortlake Crem.* Stella shivered; Jack held store in synchronicity, but this unnerved her. While a woman of action herself, Stella resented the speed at which Tina's sister and father had organized her funeral.

Tina had been Martin's adversary, winning cases that allowed his suspects – and it seemed Terry's – to get off. No one that Stella had gone out with had offered to support her like this. How did Martin know the date of her funeral? But then he was a detective.

Stella texted: *If free on Monday 2pm 17th, wd u come to Tina's funeral? x*

The reply was instant. *Yes. Jack x.*

Chapter Forty-One

November 2014

Stella and Jack walked up the broad stone steps from Syon Vista to the Palm House. An aeroplane rumbled above as they entered the glasshouse.

Palm trees stretched upwards to the soaring glass roof. Drops of warm condensation plopped on waxy leaves and splashed their faces. A soundscape of twittering and screeching birds contributed to the subtropical atmosphere. After the biting cold air outside, the clammy heat was a relief, but they had taken only a few steps before their clothes hung heavy. Stopping on the metal fret-worked gangway, shrouded by fronds, Stella bundled her anorak over an arm. In her other hand she held a carrier bag.

'The Palm House is a good place to eavesdrop on visitors,' Jack whispered.

Stella put from her mind that he could be speaking from personal experience. 'I can't stay long, I have to pick up Stanley before Jackie goes home.' She didn't add that she wanted to go back and change before Cashman came over. Again she promised herself that she would tell Jack about Martin, but not now. Besides, she argued with herself, Jack never said what he was doing.

'I'm going to supper with Jackie this evening,' Jack said, proving her wrong. 'I'm sure she'd love you to come, unless you're otherwise engaged.'

He knew! Jackie knew about Cashman because he had rung the office to speak to Stella and Jackie had answered. She wouldn't have told Jack.

'Do you remember the drought in the summer of 1976?' Jack asked, seemingly apropos of nothing.

'The woman next door had her flat fumigated because fleas from her cat bred in the heat. My mum said her legs were black with them.' She clearly remembered Suzie telling her that. Shame she didn't have better recall of more recent events, like her birthday four years ago. And whatever it was about the morning she found the dead man in the Marianne North Gallery.

Stella had suggested that she and Jack go to Kew Gardens for tea. Jackie had approved the idea. 'You need to clear your head.' Since Jack's comment about eavesdroppers in the Palm House, she couldn't shake the conviction that someone was crouching deep in the jungle-like foliage. Despite the heat, Stella shivered and, shrugging back into her anorak, when they came upon an exit she took it.

They passed a row of statues called the Queen's Beasts. Stella paused by a dog on its hind legs, posing like Stanley begging for a biscuit: the White Greyhound of Richmond.

'There should be one called the Apricot Poodle of Hammersmith!' Jack said gaily. 'Magical to think that, after dark, the Beasts leap off their plinths and have free rein here.' He stopped by one named the Yale of Beaufort. 'The Yale's horns can swivel in any direction.' He sounded impressed.

'Let's have tea.' Stella didn't want to think of any creature having free rein in Kew Gardens after dark. She set off around the lake to the café.

Jack raised his eyebrows. 'Is one of us eight years old?'

They were seated at a table near the gift shop. Jack had managed to get a mug of hot milk and she was pouring extra hot water into a pot of tea. A slice of chocolate cake coated with hundreds and thousands with two forks lay on the table between them.

'You don't like chocolate,' he added.

Stella was gratified that Jack had remembered. It was strange that Terry had got her chocolate cake. Her mum said he had wanted to keep her as a little girl and couldn't accept she had grown up. But one thing Stella did remember was that Terry had treated her like an adult from early on. It was her mum who objected to make-up and loud music. Terry had been surprised when, in her teens, she ordered a sundae; he had offered her a coffee. Yet on her forty-fourth birthday he had got her chocolate cake with hundreds and thousands. 'Terry gave it to me. We came here for my birthday in 2010.'

'A madeleine!'

'What?'

'It's a cake in Proust; the memory of eating it takes him back to his childhood.' Jack beamed. 'Are you hoping it will jog your memory?'

'The afternoon we came here is a blank.' As ever Jack had guessed right. She told him about the receipts. 'Your hunch about Dad watching that house was spot on.'

'My hunches generally are,' Jack said peaceably.

'The receipts show his movements over about five days in 2010.'

'Lucie May told me that something you said to Terry in 2010 showed him kids could lie. Was it while you were here?'

'Dad knew children lie. The police have no illusions.' Stella dabbed at stray sprinkles with her finger and licked them off. She cut off some cake with the side of her fork and popped it in her mouth, grimacing in expectation of the sweetness. 'This was the last place I'd have expected Terry to suggest for tea.' She glanced across at a woman at the next table who was tackling a green salad. 'He was a fry-up and doughnut man.'

'Maybe he knew you'd prefer this?'

'He was here for work.' As she said it, Stella saw that it was true. 'Terry bought the cake as a prop in a crime reconstruction.'

'You think someone was murdered at a tea table in Kew Gardens?' Jack was wide-eyed.

'No, it's an oblique reference. I do think cake features somehow. It was out of character for Dad to buy me cake, Mum would have told him off. It makes sense if it was a case.' Stella was now sure Terry was investigating a crime.

'But he'd retired by then.'

'Officially, yes. But he didn't stop being a detective.'

'Lucie said he was worried because he believed he'd let someone get away with murder.'

'How come she's kept it to herself?' Stella bristled. What else did Lucie May know?

'At the time I think she just thought it was a throwaway line. He didn't tell her anything else.'

Vaguely mollified by Jack's response, Stella ate another forkful of cake. The sponge was moist; she found she liked the sweetness. That day over four years ago, she hadn't liked to leave the cake, not wanting Terry to worry that he had got it wrong. Suzie said he was out of touch with his daughter. 'The cake was part of his reconstruction and so was I.

'We went to the Palm House. The heat made Dad short of breath so I suggested we leave. We came to the café.' She exclaimed: 'We sat at this table!'

Did you ever tell lies when you were little?

'I said "no" without thinking if that was true. I assumed I never lied, because Dad told me it was wrong to lie.'

Are you certain?

'It was like I was one of his suspects. He was casually questioning me. I should have asked why he wanted to know.' She ate some more cake. Like Jack's madeleine, it did prompt her memory.

If a policeman asked you if you had seen someone when you hadn't, would you lie and say that you had?

Even sitting down making no effort, his forehead had been damp with perspiration. In five months he would be dead. Tina had been able to recall the minutest detail about her dad. He had read Tina bedtime stories and called her 'Crystal'. Stella felt a flicker of envy for Tina although she was dead. She felt sad for Cliff Banks. A child dying before the parent was the wrong order.

'How did you answer?' Jack pushed the cake plate closer to her.

Stella jabbed at a morsel of sponge and ate it. 'I told him I'd never lie to a policeman. But that I said anything to stop him and my mum arguing. He was grilling me about my honesty!'

Jack shook his head. 'He wasn't testing your honesty. You'd have been his benchmark for children. I'm guessing that in June 1976 – during the drought – he interviewed a girl who reminded him of you so he believed what she said, as he believed what you said. Later – in 2010 – he suspected that she had lied and that her lie let someone get away with murder. That afternoon you confirmed it.'

'Terry wouldn't have been fooled by a little girl.' Stella cut herself more cake.

'His daughter always told the truth; it skewed his judgement. At the tea you told him that you had lied to keep the peace at home. You had taken it upon yourself to restore order. No change there then!'

'We need to find out who lives at that house. I'll look up the electoral roll.' Stella jotted a note in her Filofax, cheered by the prospect of good old-fashioned legwork.

'So many questions. Who was the child? Who was Terry asking about? Once we know who lives in Kew Villa we might get closer to that one,' Jack said.

'We need to know who lived there in 1976 and 2010.' Stella added this to her action list. 'From the receipts it looks as if after the tea Terry never resumed the stakeout. Maybe he got the answer he was looking for. This might be a dead end.' She flung down her pen.

'Or something more pressing got in the way. Here, I thought you'd be interested in these.' Jack took two newspaper clippings from his coat pocket and spread them on the table. One of the articles was by Lucie May. Stella saw the name Ramsay. Isabel Ramsay had been her favourite client.

'Did Lucie give you these?' she asked when she had finished reading them.

Jack made a non-committal motion with his head. 'The body was found in what was then called Rose Gardens. When the Great West Road was built they knocked down about twenty houses. All those homes, rooms, pavements, ways of life wiped out so that we can get out of London quicker. Non-existent.'

'Things move on.' Stella couldn't regret the loss of houses half a century ago. A clock on the wall said three o'clock. Tina was non-existent. Her appetite gone, she left the last bit of cake. Thinking of Tina, she said, 'Michelle Banks gave me this the night that Tina died.' She shoved the carrier bag across the table. 'Tina wanted me to have these things.'

Jack gathered up the bag. 'OK for me to see? They must be personal.'

'Not that personal.' Stella had been taken aback by the contents of the Boots bag. She didn't see why Tina had wanted her to have it.

One by one Jack took out the items and laid them beside the cuttings. A paperback copy of *The Cat in the Hat*. A pair of pink flip-flops. A woman's shoe, black with a silver buckle. A photograph of an elderly woman on a settee. On the back, in Tina's handwriting, it said, 'Nan (Ivy C.) three days before she died, 1970'. Tina couldn't have meant her to have it; she must give it to Michelle. She stared at the next object, heavy and cold in her hand. A silver locket. Since Michelle had handed her the bag outside the hospice, she had given its contents only a cursory glance and had missed the locket. It was the one she had found in Tina's office. The locket that Tina had insisted didn't belong to her. Jack was examining a sheet of cartridge paper on which, drawn in black ink, were the parts of a tree.

He read out the caption: '*Eucalyptus gunnii*.' He became animated. 'There's a eucalyptus above the Ruined Arch near the North Gallery. It's near here.' He gestured at the door. 'The bark is beautifully smooth. It's one of my favourite trees.'

Stella hadn't realized that they were close to where she had found the dead man. Her early-morning rides across the gardens in the dark had given her a fractured grasp of the area.

Jack contemplated the objects on the table. 'Strange assortment.'

'It's a mistake. It'll be what Tina had with her in the hospice and Michelle Banks was confused.'

'Surely that would be valuables like a watch or a purse, maybe a washbag. These flip-flops are small, even for Tina. And a woman's shoe? Why just one? Ooh, I love *The Cat in the Hat*.' Jack began to leaf through the pages.

'So did I,' Stella said more to herself. She had never told Tina so that didn't explain that it was here. 'Michelle should have this picture of their nan.' She didn't say that the locket wasn't Tina's to give away. 'It's a mistake,' she said again.

'Did you?' Jack looked surprised.

'Did I what?'

'Like *The Cat in the Hat*?'

'Dad gave it to me on my first access weekend. I was seven. Mum told him I was too old for picture books.' She paused and said, 'I didn't like the Things.'

'Thing One and Thing Two, the friends of the cat who wreak havoc in the house watched by two horrified children while their mother is away.' Jack was dreamy. 'I wished I was Thing One and could turn our house upside down, break crockery, tip up furniture and whirl up and down the staircase shrieking until my father came out of his study. I suppose that the Things made you anxious?' he said. 'The cat too. They made such a mess.'

'I liked the machine the cat uses to clean up,' Stella said. 'I wanted to use it to put everything back in our house so my mum and dad would stay together.' She puffed out her cheeks. 'Stories aren't real, they make no difference.'

'You've several of those machines now!' Jack clapped his hands. 'The story *did* make a difference – it inspired you to start a cleaning company.'

'It encourages lying.'

'Cleaning?'

'The mum asks her kids how they spent their day and they have to decide whether to lie because they don't think she'll believe the truth.'

'Yes, it ends with something like, "What would *you* tell your mother?" I used to tell my mum what I did every day. I didn't lie,' Jack said. 'We had to write letters from boarding school. Since my mum was dead, I had to write to Dad, but I wrote to her because I had nothing to say to him. I wrote that I hoped that she was happy. Wait a minute!' He dropped the book and grabbed the locket from the table.

'It says here that a locket was stolen from the Ramsays' house in the fifties. Silver, heart-shaped. Like this. Could this be the same one?'

'There must be lots of silver lockets.' Stella finished her tea and crushed the paper cup.

'True. But it might be a link between the robbery in the 1950s and Kew Villa and of course with Tina,' Jack said.

'Why should there be a link between it and Kew Villa?' Jack's brand of logic could leave her bewildered.

'Oh!' Jack stared at the locket as if he hadn't seen it before. 'No reason.'

Stella suspected that there was something Jack wasn't telling her. Mindful of seeing Martin, she decided that, whatever it was, for now she preferred not to know.

They tossed their cups and the plate in the bin and went through to the shop. Fingering the fridge magnets, Stella said, 'If the kids in the story always told the truth their mum might have trusted them.'

'It's not every day that a cat in crazy headgear ransacks your house.' Jack was holding a mug decorated with botanical illustrations, turning it around between his hands. 'We draw conclusions based on probability. If it happened yesterday, it could happen today.'

'Pretending the cat hadn't visited would have been lying.'

'It would have been less complicated than trying to convince her. Oh!' Jack dropped the mug. It smashed on the floor at his feet.

Stella stooped down and began shovelling the pieces together, avoiding cutting herself on the shards of china. A man appeared with a dustpan and brush. Apologizing, she got to her feet and saw with horror that Jack had picked up another mug. 'I'll buy it.' He nodded to the man with the dustpan. 'I'll pay for that too.'

When they got outside it was dusk and the gardens were closing. The air was brittle with cold. Their breath was like smoke in the café lights. Jack unwrapped the mug.

'Careful,' Stella cautioned.

'Look.' Jack held it up. 'This was what I'd seen.'

'*Eucalyptus gunnii*,' Stella read the italic Latin. In smaller letters the copyright was attributed to a George Watson. 'It's the picture Tina left me,' she exclaimed. Then again, this was Kew Gardens so it wasn't a coincidence to find a mug depicting a eucalyptus.

'It's by George Watson!' Jack was excited.

'Should I have heard of him?' Stella was used to Jack firing obscure names at her – usually of engineers and inventors – and expecting her to know them.

'I've met him. Twice,' Jack said after a moment. 'He was on that train where the woman died. He got off without giving a statement to … the police.'

Jackie had said a passenger had died on Jack's train. Stella had meant to check he was OK, but she had forgotten. Before she could now, Jack went on:

'I got a bad feeling about him. I was going to tell you – it might be another case.'

'A bad feeling isn't enough. Was that it?' Stella immediately regretted her curt tone. Jack's bad feelings were usually worth taking seriously.

'Yes. No.'

Now she was certain Jack was keeping something back.

'Was Tina interested in botanical drawings?' he asked.

'She told me she had lessons as a kid, but was useless.'

'Show me the drawing again.' Jack wrapped up the mug and put it back in the Boots carrier with Tina's things.

Stella brought out the paper.

Jack held it up to the light of the café lamp. 'What are these numbers: 766, 764, 34425?'

'No idea. The number of the print?' Stella hazarded.

'This is an original drawing.'

'A telephone number?'

'Why write it like that? The 766 and 764 are on separate lines when there's plenty of space to put them together. Lumped together they make six numbers. Could be part of a mobile telephone number. But why split them?'

'To hide their significance?' Stella suggested.

'A poor disguise since we've guessed it.'

'Mobile numbers begin with a nought,' Stella said.

'True. Let's assume that they're meant to be in these groups,' Jack said. 'There's probably a relation between 764 and 766. They might be from the same index system.'

'I think 764 rings a bell.' Stella held the paper up to the light and saw another set of figures a little apart from the others. 'This must be a telephone number, "940" is the exchange for Kew: "940 2418". It doesn't have the London code.'

'One way to find out.' Jack dialled it on his mobile and put it on speaker. The number rang for a while and then cut off. He rang again. No answer. 'Either they're out and have no answer machine.' He shook his head. 'Or it's not switched on.'

'When was the other time you met George Watson?' Stella tapped the drawing. Jack had said he had met him twice.

'He works at the Herbarium. He was there when I was cleaning the other morning.'

Stella hoped Jack hadn't got into trouble with any scientists at Kew. Her concern was confirmed when he said in a faraway voice, 'He *really* didn't want me there.' He had gone pale.

Stella fitted the drawing back in the bag. 'I can't throw any of this away, yet what can I do with it?'

'Got it!' Jack clapped his hands as if scaring up birds.

'What?' It was properly dark now; cold crept through the padding of her anorak. In the distance the Palm House was a dark hulk against the city sky. People were filing out of the Elizabeth Gate.

'Tina hasn't left you these things because they have sentimental value. She wasn't sentimental. She asked you to catch a murderer. She wanted you to have these because they are clues!'

Chapter Forty-Two

November 2014

'...has given to our sister *Christina*
her span of years and gifts of character.
God our Father, we thank you now for all her life...'

Jack tuned out of the service. He wasn't religious in a strict sense. He believed that his mother kept watch over him, but didn't trouble himself with the practicalities of how she achieved this. Occasionally, on night ramblings, he found a church that was unlocked and crept inside, slid into a back pew and, head bowed in a semblance of prayer, urged her to communicate with him. Sometimes she did. She did in many different circumstances: it was about making himself available.

The man intoned the prayer in a sing-song delivery. He wore a studied expression of solemnity perhaps brought on by the long procession of black limousines that had filled the turning circle outside the crematorium. On the few occasions Jack had met Banks, she was dressed in a sleek black suit and scary stilettos. Stella could be daunting in suits of charcoal or grey, but 'dressed by Jackie' looked approachable. Not a word he had associated with

Tina Banks. The funeral, with black-clothed mourners in wrap-around sunglasses, better fitted the Kray twins than a member of the legal profession.

But then criminals and lawyers, like criminals and detectives, were two sides of the same coin.

'... for every memory of love and joy,
for every good deed done by *her*...'

Jack wasn't here to mourn Tina Banks. He had been pleased when Stella asked him to come. Jackie said that she had put off Cashman from coming. He wouldn't miss the lawyer, but was sorry that she was dead. She was in her forties, too young to be meeting her maker or anyone else.

The sleek black coffin resting on the catafalque seemed large for a diminutive woman. Lucie's private nickname for the solicitor had been 'short and brief.'

Jack had lost Stella when they entered the crematorium. He had sat on the end of the last pew hoping to catch her when she appeared. After the coffin was carried in, an elderly man had made his way unsteadily over to it. His jacket bagged and his trousers had been pressed, but not in this decade. When he had reached the bier, with a shaking hand he laid a gerbera on the lid. He stood back and, with a mechanical movement, bowed to the coffin. Jack felt he was familiar, but perhaps it was his grief that he recognized.

Tina Banks had a father; her mother was dead. The opposite of Stella. Jack presumed the gerbera man was her father. Despite his mistrust of the 'deceased', Jack was sad; unknowingly he echoed Stella's thought that no parent should have to bury a child. The man had looked blown apart.

His mistrust of Tina had been mutual. This made him feel better as he sat at her funeral feeling only sadness for Stella who had lost a friend.

It had begun at their first encounter when Tina Banks had turned up at Stella's flat in Thamesbank Heights one evening when he was there. Somehow she had heard the flat was going on the market and she wanted it. Jack had fretted that Stella, no games player and liable to trust that, like herself, people did the right thing, might be a pushover.

That Banks had removed her stilettoes to protect the carpet won bonus points with Stella. But he guessed Banks was thinking of when the carpet would be hers.

Tina had offered Stella the asking price and paid extra for some of her furniture. Jack had warned Stella that what is too good to be true is usually not true. Yet as he watched the casket trundle along the catafalque towards the furnace and the curtains jerk closed, Jack admitted that he had misread the lawyer. As Jackie had said, Tina Banks was like Stella; what you saw was what you got.

'We thank you for Christina,
The years we shared with her,
The good we saw in her,
The love we received from her.
Now give us strength and courage
To leave her in your care,
Confident in your promise of eternal life
Through Jesus Christ our Lord.'

Jack mouthed, 'Amen.' He regretted that he hadn't tried to get on with Tina, not for the sake of getting to like her, or even for Stella's sake, but because it might have given him insight into her death-bed request.

No sign of Stella. With muted shuffles and coughs mourners were getting to their feet. The organ struck up and the congregation embarked on a straggling rendition of the 23rd Psalm. Something white floated before Jack. The woman next to him was holding out her copy of the funeral service sheet with the words to the psalm for him to share. He knew the words by heart, but nodded thanks and began to sing in what came out as a whisper.

259

Gradually, as if coming from a distance, he became aware of the sweetest, melodic voice. He hadn't heard such a voice since he was a boy. The notes, clear as spring water, carried across the span of years. It was his mother. *Mummy.* Jack's singing subsided until he was only moving his lips and making no sound. He let the singing surround him.

She had communicated with him at Tina Banks's funeral.

Jack's image of his mother was fashioned from a gossamer of half-spun memories and snatches of dreams. A composite of qualities he held most dear.

'... Yea, though I walk in death's dark vale,
Yet will I fear no ill;
For Thou art with me, and Thy rod
And staff me comfort still.'

He put a hand to his cheek; it was wet. Lovingly, as she would have done, Jack smoothed away the tear with the flat of his finger.

Something touched his arm, light and soft. Looking at the sheet while continuing to sing – although from her singing it was obvious she didn't need to see the words either – the woman beside him passed him a tissue. He took it and dabbed at his eyes.

If Jack had wanted to pass as bereaved, he had succeeded. Trembling with emotion, he worked the tissue into a damp ball in a clenched hand. He was the only one crying. From the pulpit, a succession of Tina Banks's colleagues and employees testified, as if giving evidence in court, to a woman who was hard-working, had a zero tolerance for failure and anything less than the best. Her mourners were dry-eyed.

Belatedly Jack resumed his seat and stole a glance at the woman. Of course she wasn't his mother, but, indulging his fancy, he imagined that she looked as his mother would have, had she lived into her forties. She would have grown more beautiful with time. Jack had lived more years than she had. At forty-eight Tina Banks had been on this earth twice the years that his mother had.

Age cannot wither her, nor custom stale
Her infinite variety...

It wasn't lost on Jack that, aside from supporting Stella, he was a 'funeral-chaser'. Unable after thirty years to comprehend his mother's death, he was drawn to coffins, of wood, of wicker, caskets of steel in low-slung hearses or carriages drawn by majestic horses. To coffins burnt in crematoria or lowered into graves. He was searching for an answer. *Why did you leave me?*

Jack made his way through the throng of mourners in the Marianne North Gallery looking for Stella. He had never seen it so crowded. Muted chatter and occasional laughter bounced off the walls; it lost definition and was like a chord sounded without pause or break. White winter light diffused by the opaque windows reflected on the glass protecting the paintings so that they resembled hundreds of tiny windows. Jack had to quell outrage that he wasn't alone in what was his true idea of a church.

In the van and on the walk to the gallery, Stella had been silent. Finding a gap in the throng in the Australian corner of the main room, Jack had turned to speak to her and she wasn't there.

It was unfortunate that Tina Banks's wake was at the gallery. Stella disliked mixing the personal with work, never mind that she had found a dead body here. Yet she was an equable soul and what could upset some passed her by, so perhaps she was sanguine. This observation prompted a burst of affection for her, and Jack stood on tiptoe to try to see her in the crowd. Jack had rather supposed that Stella was Banks's only friend, but the place was packed; cynically he guessed most of them worked for Tina or were her clients. He couldn't see Stella.

Absently, he plucked a glass of champagne from a tray proffered by a waiter dressed in a discreet black T-shirt and slacks. Tina had told no one she was terminally ill, a discretion that didn't seem to have extended to her funeral arrangements, for which no expense had been spared. It wouldn't be cheap to hire the gallery in Kew Gardens on a weekday. From where Jack stood, he had a view of both antechambers so had some chance of spotting Stella. The crowd was denser in the middle chamber. Many crowded around the gold-framed doorway, letting curiosity overcome grief to see where the Kew murder victim had been found.

'Huge turnout!' It was the woman from his pew at the funeral. Jack had looked for her outside the crematorium, but like Stella she had vanished. On a reflex, he handed her his champagne.

'Thank you. Don't you want it?'

'I don't drink. It was for you.' As he said this, Jack realized that this was true. He felt himself redden, but she didn't seem to have noticed.

'Chrissie's sister told me that Chrissie planned this years ago. I haven't even made a will. Stupid since that we will die is the one certainty!' She drank some champagne.

'True,' he agreed. The woman's voice was deep and gravelly like Lucie's; it gave no hint of her angelic singing.

'I'd prefer to sit in silence at these things and reflect on the loss. More meaningful than small talk with strangers.'

Nothing else about her was like Lucie, who favoured clothes that showed off her too-thin figure: short skirts, tight trousers, low-cut shirts and tottering heels. This woman was lost beneath layers of black: a long skirt, topped by a mid-length jacket cut in at the waist with a Gandhi-style collar, over which was draped a black woollen shawl. Jet-black curly hair framed a face done up in startling black kohl. The scent of patchouli oil topped off the trappings of a seventies hippy. Patchouli was Lucie May's perfume – no one was less like a hippy. A shadow passed across Jack's mood. It was the smell in the bedroom of the house at Kew Pond. 'I'll leave you,' he said.

'I didn't mean you! I've only seen Chrissie once in the last forty years. I'm sad, naturally, but we weren't close. I'm not going to sit about contemplating her loss, she'd have a blue fit!' The woman gave a raucous laugh.

'I didn't know her. I'm here for a friend,' Jack said, aware that the friend he was 'here for' was nowhere to be seen. 'Funerals bring back other losses,' he added by way of explanation for his earlier tears. 'I agree about sitting quietly though.' Stella would hate silently reflecting on a loss with strangers. She would prefer to get on.

'I'm Bella.' The woman put out a hand.

'Jack.' Her grip was firm. 'How did you know, er, Chrissie?' The name suggested a warmer, more immediate woman than the no-messing Tina Banks.

'From prep school. Chrissie joined in 1976 from a state primary school in Hammersmith. She teamed up with me and a girl called Emily. She was supposed to come today. Oh, speak of the devil!' She raised her glass to a woman who appeared beside them as if by magic. Bella lifted up her cheek to be kissed. The woman called Emily obliged.

'Meet Jack,' Bella said. 'I was saying how we were all friends when we were kids.'

'In another life.' The woman sounded as if she meant it literally. Pale, with long hair floating about her face, she wore a scuffed mac and sturdy walking boots, not the outfit for a funeral.

'Where were you?' Bella demanded.

'I got the time wrong.' Jack was intrigued that Emily didn't seem bothered by a mistake that would have mortified Stella, and even him.

'When we saw Chrissie last month, she looked fine, didn't she?' Bella drank some more champagne. 'Everyone says that when people die. Idiotic!'

Jack was about to contradict that Tina had been 'fine'. Stella had described her as irritable when she last cleaned her office. Stella never judged people's moods so this would have been an under-statement. Jack knew from Jackie that Banks had respected Stella, so being unpleasant would have been a sign of something amiss.

'None of us ended up doing what was expected of us,' Emily said without preamble. 'You were going to be a barrister like your father and now you're a botanical illustrator like Chrissie's father and she went into law like your father.'

'You wanted to be a teacher and you are,' Bella said flatly. Jack suspected that they had had this exchange before and had found it no more stimulating that time.

'I didn't think I'd be alive,' Emily said obliquely.

'She told my friend she was no good at the drawing lessons she had as a child,' Jack said.

'Pinches of salt for much of what Chrissie said then. Fancy her ending up doing law! The truth was a stranger to her at school!' Bella tossed back her hair and laughed. Bangles stacked up her arm jangled noisily.

'That's unfair!' Emily said, but without conviction.

Jack was keen to ask Bella what she meant, but reckoned that he would learn more by keeping quiet.

'She lied about where she lived and she lied about her dad.' Bella looked quickly around her, presumably aware that Tina's dad could be close by. 'Her dad wasn't a botanical illustrator, he was a taxi driver! We lost touch after we left that school. We went to the local comp; Chrissie went to some snooty boarding school.'

'How do you know she was lying?' Jack remembered the picture by Watson in Tina's bag. He hadn't found a way to tell Stella that Watson was a True Host who might be responsible for a death on his train. Jennifer Day had died of an aneurism. A True Host's perfect murder.

'I followed her home once. She lived in a flat in Hammersmith and the man who had collected her from school a few times wasn't a taxi driver, he was her dad! Or rather he was a taxi driver. What he wasn't was a botanical illustrator. I *knew* she was lying.'

Even after forty years Bella's triumph was palpable.

'She was only going for lessons with the man she claimed was her dad. I found out his name. And…' She tinged the side of her glass, 'in the most ginormous coincidence, I work in the same studio as the chap that Chrissie claimed was her dad. I tested my theory by telling him that I was friends with his daughter when we were small. He and his wife didn't have kids, which I suspect was an issue. *Gaffe!*' She made a cutting motion across her throat. 'If a person's committed a crime, like lying, doesn't that stop them being a lawyer?'

'Only if you're found out,' Emily murmured. 'She was young. We all did things we regret.' Jack didn't imagine Emily doing many things she regretted. She radiated goodness. Bella would take no prisoners.

Bella drew her shawl around herself, speaking without apparent bitterness. 'I was a bitch when we were kids, wasn't I, Em?' she chirped happily. Jack was getting to like Bella.

'You were unhappy,' Emily said placidly. 'Chrissie was made of tougher stuff than you.'

'You were unhappy, but you didn't take it out on anyone.' Bella swapped her empty glass for a full one from the tray offered by a waiter.

'I didn't know I was unhappy, I thought my life was normal.'

'Normal? Your mother kept trying to kill herself – how was that normal?'

'One gets used to anything.' Emily too accepted a glass of champagne from the waiter.

The crowd was thinning as people began to drift away. Jack couldn't see Stella. He wasn't being a support. Or perhaps he was, because he was talking to women who had known Tina as a child.

Emily said, 'Chrissie had come from another school. Children find that disruptive. She had lost her friends and everything was strange. She had to find her feet.'

'I was the boss and then along comes this girl who insisted on being in charge. I was well put out!' Bella's eyes glittered.

Jack knew how cruel children could be; he had been on the end of cruelty at school and he had meted it out. He suspected that Bella would be as put out now were her position in a group to be threatened.

'It never occurred to me that Chrissie would lie,' Emily said. 'My parents lied to each other, and to us kids, on a daily basis so I don't know why it didn't. Chrissie was the most straightforward of us all. Despite the lies, I knew where I was with her. She wore her pain on her sleeve.'

'I asked for proof that those people were her parents and what does she do?' Bella flicked a finger against her champagne glass, making it ring. No one spoke as the sound died away. 'She nicks a locket thingy and passes it off as her parents.' Full marks for front!'

'Tina was at a new school with new rules. She found a survival strategy. Ultimately we were all trying to survive.' Emily seemed to have tolerance for every transgression. Jack found it tiring. He wondered what got Emily riled. 'I expect she was given the locket.'

'You're too nice, Emily,' Bella retorted. 'Everyone loved you; you couldn't put a foot wrong.' Jack noted an edge to her voice. He saw the Bella who had been unkind to her friends. The tiredness went.

'I learnt to be a bystander. Head down, keep out of trouble. Hardly admirable.' Jack noticed that Emily hadn't touched her champagne.

Stella had silently witnessed her parents' rows, but she wasn't a bystander. If there was trouble, she would roll up her sleeves and face it. Jack scoured the gallery: only a few knots of people remained, mostly in the little antechamber where the body had been. Stella wasn't in the gallery. She had gone without telling him. She wouldn't do that.

'She did once tell me a secret.' Emily was serious suddenly.

The back of Jack's neck tingled. This was what he had been waiting for.

'I love hearing secrets.' Bella's eyes gleamed. So did Jack's, but he kept quiet.

'I shouldn't say anything, especially since Chrissie's no longer with us,' Emily murmured. 'She told me in confidence.'

Jack felt a burst of anger. Emily was too nice. Give him the Bellas of this world, who wore their darkness on their sleeves, any day. Stella would agree with Emily about confidence though. Stella heard her clients' secrets about broken relationships, jobs they hated, affairs and more serious transgressions, and, unlike him – because he told her – never told a soul.

'If I had been there, Chrissie would have told us both.' Bella lifted a glass of champagne from another tray. She hadn't finished the previous one.

'I don't think she saw it as lying. Chrissie believed her stories. She was trying to fit in.' Emily gave Jack a tight smile. She had sensed his anger towards her. 'I assumed it was a lie at the time, but after we saw Chrissie recently, I realized she was probably telling the truth.'

Bella said, 'Get it off your chest, Ems. Look after the living's my motto; we can't help Chrissie now.'

Good one, Bella. Jack could have hugged her.

Emily spoke so softly that Jack and Emily had to lean in to hear: 'She said she saw the Cat in the Hat carrying a box with the Two Things.'

'Is that it?' Bella mussed up her hair with frustration. 'For goodness' sake, Ems, that's *obviously* a lie!'

Emily's face was pale, almost ghostly against the rich colours of the paintings. 'It wasn't all. Chrissie told me that she had seen a murder.'

Chapter Forty-Three

November 2014

'My daughter said you was her best friend. Was she yours?' Tina's father looked searchingly at Stella. Pleading even.

Her mind whirled. She didn't know if Tina had been her best friend; nor did she know she had been Tina's best friend. She should say yes because Tina's dad wanted her to and it would do no harm. But she couldn't lie. 'She taught me to foxtrot.'

'You got that wrong!' He was adamant. 'She couldn't dance. And she refused to let me teach her.' Stella was familiar with clients rejigging the character of a loved one to suit their memory. Cliff Banks had spent the last fifteen minutes boasting about Tina's success in the law courts. Dancing didn't fit the profile. She had to agree there.

'I need some air. Fancy a stroll?' he asked her.

Stella didn't, but couldn't refuse. She looked around for Jack to tell him what she was doing, but couldn't see him. He might have left. She hesitated, scanning the crowd. Jack wouldn't leave without telling her.

Banks led her along the path away from the Marianne North Gallery, deeper into the gardens. The air was cold and crisp, the lawns pale green in the fading light. She was relieved she had kept her anorak on.

'Chrissie said she could talk to you.' Cliff Banks stopped beneath a crumbling arch and lit a cigarette. In the brief flare of the match, he looked a much younger man, more like the man in the photograph on Tina's living-room window sill. 'I'm glad she had you.' He shook the match out. He touched it with the tip of his finger and, having ascertained it was cold, dropped it in his pocket. Stella was relieved that he hadn't thrown it on the ground; she would have felt bound to pick it up.

'I talked to her too.' Stella was thankful to be able to say something that was true. It was dawning on her that she would miss the conversations about employment policies, cleaning equipment, accounting programmes, with Tina protesting that Stella under-charged her clients. *'They see you coming.'*

'I bet you girls exchanged secrets!' Cliff Banks gave a harsh laugh. 'Chrissie was a great one for mates. She told me that she had loads of friends at school. She was in charge. My Chrissie was always the boss!' He veered off the path and with gazelle-like ease – he must have been in his sixties – clambered up a slope. Stella had no choice but to follow. She balked at a length of orange plastic tape that cordoned off the top of the arch: she wouldn't trespass.

'Tina told me your dad's passed.' Cliff Banks was pacing along the loose brickwork. The surface was tufted with rough grass and scattered with stones. Stella wished he would come back; the cordon was there for a reason.

'Yes.' Stella didn't want to talk about Terry. She found the phrase 'passed' peculiar. Passed what? He didn't appear to hear her.

'This was a way out of Kew a long time ago. It took you over the road, no waiting for a break in the traffic. Horse and carts in them days. Chrissie told me. Mine of information.' He drew on his ciga-rette; the tip glowed in the receding light. 'When a person dies all they ever learnt goes too. That's mad, isn't it.' His speech trembled.

'Yes.' Stella was stumped for a reply.

Orange street lighting on Kew Road drifted over the high wall, picking out leaves and branches in high relief. Stella wished Tina were here to handle her dad. But then if she'd been here, he wouldn't need handling. He'd be driving his taxi and Tina would be working. And so would she.

'We were born on the same day. She called us twins,' she blurted out. Then she reeled at her mistake. Was it tactless to talk about Tina's birth date when she was dead? Or to emphasize that she herself was still alive?

'Friday's child is loving and giving.' Cliff Banks blew smoke towards the sky. 'That was Chrissie.' His voice cracked. 'Are you loving and giving?'

'I don't know.' Stella hadn't thought about herself in such terms. Or Tina.

'Spect you are.' He smiled at her kindly. 'Bet your dad was proud of you. Thing is, Stell, you girls have no idea what us blokes go through to keep you safe. Get you on in life.' He sucked on his cigarette, grimacing with the effort. 'I can hear her voice, but I can't see her face. Can you see her face?'

A tall tree formed a canopy over the arch. In the half-light Stella saw a label on the trunk: '*Eucalyptus gunnii*'. She stopped herself exclaiming. It was the tree in the drawing by George Watson. Jack's words came back to her.

'*There's a eucalyptus above the Ruined Arch beyond the North Gallery… The bark is beautifully smooth. It's one of my favourite trees.*'

'Do you mean…?' Was he talking about a ghost?

'Thing is, I'm frightened of forgetting her, Stella. The more you tell me about her, the more she'll be here. Know what I mean?'

Suddenly Stella realized that she did know what he meant.

Approaching the tree, stepping on sheaths of old bark splayed around the base, she touched the trunk and, as Jack had said, it was smooth, as if it had been planed flat.

'…when did he die? Your dad.' Banks lifted the tape off an iron stake and beckoned her through as if to a crime scene. She stumbled forward. He replaced the cordon after her.

Stella's mind went blank. When did Terry die: 2011, 2012? Sometimes it was as though he had died long ago, others only yesterday. 'January 2011,' she said finally.

'Bet you was poleaxed.'

Stella didn't remember being poleaxed. She did remember the drive to the hospital in Sussex. She remembered the procedure for probate and the funeral. 'It was sudden,' she said.

'Like my Chrissie. Gone just like that.' He paced about on uneven ground beneath a tree. A holm oak (*Quercus ilex*), Stella noticed irrelevantly. Soon it would be dark; they should go. Banks was above the arch, scouring the ground.

'Have you lost something?' Jack would say Banks had lost his daughter. She wished she'd brought Jack with her. He was better at grief stuff.

Cliff Banks didn't appear to have heard because when he spoke it was with another question. 'She tell you she was ill?' He faced her, a shadowy figure in the gathering twilight.

'No.' Jackie said people tried to gather up the moments of a loved one's life from everyone who had known them. As if, like Humpty Dumpty, they could try to put them back together again. Stella couldn't tell him about Tina's lie about the locket and he hadn't wanted to hear about her dancing. Tina had said he was the star of the Hammersmith Palais in the fifities. Stella guessed that Banks would have liked to teach his daughter to foxtrot. She guessed he was very good at it.

'Odd she never said nothing about it. Seeing as you're mates? She told the girls she was at school with. I just spoke to one called Emily.'

'If I was ill I wouldn't tell anyone.' This was true. Stella would do exactly what Tina had done. She would tell no one and get on with beating the cancer. She hadn't imagined Tina keeping in touch with school friends; she had never spoken about her past.

'She was my life.' He made a choking sound. The tip of his cigarette darted like a firefly against the orange-mauve sky. 'You sure she didn't talk to you? You might as well say, it can't get worse than it is.'

Tiny stones from the crumbling parapet trickled down the slope and scattered on the path below. They were metres from rush-hour traffic beyond the wall, yet it might be remote countryside.

Stella cast about for a way of suggesting they leave. If he broke down entirely she would not know what to do. Anything would sound banal in the face of his terrible loss.

'She could be watching us now,' he said. 'You feel it?'

'Er...' Stella didn't relish the idea that Tina was watching her. If she was, at least she would see that Stella was looking out for her dad. Tina would have looked out for Terry, she was suddenly sure.

'The dead know everything about us. No secrets,' Mr Banks stated. Smoke curdled around his head. She couldn't see his face, but was sure that he was crying. She considered texting Jack to come and help, but that was absurd.

'If she is watching, that might be nice.' That was a lie. She hoped Terry wasn't watching.

He came towards Stella; with each step more stones loosened and tumbled down the slope. 'She give you anything? A keepsake?' He tripped and pitched sideways towards the parapet. Stella grabbed his hand and yanked him back, just keeping her own balance. For a moment they held each other. Stella fought back her own tears.

'That was close! Thanks, Stell,' he gasped, brushing himself down. Stepping away from her, closer to the edge of the parapet, he stamped out his cigarette on the ground then, picking it up, put it in the same pocket as the match. Tina must have got her attention to detail from her dad.

Stella took charge. 'Mr Banks, we should come away from here. The gardens will be closing soon. It's getting dark.' Mr Banks had admired Tina for her leadership ability. Jackie said people who had lost a loved one tended not to be the full shilling. Her own world had been tilted on its axis.

'Cliff.' He cleared his throat. 'Call me Cliff.'

They returned down the slope. Cliff Banks ducked into an

alcove under the arch that Stella had missed on the way up. Inside a greenish light filtered through a grille in the roof. Through it Stella could see the sky. Cliff Banks must have been looking through it when he was on top of the arch.

'I hoped she had given you something.' In the cramped stone chamber his voice was strangely intimate. Stella's hand caught the wall; the stone was damp and slimy. Recoiling, she moved closer to him. For a moment, she wished with a dreadful intensity that Cliff Banks's daughter was alive and that Terry was here too.

'She didn't tell me she was ill,' Stella reminded him. She didn't know why she hadn't told him about the contents of the Boots bag. Tina hadn't said it was a secret, but somehow Stella thought that it was.

'She didn't say anything to you? Give you any clue?'

Would Terry have gone on to her friends like this if it were she who had died and he who was left? Stella was positive that he would. 'I didn't know she was ill until she was in the hospice.' It was truly dark. The temperature had dropped to freezing and Stella's ears ached. She wished she had her woolly hat, but of course she hadn't worn it to the funeral.

'Soon I won't be able to hear her voice. I can't hear my wife now. It's all a blank.' He got out another cigarette and put it between his lips. He made no effort to light it.

Even in the increasing darkness, Stella had the impression of an old man. Beaten. Defeated. 'She told me nothing. I suppose that's how she wanted it. That we wouldn't feel sorry for her, treat her differently.'

Determinedly Stella set off along the path, relieved when he followed her. Banks's breathing was rasping and, feeling bad, she slowed down. On the rare occasion that she was out with Terry, she had not slowed her pace for him. If Cliff Banks had a heart attack, Tina would never forgive her.

'Tina has died.'

At the Marianne North Gallery they stopped in light spilling on to the path from the porch.

'She didn't give me anything.' Cliff Banks's eyes glistened with tears. 'She left her estate to Michelle. That's how it should be, but I hoped for something. Stupid, isn't it? Something of my Crystal.' He forced a grin.

Out of nowhere, Stella saw Terry on the day they moved to Barons Court. He had stood on the kerb, not invited into the new flat, staring at Stella. If she died, he would grill everyone she knew for details of her last moments. What would she leave him? She could only think of Stanley. But he would go to Jack. She roused herself: 'It's not stupid. Thing is Tina didn't plan to die. Or I'm sure she'd have thought of something for you.' It was a weak response. Mentally she rifled the contents of the Boots bag. Objects that she didn't associate with Tina, that she wondered if had even belonged to her.

He smiled at her. 'Nothing will bring her back.' His eyes were exactly like Tina's eyes, blue flecked with green. Stella hadn't noticed the similarity when she had seen Tina with her dad in her flat. She had the disturbing notion that they were Tina's eyes and that she was watching.

'You visited her when she was ill. She say anything?'

I want you to catch a murderer!

'She said something about a cat in a hat.' There had been no deathbed confession, no wise words for the living. Tina had been out of her head on painkillers.

'What?'

'She recited street names. She was rambling.'

'Say again?'

'"Forward Hammersmith Road, Forward Hammersmith Broadway, Left Butterwick, Right Talgarth Road."' She remembered some of the streets because she had clients in all of them, except for Butterwick, which was a bus station.

'She wasn't rambling.' His voice was disembodied in the dark.

'Well, no, I—' He must think she was being disrespectful of his daughter.

'It's Run twenty-seven. One of the runs we have to learn for the

Knowledge. She started in the middle, which shows she weren't herself. When she was a kid, she called over all the runs for me, three hundred and twenty of them. She learnt them all. That one starts with "Leave on left Addison Road, Right Kensington High Street, Forward Addison Bridge".' Reciting the streets seemed to calm him.

Stella felt the need to justify her comment about rambling. 'Tina was hallucinating. She was on morphine,' she reminded him.

'When my mum passed they called it the "liquid cosh".' His voice was strangled. 'Bet those nurses were trigger-happy with that bloody syringe driver!' His vehemence shocked Stella. Then she remembered that Jackie said some people have to find someone to blame for the death of a loved one. Tina had had ovarian cancer – the 'silent killer', Jackie had called it. By the time Tina got to her GP with symptoms, it was too late. Jackie said grief could make you angry.

'The nurses were kind.' Stella was thinking of the woman who showed her how to sponge Tina's lips to give her moisture when she could no longer swallow. Shutting down the memory she burst out, 'She said something about a murder!'

'A murder?' He stared at her, incredulous.

'As I say, she was out of it.'

'Why aren't you a detective like your old man?'

Relieved by his abrupt change of subject, Stella answered more frankly than she had done when asked the question in the past. 'I wanted to be one until I was seven and my parents separated. I didn't see my dad much after that. I decided to be a cleaner.'

'Chrissie could have been on the cabs like me.' He seemed to have regained his composure. 'She'd have been the best. Like I say, she had the Knowledge. Not that I wanted that for her.'

Guests were leaving the gallery. Jack wasn't among them.

'Tina had a newspaper article in her flat with a picture of you. *In the Detective's Shadow!* They made out you was Miss Marple. A chip off the old block!'

The piece had been in the *Daily Mirror* and was by Lucie May. It described how Stella had solved the One Under case. She had been reluctant to do the interview, but owed Lucie. It was why she was avoiding Lucie now. She didn't want her face in the papers again. At Jack's request, Lucie hadn't mentioned him. Lucie, happy to sacrifice truth for a good story, had made it look as if Stella 'cleaned up' alone.

'What did Chrissie say about a murder?'

'She became ill so I left.'

'It was probably her work. She met all kinds of villains, that got me wound up, I can tell you.' He nodded at the gallery. 'I'm not going back in, can't face it.' He took a step away along the path and stopped. 'She must have meant that murder here.'

Stella snatched at the offered straw. 'Yes.'

'I tried to get this venue changed, but Michelle said it was Chrissie's wish. She tell you why she wanted it in here?' he wiped a hand down his face. If he was a detective, this would be the crux of the interview. *Ask the most important question casually, at the end of the interview when the culprit thinks it's over. As if you don't care about the answer.* She often heard Terry's voice.

There was no strategy to Cliff Banks's questions. He was a man grieving for his daughter.

'No she didn't.' Stella agreed that since the murder, the Marianne North Gallery was an unfortunate choice.

'The bloke that was stabbed, it was you that found him, right?' Cliff Banks might be grieving, but it seemed that he was like everyone else, tapping her for the story. 'A real-life murder under your nose – try solving that!' He pulled on black leather gloves and twitched up the collar of his Crombie coat.

'It's for the police.'

'What do they know?' He drifted away into the darkness. He called back, 'Stella love?'

She strained to make him out. 'Yes?'

'Thanks for today. You're a proper Friday's child!'

After he had gone, Stella felt bad for not telling him about Tina's bag of things. Cliff Banks had more right to them than she did. He might have known their significance. She could have learnt more about Tina too. Yet if Jack was right and they were clues, then she should tell no one.

As Banks had said, Tina must have meant the murder in the Marianne North Gallery.

'There you are!' Jack was beside her. 'We need to talk.'

Chapter Forty-Four

November 2014

Jack finished vacuuming with ten minutes to spare. He arched his back and looked around the silent space divided by the cupboards of dead materials. A faint glow seeped from the alcoves between the cabinets. The smell of naphthalene was stronger. It suggested that one of the files had recently been opened, releasing the noxious odour into the still air. Before he began cleaning, Jack had confirmed that he was alone. The True Host was not here. He leant on the rail and contemplated the floor below. It resembled the aisle of a church, plant chests housing bulky specimens – fruits and berries – lurked in the shadows. All around him were cupboards, their doors fastened shut on their ancient contents. The Herbarium was a house of questions awaiting answers.

Jack was in a quandary: one of his own making and one he had set up for himself on more than one occasion. He and Stella were a team; their skills dovetailed and got results. But he also worked alone. He had entered the large house by the pond at Kew and found articles about the man buried in the Great West Road and a robbery in the 1950s. These must have significance, probably for a woman living there, since he had discovered them hidden in a dressing-table drawer. He had felt compelled to show them to Stella and had let her think Lucie May had given them to him. He had fobbed Lucie herself off with a story about researching the 1976 drought, but she hadn't been fooled. She was judicious with her confrontations and would be holding fire.

Not telling Stella was a betrayal. She set store by loyalty. This meant she didn't know of the link between the house that Terry had been watching and the contents of the articles. He had not played fair.

They had agreed to meet up at the end of the day at her house. Jack was surprised and not a little pleased that she wasn't seeing Cashman. Although, as he had vacuumed his way around the Herbarium, he'd wondered if Cashman would be there. Was he to be part of the team?

Now Jack was agitated. The Herbarium wasn't working its magic. He would calm himself by examining a specimen. Gently he drew a folder out from the stack inside. He brought it to the table and switched on a lamp. Stuck to the top sheet were the dried segments of a plant. He felt a thrill of excitement. It had no name. It had yet to be identified. Technically, the plant didn't exist.

'Do you have permission to examine dead material?'

Jack didn't have to turn around to know that it was Watson. He felt as if caught in an airlock. His ears popped. He swallowed hard. The True Host lounged on the balcony railing, legs crossed at the ankles, arms folded. He possessed the stillness of one who practises meditation. His eyes rested on Jack, drawing him in. His brown serge suit showed off a body spare and lean. He must have moved to the alcove like a snake across the parquet.

'I don't have permission.' No point in lying: Watson knew.

'I could have you sacked,' the man observed casually as if this had no relevance to either of them.

'You could.' Jack slipped the folder back in where he had found it and fastened the cupboard. He was taller than the True Host, but that meant nothing. He must not show fear. Ultimately it didn't matter what tactic he adopted. The True Host would know it.

'Are you interested in botany?' the man asked, a smile hovering on full sensuous lips, his eyes twinkling. The thing about True Hosts was that they were whatever you wanted them to be. Jack wanted him to be a kind fatherly figure, the man his own father had failed to be. Watson was obliging him.

The dimly lit Herbarium was profoundly quiet. Dead materials make no sound. Jack wanted to convince himself that Watson *was* an ordinary, warm and generous botanist who would understand his passion for the structure of plants. Plants were the beginning of everything. But no, Watson too was dead material.

'I wanted to be a botanist.' Jack knew to offer a glimpse of his soul, enough to satisfy the True Host. Yet no matter what he did, the ending would be the same. Once he was visible, the True Host had the upper hand.

'Running away is no escape if you don't know which direction is "away",' the voice of a ghost whispered to him.

'Instead you're a cleaner.' Watson looked genuinely interested by the contrast. 'I will say nothing this time, but I don't want to catch you again. These specimens are invaluable. I am their guardian. I will stop at nothing to protect them. I think we both know that this is the second time, isn't it? Fate has brought you within the orbit of your failed ambition. Let that be enough for you.'

'It is enough.' Jack retreated along the balcony to the spiral staircase. Watson was behind him. He descended, stepping firmly on the tapering treads, the Henry in his arms like a baby. He hugged it close as if it could save him.

At the bottom Jack saw that Watson wasn't behind him after all.

Jack put the Henry in the equipment cart and pushed it along a corridor lined with glass vitrines of specimen jars and display boxes. Lights flickered on and off as he progressed. His rubber-soled shoes were silent; this was intentional, but now it unnerved him: he couldn't hear himself. Overwrought, he went the wrong way and got lost. He kept going – he would find the lift eventually – but, looking back, the corridors were a yawning maw and the vitrines vanished in the thick darkness.

Turning into another corridor he found a door marked 'Artists' Room'. He plunged inside without knocking.

Chapter Forty-Five

August 1976

'Are you sure you said here?' Bella asked for the third time in five minutes.

'Definitely. She asked if it was the place you made a daisy chain and next to the Greyhound. I didn't remember you making one, but these are the Queen's Beasts and that's the Greyhound of Richmond. There's only one.' If Emily was irritated with Bella for not believing her, she didn't show it.

The two girls were sprawled on the lawn in Kew Gardens where, weeks earlier, they had picnicked with Chrissie. In that time no rain had fallen; the earth was hard and impenetrable like concrete. There were no daisies. Unremitting sunshine beat down from a bleached-blue sky.

The Beasts, stone creatures blasted by intense heat, cast precise shadows on the path. The lake was a sheet of silver. Blinding sparks of light danced on the glass of the Palm House.

Emily and Bella had left school in July. Bella because her father had stopped payments for the daughter whose existence he barely recognized, Emily because her father had lost his job. Chrissie, her school fees paid a year in advance, was returning to the prep school in September. On the last day Emily had exacted a promise that they would be friends for ever and suggested they meet on 12 August, Chrissie's birthday, at two o'clock in the same place as before. It was fifteen minutes past two and no one was coming along the path beside the Beasts or approaching from the periphery of the lake. The girls – diminutive beneath the stone Greyhound – might be alone in the Botanical Gardens.

'A waste of a card!' Bella tossed a crumpled envelope on to the grass.

'You bought Chrissie a card!' Emily crowed with delight.

'I *made* it.' Sitting cross-legged, Bella examined indentations on her bare legs from the dried grass beneath her. 'It's a picture of a daisy.' She smoothed her Laura Ashley skirt over her knees and said gruffly, 'Like her dad *supposedly* does.'

'That's amazing, Bell! I didn't think you would have, so my card's written from both of us.'

'But I wasn't there,' Bella objected.

Emily squinted into the distance towards the Pagoda, a hand shading her eyes from the sun. 'I forged your signature.'

'That's illegal!' Bella was gleeful. 'Emily, you're a criminal!'

'Yes.' Emily took an envelope out of the pocket of her jeans jacket. She held it away from her as if it were a lethal weapon. 'Thing is, I wanted Chrissie's birthday to be perfect.'

'She's made new friends and forgotten us.' Bella got up and began bashing at her skirt; the floral-patterned material was coated with dust from the parched lawn. 'Birthdays are never perfect.'

'My mum and dad never remember my birthday.' Emily gave a little laugh as if this was a small matter. 'They remember my sister's because Mum nearly died having her. Chrissie said she would come. Anyway, I dropped a note at her house to remind her.'

'She lied,' Bella stated. 'Did you tell her to come here?' she asked again. She frowned at the Queen's Beasts. The furthest-off statues were indiscernible smudges of grey in the shimmering air. 'What house?'

'Her house. The one by the pond.'

'I told you. I don't believe she lives there.' Bella tossed her hair back. In the last weeks, she had lost the look of a little girl. In her face was a hint of the woman she would become.

'You should trust her.' Emily got up. She adjusted her denim hat on her head.

'You shouldn't trust anyone.' Bella stalked off past the Yale of Beaufort. 'Come on, let's go.'

Crushed by heat, in the glare of the sun, the girls tripped along the path past the Queen's Beasts.

It hadn't occurred to either girl to look for Chrissie Banks in the Palm House. No one in their right mind would put up with the damp heat and choking clouds of steam. Standing beneath a dripping palm, Chrissie knew that she could not join them. Her mum and dad had been chuffed that her friends had organized a party for her, but, watching through the misted glass, she might have been observing from another world.

After Bella and Emily had left, a tiny figure, indeterminate and blurred, slipped from the glasshouse and, phantom-like, passed a discarded envelope, white against the brown of the lawn. She followed a path dappled with shadow. Ahead two figures resolved into focus. The Cat in the Hat and the lady with the gobstopper eyes. Behind them, chimneys reaching to the sky, was the house with no rooms.

Chapter Forty-Six

November 2014

Bella was standing by a window, a scalpel in her hand. 'Hey, Jack, I was just thinking of you. I must have conjured you up! Come and save me from myself!' she cried, arms outstretched.

Leaving the cart by the door he followed her around a partition into a snug corner workspace. Bella pulled up a chair for him while she perched on a high stool at a drawing easel. Behind her was a table laid out with the materials of her trade: prosaic items such as masking tape and a roll of kitchen paper; and more arcane tools – a set of proportional dividers and a binocular microscope and mounted needles, forceps, a petri dish and more scalpels. The last stood in a mug identical to the one he had bought in the Kew Gardens café. Through the window beyond he saw Ferry Lane and the River Thames. He got his bearings.

'I was about to ask what on earth are you doing here?' She began sharpening a pencil with short flicks of the scalpel. Shavings flew into the air to land on a heap of curling wood on the drawing board. She handled the instrument deftly and sharpened the lead to a fine point. 'But I guess the uniform is a giveaway! You didn't say you worked here.' There was a touch of reproach in her tone as if she suspected Jack of refraining from telling her. This was true; at the funeral he had avoided giving away information about himself, intent on gathering it for the case. 'Oh my God! Was it you who found the body in the gallery?' She eyed him over the rapier-sharp pencil.

'No. It was a colleague.' Jack shifted the chair to face the door, although his view of it was blocked by the partition. 'A friend.' Stella hadn't said how finding the body had affected her; she would try to tamp down her feelings. In the last weeks she had found a dead body and her friend had died. A lot of feelings to tamp down.

'I wouldn't have had you down as a cleaner,' Bella reflected.

'What did you have me down as?' Jack asked. Hands clasped between his knees, he wriggled on his seat.

'An actor. No, a scientist. You give the impression of having your mind on brilliant things. Day-to-day stuff is not so much beneath you as beyond you.' She put the tip of the pencil to her lips. 'Goes to show how easy it is to be bound by preconceptions. No wonder Chrissie lied about her background. At that prep school a taxi driver was on the spectrum with a mad axe murderer. In the end none of us measures up.' She did a Lucie May laugh. Shunting the curls of wood into a cupped hand, she scattered them into a dustbin behind Jack. 'I did my first botanical drawing for Chrissie,' she suddenly announced.

'When? I thought you didn't get on at school,' Jack asked.

'Emily had organized for us to meet in Kew Gardens and have tea. We pooled our pocket money. By then we'd left the school. Neither of our parents could afford to keep paying the fees. Ironic when you think about it. Chrissie thought we were posh, but it was her that had the private education and ended up earning the big bucks. Me and Emily scrape our livings! And I lied about my dad too.'

'You said he was a barrister. Was that a lie?' Jack found he rather liked the idea that Bella told lies. Putting Watson the True Host from his mind, he began to enjoy himself.

'Sort of. At the prep school, I didn't tell anyone that he had never lived with my mum. I was illegitimate. I nearly told Chrissie, but I fudged it and said he had left us so we'd had to move. I had never as much as seen him. All I knew was that he wore a wig and sent people to prison.' She gave a husky laugh. 'He probably wasn't impressed by having a daughter; Mum said that he had four already. I pretended that he loved me,' she said. 'Sometimes I still do.'

Jack nodded. He was used to make-believe.

Bella's speech flowed with the ease of one used to telling the story for laughs. 'No prizes for why I was a cow to Chrissie. I was jealous of her for having a dad who lived with her. I made her dad into the perfect dad. Except he wasn't her dad. Although she still had a dad which is more than I...' Her voice trailed off.

From behind the partition, Jack heard the door open and close. Then nothing. He stiffened.

'Is he bothering you, Isabella?' This time Jack didn't meet his eyes.

'He's my friend.' Bella sounded lackadaisical, but Jack sensed her body tense.

'You're so democratic in your relationships.' Watson spoke as if he genuinely cared. His hands were like white fish; his nails were clean and trimmed. Jack knew that if he reached out and brushed the man's skin it would be as cold and unyielding as the marble bust of Joseph Hooker. This man worked with plants. He was used to cutting and splicing, to rendering the whole into parts. He knew what was beneath the skin. He gave names to dead material. He gave plants existence.

'How is the plate coming on?' he enquired smoothly.

'I've added in the fruit as you asked. But since you didn't tell me until I'd nearly finished the plate, I've had issues fitting the fruit into the layout.'

'If it's too much for you, I can ask one of the others.' So kind, so thoughtful. Jack saw the muscle above Bella's cheekbone flick.

'It's not too much.'

'Please could I see what you've done so far?' He did a washing motion with his hands in happy anticipation. Jack kept still.

Watson's request was a preamble to something he had planned. From the set of her shoulders Bella guessed this too. Jack was helpless; if he interfered it would have repercussions for her.

Bella lifted a sheet of paper off the easel and laid it on the table behind her stool. Jack looked at the most beautifully executed drawing. Better even than the one of the *Eucalyptus gunnii* from Tina's bag that Watson himself had done. The lamp-black ink lines were sharp against the cream vellum; different thicknesses in the lines showed dimension. Jack knew from his hours of reading that the intention of a botanical illustration was not to make the plant look 'real', but to aid the work of identification for the botanist. Precise and uncluttered, the drawing displayed the elements of the specimen in logical flow. The leaves had been positioned to show the way they grew on the stem, the patina of the bark was depicted with uneven lines and stippling.

In the centre of the plate was a pencil sketch, but it wasn't, Jack fretted, ready for inspection. The True Host's late addition had given Bella a tricky puzzle because the only space on the plate was too small. One side of the fruit was hard by the length of bark that framed one side of the plate and balanced the stem depicting leaves that reached across the top of the drawing.

However, the objective was about science, not art, and Jack felt triumph for Bella, because for the purposes of a botanist, she had solved the issue. This was short-lived: True Hosts didn't like to be thwarted; their objective was neither science nor art, but death.

He tried to catch Bella's eye and let her know he was there for her. But she was looking at the drawing.

'It's going to be the wrong scale,' Watson said at last.

'It will be the same scale.' Bella was still holding the scalpel.

'This isn't what I envisaged.'

Jack saw the dynamic. At one time most botanists were artists: a necessary skill because out in the field it was the only way to capture the plant. Joseph Hooker, a fine illustrator, had been self-taught. On a scientific voyage in his twenties he had filled notebooks with drawings done exactly as he required. It seemed that Watson wasn't an artist, but as the botanist, he was the boss and Bella must do his bidding.

'Do you know, I wonder if it would be preferable to do it again? A fresh start.' The words of Stella's company strapline. Jack shuddered.

'If that's what you want,' Bella replied, apparently unruffled.

'It's not about what I want. It's what works. We're both of us servants.' He lifted the plate up. It was centimetres from Jack's face. Watson seemed to have forgotten that he was there. But he would be only too aware. Seconds later Jack was proved right,

'What is the opinion of our esteemed botanist?' He was looking at the plate, head cocked to one side as if considering a decision, but he was addressing Jack.

Jack thought fast. Watson's decision was already made, so anything he said would make it worse. True Hosts despised flatterers and didn't suffer contradiction or obstacles. They toyed with their victims. Watson had Jack in his sights. He had been in the sixth car that night when Jennifer Day died. He knew that Jack drove the Dead Late shift on the District line. Watson had only to bide his time.

Showing the right amount of deference, appealing to the man's professionalism, often an Achilles heel, Jack chose his words carefully. 'It is whether this drawing helps you identify the plant. If it doesn't, then it would be advisable to redraw it.' He avoided looking at Bella.

'I will accept it.' Watson handed the plate to Bella.

Bella waited until she heard the door to the Artists' Room close behind Watson. 'Thanks, Jack!' She sounded heartfelt.

'I didn't do anything.'

'You saved me a load of work. As it is I'll make nothing on this job, he's asked for so many revisions. He gives crap briefs, and then changes his mind halfway through. Shaves off my margins.'

'You're paid by the drawing?' Jack was taken aback. 'Aren't you on a salary?'

'Yes, to the first question. The budget is tight. I'm "lucky" because, though you'd never know it, he likes my work, so chooses me over the other artists. I get steady work.' She gesticulated across the room to an empty chair in the other corner. 'My colleague there scratches in the dirt. Shame because he's good, been at it for decades. Mr Fusspants treats him far worse than me. He once made him scrap a plate because they found another specimen in Melbourne and didn't need it. It's because he knows he's dealing with a frustrated botanist – he enjoys torturing him. Demeaning him.'

'That's fair enough, I suppose.' Jack was loath to defend the botanist. 'I mean about finding the plant already existed.'

'Except he knew it all along.'

'Would he waste resources deliberately?' Stupid question. True Hosts were sadists and every act was a rehearsal of murder.

'Who knows? We have to accept it. No such thing as a kill-fee.' Bella jumped off the stool and grabbed Jack's hand. 'I'll treat you to tea in the canteen!'

Jack was surprised to find the bright airy room on the top floor of the Herbarium, with windows on two sides, teeming with staff so early in the morning. Did scientists ever sleep?

'Have this mug. The man it belonged to is dead,' Bella said cheerfully, thrusting a mug decorated with a picture of Kenny from *South Park* – not botanical – into his hand. 'We have our own mugs – a taxonomy of china, if you like! We used to have our own seats; woe betide you if you sat in the Succulent Corner if you were Palms.' Bella was matter-of-fact. 'Artists were nobodies, we had to balance on the door knob. Things have improved. Tea or coffee?'

'Would it be possible to have hot milk?'

If Bella thought this request odd, she gave no sign. She took the mug off him, filled it with milk from a carton on the counter and set the microwave going.

'If Chrissie told me now about that murder in the Marianne North Gallery in the seventies, I'd believe her like a shot. I pity the police trying to find the killer of the bloke your friend found there. Murder is the natural end game for thwarted ambition and hubris. It's only a wonder that it doesn't happen here more often.' Bella hooted with laughter.

She gave Jack his milk and they found seats facing the terrace. It was now properly light, but heavy cloud shrouded the view of the Thames, giving everything a monochrome aspect.

'You mentioned at the funeral that you had seen Tina recently. How come?' He tried to sound casual. Bella was capable of saying it wasn't his business.

'That woman opposite is an expert on angiosperms. Legumes to be precise. That's beans to you and me. She's retiring next week and she'll take her knowledge with her.' Bella settled back in her seat. 'Sorry, what did you say?'

'I wondering how come you saw Tina, given that you'd been out of contact. I no longer see any of my school friends.' This was true.

'She got in touch with me. Out of the blue. And there was Emily. She hadn't mentioned she was asking her and she hadn't told Emily that she was asking me. Control shit – typical of her. I said we shouldn't go because the last time we agreed to meet when we were kids she never turned up.'

'So you were still in touch with Emily?' This struck him as unlikely.

'Yes. We have nothing in common except shit childhoods, but that is enough. We go for walks, cinema and a meal at least once a month.'

'Why did Tina want to see you?' Jack couldn't refer to the sharp, no-messing woman that he had met as 'Chrissie'.

'She told us she had cancer, but she would beat it. She said that if she atoned for her wrongs, gave something back, that would save her. Poor thing was desperate, I suppose. All the same, if I get a terminal illness, I'll fight tooth and nail just like her. Emily's more "so be it". Touch wood, I'm fit as a flea.' She patted the coffee table, making the tea slop over her cup.

'Did Tina say what she had to atone for?' This wasn't the

answer Jack had expected – he didn't have the lawyer down as superstitious.

'She said something about being sorry for running off one time when we were kids. Hardly a sin! She said she ended up in the North Gallery. We now think that was when she saw the murder Emily told us about at Chrissie's funeral. She had been hiding in a cupboard in the gallery and saw some character in a book. I thought at the time that she was probably in shock, but Chrissie was too level-headed for that: the diagnosis spurred her to action.' Bella took a Bourbon Cream from a plate on the table and bit into it.

'What was the character?'

'The cat from *The Cat in the Hat*.' Bella hooted again, then became serious. 'When we were at school she told us that it was her favourite book. I didn't believe her. Now I think that at least wasn't a lie. Poor Chrissie, what a bitch I was!'

Jack found himself feeling sorry for the little Christina Banks. Bella wouldn't have changed over the years; she would have been as implacable then as she was now. Yet he'd found that he liked her.

'She admitted that she'd stolen this love charm off the Watsons. It had a picture inside that she said was her mum and dad. I was jealous. I had no pictures of my parents kissing. My dad tried to pretend his affair with Mum never happened. Such a picture would have been high on the yuck scale, but it did make Chrissie's parents seem glamorous. And it was incontrovertible truth. Emily was convinced. I wasn't because Chrissie was like me, I too lied about my home life.'

Jack had several photos of his mum and dad kissing on their wedding day. He couldn't remember seeing them kiss in real life. Hurriedly, he blocked the idea and tuned back to Bella.

'…I tried to make up for it with Chrissie's birthday card. But she never turned up.'

'Did you worry that something had happened to her?' Jack asked.

'We presumed she had forgotten. I wonder now if she bottled out. I would if I was her. Shame – it was a rather good drawing!' She squeezed Jack's knee. 'You can see I'm the modest sort!'

Jack retrieved his cart from the Artists' Room. He would be late reporting in to the Estates Office although he had completed the job within the allotted time. In the corridor, he turned back to Bella, standing by the Artists' Room door. 'Take care, Bella. Watch your step with George Watson.'

'Blimey, Jack, I can handle George. He's a sweetie-pops!' Another Lucie May laugh.

Jack couldn't explain without telling her everything, that a 'sweetie-pops' was far from what Watson was. Nor could he explain about True Hosts. He repeated lamely, 'Just take care.'

'Honestly, George is harmless.' Bella closed the door.

Chapter Forty-Seven

November 2014

Stella took some time to understand how the slim red-backed volumes were set out. At first she had assumed she had the wrong book, but there were no others. A typical frustration for a detective was a missing or misfiled record. She had been looking in the wrong 'ward'. She found Priory Road. To her dismay the names of occupants registered to vote were listed by house number, sometimes with as many as eight in one dwelling. She didn't know the number of Kew Villa. Then the words 'Kew Villa' leapt off the page. She was in business.

Stella had come to Richmond Library intending to establish who had lived in the large house by the pond when Terry had staked it out in 2010, and who was there in the seventies when Lucie May believed Terry had been lied to by a girl of a similar age to herself. A detective, Terry used to say, was like an electrician: *Isolate the issue by testing all other scenarios one by one.* It was a dictum that Stella followed when cleaning, stain by stain.

There were only two names registered at Kew Villa in 2010. Given the size of the house, eight occupants would have been a breeze. George and Rosamond Watson. Stella noted the names in her Filofax. His name struck a chord. She didn't dwell on this. Terry had stressed it was important to avoid being bogged down with hints and hunches.

Everything rises to the surface in time.

She drew a grid with 'Year' running horizontally and 'Name' at the side. Starting with the present, she listed the residents, trawling back through the decades, volume by volume.

Forty minutes later she reached 1976. George and Rosamond Watson had been there continuously to 2013, the publication date of the last electoral roll.

If the Watsons had had children they had either moved away before they were old enough to register to vote or hadn't registered. She shouldn't rule out children; after all, her name wouldn't appear with Terry's under Rose Gardens North. His would be the only name listed, giving the impression that he had no children, when he had been a father of two. She recalled his advice: *Set a framework of investigation and widen the boundaries only if necessary. Keep the task manageable.*

Flicking back in her notes she found why the name was familiar. A George Watson had signed the drawing in the Boots bag that Tina had given her. The Watsons had lived there for over forty years.

Riddled with unknowns and assumptions, the task was barely manageable. Terry may – or may not – have made an inquiry at Kew Villa in 1976. The crime – if there even had been a crime – could have been any time before. Like a headstone, the electoral roll offered the bones of a story. Despite Terry's advice, Stella ventured further back in time. In 1962 one James Hailes appeared alongside the Watsons. He was still there in 1958 which she decided was her end point. In 1961 George Watson disappeared and Rosamond Hailes replaced Rosamond Watson. Another name joined them in 1962. Harold Hailes. Since she was going back in time Stella had to stop and take stock of the permutations. She entered them on her grid. First assumption: the house had belonged to Harold Hailes. The second was that James and Rosamond were his son and daughter. Third, Rosamond married

George and became Rosamond Watson. In 1962 Harold left the house, perhaps he had died. Perhaps the Watsons had bought James Hailes's share. He too had left. She had no evidence for this, just a dance of names in small print in fusty-smelling books. She would go with the scenario until she came up with evidence to the contrary. This was thinking as Terry had taught her. Stella glanced up almost expecting him to be there.

She left the library and took the District line to Hammersmith station.

The Hammersmith Archives were housed in the central library on Shepherd's Bush Road opposite the police station where Terry Darnell had spent much of his working life. As a girl, Stella had sat in the lobby of the station waiting for him, her lips working silently as she read the names of fallen officers carved in plaques above reception. She had clutched a pen and paper given to her by an officer at the desk, obediently following the instruction, 'Do Daddy a picture.' She had spent more time there than with Terry.

Stella found herself a seat at a long table in the centre of the archives, a hushed room with stained-glass windows at each end.

She spread out Jack's newspaper cuttings before her. She had supposed that he had got them from Lucie but, as she looked at them again, realized that he hadn't actually said so. They had agreed she would start by finding out which house in Rose Gardens fitted the location of the hole in the Great West Road in which the murdered man had been found in June 1976. She referred to this incident in her Filofax as Case Two. It would be easy to confuse her research with the Kew Villa Case – Case One.

The archivist brought her the only Ordnance Survey maps on file for that period: five large sheets spanning 1955 to 1957. The last map showed the area when the six-lane carriageway had been completed. Usefully, while the other maps were paper, this map was transposed on to plastic film. By laying it over the map for 1956, Stella had a double image that showed which houses had been demolished and where they had been located. She snapped this with her camera app. As Jack had said, Terry's street used to continue around a corner with twenty houses either side. This was no surprise to her: the end house of the existing cul-de-sac had a sheer wall as if smoothed with a palette knife. But she had imagined that Rose Gardens, like the adjacent Black Lion Lane, had run down to the river. Instead it had been L-shaped.

Stella lived at thirty-one. All the numbers in her cul-de-sac were odd with thirty-three on one end and twenty-seven at the other. Numbers 23 and 25 had been knocked down. In the 1950s, around the corner on the nearside of the street, the houses had numbered twenty-one to one. All now demolished. The crater in the Great West Road had appeared in the eastbound left lane where the houses had stood.

Stella examined a photograph of the hole that Lucie had given Jack. In the distance, she made out houses on the south side of the Great West Road. According to her map, they were the even numbers in Rose Gardens. She had a client at number 22 Rose Gardens: now a beleaguered terrace with traffic streaming by just feet from the front doors.

She snapped a picture of the photograph and enlarged it on her phone screen. Through the pixels, she deciphered two house numbers, 22 and 20, on the houses beyond the crater. Placing her pen on the map overlaid with the old map, one end by the two houses, Stella traced a line, following the angle of the camera lens, to the north side, where she lived. She sighed with satisfaction; this was why she liked this work. The crater had opened up where number 25 Rose Gardens used to be.

Consulting the electoral roll, a task at which she was now adept, Stella found that in 1954 and 1955, 25 Rose Gardens had had a sole occupant: a Mrs Ivy Collins. She trawled back in the volumes as far as 1939 but found no Mr Collins. Perhaps he had been killed at the start of the Second World War which had started that year or Mr Collins had never existed and Ivy styled herself 'Mrs' for respectability. Number 25 had no entry in 1956, presumably because it had been demolished around then. By 1960 the street had two suffixes, 'North' and 'South'.

The archivist found her a folder of articles and photographs specific to Rose Gardens. On the top were the articles from the seventies that Jack had given her covering the Ramsay robbery in the fifties and the body unearthed in the crater in 1976 when tarmac had melted.

The file included black-and-white prints of Rose Gardens before the A4 was extended. Writing on the back said the photos were donated in 1954 by William Britton, a local amateur photographer. One was shot looking towards the junction with St Peter's Square. Counting along Stella made out Terry's house. Opposite, where there were now bushes and a scrap of grass, was a wire fence bounding back gardens in Black Lion Lane. A man with a dog about the size of Stanley was standing beside a curved iron lamp-post that looked Victorian. The position of the post was where the faulty lamp was now and this helped Stella get her bearings.

Two doors down from Terry's, closer to the camera, a boy aged about fourteen was sitting on the wall. He was outside number 25, Ivy Collins's house – now an end of terrace – grinning at the photographer. Flipping the picture over, she found a date stamp: March 1954. Given his confident – cheeky – pose, the chances were that the boy had lived there. It was likely he was Ivy Collins's son. She could see from the photo that he was too young to vote.

The article about the robbery said the burglars were likely to be boys thin enough to have climbed through a narrow window at the back of the Ramsays' house. Stella knew the window from when she had cleaned for Mrs Ramsay; there was no way an adult could get through, unless they were very small in stature. Could this boy have been the robber? Not a link possible to make in the 1950s because the man's body with the signet ring was not found until 1976. By then Ivy Collins and her son would have been rehoused. The police would have done house-to-house inquiries after the man's body was found in 1976 – with fewer houses in Rose Gardens and many of the occupants who had lived there in the fifties having died or moved on. Still, it was inconceivable that detectives wouldn't have worked out that Ivy Collins had a son who was a prime candidate for the crime. Perhaps they had and the boy had an alibi – or wasn't even living – or they hadn't been able to trace him. Terry had probably known. She could never ask him.

Stella photographed the picture of the boy and tried enlarging his image on her phone, but the result was too grainy to do more than confirm he was smiling.

Stella got out her phone. No one had texted. She had hoped for one from Tina.

Let's do coffee, I need decent human interaction!

An idea occurred and before she could change her mind, Stella texted Lucie May. The reporter had access to resources and possessed investigative skills that Stella – and Jack – had yet to hone. Stella would use them. She was learning that detectives couldn't work alone. Terry had trusted May; she would trust her too. Armed with Ivy Collins, the name of the woman who had lived in the 'murder house' in Rose Gardens with her son in the fifties, and having established the names of all those who had lived in Kew Villa, Stella called it a good morning's work.

It was raining when she stepped out on to Shepherd's Bush Road. Head down, hood up, she ran towards the Metropolitan Underground station.

'Want a lift?'

Her hood didn't move when she turned her head, blocking her view. She wrenched it back and was hit in the face by a squall of rain.

A taxi was crawling along the nearside kerb and through the open window the driver was gesticulating at her. It was Tina's dad. She couldn't say no without sounding rude, but she didn't want to talk about Tina. She splashed across the pavement to the kerb.

Cliff Banks was wearing a green polo shirt, the same colour as the Clean Slate uniform. He was leaning across the front luggage space grinning. 'Climb in, Stell. It's cats and dogs, I'll take you to wherever you're going.'

'I can get a train.'

'You'll be soaked before you reach the Broadway. Chrissie wouldn't forgive me for passing by. Hop in, love.' Stella heard the click of the door locks being released and admitted that she was grateful to accept.

As soon as she settled in the back, she felt awkward. On the rare occasions that she took a taxi, she avoided small talk with the drivers. It was hard with Cliff Banks; his 'talk' would be far from small. Thinking where she had just been, Stella said the first thing that came into her head, 'I heard that Tina had drawing lessons when she was young.'

She thought that Cliff Banks hadn't heard, but then saw that he was looking at her in the rear-view mirror.

'That's going back.' He did a U-turn and headed up Shepherd's Bush Road. 'It was with an old mate of mine, George Watson. Mucked about together as boys. He only goes and marries some heiress. He finds himself living in a flippin' mansion by Kew Pond and drawing flowers for a living!' Stella couldn't decide if he was being sarcastic or was impressed. *Kew Villa*. Tina had had drawing lessons with George Watson. Were they the people that Tina had told her friends Bella and Emily were her parents? An odd thing to lie about. But Tina having had drawing lessons was odd. She had been a woman of surprises. Foxtrotting being one. Dying another.

'Drawing flowers is a far cry from being a solicitor.' Stella had decided that Jack had got it wrong about Tina's drawing lessons. It didn't fit with Tina. It seemed that she hadn't known Tina at all.

'I wanted her to mix with different people. They didn't have kids so it was nice all round. Chrissie did some lovely pictures. Rosalind Watson baked cakes – she used to give Chrissie her tea,' he said, as if this was important.

'Rosamond.' Her notes fresh in her mind, Stella coughed to disguise the correction. Looking out of the window as they swung on to Shepherd's Bush Green she met the gaze of an elderly man waiting on the kerb. He was wet through, but seemed not to care. His hands plunged in the pockets of his sodden windcheater, he stared at her without expression. *Harry Roberts.* The man from Stella's childhood nightmares. She turned in her seat, but rain was streaming down the glass and the man was a ghost shape and then was gone. It wouldn't be Roberts; she doubted he was allowed to set foot in the borough where he had killed the policemen. Banks was talking:

'So Chrissie talked to you about her lessons?' He was smiling in the mirror.

'No. I found out from the funeral.' This was true. There was nothing wrong with Tina's friends looking back on her life, but Stella decided not to mention Jack's conversation with the women called Bella and Emily. Luckily Banks chose to change the subject. He asked her if she would continue cleaning the flat until it was sold and she agreed that she would.

'I'll let you know a good time to go,' he said.

When they got to the Clean Slate office at Shepherd's Bush Green, Cliff Banks refused payment. 'Chrissie'd have conniptions if I charged you! She's watching over us and is grateful you're humouring her old dad. It wasn't just luck that I was passing.'

Stella was sad. How could he know that Tina was watching? As for 'old', Cliff Banks didn't look old. He was one of those men who could be anything between fifty and seventy. His hair was short with a flick at the front; he was natty in the polo shirt, he was good-looking and, despite the smoking, gave off an impression of vigour and health. She remembered the photograph in Tina's flat and how she had mistaken Banks for a fifties matinee idol. With a shock, Stella acknowledged that her own dad hadn't looked as fit as this since she was in her teens. Terry had died before his time. She could have driven with him in his blue Toyota Yaris chatting as she had with Cliff Banks in his taxi. Tina had still had a dad. *'Tina has died.'*

She was passing the mini-mart when Cliff Banks called her back. 'Take this for your books.'

It was a blank taxi receipt. Before she could protest that she wouldn't claim for a trip that she hadn't paid for, the taxi had joined the stream of traffic heading towards Holland Park and the Westway. She pocketed the slip of paper.

Banks had known to bring her to Shepherd's Bush Green although she hadn't told him where she was going. Terry used to second-guess her. He had once saved her from walking in front of a lorry. Berating herself for getting like Jack, Stella stomped up the stairs to the office.

Chapter Forty-Eight

October 1976

Bella hopped about on the pavement impatiently. It was bang on half past three. Emily was due to call. Their plan was going wrong because there was a man in the telephone box. She had never seen anyone in there before and she was cross. It was unreasonable to be cross – she could hear Emily herself telling her – it was a public call box so anyone could use it. But the man wasn't talking on the phone. He was holding the receiver as if he didn't know how to work it. All the time he was doing that Emily would be calling and getting the engaged signal. Soon Emily's mum would wake up and catch her on the phone. Bella didn't want Emily to think that she had forgotten their agreement. When Emily didn't come to school she was to ring Bella at the telephone box outside Kew Gardens – Bella was there to draw flowers – and Bella would tell her what she had missed at school.

Bella could bear it no longer. She pulled on the heavy door with all her might and heaved it open. She leant against it to stop it closing again.

'There are people waiting. If you're not going to make a phone call, please could you get out of the way so that others can?'

She loosely echoed the words a woman had once said to her when she had been waiting in the box for Emily to call.

The man turned around.

'Oh!' Bella stepped back. She had seen him before. It was Chrissie's dad. Or the man Bella had decided was her dad because he had come out of the big house by the pond when she had watched it after school, waiting for Chrissie to come home. The man that Bella didn't believe was her dad. Memories of the hot summer months earlier flooded back. 'How's Chrissie?' she spluttered.

'Who?'

'Chrissie? Your daughter.' The sense of triumph that she would have experienced months before was muted now that she and Emily didn't see Chrissie. She had disappeared from their lives.

The man towered over her. Although the sun had gone in, he had clip-on sunshades over his glasses so she couldn't see him properly. He looked like a giant insect.

'She's not my...' He looked about him as if checking that they were alone. Bella wasn't supposed to talk to strangers, teachers were always saying so, but – cross that this stranger was in the telephone box – she had forgotten. She felt an ice cube of fear slide down her back. 'She's fine,' he said.

The telephone in the call box began to ring.

Bella was frozen to the spot; the weight of the closing door dug into her shoulder. She watched as if tied up as the man leant back into the box and lifted the receiver.

'Hello,' he said. 'Yes, I think she is.' He looked at Bella. She could just see his eyes out of the side of the sunshades. 'A girl on the line for you, *Bella*.' He gave a funny smile. One of his teeth looked like a gravestone, grey and crooked. He moved so that Bella could come into the box with him. She remained on the pavement. He held the receiver out to her, but the metal cord didn't stretch beyond the box. 'You will have to come here.' His voice grated.

Quickly Bella ducked under his arm. She felt a nudge in her back and saw that it was the closing door. The man had left the telephone box.

304

The cubicle smelled of tomato sauce. Bella's throat constricted with revulsion.

'Who was that?' Emily's voice sounded as if she was small and far away.

'You'll never guess!' Bella peered through one of the grimy windows in the box. Beyond the sweep of pavement were the wrought-iron gates to Kew Gardens. The man had gone. 'It was Chrissie's dad! Except I think I was right and—' She stopped. 'Ems, are you OK?'

'My mum's done it again.' Emily spoke in a monotone.

'Done what?' Bella knew what Emily was going to say. 'Is she... Is she—'

'Dead. I don't know, I'm at the hospital.'

'Charing Cross?'

'Yes.'

'I'm coming.' Bella slammed down the phone and pushed out of the acrid-smelling cubicle. She had come to Kew Gardens after school to draw flowers. Now she would go to the hospital instead. She wouldn't tell her mum where she had really been; her mum would say it was none of her business. Bella would lie to her.

Chapter Forty-Nine

November 2014

Stella reached around in her seat and gave Stanley a rice bone. Not normally advisable because he could turn nasty to protect his 'kill'. If she needed him to move, he would refuse until he had finished the bone. But this afternoon she was going nowhere and it was vital to keep him occupied.

Given a choice, Stella wouldn't have brought Stanley, but Jackie had gone to see her son Nick dancing in a matinee in the West End and Beverly had enough on her plate managing the office single-handed without dog-sitting.

She was on the second stage of her legwork, working on Case One. Ensconced in the van, she laid her Filofax on the passenger seat next to her, hoping that, in her black suit, she might be mistaken for an estate agent, not that they generally drove white vans. She also hoped that a woman sitting for a long period in a parked vehicle might be less conspicuous than a man. Both hopes were slim.

She reviewed what they had. Potentially two cases. Tina's bizarre request to 'catch a murderer' and Terry's comment to Lucie that he had 'let someone get away with murder'. Jack had related his conversation at the funeral with Tina's childhood friends.

At the time of the drought, Tina had confided to the one called Emily that she had seen a murder. Both women told Jack that Tina often told lies. So, like the boy crying wolf, Tina hadn't been believed. But for the locket, Stella would have objected that Tina wasn't a liar. She still harboured doubt. Tina must have had a reason for claiming that the locket wasn't hers. Case One was flimsy but Stella owed it to her friend to follow up on her deathbed request.

For these cases all they had to go on was a bag of strangely assorted items: a jumbled text, images of Terry on Street View and a bundle of receipts. Many detectives worked with less.

She was parked up outside Kew Villa, overlooking Kew Pond, in the same space where Terry had been four years earlier. The police set store by the re-enactment of crimes, hoping to jog memories of witnesses and of those who hadn't realized that they were witnesses. Stella was doing this in reverse. She was reconstructing the detection process hoping to identify the crime. Stella was on a stakeout.

She took a sip of tea from Terry's flask and placed the cup on the dashboard. Steam clouded the windscreen, blurring her view. She wiped the glass with a gloved hand. She had put the heater on full blast coming from Shepherd's Bush to build up a store for when the engine was off. This had abated and the van was like an ice box. Terry had been here on a summer's day.

She was hungry. She'd planned to hold off having the pork pies that she'd bought from the Tesco Express outside Kew station – faithful to Terry's MO – until at least an hour into the stakeout. But with Stanley crunching on his bone behind her, she couldn't wait.

Biting into the first pie, she washed it down with tea and scanned the house. The lace curtains in the downstairs windows hadn't as much as twitched and no one had come out or gone in. She opened the copy of the *Daily Mirror* that, like Terry, she had got from the newsagent's in Kew Gardens station and spread it across the steering wheel. Her eye was caught by a headline: *Police Killer Free*. She rattled the paper and shifted in her seat. Harry Roberts was out of prison. The article said that he was being closely monitored. A police chief described it as 'sickening'. She checked her phone to see if Cashman had been in touch. She hadn't seen him for a couple of days, he had been unable to leave work. No one had texted. She blinked from her mind the image of the blank-eyed man she had seen on the kerb in Shepherd's Bush, telling herself that he had not been Roberts.

With a start she looked up. The paper was a prop; she shouldn't actually be reading it. She could see how detectives lost concentration at crucial moments. The lace curtains hadn't moved. If she was being watched she had better look like she was outside for a reason. She flipped to the page in her Filofax on which she had written Tina's text.

Please never shed fruit was sleet, how dear hehe No Kesto Mar.

She had told Jack that Tina never did crosswords, but she didn't actually know that. It could be an anagram. She wrote down the individual letters in the sentence in her Filofax in no particular order, breaking up the twelve existing words (not that hehe, kesto or mar were words) to start the process. There were 50 letters. She began a list of new words – sheet, stone, devil, dead – there were many possibilities. Too many. Tina wouldn't have made it this hard. And while she was trying to work it out, she wasn't watching the house.

The tea was already lukewarm; Terry's flask was less than effective. Still no movement in any of the windows. Catching the last crumbs of the pie, munching, Stella remembered Cliff Banks's request for her to continue cleaning the flat. She was pleased: it was something concrete that she could do for Tina. Well, not for her since she was dead... She forced herself to concentrate. She hadn't considered how boring a stakeout was. Something needed to happen soon to keep her alert.

Something did.

The front door opened and a woman came out. Stella angled herself so that she could watch in the wing mirror. The woman was black and wore red-framed spectacles that matched a red woolly coat. She was in her forties, so too young to be Rosamond Watson, and was lugging a gym bag. Stella jerked the flask cup and splashed tea on the newspaper. Harry Roberts's face was obliterated in a pool of tea. Stanley barked, straining on his car belt in search of the enemy.

It was Donette, one of the first cleaners that Stella had employed and a friend from school. She was a senior operative at Clean Slate. She wasn't carrying a gym bag; Stella didn't need to be a detective to spot the Clean Slate logo on the green and blue equipment bag. Donette did specialist cleaning in industrial areas and schools. She had qualified in rock climbing and abseiling specifically to scale high walls and ceilings and to crawl along gantries and beams of commercial buildings. What was she doing on a domestic job in Kew? Stella squirmed down in her seat, but the steering wheel was in the way so she couldn't get below the line of the dashboard. If Donette saw her, she had no good explanation for being parked in her van drinking tea and eating a pork pie on a weekday afternoon.

Donette hurried past without noticing Stella. A few moments later, twisting around, Stella saw a Clean Slate van pull out of a space along Priory Road and drive off. She slumped in her seat. Stanley resumed his bone.

Gathering herself, Stella reached to her phone on the dashboard and dialled the office.

'Clean Slate for the freshest of fresh starts, Beverly here on the line especially for you!' chirruped the voice at the other end of the phone.

Stella grimaced. Beverly's recent customer-service training course had encouraged her to express her true self so that customers were encouraged by speaking to a real person. Stella barely recognized her.

'It's Stella.'

'How funny that it's you!' Beverly laughed gaily. 'What service can I interest you in? We do a winter warmer package that—'

Stella contemplated the damp newspaper with the stained photograph of Harry Roberts. 'Bev, is Jackie back?'

'No. I'm still in charge. Do you want your messages?' Beverly was on top form, Stella had to give her that. She rarely passed on messages.

'Not now, thanks.' Stella decided to risk letting Beverly loose in the database. Suzie would have forty fits because the last time Beverly had gone into it, she had inadvertently deleted half the records. Not a disaster as Suzie kept a backup, but Beverly was banned from it after that. Suzie was still in Sydney (an Instagram of her mum in Dale's phantom-grey Holden Cascada convertible on the Harbour Bridge in Ray-Bans and a headscarf had pinged in that morning. Had she not grown used to the daily photographs of her mum in a variety of guises, Stella wouldn't have recognized her. 'Revisiting my misspent youth!' said the caption). At this moment Suzie was presumably asleep so need never know about Beverly's trespass.

'I want you to look up a client.'

'But I'm not—' Beverly was incredulous.

Stella interrupted her with the password.

There was a tapping sound down the phone. 'I'm in!' Beverly cried. 'What's the name?'

Stella glanced down at her Filofax. 'Watson, Rosamond.' It was usually the woman in a household who hired Clean Slate.

'Watson, Rosamond.' Beverly echoed and Stella heard a laborious pecking. 'Whoops!'

'What?' Stella stopped herself yelling.

'I pressed a button and everything went blank. It's all back now.' Beverly was calm. 'Here we are.' Her breathing was laboured with concentration; Stella pictured her, tongue between her teeth, moving the mouse on the mat with exaggerated care. 'The operative is Hannah, that new girl.'

'Woman,' Stella absently corrected her.

'Ooh, I forgot: that was one of the messages. Hannah rang in sick this morning. Donette was in the office, so Jackie asked if she would take it to "to stop Stella doing it". I wasn't meant to say that.'

'And the client?' she reminded Beverly.

'Mrs Rosamond Watson. No key. Light clean. Weekly. Downstairs only.'

Stella looked at the house. There were five floors. Even assuming an extension, Clean Slate was only covering about 20 per cent of the property. 'No key' meant that there would be someone at home to admit the operative. Mrs Watson presumably. A thought occurred. 'When was the contract signed?'

'The thirteenth of August 2010.'

The day after her birthday and just after Terry had done his stakeout. She felt the back of her head tighten as the notion presented itself that Terry had recommended Clean Slate to the owners as a means of getting inside the house. But if he had, he would have asked her to help him gain entry. And anyway, whatever her mum said, Terry wouldn't have compromised her business for his case.

'How did Mrs Watson hear about us? Look at the last box on the right-hand side of the screen.'

Beverly hummed a snatch of Daft Punk's 'Get Lucky'. At last she exclaimed, 'Ah, *right*-hand side, OK. *Saw. Fan. In. Street,*' she haltingly read. 'Fancy Clean Slate having fans!'

'It must be a typo.' Behind her, Stanley was washing himself, his tongue clicking and slapping. 'It should be "van".' People often called them having spotted the van parked in the street. It was why she had kept her own van plain white. She didn't want to be noticed.

'Shall I correct it?' Beverly asked.

'*No!* . . . No, thanks. My mum will do it.' Then, struck by an idea: 'Please could you do a search on Priory Road? See if we have other clients in this – er – in that street?'

Beverly named two addresses in the road. One was only three doors down from Kew Villa. Wendy had been the operative for all three jobs and had come off when Stella promoted her to manage the Kew Gardens account. Hannah had taken over.

She talked Beverly through shutting down the database, thanked her and rang off.

Stella stole a glance up at the house. At any time while she was on the phone, Mrs Watson might have looked out and seen her van. Stella felt a wave of certainty: Terry *had* suspected the Watsons of a crime. He was a good detective, but, as Jack often said, to successfully stalk your prey, they must be oblivious even to the possibility that they were being tailed. If they had done a crime they would be more alert than the average citizen. Someone in Kew Villa had seen Terry's Toyota parked where her own van was now. Stella had no proof of this, but was positive that Terry watching the house and Clean Slate getting a contract to clean there days later were connected. The first the cause, the second the effect.

She craned around in the seat. Stanley was engaged in a grooming session, nibbling at the end of a front paw, toe by toe.

'Wait there,' she commanded superfluously. Stuffing her Filofax in her rucksack, she hauled it from the footwell and got out of the van.

Stanley looked up, a damp paw raised.

'I won't be long,' Stella reassured him, unsure if this was true.

She opened one of the gates. It was rusty and could do with a coat of paint, but the hinges were oiled. She counted her paces to the front door – eleven – alert for every detail, however apparently irrelevant.

She lifted the knocker, also flecked with peeling paint, and knocked twice.

A minute went by. Ten more seconds. *No key.* There must be someone there. No one had left the house since Donette. Not true: there might be a back entrance.

... nine, ten. Another ten seconds. She was turning to go when the door opened and a man peered out. There was no sense of motion in his pose and Stella got the wild sense that he had been on the other side of the door all the time. He looked faintly familiar, but she couldn't think why. But she met many people in the course of her work: lots of people in West London looked familiar.

'Can I help you?' He addressed her with unsmiling eyes.

'I do hope so.' Jack had once said that if you didn't have a plan then the best thing to do was to open your mouth and start speaking. Stella had never understood this tactic. She had always made sure that she did have a plan. Until now. She opened her mouth and words came out. 'I'm from Clean Slate, the cleaning company. One of our operatives has completed a session here. As you know from the contract, we do ask if periodically a senior member of staff can visit to check on the quality of the work. To ensure it's up to standard. Would you be Mr George Watson?'

He blinked rapidly. 'Yes, but my wife deals with the cleaning.'

'Yes, Rosamond Watson,' Stella said as if he had more than one wife. Of course he might. Was bigamy the crime Terry had suspected? Her thoughts were racing. 'I wonder, could I speak with Mrs Watson a moment please?'

'No!' He retreated into the gloom of the hallway. 'She's just popped out.'

Stella had been outside the house for nearly two hours; she must have arrived moments after Donette. She wasn't practised at keeping watch on properties, but wouldn't have missed anyone 'popping out' of Kew Villa. She was convinced Watson was lying. His wife was there, but he wouldn't admit it.

'Would it be possible, as I'm here, to do a check?' She moved towards the hall. 'On the cleaning.'

She could tell that Watson was casting about for a reason to refuse, but evidently he couldn't think of one because he said, 'I suppose so.'

'Where shall we start?' Stella flourished her Filofax and clicked on her biro. Ostentatiously she ran a finger down the side of a grandfather clock by the door. On her pad, she wrote 'RW popped out', for good measure adding: 'No dust'.

She did the same finger-check on the banister. A woman's coat was slung over the newel post; she didn't think it appropriate to touch it. But her powerful sense of smell told her that it reeked of a mix of patchouli oil and camphor. Mrs Watson – like Lucie May who also wore patchouli – must be stuck in the seventies.

'Are you happy with this room?' Reverting to her 'day job',

Stella noted vacuum tracks on the carpet, no rucks in the rug and a whiff of polish. It was unnecessary to monitor Donette's work: it was flawless.

Her question seemed to confuse George Watson because he blinked again, his eyes staying shut for at least two seconds at a time. He stared about him as if he didn't know where he was. 'Really you need to ask my wife.'

'I can come back,' Stella offered without enthusiasm.

'You're here now.' He led the way down a passage, touching the walls to steady himself. Stella put him in his early seventies, but frail with it. He would have been in his thirties in 1976 and presumably capable of anything.

The sink gleamed; the taps were old, but Donette had encouraged a shine. The wooden table had been scrubbed: there were patches of damp where it was still drying. There was not a speck on the floor. Despite this, Stella detected a tired air, as if the room wasn't much used.

'How did you know my name?' The man was leaning on the back of a chair as if it was an effort to stand up.

'It's on our database.' As she spoke, Stella realized this wasn't true. The only contact was Rosamond Watson. She knew his name because she had seen it in the electoral roll and on Tina's drawing. She knew his father-in-law and brother-in-law's names too. With a jolt Stella remembered where she had seen Mr Watson. He had been at Tina's funeral.

'My wife took out the contract; I had nothing to do with it. My name *shouldn't* be on your database.' He seemed disproportionally annoyed.

Stella was horrified. Watson might be frail, but his mind was as sharp as a pin. Again she let her mouth do the talking, 'Your wife probably told our operative your name. Having a rounded picture of our clients helps us do a good job.' She held her bright smile, cringing inwardly at the ghastly customer services spiel. 'If your wife is away – or out – you are our contact. Our records are confidential.'

'My wife is always here...' He subsided into silence.

Vaguely aware of a bell ringing in the distance, Stella did a circuit of the kitchen, taking in empty glass jars on a shelf labelled 'Flour', 'Sugar', 'Baking Powder', and a tin of chocolate powder. Beside the jar for flour was a plastic pot of hundreds and thousands. If the elusive Mrs Watson planned to make a cake, she had run out of core ingredients. Perhaps this was what she had 'popped out' to get. *Chocolate cake coated with hundreds and thousands.* She wrote the words down on the pad and quickly tilted the page to avoid Watson seeing it.

'If you're happy with this—' She turned around. Mr Watson wasn't there.

Quickly, although she had a legitimate excuse, Stella opened the fridge. The first thing she saw was a shepherd's pie, a ready meal made by the same company that Dariusz Adomek sold in the mini-mart. There was a half-used carton of milk in the door. She hoped that Rosamond Watson had gone shopping because they had little to eat.

Her eye caught something on the kitchen table. It was a slip of card. Confirming that she was still alone, Stella snatched it up. Her heart crashed in her chest. Looking at clients' belongings was not part of the job. The card was bent and scuffed, suggesting that it had been on the floor. Donette would have found it when she was cleaning and left it out for the Watsons. Operatives did not throw away any papers found on the floor or behind furniture. Dirty tread marks and creases made the card hard to read, but she made out that it was an Air India boarding pass. Departure date: 22nd October 2014. Madras to London. Seat number A22. Economy class. The name was 'J. H. Hailes'. Stella caught a faint odour of sweat, like tomato sauce. She raised the pass to her nose, but it didn't come from there.

'I'll have that.' Watson reached around her and took the card.

'We found it on the floor.' Stella felt herself redden. He had seen that she was looking at it. Her thoughts tumbled over themselves. Donette might not have put the card on the table. His wife might have left it there. Watson might know that.

'It blew in from the street.' Watson stuffed the pass into the pocket of his cardigan. The sharp tang of sweat came from him. Her face prickling with the shame of being caught red-handed with the boarding pass, Stella distantly perceived that his agitation seemed more than simply resentment at her intrusion.

She had the eerie sensation of déjà vu. It was like Tina and the locket. But in an office anyone could have dropped the locket, although since it was in the Boots bag Tina had left her it must be connected to her. It was possible that the pass had come from outside as Watson said. Yet Stella didn't believe him. It wasn't unusual for Clean Slate staff to encounter erratic behaviour in clients; they were trained to take it in their stride: *No judgement, keep cleaning*. She said, 'If you're happy with the kitchen then we'll move on so that I can leave you in peace.' She made a mental note *not* to cold call ordinary clients for a spot check; annoying them could undo the good work of the operative.

George Watson was no ordinary client. Terry had staked out his house for several days. A darker suspicion was forming. Unable to shed light on it she let Watson take her through to what he referred to as the drawing room. At the door, he paused to let her go first, less from politeness, Stella guessed, than to keep her in his sight.

Here too Donette had done a top-level job. Privately Stella appreciated the beeswax-polished furniture and forensically clean carpet. Maintaining her charade, she confirmed the sheen on a coffee table beside a plush sofa.

'It seems fine to me, but of course it's not me that matters.' She heard the false ring in her voice; she wasn't used to talking to a client with no interest in Clean Slate's work. Specifically she wasn't used to being a detective posing as a cleaner.

A painting hung over the mantelpiece. It was of a tree on a mountainside. The sky was turquoise with white clouds. The impression was of greens, blues and grey. All except for the tree which bloomed with vivid orange flowers. Stella wasn't so observant that she had absorbed such detail in seconds. She had seen it before. Tina had the painting in her flat. And it was in the Marianne North Gallery.

'Lovely picture.' Stella doubted that she was convincing him that she was sincere any more than she was herself. Although as she spoke, she admitted to herself that she did quite like it.

'Marianne North was a brilliant artist.' Watson was transformed. His agitation went and his eyes – blank and dull – became bright and alive. 'That's the Australian fire tree. Marianne travelled to the Antipodes; she put up with extreme discomfort to capture species now extinct. Thankfully the fire tree isn't extinct. Marianne has left us with an invaluable record of flora in the nineteenth century. Many of her paintings depict vanished landscapes. Her gallery is a shrine—' He appeared unstoppable.

'A man was murdered there recently.' Stella was horrified. She had smashed into Watson's rapturous musings about the artist with talk of a dead man. Her job – as a detective or a cleaner – was to listen.

As if hit by an electric shock, Watson returned to his previous self with a jerk. He fixed her with a lifeless stare. 'I know nothing about that. It's Marianne's work that counts.' He was by the hall door now. 'Finished?'

'Yes.' Stella felt a thrill of fear. In a wild bid to defuse the feeling she said, 'I think you knew Tina Banks. She was my client... she was my friend.'

'Who?' He looked at her furiously. She should have done this with Jack. She was treading on mines that she herself had planted. She was tempted to cut and run. As a cleaner she should because she had infuriated Watson enough. As a detective undercover she mustn't squander the chance to pick up clues. Floundering, she went on, 'Tina said you gave her drawing lessons.' Not strictly true. Tina hadn't told her who had taught her.

'It was a long time ago. Christina will no doubt be missed.' He didn't suggest that he himself would miss her. He indicated for her to precede him into the hall. He said in a perfunctory tone, 'My wife is happy with your cleaning.'

Stella's heart seemed to rip loose from her chest and bash against her ribs. She made a show of scribbling down the comment.

Her pen froze. On the facing page was the timeline for the occupants of Kew Villa that she had made at Hammersmith Library. James Hailes had lived there from 1958 – the year she had stopped her search - until 1962. The name on the boarding pass she had found in the kitchen was 'J. J. Hailes'. It was too much of a coincidence that a boarding pass with the name of Watson's brother-in-law had blown in off the street. He had lied to her. Could it be Hailes that she had found in the Marianne North gallery?

Follow the evidence, don't try to pre-empt it.

She rested a hand on the newel post. As she had noted already, the hall was immaculate. The glass on the longcase clock face was so clean she couldn't see a reflection. The clock was stopped at eleven-forty-three. There were coats hung on hooks above an umbrella stand. She hadn't noticed that the oak newel post was polished to a rich dark brown.

That was it. When she had arrived, a woman's coat – Mrs Watson's presumably – had been slung on the post. It now hung with the others on the hooks. Who had moved it?

'This has been helpful,' she told Mr Watson. 'Do contact us if you have any issues.' She avoided the word 'complaint'.

'My wife will call if we require anything.' Watson was tight-lipped.

Outside on the path, cold air hit her face, numbing her cheeks. She zipped up her anorak and rummaged in her pocket for her gloves. As she started the engine, she looked up at Kew Villa. She saw a movement at one of the upstairs windows.

'Do you see the problem?' she asked Stanley as they drove past Kew Pond. When he didn't reply, she said, 'It's freezing, so why didn't his wife take her coat?'

Had Mrs Watson been there all along?

Fifteen minutes later, she was at her desk in her old bedroom, sifting through the receipt bundles. She lingered over the taxi receipt. The flower motif was a four-leaf clover.

There was no fare given on the taxi receipt; Stella guessed that, like Cliff Banks today, the driver had left it to Terry to fill in, assuming he would inflate his expenses. In a three-week period between 4 August and the 24th, Terry had bought and, Stella assumed, eaten, twenty pork pies and four sausage rolls. She searched his desk for any receipts that she might have missed, but found none.

However, she did find Tina's bag, where she had bundled it in the knee-space of the desk. She lifted it up and spilled the contents on to the desk.

She had thrown a lot of things away when she moved into the Brentford flat. She supposed this had included the copy of *The Cat in the Hat* that Terry had given her. Flipping Tina's copy open at random Stella frowned at a picture of a fish leaping out of a teapot and a toy boat wedged in cake with icing dripping on to the carpet. A milk bottle lay on its side, the milk spilt, and a book lay spine up, pages splayed. The cat sat against the wall regarding a bent rake with a baffled expression. Stella shuddered. As Jack had guessed, the story had made her anxious. Although at ten she was old enough to know it was just a story, whenever her mum went to buy food from the shop by Barons Court station, leaving her in the flat, Stella had worried that the Cat in the Hat would visit and make a mess.

Her mobile phone rang. Martin Cashman.

'All right, Stell!' He sounded hearty.

'Hi.' She lined up the items from Tina's bag and took a picture of each of them on her phone. She didn't have a photographic memory, so wanted them to be easily accessible. She focused in on the pencilled figures scribbled under the botanical drawing. The two groups of three numbers – 766 and 764 – and the five numbers underneath: 34425. And the telephone number. Martin was talking:

'...full on. Not going to make it tonight. Sorry. Another time, yeah?' He spoke in abbreviated sentences, as if he was texting. Stella started to say that she had Jack coming and that she and Martin hadn't arranged to meet, but it would sound churlish. He didn't give her a chance.

'Gotta go!' The line went dead.

Stella felt mild irritation that he had taken it for granted that he was coming over without asking. She had been thinking of telling him about Terry's stakeout of Kew Villa and finding the boarding pass, but was glad that he hadn't given her the chance. If she heard herself telling Martin, it would demonstrate how flimsy their so-called case was. He would laugh if she suggested he chase up the name Hailes in India on the basis of one boarding pass in a client's kitchen. She didn't mind that Martin wasn't coming, she wanted to see Jack.

She put Tina's things back in the Boots carrier. The book, the black shoe with a silver buckle, the silver locket, the photograph. She hesitated over the drawing. It was of the parts of a eucalyptus. The tree could be significant and the numbers mean nothing – Tina might have had nowhere else to write them at the time. She reread the name on the drawing. George Watson. According to the Richmond electoral roll he had lived at Kew Villa since the early sixties. According to Cliff Banks he had given Chrissie drawing lessons in a huge house Jack told her Tina had pretended to her friends was where she lived. Kew Villa. The house outside which Terry had conducted a three-week stakeout in 2010.

Stella jumped up and, with Stanley at her heels, ran down to the kitchen. She opened the freezer and got out two shepherd's pies. As she ripped off the packaging and pierced the cellophane tops, Stella reflected that it wasn't much of a leap to work out that the two cases were one!

Chapter Fifty

November 2014

Jack came out of Kew Gardens station. The True Host was nowhere to be seen. He had hung back when Watson got off the train – he had to be careful since the man knew him now. Watson was more than capable of taking out anything Jack did on Bella.

A few metres away, outside Lloyds chemist, he saw a familiar face. It wasn't George Watson. It was Cashman. He was with Stella.

Jack ducked out of sight behind a tree, his heart doing cart-wheels in his chest. He broke into a flop sweat. Then the heat vanished and his teeth began chattering with cold.

He was furious with himself for lurking behind a tree trunk as if it were he who had something to hide. He should go over and say, 'Hey!' When he had recovered a semblance of equilibrium, Jack snatched a look.

Cashman was kissing Stella. They were making a thing out of it, like teenagers. Stella, usually private and discreet, didn't seem to care who saw her. Jack fought the urge to scurry back into the station, over the bridge and far away. It was dusk; Cashman and Stella stood outside the light from a lamp-post, as indistinct as phantoms.

He should confront them. Not confront, he corrected himself, Stella could go out with whom she liked; he had no right to mind. He could shake Cashman's hand to reassure Stella that he was pleased for her. But the Jack who could do that, warm and friendly with an open heart, didn't exist. Somewhere in the dark, the True Host was watching him.

Hunting and hunted, Jack shook with emotion; hands rammed in the pockets of his coat in imitation of a *flâneur* out for an evening stroll, he wove between the parked cars and returning commuters homing in on the loving couple.

'Fancy seeing you here,' he exclaimed, furious at the crass line, however ironic.

'Sorry, mate.' Cashman made as if to step aside.

In all his fantasies of an encounter with Martin Cashman and Stella, Jack hadn't envisaged that the detective would pretend not to know him. He was dismayed. He had expected that, however much he despised Jack, Cashman would play fair. Desolation enveloped him. He was a tiny boy crouched beneath a statue in a clearing, numb to traffic sounds and the cold concrete pressing into his back.

'Oh, it's you.' Cashman didn't smile.

'Yep.' Jack found he could hardly speak. He turned to Stella. 'OK?'

The woman wasn't Stella. Jack never forgot a face. The woman holding Cashman's hand was his *wife*. Cashman had been kissing his wife.

'I thought you were Stella,' Jack said without thinking.

'Stella who?' his wife asked Cashman.

'Stella Darnell. Terry's daughter, you know. This is her *friend*.' Cashman glared at Jack.

'Jack.' Jack shook her hand and was momentarily caught off balance as his knuckles crunched in her grip. 'Stella has said what friends you both were to her dad.'

'Coppers – try prising them apart! Karen. Nice to meet you.'

Jack avoided Cashman's furious face. Hating himself he said, 'I'll tell Stella I've seen you. Both of you.'

Cashman muttered something unintelligible and, moving away, stepped on a discarded fruit drinks carton lying on the kerb. It squirted out the remainder of its contents on to his shoe.

Then they were gone.

It was properly dark. Jack caught his reflection in the chemist's window. Indistinct in the lamplight, tall and pale, he was a man in the crowd. No sign of the True Host.

Cashman had gone back to his wife. Jack was sure that Stella didn't know this. He was due there in half an hour. He texted her: *On my way.*

Chapter Fifty-One

November 2014

'I'm seeing Martin Cashman.' Stella held a mug, wisps of steam rising up from the drink like smoke in the night air.

'You're *seeing* him?' Jack took the hot milk from her and closed the front door. Stanley usually greeted him – Jack looked forward to the fuss – but there was no sign of him. Was his fuss now reserved for Cashman?

'He's left his wife. They've left each other.' Stella was walking up the stairs. 'It's amicable; they ran out of steam. He's really quite nice.' For Stella this was praise indeed. Jack got a glimpse of her feelings about Martin Cashman. They were stronger than she knew herself.

All the way to Stella's house he had wrestled with how to tell Stella that he had seen Cashman kissing Karen Cashman. He see-sawed between saying nothing because he didn't want her to be hurt to concluding that she would be hurt anyway so he should tell her. He had wondered if Stella was aware that Cashman was back with his wife and didn't care. She shunned any partner who wanted her full-time attention so Cashman, in CID and married, was potentially perfect for her. But Stella had always been clear: she would be no one's mistress. From Karen Cashman's response, Jack had gathered that she didn't know about her husband's liaison with Stella. Sitting in what was now the study, sipping his drink, Jack was equally certain that Stella didn't know about Karen Cashman.

'So that's that.' Stella sat down at the desk and wheeled herself closer to it. She indicated he pull up his chair and join her. 'I've had a hunch about Tina's text.'

The subject of Cashman, barely opened, was closed.

Stella pushed her Filofax towards him. 'It was talking to Beverly that got me thinking.'

Preoccupied by his encounter with Cashman, Jack made himself concentrate. He read the transcribed text on the notes page, written in Stella's careful script.

'"Please never shed fruit was sleet, how dear hehe No Kesto Mar".'

'You told Beverly?' They had a rule not to share information with other people unless they both agreed. He didn't mind that Stella had shared information with her office assistant, but was faintly ashamed by his surprise that Beverly had given Stella a hunch.

'She spotted a typo on Mum's database that alerted me. I reckon most of this text is wrongly spelt. Tina dictated everything, emails, documents, letters and texts. It was quicker.' Stella opened the Message app on her phone.

Jack nodded slowly. 'I remember you saying.'

Stella pointed at a symbol of a microphone by the space bar. 'By the end her speech was slurred. The voice-recognition software offers the most likely words, like predictive texting. When she texted me, Tina would have been very unwell.' She bit her lower lip. 'She was dying. She probably didn't check the message before she sent it. We have to work out what she actually meant.'

Jack frowned. 'Shame we can't use Google Translate.'

'I've had several goes. It's difficult to say the words wrongly and in a different voice. So far I've only got a fresh load of gobble-degook.'

'You dictated the message into the phone in a disguised voice?' Jack was delighted.

'Then I tried being Tina, but I was doing her when she was well.' Stella didn't notice Jack's excitement. 'She didn't sound the same in the hospice. I was about to try a different accent when you arrived.'

'Go on then.' Exuberant, Jack settled into his chair.

Stella cleared her throat and, without a trace of self-consciousness, the phone held to her mouth, she growled into the microphone speaking in an accent that reminded Jack of Dariusz Adomek.

'Perleese never shed frowt wasss sleet, how dear hehe Nooow Kesto Ma.' Heads together, Jack and Stella peered at the result on the screen.

'"Please never shed throat was sleet, how dear hehe no Bisto Ma",' Jack read out the sentence. 'Something about the weather in there?'

'"Police"!' Stella banged the desk. 'Not "please". I'm being dense. She was dictating. "Kesto Ma" is "Question Mark". It's a question!'

'Could "sleet" be "slit", do you think?' Jack pondered.

'It's a contender,' Stella agreed. '"Throat was slit" makes more sense.'

Jack grabbed a pen from a pot of pens and pencils on the desk and began to write out the revised sentence.

'The "hehe" could be a hesitation, rather than mean a joke. Try crossing out the second "he". Tina found it hard to get her words out. She might have repeated it. "No" could be "know".' Jack was enjoying this.

Stella read out the result. '"Police never shed throat was slit, how dear he know?"'

'"Police never said throat was slit, how did he know?"' Jack flung down the pen. 'Stella the Wonderhorse!'

'How did who know what?' Stella asked. 'Let's leave this for now.'

'How come you have this?' Jack picked out a scalpel, the blade sheathed in plastic, from the pot of pens and pencils.

'It's not mine, it was Terry's.'

'How come he had a scalpel?' The metal handle flashed in the light of the anglepoise lamp.

Stella shrugged. 'It's always been there.'

'What you mean "always"?' Jack asked.

'It was in that pot when Dad died.'

'Another question for our list: "Why did Terry have a scalpel?" The man who isn't Joseph Hooker was killed with a scalpel.'

'He had lots of tools,' Stella said. 'They're in the cupboard under the stairs.'

'Precisely. Why is this on his desk? What would he use a scalpel for?' Jack held the implement up to the light of the lawyers' lamp. 'Detectives get into the role; they inhabit the mind of the killer. This scalpel was a prop. So far our prime suspect for a crime we haven't identified is George Watson.'

Stella nodded. 'You could be right. Dad was staking out the house of a man who is a botanist. And that's not all – look at this.' She had laid the collection of things that Tina Banks had left her on the desk. 'In that article that Lucie May gave you, it said that an item stolen from the Ramsay house was a heart-shaped locket.' She pulled forward the silver locket from between Watson's botanical drawing and *The Cat in the Hat*.

'So it could be the same one.' Jack wanted to tell her how he had actually come by the cuttings. He couldn't find the courage.

'The initials on the back are "G" and "R" which could stand for "Gerald Ramsay". Tina was a criminal lawyer, she might have represented the burglar who stole this. For another crime, obviously, as she wasn't born when the robbery took place. When I found this on the carpet in her office, Tina insisted that it wasn't hers.' She laid photocopies of the articles on the desk and placed the locket on top of them. 'I've started establishing links.' She flipped over the page in her Filofax. Each item was written on the page, in the same order as she had arranged them on the desk, a circle was drawn around them. Outside the circle she had printed the word 'Articles' and drawn an arrow from it to the locket. Further along the page, also outside the circle, she had put names: George and Rosamond Watson; Harold and James Hailes. Arrows from these pointed to 'Kew Villa'. Another arrow connected Kew Villa to 'Botanic Drawing' written inside the circle, as did an arrow from Botanic Drawing to George Watson.

'Tina went for botanical drawing lessons with George Watson.' Stella pulled forward the picture of the *Eucalyptus gunnii*. 'That's why!' She sat back, arms folded.

'What's why?'

'Hailes is the name of Rosamond's brother. It comes up on the electoral roll. It was her maiden name. Then she married George Watson and he moved into Kew Villa. When I was at Watson's house, I found a boarding pass from Madras belonging to a J. H. Hailes. Watson said it wasn't his.'

'That was true, I suppose.'

'He said it had been blown inside by the wind. Why bother with that detail? It would have to be a strong wind to lift it off the pavement, blow it up the steps and into the house. I checked with Donette and she didn't find it when she was cleaning. That means Watson or his wife left it on the kitchen table. James Hailes is Rosamond's brother, so what's the bet that J. H. Hailes and James Hailes are the same?'

'So Watson lives at Kew Villa.' The man he had seen on the stairs had been visiting and had left in a taxi. It began to make sense. When he had seen Watson go to Kew Villa on the night Jennifer Day died, he was going to his own house. The man on the stairs was possibly Hailes, the brother visiting from India. Jack said nothing; he couldn't discuss this with Stella.

'I've put this chart together.' Stella jiggled the mouse and the computer screen was filled with a colour-coded spreadsheet of names and dates. 'Watson's been in Kew Villa since 1962 when he married Rosamond Hailes. She was living there with, and I'm guessing this, her father Harold and brother James. There was no Mrs Hailes back to 1958 when I stopped.'

Stella had constructed a timeline showing who had lived in Kew Villa and when. 'George Watson' was in bright red. *Red hot.*

He couldn't tell her that the cuttings about the Ramsay burglary had come from Watson's house and not from Lucie May. This meant that they couldn't speculate on why his wife Rosamond had hidden them in her desk. 'Stella, I've been in—'

'In 1962, as you can see, both Harold and James disappear. They may have moved to let the married couple have privacy,' Stella said.

'Or the father died and the brother left,' Jack murmured. 'Or they both died.'

'Or maybe the Watsons bought one or both of them out,' Stella said. 'Whatever, the Watsons were there in 1976 and were still there in 2010. Their names are still on the electoral roll.'

'I met Watson when I was cleaning. He's a nasty piece of work. Bella works with him. She said she put her foot in it by referring to Tina as his daughter. As I said, when they were kids, Tina told Emily and Bella that the Watsons were her parents. Not that she said they were called the Watsons. Bella didn't believe her. She did some detective work of her own. She trailed Tina and hung about outside the Kew Villa. She realized that Tina didn't live there. Enterprising!' Jack wished he had known Bella Markham when she was a girl.

'When I went into Kew Villa this afternoon, Mr Watson said his wife had just popped out. It was odd because her coat was there. She could have been upstairs, I suppose.' Stella pressed 'print'. Moments later a copy of the Kew Villa timeline slid on to the printer tray. 'I've asked Lucie May to give us background on Rosamond's family.' Stella handed Jack the timeline. The red ink highlighting Watson's name was damp. It glistened like fresh blood.

'Is that wise?' Jack was so astounded that Stella had asked for Lucie's help, he forgot to be annoyed that she hadn't run it by him. He would have said 'yes' if she had.

'It comes with a price.' Stella went on with her story. Jack was rapt as she described how she had inveigled herself into Kew Villa.

Stella clicked the mouse and opened Suzie's database. She pointed at an entry: 'Jackie did the original estimate. Read this.'

'Mr Watson said his wife had popped out, but had left

instructions. He apologized that Mrs W's knitting was on an armchair and for a mug of cold tea beside the chair. He offered me a slice of her homemade chocolate cake, which out of politeness I accepted. Only the downstairs rooms are to be cleaned. Mr Watson said that his wife preferred to do the rest of the house.'

'Watson used the same phrase – "popped out" – today. As I said, her coat was there.'

'She might have more than one coat.'

'True,' Stella conceded. 'We are no nearer to establishing why Terry was watching the house. He suspected someone had got away with murder. It's safe to consider the possibility that that someone lived, or is living, in Kew Villa. Today, I'm sure George Watson was hiding something. He wasn't just cross that I was being inquisitive. He didn't want me to see Hailes's boarding pass.'

'I can see Watson committing murder,' Jack said. He couldn't admit breaking into the man's house. 'I still wonder if he had a hand in the death of that woman in the sixth car.'

Stella pulled a face. 'I thought she died of an aneurism.'

'She did, but . . . go on with your story.' No point in adding more mud to muddy waters.

'I spoke to Wendy. She used to clean for the Watsons. She told me she met Mrs Watson at her first session.'

'So whatever the crime, Mrs Watson wasn't the victim.'

'I thought that, but just before you got here, Wendy rang back. She had mixed up Mrs Watson with another client in Priory Road, partly because, like her other client, Mrs Watson leaves her cake to eat in her break. She's never met her. Whenever she's gone there, Mrs Watson has just "popped out". Mr Watson used the same phrase to her. Or she's upstairs having a lie-down. The last time Wendy went, Mrs Watson was on the phone. It's always Mr Watson who she sees. One time a man she didn't know answered. We've got a woman called Hannah cleaning there now, but she's off sick so I haven't called her.'

'I suspect she'll say the same thing. From Jackie's database entry, it seems that Watson was at pains to draw attention to the knitting and mug of tea.' Jack reread the database entry.

'If clients take ages to answer the door it's often because they're scooting about tidying. The last thing they do is point out mess. Oh!' Stella slammed down her mug.

'What?'

'When I had tea with Terry in Kew Gardens, he ordered chocolate cake with hundreds and thousands. I did too when we were there, to prompt my memory, as you know. There was a pot of hundreds and thousands in the Watsons' kitchen beside empty jars for flour and sugar. Tenuous, but could that be the cake Mrs Watson made for the girl? Was that why he bought it for me that day? He was trying to jog my memory.'

'More than likely. Did you check the sell-by date on the sprinkles?'

'I couldn't have justified it. Cleaning cupboard contents is part of one of our intensive packages.'

Jack knew this. 'Getting Ready for Spring' was his favourite one: it was full of hope and fresh alacrity. His mood was not springlike now. Stella had found a way into Kew Villa using her roles of cleaner and detective. She hadn't lied. He had sneaked in as an intruder and now had to hide critical information from her.

'Actually, I *did* have a chance to check the date because Watson went out of the kitchen, but I only realized when he returned.'

'What was he doing?' Jack's antennae were up.

'I think he was moving the coat.' Stella blew out her cheeks as the realization dawned.

'There was no sign of this James Hailes?'

'He could have been upstairs with Rosamond. Yet I am sure we were alone in the house.'

Jack and Stella were silent as each considered what they had so far.

'You said Rosamond Watson called Clean Slate just after Terry

stopped watching the house. What if these events are connected?'
Jack straightened the black shoe with the buckle in line with the
flip-flops.

'I wondered.' Stella took Terry's scalpel out of the pot.

'Perhaps Watson saw Terry and recognized him as a police
officer. A clever response would be to hire the detective's daughter's company in your wife's name. Good cover.'

'A cleaner goes into the furthest corners. If you've something to
hide that's the last type of person you'd want in your house,' Stella
objected.

'If you want to hide something, put it in plain sight.' No one
knew that better than a True Host. Jack should tell Stella about
Cashman; she wouldn't thank him for allowing the police officer
to humiliate her. He looked down. Stanley was sitting at his feet
staring up at him as if he had read his mind.

He tried again. 'Stella—'

Stella's mobile rang. Jack could see that the screen said *Cashman*.

'Hang on.' Stella swiped open the line. 'Hi, Martin.' She broke
into a wide smile. Jack clutched his hands to stop them shaking.
Cashman was going to tell Stella right now with him there.
He made to get up, but Stella mouthed to him to stay.

Jack could hear Cashman talking through the earpiece, but not
what he was saying.

'I only suggested that the man wasn't Hooker. You'd have
thought of that too.' She made a batting movement with the hand
holding the scalpel. Jack winced. 'Did you get prints off the cigarette packet?' She paused for Cashman's reply. 'Wiped clean? That's
weird. OK, so he wore gloves outside, but he'd have touched them
with his bare hands at some stage. Actually, Martin, I did some
digging on Winfield… You've done that. Good. OK then.' Stella
nodded vigorously as if Cashman could see her. Had he repri-
manded her for sticking her nose in? Jack felt a rush of fury, but
then Stella went on unperturbed. That Cashman had encouraged
her made Jack feel no better. Again he tried to go, but Stella
motioned him to stay, the scalpel blade flashing in the lamplight.

'It's about Winfield soft packs.' Pause. 'They stopped making the twenty king size in 2008. The soft pack you found on the body has to be six years old minimum. Could whoever planted the fake ID on the body have also planted the cigarettes?' Pause. Cashman's voice buzzed like an insect through the phone. The buzzing stopped. Stella said, 'To make you think he was Australian. The killer might have a magpie temperament, he or she collects stuff to use when the time comes. Not as trophies but as props like in a play. Mum does that. Not that she kills people.'

Jack guessed that Cashman was doubting that the killer would have kept the cigarettes for so long. Glowing with pleasure at Stella's detective skills, he felt that she had lit upon the truth. True Hosts were often collectors. They kept trophies from killings and disparate items left on trains and buses, in taxis and cafés. He had seen gloves, scarves, wallets, broken necklaces, books and mobile phones stored in cupboards in True Hosts' homes. *Finders keepers.* A True Host would, as Stella was suggesting, construct a fake personality from such objects. Jack's most recently discovered True Host was a botanist. George Watson had at his disposal a vast collection of dead plant specimens. Many waited to be given names and placed within the order. What crime had Watson constructed?

Jack's pleasure at Stella's prowess vanished. Cashman was treating her like one of his team. As she talked, Stella tapped the scalpel on a page in her Filofax. The blade was making indentations in the paper. Jack wanted to point this out but then Cashman would realize that he was there. Then Stella said, 'Tonight? Thing is, I've got Jack here.'

Jack froze. Cashman hadn't told her about his wife. He wanted to say it in person. He would suppose that Jack had told Stella that he had seen him kissing his wife. He would guess that Jack had said nothing or Stella wouldn't have been so friendly.

'Tomorrow? Sorted. Me too. Bye then.' Stella put the phone down. 'That was Martin,' she said superfluously.

'Oh.' Jack couldn't say anything. It would compound his failure to tell her about Cashman and his wife. It was usually Stella who did the leaving; he feared for how she would take it.

'They've found CCTV of the man from the Marianne North Gallery in the arrivals lounge at Heathrow. Cashman reckons it won't be long before they establish where he flew in from.'

'I wouldn't bet on that. Sounds like they need you on their team.' He was ashamed of the nasty edge in his voice.

'I'm on *your* team,' Stella replied. Jack felt worse.

'Cashman may know of Terry's suspicions.' This was as close as Jack would go to suggesting she ask Cashman to look on the HOLMES computer.

Stella shrugged and Jack didn't push it because the last thing he wanted was to encourage her to ask Cashman a favour when the man was two-timing her.

Stella was too involved in Cashman's business. She would be hurt when he shut her out. Jack went back to his earlier idea. 'Watson could have hired Clean Slate to prove that he had nothing to hide. He went out of his way to highlight to Jackie that Mrs Watson had been in the house. He gave access to the house – only downstairs – to line up witnesses who would shore up his story. Wendy's first response was that she had met Mrs Watson. The contract is in Rosamond Watson's name. He may not have known of the connection between you and the detective staking him out.'

'And his story is?' Stella appeared to catch herself waving the scalpel about; she placed it on the desk beside *The Cat in the Hat*.

'That Mrs Watson is alive—'

'—when she's dead!' Stella cried. 'The murder that Terry let someone get away with was of Rosamond Watson.' She picked up the scalpel again and, considerations of health and safety apparently forgotten, carved the air. 'James Hailes returns from India to see his sister—'

'So Watson has to stop Hailes finding out that she's dead.'

Stella dropped her voice as if, in the silent darkened house, someone was listening. 'George Watson murdered James Hailes in the Marianne North Gallery. With a scalpel.'

'But we have absolutely no proof,' Jack said.

Chapter Fifty-Two

November 2014

Stella didn't go to bed after Jack left. She sat at the desk ruminating over Tina's 'clues' ranged before her. Pink flip-flops, a child's story-book, a black shoe with a buckle, a botanical illustration of a eucalyptus scribbled with numbers and the silver locket and the picture of Tina's nan. Tina had been upset when Stella had suggested that the locket was hers, a reasonable assumption since it was under her desk. Since Tina had died, Stella had decided that it was the cancer that had upset her. But now she wondered. Tina had behaved as if the locket was the last straw. She had received a call and left the office. Who had called her?

Where was Tina's phone? Michelle Banks must have taken it from the hospice. Stella was about to text her but then saw the time. Michelle wouldn't thank her for waking her up at past one in the morning. She made a note in her Filofax to call her tomorrow, hoping that Michelle hadn't wiped the call log.

Stella went over what Tina had said that morning. As Jack had pointed out, Tina was a lawyer: she used words precisely.

'Is this yours?'

'No ... A client must have dropped it.'

Stella had supposed that Tina was denying knowledge of the locket as well as ownership. Jack had also said that lawyers were adept at skirting truths without lying. Had Tina been truthful, but not completely so? The locket didn't belong to her, but she had known whose it was. When Tina asked to see Bella and Emily before her death, she told them that she had stolen the photo to prove to Bella that the Watsons were her parents. Were the people in the tiny heart-shaped photograph George and Rosamond Watson in happier times?

Stella opened the casing and looked again at the photograph of the young man and woman kissing. If the locket was the one stolen from Judge Ramsay's house in the 1950s, then originally it must have contained pictues of Judge Ramsay's father, and his wife. Watson must have removed them.

The man had dark hair; George Watson was now grey. This man had a mole at his jawline; she hadn't looked closely at Watson so couldn't vouch for a mole one way or the other. Jack would have noticed. There was something about the bone structure that suggested the elderly man who had shown her round the downstairs of his house that afternoon, but the resemblance was passing.

She weighed the locket in her cupped palm. It was solid, yet light; the silver was cold. She put it down and absently opened *The Cat in the Hat*. The story was still fresh in her mind. The drawings were as disturbing, and the same coil of disquiet stirred within her as the cat created more and more mess. On page twenty-eight something fell out and sailed to the floor. Stanley's head shot up from his bed; rising to his feet, he prepared to investigate.

'Stay!' Stella scooped up the paper.

It was a photocopy of two newspaper cuttings. The same ones that Jack had given her and that she had seen in the archives.

The quality of the silence had altered. She swivelled around in her chair. The attic hatch remained shut. Jack had closed the study door behind him when he left. The feeling she had had earlier that they were not alone returned. Stella got up and approached the door. She stood, her ear to the wood, and listened. She could only hear the blood pulsing in her head. Stanley sat up in his bed, ears cocked, eyes liquid dark. He had heard something. Stella pulled open the door.

Stanley flew past her and down the stairs to the hall, snorting and panting. Dogs were meant to provide company and protection and allay fears. More often Stanley caused fear or, like now, exacerbated it by behaving as if there truly was an external threat. Stella crept to the top of the stairs and looked down into the hall. Diffused light spilled through the glazed panels in the front door. A shadow flicked across one panel and she prickled with rising terror. The shadow was of the tree opposite. There was no one there.

She looked along the landing to what had been her parents' bedroom and where, for the last forty years, Terry had slept. Raised voices carried through the closed door: her mum and dad were arguing. Lack of sleep was playing with her nerves.

Beckoning Stanley – Stella couldn't have used her voice had she wanted to – she returned to the study and slumped back in the chair. The change of state had been in her mind; it had signified a shift in perception. She and Jack had amassed clues and connections; it was like a thousand-piece jigsaw with a choice of pictures. George Watson had murdered his wife. Hailes had murdered his sister. Rosamond Watson was alive so no one had murdered her. Or she had died of natural causes years ago and there was no mystery? Stella rubbed at her temples as a headache threatened.

On page twenty-eight of *The Cat in the Hat*, she had found another clue. Another connection. Reaching for her diagram, Stella drew an arrow from *The Cat in the Hat* to the 'Newspaper Articles' and one from each to Tina.

Martin wouldn't thank her for talking to the press, especially Lucie May. She dialled her.

'Surprise, surprise!' Lucie May was being Cilla Black.

'Can I see you?' Stella asked.

'Yes, Detective Darnell, you *so* can!'

*

'He kept his cards close to his chest!' Tented in a man's woolly pullover, arms wrapped around her knees, Lucie May contemplated her e-cigarette. It wasn't switched on, but Stella assumed that she realized this; she vaguely remembered that Lucie had been trying to give up. 'We had a pact. Terry gave me the heads-up on a case and I kept stuff out of the paper until he gave me the nod. We were a team.'

'He said he had let someone get away with murder. What did he mean?'

'I took it as a turn of phrase. I told Jack that Terry said that, because of you, he'd been misled. That's the polite word. In June 1976. But you know this. What have you got for *me*?' Lucie May was ruthless, but Stella liked that she didn't hide this.

'My friend Tina left me these.' Stella emptied out the Boots carrier bag and explained why she had it. 'I found this in the book.' She gave Lucie the photocopy of the newspaper articles from *The Cat in the Hat*.

'Jack's already shown me these.' Lucie flapped the piece of paper impatiently. 'I wrote this one so I have a copy in my files. C'mon, Stella!'

Stella kept her face expressionless. Jack had told her that Lucie had shown the cutting to him. Or had he? Jack could be prudent with the truth.

Lucie guzzled from a bottle of Evian mineral water; she dashed a drip from her chin with the back of her hand. 'The robbery was from the home of that family in St Peter's Square you used to clean for. Ramsay was the name. Obviously you weren't cleaning for them then, you weren't a speck in your pa's eyes. Lah de dah.' She gave a peremptory sniff and tossed her e-cigarette into a fruit bowl on the coffee table that was filled with packets of painkillers and cold-relief tablets. Stella picked up a strange, not entirely unpleasant smell in the room. Not the e-cigarette. She identified it as a dog-calming spray called Placid Pet and, looking around, spotted the canister on the mantelpiece. She hadn't brought Stanley, thinking of the havoc he might cause with the papers in Lucie's front room. Perhaps he would have gone to sleep.

She updated Lucie with all that they had so far. 'Tina's friends told Jack that, in the seventies, Tina pretended to them that the people living at Kew Villa were her parents. In fact she was having botanical drawing lessons with George Watson. She had moved to a prep school from a state primary and couldn't tell them her dad was a taxi driver or that her mother was a cleaner.' Stella had been proud that her dad was in the police.

'When I won the scholarship for a place at Burlington Grammar, as it was then, everyone was snooty poo. My sister hated me. I acquired a new accent along with the uniform.' Lucie May rummaged in a bag of chopped carrots on the sofa and grabbed one, sticking it between her lips. 'My old man was a prison officer; the girls I knew wouldn't have seen the difference between him and villains in the Scrubs!' She gave a shout of laughter.

Stella realized she knew little about Lucie, she had no idea that she had a sister. She referred to the notes she had made before leaving her house. With Lucie it was easy to lose the thread. 'Did you hear of a body in the Marianne North Gallery in the seventies? It would have been during the drought in June, around the time you think that Terry talked to this mystery girl.'

'You don't have to tell me when the drought was, I was there! The heat was crap for eye make-up, melted soon as you applied it.' Lucie pinched a bead of wool off her jumper. 'Deaths galore – the heat saw off the young and old.' She pulled a face. 'Nearly saw me off.'

'Tina told her friend Emily that she had seen a murder.'

'A murder in Kew? No chance. I'd have been all over that. Look at the fuss about that bloke you found. By the way, Agent Darnell, you owe me an exclusive on that!'

Stella could not break Martin's trust. Lucie was adept at turning fiction into fact. She did tell Lucie about her visit that afternoon, including seeing the coat on the banister and finding the boarding pass belonging to James Hailes. She told her about the Clean Slate contract and Jackie's database entry.

'You're your daddy's girl!' Lucie used Tina's old phrase. She embarked on another carrot, half shutting one eye as if screening smoke. 'I've actioned your request for information and done some ferreting.'

'And?' Stella asked.

'And *nothing* unless you cut me a deal. This better not be a waste of time for us both.' Lucie May was steely.

It didn't pay to forget that Lucie was a ruthless reporter before anything else.

'When the police investigation is over, I'll tell you about finding the body.' Martin couldn't object to that.

'You strike a hard bargain,' Lucie huffed. 'Cashman's mind's not on his job so it might not be over in our lifetime!'

'Done!' Stella could be ruthless too.

Lucie nestled into the sofa. 'OK, so this is the background check on the Hailes family that you asked for. Kew Villa has been in the Hailes family since the Second World War.'

'I know that,' Stella barked.

'Patience! I can't work without context. The daughter Rosamond was born and grew up there as did an older brother James. She married George Watson in 1962. No kids. So it wasn't their little girl who put a spell on Terry. The mum died having Rosamond; the death certificate is dated the day after Rosamond was born. Says "Cause of death: pneumonia". Old Harold Hailes – the dad – shuffled off in 1962 and, according to his will, left his son a hundred pounds. Sounds OK until you see that little sis, the fair Rosamond, got Kew Villa. Jimmy must have been incandescent. I haven't made a will – God knows who'll get this – my sister, unless I pull my finger out.' Lucie May essayed a sketchy wave taking in the living room cluttered with books and files. 'You could preserve it for posterity. Over-awed visitors could troop in to view the sit-up-and-beg Remington on which the Great One bashed out her stories.' Lucie's corncrake laugh halted mid-flow, perhaps picturing the cold reality of life after her death. 'Jimmy does a vanishing act – it's as if he doesn't exist. If he went to India that explains it. Here's my take: Rosamond Watson was done away with by the big brother.'

'If he'd murdered her, would he have inherited the house?'

'It was left in trust to Rosamond. After her death it would go to Jimmy, not Watson. Motive!'

'Not if he was in India in 1976 when we think she was murdered.'

'Who says he was? I'll chase that up.' As Stella had feared, like a rugby ball detached from a scrum, Lucie had hold of the case and was off down the field.

'But he didn't inherit in 1976,' Stella pointed out.

'Maybe he was playing a long game,' Lucie said, looking fleetingly deflated.

An idea struck. It was a leap across an abyss with no accompanying evidence. 'Was the little girl that Terry spoke to Tina Banks?' A blurred jigsaw picture was emerging. 'Tina had drawing lessons at Kew Villa in the mid-seventies. If Terry went there, perhaps he saw her.' Stella argued with herself: 'Why would he have gone there? For the same reason he had staked out the house decades later.'

'Easy enough to find that out,' Lucie muttered to her carrot.

Stella changed tack. 'Terry took me to Kew Gardens for my birthday in 2010, just after he'd been staking out the house. I don't believe he chose the Botanic Gardens because he thought I'd like it there; he was working.'

'I got to claim credit, Honey-Bee. I warned Terry not to be like my dad, a stranger to his daughter. If you don't put the work in, you die alone. I dare say I'd have popped in on him in some care home. You enjoy the outing? The dogs at White City were more my dad's thing, not that he took me.' She looked briefly pensive.

In that instant, more of the afternoon in Kew came back. Stella had trodden on a goose dropping. Terry had offered to clean her shoe. She had refused. She shifted to the edge of the sofa as her thoughts clarified. 'From what you say, something in 2010 made Terry change his mind about an interview or conversation with a child in 1976. It can't have been what I said at the tea in Kew Gardens because by then he was already staking out Kew Villa.'

Lucie was working her way through the bag of carrots at a scary rate. 'If I could get my hands on Mrs Watson's bank account, I'd lay a big bet that we'd find it's in regular use.'

'So you don't think she's dead?'

'I *do* think she is. But our George is playing us. With a flick of his wand he gives the impression that Rosamond has just "popped out", whipped up a chocolate cake or laid down her knitting needles.' Lucie seemed to have forgotten that moments before she had her money on the brother, Jimmy Hailes. 'So your prime suspect is George Watson.'

'Possibly.' Stella was cagey. 'Jack thinks Clean Slate was hired to ensure that Rosamond's name was on the client database. Watson told me the cleaning is his wife's domain; he has nothing to do with it.'

'Listen, Stella Darnell.' Lucie looked stern. 'Jack refused to get you to lean on Cashman to interrogate the HOLMES computer. But seeing as Scotland Yard's gone back to his wife – and don't they all – I'm guessing you'll be up for twisting his arm a little?' She did a half-Nelson gesture and bared brilliant white teeth.

Stella gaped at her. No words would come.

'You didn't know!' Lucie May looked genuinely shocked. 'The *Shit*-Bird!' She tossed the half-eaten carrot across the room. It landed in the wastepaper bin.

'How do you know?' Stella's voice was weak.

'I'm a reporter, it's my business to know.'

The last few nights Cashman had been too busy to come over. It was a high-profile murder; the bosses were on his back. Lucie and her fellow hounds were snapping at his heels. Stella had never doubted Cashman was telling her truth. She observed, more to herself: 'He could have told me.'

As if on cue, she got a text. Martin's name was on the screen. *Can I see you?* Dazed, she let Lucie take the phone off her.

'Speak of the Horned Devil! Is he going to give you the happy tidings after all? Listen, Stell, here's a plan. Dump him before he dumps you. You got to come away with your pride.' She scooted across the room and set about assembling a gin and tonic. 'A nippet or three for the road? '

Stella refused the drink and began texting Cashman.

'Don't reply now, make him sweat!' Lucie brandished her lemon-slicing knife.

Stella wasn't a games player. *Tomorrow. 8pm?* She sent the message.

She pulled an envelope out of her bag and emptied it on to the coffee table next to the bowl of pills. Photocopied pages fanned out. The photographs she had taken in the archive including the boy outside number 25 Rose Gardens; the details of the electoral roll for Kew Villa and Rose Gardens; her Filofax notes and her report of the stakeout of Kew Villa. 'You're good at jigsaws,' she told Lucie. She zipped up her anorak.

'I'm the best,' Lucie remarked, possibly in response to Stella's comment, but more likely because the idea had just occurred to her.

'See what you can make of this stuff.' Stella slung her rucksack on to her shoulder and left.

'Make him pay!' Lucie cried after Stella as she went down the path into the darkness of British Grove.

Stella didn't reply. By then she had decided what she would do.

Chapter Fifty-Three

November 2014

'George Watson has been murdered,' Bella said.

Jack dropped his spoon. It clattered into his bowl, splashing tomato soup across the table. He dabbed ineffectually at the stains spreading across the white cotton cloth. 'How?' Watson was dead. This changed everything. *Every True Host had an enemy.*

He was having lunch with Bella in a French restaurant near Kew station. The only other diners were a middle-aged man and woman eating in silence a few metres away and a young man in a corner who, between mouthfuls of food and slugs of beer, was absorbed with his phone, his finger whizzing over the screen. A waiter, a windblown-looking man, brooded out of the window at the street. No one appeared to have heard Bella.

'When did this happen?' Jack pushed his bowl away, his appetite gone. Someone had taken revenge on their prime suspect.

'Just before I left to meet you.' Bella was tucking into her smoked salmon roulade.

Jack had told Stella that he would meet up with Bella and Emily to see what else he could learn about Tina's claim to have seen a murder. Emily couldn't come and as Jack walked with Bella across

Kew Green from the Herbarium, he was pleased. He rather wanted to see Bella again for herself. Bella Markham had, by her own admission, been an unkind child and, he suspected, wasn't always a kind adult, but he liked her energy and honesty. They had ordered their food and begun to eat. Then she had made her announcement. Bella worked with dead plants; maybe dead people didn't faze her.

'I should have seen it coming.'

Jack had told Bella to be careful of Watson. It hadn't occurred to him that the True Host himself was in jeopardy. 'Did you call the police?'

'Unfortunately it's not a crime.' Bella drank her wine.

'How is murder not a crime?'

'No one's actually been murdered, or not yet. Only a matter of time – that Matthew's a psychopath.'

'Who's Matthew?'

'You met him.'

'When did I meet him?' Jack was reeling.

'When you came to the Artists' Room. The sadistic botanist, remember?'

'The man who wanted you to redo the plate?' The tomato stains on the cloth appeared to grow, to join up. A haze of red.

'Yes! Thought my memory was dodgy!' Bella flashed him a smile. 'You warned me about George but it's Matthew who is likely to slit your throat and fix you in a jar of Kew Mix. Old George is harmless, spineless even.' She dabbed at her mouth with her napkin, leaving lipstick kisses on the fabric.

'Anyway, Matthew told George that he'd found a new plant species and that he planned to name it after George. It was a secret, but George couldn't resist telling me. Never seen him so exercised. Matthew asked George to draw the specimen. He'd found it in the Herbarium – as you know many of the plants in there are yet to be identified. Botanists don't need to be hoofing off to distant parts of the world, just a rootle in those cupboards could make their name.' She cackled happily. 'So, as per, when Matthew saw the plate, he had George redo much of it. Unlike me, George never complains. Matthew was feeding his ego, going on about how *Rosulabryum watsonii*, the new species, would be accepted by the botanical community and entered in the taxonomy. A lasting tribute to George – and his wife – her name is Rosebud or some such.'

'Rosamond.' Too late Jack remembered he wasn't supposed to know. He morphed the name into a sneeze. Luckily Bella didn't seem to have noticed his slip. He reached over and toyed with the remains of his soup, stirring the spoon about in the bowl.

'The specimen was among the bryophytes, non-vascular plants – mosses and liverwort to you.' Bella paused for some more wine.

'What happened?' Jack tried to breathe evenly. *Two seconds in, two seconds out.*

'Matthew slinks into the Artists' Room, all smiles. First clue. He only smiles when he's about to twist the scalpel. He tells George, loud enough for us all to hear, although it was supposed to be their secret, that: "Our hard work has been in vain." Pompous and puffed-up like a cockerel. "Blame *Rosulabryum andicala* (Hook.) Ochyra. The species was approved for Kew's Plant List on the eighteenth of April 1892".' Bella tipped up her glass and drank the last drop. 'In other words, what George had bust a gut drawing wasn't a new species – it had existed over a hundred years.'

'Does it matter?'

'People dream of achieving immortality through botany. Your name on the Royal Botanic Gardens database and published in botanical journals all over the world. For George, *Rosulabryum watsonii* was the pinnacle of his ambition. Some artists, and I'm one, get pleasure from bringing dead material to life through drawing. George is a good artist, but it means nothing because he sees himself as a failed botanist.'

Jack tried to gather his wits. Watson *was* a botanist.

'. . . sits in his corner, following orders, at the beck and call of the botanists and good as gold. Keeps himself to himself, doesn't hang out with the rest of us artists.' She drank some mineral water and went on, 'George once let slip that his wife is disappointed in him.

346

So I guess *watsonii* – having his name immortalized – would have been ample compensation. Ayrton is a bastard!'

'Matthew Ayrton was the man I met?' Jack gripped the edge of the table.

'Yes, ol' Fishy Fish Eyes. He's dead material!' Bella did the Lucie May laugh and Jack saw what Lucie would have been like when she was younger.

'Isn't Ayrton something to do with Kew?' Jack racked his brains. 'I mean a long time ago.'

'Yes, Acton Smee Ayrton was the first commissioner of the Office of Works in the Victorian times. He tried to turn Kew Gardens into a park and bundle everything off to the Natural History Museum. He and Joseph Hooker fought tooth and nail. Hooker won. Probably Matthew's ancestor.' Bella nudged Jack's arm away from the tomato soup stains on the cloth.

'It must often happen that a species exists already. Joseph Hooker was constantly lumping plants into one species and wiping out the mooted names of his poor old collectors,' Jack mused.

'Listen to you, Mr Botanist! Yes, it does happen. But in this case Matthew raised George's hopes expressly to dash them.'

'You're saying that he deliberately chose a specimen knowing that it existed?' Jack was dismayed. 'No botanist would do that.' Yet this was the second occasion that Bella had suggested such a thing.

Bella raised her eyebrows. 'Ah to live in your world, Jack. I imagine that London Underground drivers don't try to derail each other. But in the sweet-scented gardens of Kew, it's dog eat dog! No one could prove it, and if they could, they'd probably bury the evidence because Matthew's a brilliant botanist.'

'What a waste of time and money,' Jack murmured.

'You can bet Matthew never submitted George's invoice for the drawing. George won't have chased it because he was focused on *watsonii*. Plus he needs work from Matthew. So lose-lose.'

'There'll be other plants and other chances.' Even Bella seemed to have lost a sense of perspective. More serious was that in a few hours Stella was meeting Cashman. Although surely Cashman didn't hold all Stella's hopes and dreams.

'It *is* death!' Bella insisted. 'Once your name's been allocated to a specimen it's made a taxonomical footprint. It can't be reused. George can never have a species named after him. *Watsonii* is extinct. Matthew killed him!'

If the True Host was called Matthew Ayrton, who was George Watson? Jack realized he had never seen him. When Stella was talking about meeting him at his house, he had pictured Ayrton.

Bella's eyes glittered. 'Let's slip Kew Mix into Matthew's Martini!'

'"Kew Mix"?' It was the second time Bella had referred to it.

'It's for preserving specimens. Ethanol, glycerine and the one that would finish him off: formaldehyde. If you think Wing C in the Herbarium is full of ghosts, Jack, visit the Spirit Collection in the basement!' She was teasing him. 'Or there's *Abrus precatorius* – cute little red and black beans – just five of them ground up into his coffee will make Matthew extinct!'

Jack was too attracted by the idea. Hastily he asked, 'Have you met Rosamond Watson?' He needed to lock down facts. So far he had been way off.

'Once.'

'When?' Their theories were becoming extinct too.

'We were kids. She answered the door once when Emily and me went with Chrissie to her lesson. We didn't meet her. Chrissie made sure of that. I did see her though.'

'Have you met her as an adult?'

'No. George says she's a sociophobe. She hasn't got any friends and is dependent on him. Shoot me if I get like that!'

Jack hadn't noticed the arrival of the main course. The man he had seen on the stairs in Kew Villa *had* been George Watson. He wasn't a visitor who left in a taxi. The man he had seen in the sixth car and followed from Kew station was Matthew Ayrton. He had called on Watson, probably to make him redo the *watsonii* plate. When Bella had described him as harmless, she hadn't meant

Ayrton, whom Jack had mistaken for Watson, she had meant Watson. Today she had called him spineless. Jack was stunned. Watson wasn't a True Host. That changed everything.

Was his wife alive? The case was in tatters. Numbly Jack traced the root of his mistake. When the Herbarium receptionist had told him that George Watson was upstairs, he had assumed that Watson was the man who had caught him looking at a specimen. In fact that was Matthew Ayrton.

He had defined True Hosts as those who had murdered, or would murder. He spotted them intuitively, a skill based on early experience, but his focus had been narrow. Murder wasn't only about the extinguishing of life, but of killing all hope.

His conclusions were based on erroneous assumptions. Matthew Ayrton had been in the sixth car when Jennifer Day had collapsed and died. Jack had thought it impossible that, as a True Host, he hadn't been instrumental in her death. But sometimes situations were what they seemed. Jennifer Day had suffered a cerebral aneurism. No one had murdered her. The botanist had lingered briefly because True Hosts were drawn to the proximity of death. He had then left because his sort didn't waste their lives helping members of the public or the police.

'A penny for them?' Bella probed.

'*Rosulabryum andicala* was there all along,' Jack said quickly. He couldn't share his real thoughts. 'Without a name, something doesn't have a place in a taxonomic system. Botanically it doesn't exist. Yet it *does* exist. We invent classifications and then we reinvent them. Names change. They make up our reality. If we lose our name, our identity, we don't exist.'

'Chrissie said something about not existing the last time we saw her.' Bella piled creamed potato on to her fork. 'After she apologized for running off when we were kids.'

'That was honest.' Jack couldn't imagine the hard-nosed lawyer capable of being so frank. Another fundamental error.

'When people get a life-threatening illness, I guess they go all existential and consider the meaning of life.' Bella ripped off a piece of olive bread and mopped it in the jus. 'She showed us this cupboard in the Marianne North Gallery where she had hidden from us. It's still there. I said I'd've found her straight away.' Puffing up with ill-concealed pride, Bella gathered more potato on to her fork. 'S'pose that was a bit mean,' she remarked placidly.

'That's when she saw the murder? Hiding in a cupboard.' Jack chopped a sliver of meat off one of his lamb cutlets and nibbled it.

'She didn't tell me. It was her secret with Emily.' Bella rolled her eyes. Jack guessed that this still irked her.

'She did tell you that she had cancer.' Although she didn't need it, Jack felt an urge to bolster Bella's feelings.

'She claimed we were the only ones she told, not her family or someone called Stella. Not even her dad. Emily met him at the funeral. She said that he was upset about that.'

'She must have trusted you.' But Bella wasn't listening.

'My father's family didn't tell me that he was dead until months afterwards, and only then to find out if I wanted a pair of crappy cufflinks. I told them where they could stuff them!'

'Did Tina mention George Watson? Jack was in a fog, feeling his way. 'I mean apart from when he taught her as a child.'

Bella dabbed her mouth with her napkin. 'She said his wife makes good chocolate cake and that I should suggest that he brought some into work.' She laughed. 'Funny what makes an impression on kids!'

Jack gave up pretending to eat and set his knife and fork together on the plate.

'Have you asked him? To bring in her cake?'

'I wish I hadn't! When I said what Chrissie told me, George behaved as if I'd hit him. At her funeral he looked in pieces. Did you see him with that flower?' Bella signalled to the waiter and made a sign for the bill. 'Matthew said the Rolex George wears is one of the originals. It's worth thousands and he wears it as if he bought it on the high street. Matthew's obsessed with it. I felt like saying to George: Give Ayrton your Rolex and he'll name ten species after you.

'Emily said on the phone last night that she had remembered more about the secret that Chrissie told her – about the murder she claimed to have seen in the Marianne North Gallery. She was so frightened that she rushed out without her flip-flops. Chrissie spun Emily some tale that a taxi driver picked her up from her drawing lesson and had been given them by her mum. We guessed that the taxi driver was her dad and, since I worked out who lives at Kew Villa, her supposed mum had to be Rosamond Watson. Chrissie told Emily that it didn't make sense. She had left the flip-flops in Kew Gardens so how had "the lady" got them? A consummate liar sprinkles their lies with truth, but it's such a convoluted story, we think it might all be true. Chrissie did see something in the gallery. Not a murder obviously since there was no body.'

'The lack of a body doesn't mean she didn't see a murder.' Jack flipped open his wallet. 'What colour were her flip-flops?'

'Bright pink, since you ask!' Bella handed her debit card to the waiter and asked him to split the bill. 'I had the same ones in blue.'

Included in the Boots bag that Tina had left for Stella was a pair of pink flip-flops. And included in the burglary at the Ramsay house in the 1950s was a Rolex watch.

351

Chapter Fifty-Four

November 2014

'You mustn't say anything, Jack. Do keep out of it.' Jackie put a plate of chilli down in front of him. 'Eat!'

'How can I face Stella knowing that Cashman is two-timing her?' Jack wailed.

'It's frustrating, but not your business.' Jackie sat down at the table with him, nursing a bulbous pottery mug of camomile tea.

Jack had gone to Jackie's to get her advice about Cashman, but as soon as she had welcomed him into her terrace house in Chiswick, he knew he had come home.

Jackie sipped her tea. 'You'll upset her.'

'Upset who?' Graham, a mild-mannered man in suit trousers and shirt sleeves, with glasses pushed up on his forehead, wandered into the kitchen. He replenished his mug from the cafetière on the counter.

'Stella. Her policeman's gone back to his wife.' Jackie pushed a carton of milk across the table towards her husband.

'Nice enough bloke, but he wasn't good enough for her,' Graham commented.

'No one is, in your eyes!' Jackie said.

'Nor yours,' Graham replied.

Jack would normally have minded that Jackie had told his secret – not that it was his secret – to someone else. But Graham was family. Sitting in the Makepeaces' cosy kitchen savouring chilli doused in tzatziki and tucking into a fluffy baked potato (Jackie always did an extra one) he was sanguine.

'I can't lie to Stella.' He had received a text from her an hour earlier suggesting the identity of the little girl that Terry had spoken to. Burdened with his knowledge about Cashman and his secret visit to Kew Villa he had yet to reply.

'It's not lying. Has she talked to you about seeing Cashman?'

'She told me yesterday. I didn't know what to say.'

'That would have been hard,' Jackie agreed.

'Someone needs to tell her before she finds out.' Jack mashed chilli into his baked potato.

'Remember what happens to the messenger. Don't even go there, mate!' Carrying his mug of coffee, Graham left the kitchen.

Jackie shook her head at the closing door.

'You said he was Stella's "Mr Right".' Jack scraped his plate.

'Did I?' Jackie looked sceptical.

'Stella said you did.'

'I know my memory's bad, but I'm sure I didn't. Stella decides what I'm thinking and is, without exception, wrong. It's how she makes difficult decisions: she puts them on to others. We all have our strategies. If they had met in their twenties, Cashman might have suited her. Unlike Suzie, Stella doesn't need constant attention, and he's like her dad, always working, which allows her to work too. I may have said that once. But Cashman sets too much store in family to leave and start again. Karen probably asked him to pick his socks off the floor and he took that as grounds for divorce. Stick that in the dishwasher,' she said as Jack took his plate to the sink.

'She will be upset.' Were it him, he would be ripped to shreds.

'She will,' Jackie agreed. 'Then she'll lick her wounds and move on.'

'Anyway, he hasn't dumped her, he's still seeing her.' Jack slammed shut the dishwasher door. Filling a mug with milk, he put it in the microwave. Tonight, as he often did when he was here, Jack wished he lived at Jackie's. Then he wouldn't have to stay perfectly still in dark corners of the homes of strangers as their secret guest. Here he was legitimate. But, he reminded himself, he was welcome in the Makepeace home because he was *visiting*. Although they treated him like one of the family, he was a cuckoo and this was not his nest. Still, if anything happened to Jackie, he didn't know what he would do.

'I nearly hit him yesterday, right outside Kew Gardens station,' Jack confessed as he stirred runny honey into the steaming milk.

'Best not clobber a police officer in a public space,' Jackie advised. 'Stella will miss talking with Martin about the case. Still, she's not in love.'

'Could Stella be in love?' Jack pondered aloud.

'Oh yes.' Jackie got up and fitted her mug on the crowded top rack of the dishwasher. She began laying the table for breakfast with the efficiency of a nightly routine. Jack's routine was driving a train at precise times or cleaning for Stella. His nights were open to chance.

Jackie placed a tablet of soap in the dishwasher and set it going. 'Stella wouldn't admit it to herself, but she'll have appreciated emerging from her dad's shadow and being Martin's sounding board. She'll have been solid gold for him. Have you seen him on the telly? Rabbit in headlights. He's no nearer to finding who killed that man, poor lad.' She placed a jar of muesli on the table beside a packet of cornflakes. 'You and Stella are a good team.' She rinsed out the cafetière and put it by the kettle.

'Stella is thinking that the little girl Terry spoke to might have been Tina.' Jack tried the idea out on Jackie.

'Tina sought Stella out, remember. She apparently wanted to buy her flat, but there were others on sale in the block and Stella hadn't advertised. Have you thought that Tina came to Stella because of Terry?'

'Why didn't Tina just tell Stella about the murder? Buying her flat and taking out cleaning contracts was a complicated and expensive route to her.'

'Tina Banks needed a flat and a cleaner.' Jackie put out bowls and spoons. 'I suspect she wasn't ready to tell her. She wanted to, but couldn't, but unconsciously she did the groundwork.'

'She was using Stella!' Whatever else, Jack had come to think that Tina had liked Stella for herself.

'No. She genuinely liked her. But she had to be sure that she could trust her. Then she got ill and things came to a head.' Jackie spoke over the hum of the dishwasher. She put out mugs and a bottle of vitamin C tablets. 'Stella was round here a few times asking me if she could trust Tina. She knows how to look after herself.'

Jack shouldn't have been surprised that Stella had confided in Jackie. The evening when Tina Banks had come to the flat, she had said she wanted to buy it, but spent most of the time quizzing Stella about the Rokesmith case. Jack had assumed she hoped to get Stella onside with flattery, not knowing that Stella was impervious to such tactics. But had she actually wanted to know about the case?

Jackie was filling tumblers with water from a filter jug on the counter. 'It could have been Tina that Terry spoke to. She was exactly Stella's age and they got on because they were alike. Terry probably saw that.' She pinched fluff off Jack's sleeveless pullover. 'Give that to me when you go, I'll handwash it. You can borrow one of Nick's; he's about your size.' She tapped the jar of muesli. 'Your favourite.'

Jack looked properly at the table. Jackie had set three places. There were three glasses of water for bedtime. He felt a glow of happiness. He was staying the night.

In bed that night, Jackie lowered her book and told Graham about her conversation with Jack. 'I wish Jack and Stella would sort themselves out.'

'Careful what you wish for.' To wind down, Graham Makepeace – a surveyor for Hammersmith Council by day – designed buildings on a computer-aided design app loaded on to his mini iPad. He placed a green-planted roof on to the sustainable three-bedroomed house.

'I am careful.' Jackie took up her book and proceeded to read the same page for the third time.

356

Chapter Fifty-Five

November 2014

Cashman's knock was tentative. Had Stanley not succumbed to a tirade of barks, Stella wouldn't have heard it.

'You've seen your friend Jack?' he demanded gruffly when Stella opened the door. 'You know he was questioned by one of our officers for the Kew Gardens murder? He was in the vicinity of the gardens the following night.'

'Jack does night shifts; he frequently walks home afterwards.' Jack hadn't told her.

'He had no alibi for the morning of the murder.' Cashman stamped his feet on the mat in the hall.

'Is he a suspect?' Stella called a halt to Stanley's barking with a tip of the hand. Instant quiet. The dog remained close to Cashman, eyes black with suspicion.

'We can't rule him out. You saw him last night.' It wasn't a question, but she gave a nod of confirmation.

'Did he say he saw me?'

'No.' His question told her everything. Jack must have seen Cashman with his wife. Cashman had worried that Jack had told her. She had noticed that Jack was silent when she told him about seeing Cashman. And now Cashman had come to explain. He had left it twenty-four hours so she'd have had time to digest the information and would perhaps not be so angry.

Stella flicked the switch on the kettle. 'Tea, coffee?' She had forgotten which he preferred.

'Neither – I can't stop. Things are hotting up. We've got a print at the gallery. It's in the back yard, at the side of the tap.'

'Is it on the system?'

'Yes! You're not going to believe this. It came up on a robbery round the corner from here in St Peter's Square!'

'When was that?' Before he died, suspecting an intruder in Rose Gardens North, Terry had changed the locks. The houses in St Peter's Square were bristling with grilles, CCTV and state-of-the-art alarms.

'Nineteen fifty-six!'

Stella moved Tina's bag, which was on the table after her visit to Lucie May, on to the floor out of sight as a truth began to dawn.

'Police thought the job was done by boys and orchestrated by a Fagin-type character. This was fifty-eight years ago so add another sixteen or so years and the owner of the print would be in his seventies. Perfectly able to wield a scalpel. This is the break we needed, Stell!'

Stella imagined the Ramsay locket burning a hole in the bag. She didn't speak. Now was the time to mention the James Hailes boarding pass. She remained silent.

'There's more!' He sat astride 'Jack's chair', leaning on the back rest, his usual position. 'We've found more footage of the man from the gallery alighting from a Piccadilly train at Chiswick Park and boarding a District line train to Kew Gardens. He leaves the station in the direction of Leyborne Park. We've got him crossing at the zebra on the South Circular and going up Forest Road, then nothing.'

'That's not the way to Kew Gardens.'

'Like you said, he probably met someone and went there with them.' It was the way to Kew Villa. Stella didn't say this.

As was typical if she wanted him not to touch something, Stanley began nosing around the bag. Stella snatched it up and put it on the counter. She remembered what Jack had said about hiding something in plain sight and hoped it would work.

Perhaps Cashman thought that discussing the case with her would be a good lead in to finishing with her? He would have to do it by himself. Perhaps Lucie was wrong and he hadn't gone back to Karen Cashman. She remembered the look in Jack's eyes and this slim hope died.

'I must go.' Cashman leapt out of the chair and swung it around with one hand, tucking it under the table. 'I wanted to keep you in the loop.' He wasn't going to say anything. Where Lucie May would have been enraged by Cashman's cowardice, Stella was faintly relieved. It made her plan easier.

'Martin, could you do me a favour?'

'Anything for you, Stell.'

Stella explained what she wanted, poised for his refusal.

Cashman's reply was immediate. 'I'm on it!' He kissed her on the forehead and, escorted down the hall by Stanley, left the house.

Later, with Tina's locket on the table in front of her, in a voice that lacked conviction, she took a leaf from Tina's book and dictated a text to Cashman. She didn't compose it in a mood of revenge as Lucie had urged her to do. She was letting Cashman off the hook since he was obviously bad at endings. Her message was identical to one that she had sent to a previous partner on the day that her dad had died.

Let's call it a day. We know it's not working.

Chapter Fifty-Six

November 2014

A keen wind pushed at bare trees and rustled bushes; it raced across the lawns that were grey in the dying light. It was only ten to four in the afternoon, but the lowering sky was hastening the night. The muted roar of an aeroplane, lost in cloud, made the air throb.

Taking the path from the Elizabeth Gate, Jack timed the interval between planes. One minute and fourteen seconds. Risk measurement relied on the premise that if something happened yesterday it might happen today. Yet there was much that had happened yesterday that no one knew about. Fred West had murdered for years before he was discovered, a True Host who had welcomed his victims into his home of ever-expanding rooms. Murders committed on a hundred yesterdays lay undiscovered in makeshift graves and beneath concrete footings. Unrecorded, they didn't exist. While his visit to Kew Villa remained a secret, could it be said to be non-existent? However much Jack tried to be open and honest, secrets held him in a vice. He was in no position to judge Cashman.

True Hosts relied upon most people's cosy assumption that a bad thing was unlikely to happen.

Jackie said: 'We can't live waiting for something bad to happen.' She left the front door open when she put bottles in the recycling bins; she pulled the curtains after it was dark giving anyone in the shadows a chance to map her living room. She wouldn't notice if someone was trailing her, learning her habits and routines. Yet Jackie wasn't naïve; she feared for the safety of her sons, particularly Nick who rode a motorbike, but she expected only good of life. Jack lived in fear of something happening to Jackie. It was a 'fact' that the good die young.

No wonder Bella had laughed when he had warned her about Watson. The man with the gerbera at Tina Banks's funeral, who he now knew wasn't Tina Banks's father, wasn't a True Host. He lacked the precision of step and the cold certainty; his hand had trembled when he laid the flower on the sleek black casket. True Hosts are psychopaths, unable see beyond themselves. Other people kill on impulse and out of desperation or cowardice. Watson mightn't be a True Host, but had he killed his wife? Or had Matthew Ayrton committed an actual murder? Jack felt the case, already nebulous, drifting into fog.

He shouldered through the doors of the Marianne North Gallery and was enveloped by the quiet. He gazed at the richly polished wood panels and the octagonal pattern in the tiles at his feet. His heart leapt at the beauty awaiting him in the hundreds of paintings on every wall. Thin morning light trickled down from the windows high above. He thought he was alone and gave a start when he saw Stella sitting on a bench facing the chamber where she had found the body, her rucksack at her feet. She was leafing through a bundle of papers.

'All right, Jack?'

Her tone gave nothing away. Had Cashman told her?

'The police got an anonymous phone call about Rosamond Watson. The exact words were: "Ask Watson where his wife is." Although it wasn't a job for CID, Terry went along. We were right about one of those sets of figures on Watson's drawing: it's the telephone number for a public phone box outside the Kew Herbarium.

It's still there. I've just checked it and, apart from the area code, it's the same number: 0208 940 2418.'

'How do you know this?' Jack was astonished. Stella must have asked Cashman to go on the HOLMES database. And he had agreed.

Stella handed him the papers.

Jack joined her on the bench and, fumbling for his reading glasses in his coat, put them on. The sheet was headed *Enquiry Kew Villa – telephone call.*

'Martin Cashman emailed it this morning.' Stella didn't look at him. Jack blinked as the floor tiles seemed to reconfigure, merging and separating. Cashman hadn't confessed that he had gone back to his wife. *Stella had told him about their case.*

```
I spoke to Mr George Watson, the owner of
Kew Villa, the address cited in the call.
I explained that the police had received a
telephone call that raised concern for his
wife's safety. I regretted that I wasn't at
liberty to say who had rung. I refrained
from informing Mr Watson that the call was
anonymous. I enquired if he could surmise
who would initiate such a call.
    It is my suspicion that Mr Watson knew the
identity of the caller but was unwilling to
divulge a name. He assured me his wife was
fine and invited me to stay for her to return.
    A girl was present during this exchange.
Christina Banks, aged 9 years, was of a calm
and honest disposition. She told me that
Mrs Watson gave her milk and 'chocolate cake
with hundreds and thousands' and then 'popped
out'. Her account and a reference to a locket
worn by Mrs Watson was credible. On this
basis, I considered it unnecessary to wait.
    Conclusion: hoax call intended to malign
```

    Mr Watson. Perhaps arising from a disagreement
    at Mr Watson's place of work or a domestic
    issue now resolved. Unless there are further
    calls, no action required.

'Lucie said Dad "let someone get away with murder". Here's the proof. On the basis of Dad's report, the file was closed.'

Stella played with the zip of her anorak. In the silence, Jack became aware of the drone of the air-conditioner. He glanced about him; they were alone in the gallery.

'Something happened to change his mind.'

Stella had got the transcript from Cashman. He couldn't bear that she was being duped. Regardless of Jackie's advice he began, 'Stella, I need to tell—'

'Later perhaps Dad saw that leaving without seeing Mrs Watson was a serious slip. He had taken the word of a girl – Tina – and the husband. Both unreliable sources.'

Jack flapped the papers. 'This suggests that Terry was swayed by Tina's "testimony", not the husband's. It wasn't Tina he saw, but you, his honest daughter.' The Stella that Jack knew would never have asked Cashman for the file. Jackie was wrong; she must be in love. 'Around summer 2010 something that you said made him review this visit in 1976.'

Stella got up and went into the antechamber where the body had been. A disembodied voice replied, 'He had an argument with Mum.'

'I thought they didn't meet after you got too old for access weekends.'

'It was on the phone. Mum accused him of putting me on a pedestal.'

Jack heard the scrape of a footstep. Behind him the doors to the porch were closed. The gallery, clad in glass, wood and tiles, played tricks with the acoustics. The sound was Stella.

'She told him I hated the dolls he used to give me and had lied to please him.'

Suzie Darnell was still tough on her ex- and now dead husband.

'Dad had tried to get hold of me when he heard about that taxi driver going on a shooting spree in Cumbria. He was worried I was OK. Mum told me later: I think she felt bad for what she'd said.'

'The second of June 2010.' Days of death were burnt into his soul. 'Were you in Whitehaven then?' Stella seldom left West London.

'No. Terry was just worried I might be. He got in touch after the Hungerford massacre in 1986. I've never been there either. He checked on me after any major incident. During the London bombings he was frantic. Mum says he was neurotic.'

'More likely he was well aware that the unlikely can happen. It was proof that you were never far from his mind.' Jack knew that in the face of a disaster he too would check that Stella was all right.'

Stella was in the doorway of the antechamber. 'I can't see that it would prompt him to review his visit to Kew Villa in 1976.'

'It might have. At the tea in Kew Gardens, you confirmed to him that when you were little you lied to keep the peace. He could well have faced the likelihood that Tina had lied to him so staked out Kew Villa to catch a glimpse of Mrs Watson.'

'Why didn't he just knock on the door and ask for her?' Stella's voice rang around the gallery.

'Maybe he did. Or maybe he thought Watson would remember him. If he was guilty, he might have feared your dad would return. There's so much about this that we don't know.' Jack looked about him. North's paintings held their counsel.

Stella went on: 'Unless Tina was telling the truth and Mrs Watson was alive when Terry went round.'

Jack told her about his conversation with Bella. How he had mistaken Ayrton for Watson and that Tina had admitted to stealing the locket when she saw them shortly before her death. 'The hoax call suggests that someone knew she was dead or in danger. An obvious suspect is Matthew Ayrton, but if he was suspicious about Rosamond Watson he wouldn't have stopped at one call. He's sadistic, he would have terrorized Watson.'

364

'This means that we have two suspects: Ayrton and Watson; and a likely victim. Still nothing concrete.' Stella sighed.

'Tina had stolen the locket from the Watsons. Maybe Watson found out and that was why Tina lied for him.'

'Bella told you that Ayrton bullies Watson. He could have been blackmailing Watson all this time.' Stella sniffed the air. 'When I found the man in here, I had smelled stale tobacco smoke. When they found the pack of cigarettes on the body I thought that was the source, but the killer could have been here when I arrived, or just left.'

'Watson gets into work early. That's how I came to mix him up with Ayrton. He could easily have been in the North Gallery and then come to the Herbarium. The receptionist commented that Watson often forgot to sign in. Ayrton hadn't either. Less an oversight than a deliberate intention to mislead.' Jack was still cross with himself for mistaking Ayrton for Watson. He went back to Stella's observation. 'Apart from smelling smoke, was there anything else you noticed?'

'Cashman asked me that. There was, but it's gone.'

Jack was piqued that Cashman had got there first. He noticed that Stella hadn't called him 'Martin'.

'Odd that Dad didn't tell Lucie,' Stella said. 'He only dropped hints. He didn't even tell Cashman.'

'It was a basic error not to have waited to see Mrs Watson. Perhaps he wasn't keen to admit that to Lucie and maybe he didn't trust Cashman as much as Cashman likes to imagine.' Jack bit his tongue to stop the sniping.

'Cashman could easily establish if Rosamond Watson's dead or alive,' Stella said. 'The locket Tina gave me has to be the one that was stolen from the Ramsays. I think the man who died in here was James Hailes. Lucie said Kew Villa was left in trust to Watson and if Rosamond died it was to go to Hailes. That gives Watson the motive to kill him. And he has the means to enter the gallery after hours. We should tell Cashman.'

'If we give him a bunch of screen grabs from Street View, tell him about a boarding pass and show him Tina's bag of odds he'll send us packing.' Not true. Cashman would listen to Stella. He would take over the case. He would keep Stella involved, but would cut Jack out. He would see Stella and his wife. 'Have you said anything?' He was torturing himself.

'Of course not. It's conjecture. You and I need to agree before I speak to him. And there are lots of silver lockets.' Stella didn't sound convinced.

Not with 'G' and 'R' on the back, Jack thought, but didn't say.

Stella went through to the back gallery where Tina had told Emily she had seen a murder. Jack followed her.

A dull glow emanated from a screen on which was scrolling Marianne North's timeline. A grainy photo of the artist in voluminous skirts painting on a veranda appeared with the caption *Marianne North in Ceylon*.

Stella was peering into an old wooden cupboard opposite the rear exit. 'This must be where Tina hid.'

One side of the cupboard was given to shelves, but on the other side was a compartment with enough room for a child to crouch. Bella had boasted that she would have found Tina if she had looked for her. Successful concealment, as Jack knew, relied on a person not properly looking. The space was now crammed with plastic signs. He flipped through them: 'Cleaning in Progress', 'Marianne North Gallery', 'Shirley Sherwood Gallery'. He felt a tingling and looked beyond the signs into the shadows. He imagined whispering to the frightened girl that it would all end happily. But it wouldn't be true. There was no such thing as a happy ending. Yet, he suspected that even at nine, and since she had read *The Cat in the Hat*, Chrissie Banks had known that.

'Chrissie told Emily that she saw the Cat in a Hat carrying a box with two things,' he remembered Bella scoffing that it must be a lie.

'Pages twenty-eight and twenty-nine,' Stella said. 'The Two Things wreak more havoc.'

'You remember the page numbers.' He was thrilled.

'Because I found a copy of those cuttings you showed me in Tina's book. It was tucked between those two pages. Everything that Tina did was deliberate.'

Jack felt his way as the fog in his mind thinned. 'Tina saw a *man* not a cat. He had a box holding two things. As in *items*.' He crouched beside the cupboard and, with a child's eye view, surveyed the room. The vanilla and terracotta tiles fanned away. The pictures seemed to crowd around him. 'Read the notes from your visit to Tina in the hospice.'

Stella flicked through her Filofax. 'Forward Hammersmith Road, Forward Hammersmith Broadway, Left Butterwick.' She stopped. 'Cliff Banks told me this is one of the runs taxi drivers learn for the Knowledge, so Tina wasn't rambling.'

'I doubt she was ever rambling. Skip the street names then.'

'"Cat in a hat. Two things. Fork. Bag. Look behind the fire,"' Stella read with Tina's halting speech.

Jack scrambled up. He knocked against one of the signs. 'Fire Exit'. It depicted a stick figure running. 'From her hiding place Chrissie had seen the murderer enter the gallery through the rear door. He carried two things, a fork and a bag. Assuming the fork wasn't cutlery, but a garden fork, he was going to bury the body.'

'So why couldn't she have said that?' Stella pinched the bridge of her nose ruminatively. 'I suppose she was too ill.'

'Too painful. I didn't speak for weeks after my mum died. Tina – Chrissie – saw Rosamond Watson being murdered by her husband. It must have made no sense. She wiped it. Only when she was dying did it return and she knew she must tell you. She needed to tell you; she hoped it would save her.'

'How could telling me cure the cancer?'

'It couldn't, but people do a lot to avoid death.'

There was a ping. Stella had received a text. Jack guessed it was Cashman. 'Is that Cashman?' He could have kicked himself.

Stella read the text. 'Cliff Banks wants me to clean Tina's flat tonight.'

Jack hadn't seen Banks at Tina's funeral; he had mistaken

Watson for her grieving father. From Stella's description, he sounded devastated by Tina's death. Stella missed her father. If each could assuage the other's need, that could only be good. Especially now that Stella had lost a friend too. No one could replace Jack's mother, but Jackie came close. Not that Jackie needed a son; she had two already.

'George Watson doesn't look as if he'd hurt a fly,' Stella said as she replied to Banks's text.

'Reginald Christie looked like a bank manager, but he strangled at least eight women before he was hanged at Pentonville in the fifties.' Jack thought back to Tina's words. 'Odd to bring the fork in here. He would have had to lug it out with the body.'

'Murderers make mistakes,' Stella said. 'A small error given he got away with murder.' She opened the back door and made her way out of the disabled exit. Jack went after her. 'We need to get inside Kew Villa again,' she said over her shoulder.

Locked gates gave on to the Kew Road. Evening rush hour was in full swing, with traffic nose to tail in both directions. They took the path that ran past the galleries and went deeper into the gardens. They stopped beneath the Ruined Arch.

'Are you free this evening?' Stella pushed aside tresses of thickly growing ivy and went into one of several bricked cavities within the arch. Daylight was fading; she was an indistinct shape.

'What had you in mind?' He pictured shepherd's pie at Stella's, but she was going to Tina's flat. Jack got out his phone and switched on the torch app. Patches of lichen and moss on the crumbling stone shone vivid green and brown in the bright light.

'I want you to clean Kew Villa. I've taken Donette off the job. The remit is only downstairs, but do what you can.' Stella stepped into the light. 'We need hard evidence before we tell Cashman.'

Jack felt a leap of excitement. This was a new side to Stella. The wishes and needs of the client came first – within reason; to arrive late or unannounced was, according to her manual, a *No*. It seemed the rules for investigating cases were different.

He saw a hidden advantage to her plan. He could say that he

had found the cuttings while cleaning. He could show Stella the link between the burglary, the body beneath the Great West Road and Kew Villa. Then he saw that he could never do that. It would be a lie.

'A good place to bury a body close to the Marianne North Gallery would be up there, off the beaten track.' Stella pointed at a steep slope beside the Ruined Arch covered with dense foliage.

From the mass of bushes a tree trunk rose skywards. Jack aimed the beam at a notice nailed to the bark. '*Eucalyptus gunnii!*' he breathed.

Chapter Fifty-Seven

November 2014

From across Kew Green, St Anne's Church chimed seven. A pigeon landed on the window sill, strutted up and down and then flew away. A plastic clock on the table read twenty-three minutes past eleven. The second hand jerked with each tick, but didn't move forward.

George Watson didn't notice. When he needed to know the time he consulted his Rolex watch which, although nearly a century old, kept perfect time.

In his studio at the top of Kew Villa, he contemplated the liquids with which he brought his dead materials back to life. The Copenhagen Mixture of alcohol and glycerine water and the Kew Mix, a lethal concoction that must on no account leave the Herbarium. George smiled grimly as he imagined Matthew Ayrton's reaction if he could see the tumbler of Kew Mix beside his scalpel.

Chin chin, Matthew!

Methodically he finished the inking in. There was little blank space left on the sheet of acid-free paper. He executed final curves and flourishes. His hand had been steady as he traced the pencil sketch. He was the best artist in Kew, in the world. Ayrton could not do without him. He knew more about botany than Ayrton did.

He had realized who made that telephone call in 1976 as soon as the policeman told him about it, but said nothing. He had understood, before it was laboriously explained to him, that it was an insurance policy. A warning shot across his bows in case he should feel tempted to confide in anyone else.

'*Get a grip, George. You must learn to keep secrets.*'

Then Jimmy Hailes had turned up and the nightmare started again. He could keep secrets. When he found the flip-flops outside the gallery he had kept to himself that the child must know and pretended she'd left them at his house. He had saved her life with his silence. But then even she turned on him at the end, after all he had done for her, threatening to reveal everything.

He slipped a fresh blade out of a protective sheath of folded paper. He picked up the handle of the scalpel from the gutter of his drawing board and, with dexterous fingers, fitted the blade on to it. The fine steel caught the light from his lamp. He touched his finger to it and cut the skin. A light cut, so no blood. The slightest pressure and he could slice his finger in half.

He drew a line along the bottom of the plate and wrote his name. He gave his drawing a name: *Rosulabryum watsonii*. He added the copyright sign. Copyright for botanical drawings was assigned to the botanist. The artist was the botanist's amanuensis. But this drawing was his alone. *He* was the botanist. He had the knowledge. He should have been in Ayrton's place. Instead of a corner of the Artists' Room he should have had a large office with a curving wall in the Herbarium covered with specimens and accolades. The accolades were meant for him. Too late Rosamond understood the nature of his shackles. He laid the finished plate on the drawing board. It was his best. He looked at his Rolex. One thing he could say about it was that it kept perfect time.

It was the perfect time.

The air shifted in the room. Someone had opened the front door. George Watson picked up the scalpel.

Chapter Fifty-Eight

November 2014

This time when Stella smelled the stale tobacco smoke she knew it wasn't Tina. It wasn't the smell of a cigarette that had been smoked in the flat, but the residual odour on a smoker's clothing. Cliff Banks was here. Her heart sank; she had wanted to clean alone.

'Hello?' There was no reply. But, as she knew well, the walls were thick. The fire doors didn't allow sound to penetrate. She pushed the equipment cart along the corridor, making no sound herself as she approached the closed living-room door. Surely she wasn't about to catch Cliff Banks doing the foxtrot, although Tina had said he was a star at the Hammersmith Palais when, as Tina had liked to imagine, their dads had vied for partners on the dance floor.

The living room was empty.

'Anyone here?' Her voice resounded in her head. The words hung in the air. She crossed the hall to the little room that, in her day, had been her study. It was Tina's study too. A state-of-the-art computer sat on a curving work station. She caught a fading whiff of Eau Libre and her throat constricted. The desk lamp was on; a pool of light accentuated shadows in the corners of the room. She shifted it to confirm that there was no one there.

Stella was puzzled. She never left lights on. Perhaps Cliff or Michelle Banks had been sorting through Tina's things. She heard a faint whirring, like a trapped insect, and, squatting on her hands and knees, traced the noise to a timer mechanism plugged into a four-gang socket. The light had come on automatically. The timer wasn't there the last time she cleaned. Tina's dad was, like Terry, security-conscious.

Stella sensed a movement and wheeled around in time to see the door swinging shut. The latch clicked. Someone had oiled the hinges since she lived there, a task she had never got around to.

She checked Tina's bedroom. Tina's bed had been stripped; the little cupboard where she kept her make-up and hair products was empty. Tina's clothes were gone from the wardrobe and the drawers of the cupboard. Nothing remained that might distract a buyer from imagining how to make the flat their own. Stella hadn't expected the Bankses – Cliff and presumably Michelle – to act so quickly. But Tina used to tease her for taking so long to sell her dad's house. She never had sold it. If she made a decision, Tina wasted no time actioning it.

Having established that she was alone, Stella went to the kitchen and began to clean. She couldn't have foreseen how calming it would be to go through the familiar actions in a flat that had been hers, but now felt very much Tina's. Her friend seemed closer. For the hour that it took to move through the rooms – still clean from the last session – Stella allowed herself to believe that Tina wasn't dead, but at her office. She would return soon, kick off her high heels and be pleased to see the windows sparkling and the surfaces gleaming. She would appreciate the scent of lavender oil.

Stella had another go at the stain in the living room that Cliff Banks had pointed out. It was her 'loose end'. After fifteen minutes she thought it might be fainter and admitted defeat.

It was seven o'clock. Jack would be arriving at Kew Villa. After tonight, they would go to Cashman with their suspicions that James Hailes was the body in the Marianne North Gallery and that George Watson had buried his wife by the Ruined Arch. If he dismissed it, they would have at least done all they could.

She hadn't brought Stanley. She realized that it was years since she had been in the flat without him. The sight of the square of lamb's wool that Tina put out for him was unsettling. The sealed quiet had an uncanny quality: not the quiet of being alone, but of muted presence. No longer calming, the stringently cleaned rooms accentuated the abandoned air. Tina wasn't coming home later. She wasn't coming home at all.

Abruptly Stella was gripped with the conviction that she must leave. Job sheet in hand she hurried from room to room, confirming her checklist.

Her mobile rang. On a cleaning shift Stella usually kept the ringer on silent and only took emergency calls. But it could be Jack and there was no one to mind if she answered. She raced back to the living room and fished it out of her anorak.

The screen said *Tina Banks Mob*.

Stella felt as if she was deep underwater, the pressure building and her senses dulled. At her feet the stain grew, filling her vision. She put the phone to her ear.

'Stella Darnell?'

'Hey, Stell, fancy a coffee and a natter!'

'It's Michelle. I've found Tina's mobile. It was in her coat.'

Stella had forgotten she had wanted to know about Tina's early-morning call in the office and had asked Michelle Banks about Tina's phone. The weight of reality returned. She lowered herself on to the sofa, her energy sapped.

'You wanted Tina's phone log? I've no idea how to send it to you, but if you've got a pen, I've transcribed the calls. There aren't many because Tina mostly used her work phone.'

On automatic pilot Stella pulled her Filofax from her rucksack. Her hand was trembling. 'I only need the ones for the day that Tina was admitted to the hospice,' she said, pen poised.

'That's easy. Tina phoned to tell me she was being admitted. Mad – I didn't even know she was ill. An hour later she called again and asked me to call you.' There was a pause, but when Michelle spoke again she gave no hint of judgement that Stella hadn't gone to see Tina as soon as she got the message. 'Looks like Dad phoned her too.'

'Was that it?' Perhaps Tina had received the early-morning call on her work phone, but Stella didn't think so.

'No. There are two more. One at six for ten minutes and then again at a quarter past six for one and a half minutes. I thought at first they were on the previous evening, but it looks like someone rang her early on the day she went into the hospice.'

'Who is the caller?' Stella breathed in the scent of the lavender air freshener to steady herself. She had a hunch that what Michelle told her next would be the key to the case.

'It's an unregistered number.'

'You mean "Withheld"?' Stella was stunned with disappointment.

'It's not in her contacts list. It has no name.' Michelle was patient. 'Do you want it?'

'Yes.' Crestfallen, Stella would take it anyway.

'It's 0208 940 2418. Does that mean anything to you?'

'No.' *But it did.* Stella thanked Michelle, told her she had cleaned Tina's flat and would get the key to her as arranged.

Stella prepared to leave. The living room, lacking many personal items, looked much the same. Probably the Bankses had decided that the two pictures by Marianne North would convey a sense of home to any buyer.

Now more familiar with North's work than she had been when she first saw the prints, Stella wandered over and looked at them properly.

At the bottom of the print of the tree was the label, '*Study of the West Australian Flame Tree or Fire Tree*, Marianne North'. The number in the corner of the print was 764. She looked at the other print, a detail of one of the flowers from the fire tree. It was 766. Stella felt a return of the prescience that she was getting closer to the truth.

She brought up the photograph of the botanical illustration from Tina's bag. Scribbled on Watson's drawing of the eucalyptus were '764' and '766'. She was about to swipe the photo closed when she saw the telephone number for the call box outside the Herbarium at Kew. Her hunch was not misplaced. What she had told Michelle was untrue; the number did mean something to her: 0202 940 2418 was the number in Tina's call log. She had received two calls from someone in the telephone box early that morning.

She had written the number on George Watson's illustration. It wouldn't have been because it was the nearest thing to hand; as Stella had said to Jack, everything Tina had done was deliberate. It would be because she wanted to point Stella's attention to Watson. He worked at the Herbarium. Jack had said he arrived at work early; it was why he had mistaken him for the botanist Matthew Ayrton.

She remembered what she had heard Tina say before she went out of the office – Stella had come in on the end of the first conversation. Tina had left the office to take the second call. She had referred to Stella as the cleaner. She tried to recall the first conversation, but it wasn't a case of recalling: adept at tuning out to clients' business as she cleaned, she hadn't listened in the first place. She did remember that Tina had said 'Twat!' because although Tina used to lose her temper with bits of equipment, she never swore.

She shut her eyes and tried to re-create the morning. It wasn't a pleasant memory. Tina had been angry and impatient. When she found the locket she had accused Stella of suggesting she was lying. Stella heard Tina's voice: *'This is about truth and lies. It always has been.'* She had supposed she was talking to a client. But what client rang at six in the morning from a phone box? They might ring at that time, but why not from a mobile? Unless they didn't want the call to register on their phone. She had no hard proof, but Stella was now certain that the caller had been George Watson. *'It's a bloody name. It means nothing.'* Jack said a plant didn't exist until it had a name. Tina was wrong. A name was important. Watson had hoped to have a plant named after him.

Stella opened her eyes and the phrases that Tina had uttered in the office echoed in her mind.

'Time is not a luxury at our disposal... Everything must come out...'

Tina had told Watson that she was going to say what he had done. She had been going to catch a murderer.

Without Stanley to alert her, and preoccupied, Stella had no idea if she was still alone in the flat.

She grabbed her Filofax from her rucksack and flipped to the page where she had written down what Tina had said to her in the hospice.

'Cat in a hat. Two things. Fork. Bag. Look behind the fire.' Jack had said he doubted that Tina was ever rambling; everything she said made sense. *Look behind the fire.*

She looked about the living room. Of course there was no fire. She knew that. Her eye fell on the only colour in the room, the Marianne North prints, and she felt a flash of guilt. She hadn't cleaned them. She lifted the tree print down, took it to the dining table, laid it carefully face down on the glass top. A card was tucked into the edge of the frame. *Look behind the fire.* Tina hadn't finished her sentence. Look behind the *Fire Tree*.

Stella prised it out. It was a photograph of a teenaged boy sitting on a wall outside a house. Above his shoulder on the wall of the house was marked either a '5' or an 'S'. Stella knew it was a five and behind him would be a two. It was a copy of the photo in the Hammersmith Archives. She had believed the boy to be Ivy Collins's son because he was outside 25 Rose Gardens. Now another thought occurred.

She grabbed her phone and brought up the snaps she had taken of the contents of Tina's Boots bag. She found the photo of Tina's nan. She had also photographed Tina's writing on the back of the photo. 'Nan (Ivy C.) three days before she died, 1970'. Stella had dismissed its inclusion in the bag as a mistake, thinking it was meant for Michelle. Now she saw that Tina had definitely meant it to be there. Ivy Collins was Tina's grandmother. That meant the

377

boy in the picture was Tina's father. She knew from Tina that her father had been an only child.

Stella fetched down the other print, the flower of the flame tree, but found nothing behind it. Yet Tina had noted the number on the illustration. She was about to return it to the wall when she saw something on the carpet by the skirting. She rested the print beside the *Fire Tree* against the wall and picked up the slip of paper.

It was a blank receipt, identical to the one that Cliff Banks had given her, with a four-leaf-clover motif in the top right corner. And, she realized, it was the same as the taxi receipt in Terry's desk drawer. She went to the table and, her back to the living-room door, abruptly sat down, her thoughts rushing in. Had Terry been in Cliff Banks's taxi? This receipt wasn't blank. Scrawled in Tina's hasty hand were the letters: 'JH – KV, RW@ EG'.

There were too few characters after the at sign and no domain name so it wasn't an email address. A code? Too easy.

Outside was darkness. There were no lights on the River Thames or on the far bank. The pane reflected her black-silhouetted figure in the white-walled room. She didn't notice that the smell of stale tobacco smoke was stronger.

Stella quickly decided that 'K' stood for Kew and that 'KV' could be Kew Villa. It was a short hop to conclude that 'JH' were the initials of James Hailes and 'RW' stood for Rosamond Watson. 'G' might be George, yet it came second. What was the 'E'? It needed two minds; she would show Jack.

'All right, Stell!'

She hadn't heard Cliff Banks come in and nearly shouted with fright. The reek of stale smoke was overpowering. He was grinning. Stella dropped the slip and it sailed to the floor and landed at his feet. Cliff Banks snatched it up.

'Let me put these up for you?' Scrunching up the receipt, he grabbed the prints from the skirting, carelessly wielding one in each hand, and hung them up. He had swapped them around, but Stella didn't say so.

'What's this?' He was smoothing out the receipt.

How had she not heard Banks arrive? One law of being a detective was to be aware of your surroundings. 'You gave it to me,' she lied, her head spinning.

'What does this mean?' He jabbed a finger at the writing. He had the same look in his eyes as when he had asked about Tina's keepsakes. She had lied then too.

'They're, um… It's a file reference. In my office,' she floundered.

'Funny file reference.' Still grinning, Cliff Banks flicked the paper across his fingers. He didn't give the receipt to her. 'Your problem is you work too hard. You and Chrissie. She never knew when to stop either. Don't make the same mistakes as my girl.'

It sounded like a threat. But Jackie often said the same to her.

'If I was you I'd come up with a more logical filing system.' He handed her the receipt.

'If you're happy with everything, I'll be off.' She put the slip in her trouser pocket. He knew she was lying. She felt herself redden. She could have told the truth. Yet if Tina had wanted him to know about what was behind the pictures, she would have told him. *Why hadn't Tina told her dad?*

'Very happy.' Banks put up the collar of his denim jacket. 'Don't worry about locking up, I'll do it.'

Stella wheeled the cart along the passage and at the end glanced back. Cliff Banks hadn't followed her out of the room.

Out on the landing she waited for the lift. Her heart thumped as she willed it to arrive. She smelled stale tobacco smoke here too. She listened for the mechanism inside the shaft. Nothing. The flats had been acoustically engineered to dampen sound. The silence was complete. Stella felt uneasy. She was just about to lug the cart down the stairs when the lift door slid aside.

The taxi was parked beside her van in a visitor bay. Stella shoved the cart into the back of her van. In the driving seat, she fitted her phone into the dashboard cradle. It was eight o'clock; Jack would be finishing at Kew Villa.

'KV'. She flooded with hot panic. Keeping an eye on the lobby door for Cliff Banks, she cursed herself.

'*My wife took out the contract; I had nothing to do with it. My name* shouldn't *be on your database.*'

'*Your wife probably told our operative your name. Having a rounded picture of our clients helps us do a good job.*'

Watson had murdered his wife, so he would have known that she was lying. She couldn't have spoken to Rosamond Watson. He would know that Jack wasn't there to clean. Jack was alone at Kew Villa with George Watson.

Stella fumbled with the key in the ignition. Nothing happened. She had turned it the wrong way. There was only one way to turn it. The van wouldn't start in drive. The automatic gearstick was at neutral. She tried again. Dead. The battery was flat. How could that be? She hadn't left the lights on. She hadn't left anything on that could have drained it.

'What's occurring?' Cliff Banks was at the window.

'My battery's flat,' Stella shouted through the glass. 'It's fine,' she added stupidly.

'I'll jump start her.' Banks pulled open her door. She was enveloped in cold air and spattered with drops of rain. She was tempted to pull it shut again and lock it.

Banks reached into his car and sprang the bonnet. He bent down and tweaked the lever under her dashboard. She caught a whiff of stale smoke. He had her bonnet propped up and was attaching his jump leads to the battery points by the time she climbed out. He gunned the taxi's motor. The noise of the cab's diesel engine carried across the grassy slopes.

The morning she had found the body in the Marianne North Gallery she had heard a diesel engine start up and drive away. She had supposed it was a delivery van. *Who was delivering to the gallery at that time?*

Frantically, she turned the key in her van. Still nothing.

Banks gave a strange giggle, high-pitched like a woman's. 'No point. Your battery is shot.' He detached the leads, gathered them up and slammed shut the bonnet. 'Hop in, I'll take you.' Another giggle.

'I can get a bus.' Rain stung her cheeks.

'It's freezing and wet. Chrissie would never forgive me.'

'I want you to catch a murderer!'

Mechanically, Stella got into the back of his taxi. 'Please could you drop me in Kew? I'm meeting a friend.' She spoke through the gap in the glass partition, her voice a monotone.

'Make yourself at home.' Cliff Banks slid shut the panel. In the dark, the rear-view mirror reflected nothing so Stella couldn't tell if he was looking at her. Strains of music seeped through the rear speakers. Mantovani's 'Dancing with Tears in My Eyes' had been her nan's favourite. Had Ivy Collins liked it too?

On Kew Bridge lights from the traffic strobed over Banks's registration certificate above the jump seats. Stella read the number: 34425.

'I want you to catch a murderer!'

She sat forward in her seat.

'All right, Stell?' The speakers were close to her. In the reflection of the windscreen Cliff Banks was a distorted Harry Roberts. The robber's lank hair fell over his forehead, dark eyes betraying no feeling.

Those numbers: *34425*. Tina had scribbled them on the eucalyptus drawing.

'My dad was my hero.' When had Cliff Banks stopped being his daughter's hero?

'Drop me here!' Stella looked up and was appalled to see no lights outside. No traffic. Only impenetrable darkness. The music swelled in volume. 'I'll get out.' Thinking that she mustn't sound scared, while knowing she sounded very scared. She wrenched at the door handle, but black cabs locked automatically when the vehicle was moving.

Mantovani rang in her ears. She delved in her anorak for her phone. Her fingers closed over nothing. She pictured her mobile in the dashboard cradle. She had left it in the van.

Chapter Fifty-Nine

November 2014

Jackie was alone in the house. Graham was at a surveyors' conference in Cambridge, Nick their eldest son was in a show and wouldn't be back until the early hours. He lived at night and slept by day. Her other son Mark lived in Manchester. She made herself a cup of camomile and, while it was steeping, began to lay the breakfast table for the next morning. Absently she laid four place settings and then remembered it was just her. Mark had left home and Nick would go as soon as he and his mates had found the right place. Then it would be her and Graham. She would relish the peace. She wasn't like some women she knew who dreaded being left alone with their partners after the birds had flown. Jackie never tired of Graham's company and if anything she loved him more now than when they had met. She would welcome Nick leaving. While he was under their roof she knew where he was, or rather where he wasn't. She couldn't properly go to sleep until she heard him come in at some unearthly hour and set the downstairs alarm. If he was in his own place, like Mark way up north, he could get up to all sorts and she needn't know. Not that she'd be without someone to worry about. There would always be Stella and Jack.

Jackie was startled out of her reverie by a knock on the door. Who could be calling at this hour?

Hurrying to the hall, she went through a roll call of loved ones who might be injured or worse. Nick would still be on stage, but he had that terrible leap from a cupboard in the second half. Graham had been the victim of a freak accident, a bus crash or flash flood. Or Mark…

Without hesitation she opened the door and Lucie May swept past her into the kitchen. Cobwebs fluttered in her hair and she was flecked with a dusting of grime.

'You have to help me,' she trumpeted.

'Do I?' Lucie May was not on Jackie's list of loved ones. 'Coffee?' She flicked the switch on the kettle. 'Or a shower perhaps?'

'There isn't time!'

Refusing to be ruffled, Jackie leant against the sink, sipping her camomile tea. She had the measure of the reporter and her tendency towards drama and catastrophe, but she wasn't ready for May's reply.

'I want a job with Clean Slate.'

Chapter Sixty

June 1976

The silence was all-encompassing, as if the heat had absorbed sound as well as moisture. No flies buzzed; no birds sang. No breeze stirred the dried stems and grasses browned as if scorched by fire. All was devastation. Even aeroplanes didn't penetrate the deathly quiet. Evening was approaching, but it was so hot that it could have been the middle of the day. The stifling temperature obliterated all sense of time.

Chrissie emerged from a tunnel of pines and japonica bushes into intense sunshine. She raced across the grass to an asphalt path. It was swollen and blistering; cracks where weeds had forced their way up had opened wide. The weeds had wilted and died. The soles of Chrissie's flip-flops stuck to the tacky bitumen and, tripping, she yelped when the ground burnt her foot.

Thirty metres away, amidst grasses of brown and faun, was a house. Palatial Victorian red brick, it was better suited to the leafy suburbs of Epsom or Ascot than the Royal Botanic Gardens in Kew. A mantle of ivy, shrivelled to raffia, trailed across the walls and entwined rusting drainpipes. A veranda skirting three sides of the building was topped with a glass canopy thick with dirt and bird droppings. The canopy was supported by wrought-iron uprights with exuberantly curling supports. Steps led to an external porch. Paint on the window frames above the veranda was flaking; the sashes were rotten.

The house had seven windows and two big chimneys. The heat warped the air and it seemed to the girl that the house was made of jelly.

Although drenched in hot sun, the house had a desolate aspect that sent a shiver down the child's spine. With a swoop of shock it dawned on her that she was lost.

Dizzy and thirsty, she made her way across scrubby grass to the villa. She grasped a metal handrail beside the steps to the porch; it burnt and she snatched her hand away.

A papery pile of leaves lay outside the porch. It was as if the seasons had telescoped. Everything was parched and dead.

The quiet wasn't absolute. Chrissie felt a trickling at the back of her neck and smacked at it. Her hand came away wet. Even in the shadow of the canopy it was like an oven.

She shuffled out of her flip-flops and placed them side by side by the porch. One of the doors was open and without pausing to consider if it was wise or if she was allowed to, the girl insinuated herself through the opening between the doors. She called out, 'Hello?'

Light spilled through dirt-encrusted windows on either side of the porch. Chrissie ventured further in. Her dad had told her often enough that she was better than everyone, and had nothing to be frightened of. She was lost so she would ask the people who lived in the house to tell her the way home.

A woman appeared. *A ghost.* Chrissie gaped at the face floating before her. Then the apparition solidified to a head and shoulders on a block of stone. Telling herself that she wasn't scared, Chrissie strode across the vestibule. She opened one of the two doors ahead of her. Out drifted the deadened air of a tomb. Confounded by heat and, although she couldn't admit it, fear, Chrissie crept inside.

It wasn't absolutely dark; light seeped in from grimy windows in the pitched roof. Gradually shapes of light and shade resolved into a balcony. There were no walls. The house had no rooms. Across the tiled floor was a doorway with no door.

'Hello?'

Chrissie stopped in amazement. Every wall was covered with paintings framed in black wood. They hung so close together that her impression was that they *were* the walls. The glass in the frames reflected paintings on the other walls.

In one painting was a tree with bright orange flowers. She had thought that flowers and trees were different things. She fumbled with the title, her lips working silently. *Study of the West Australian Flame Tree or Fire Tree*. It was numbered 764 and was painted in 1882. Chrissie did a sum and worked out that it was painted ninety-four years ago. She didn't know anybody that old. The white-blue sky in the painting was the same as the sky outside. Near the tree was a mound of smooth rocks that would be too hot to lie on. The only shade was under the tree. She could shelter there, her back to the tree trunk.

There was someone lying there already.

Chrissie went closer. Holding on to a wooden rail, she peered at the picture. A woman was lying on the ground. One hand was stretched towards Chrissie. She wasn't on the grass and stones beneath the tree; the painter had put in tiles for her. The tiles were like the ones that Chrissie was standing on. She whirled around.

The woman was lying in the place with no door behind her. Chrissie went over to the doorway. White teeth, white eyes, white hair. Chrissie clamped a hand to her mouth to stop herself screaming.

'Are you all right?' she tried tentatively. She kicked something. A shoe, black with a silver buckle. The other shoe was on the woman's foot. She leant on a tall cupboard to get her breath. 'Do you need help?' she asked in a quavering voice.

The lady's face and neck were pink as if she had been in the sun too long without her sun lotion on. Chrissie knew the lady. She looked like Mrs Watson.

There was a noise. Without stopping to think, Chrissie wrenched open the cupboard door. There were shelves piled with books, with nowhere to hide. Then she saw that the shelves were only on one side. There was a space on the other side. She pushed herself inside and, twisting around, hauled the doors shut. It was a stupid hiding place because if Bella and Emily looked they would see her straight away. Her dad told her off for acting without thinking. There was a hole in one of the doors; she poked her finger in and held it shut. She should have run out the way she came in. Her dad would be cross that she was hiding in a stranger's house when she should be outside playing with her new friends.

She squinted through the slit between the doors. It didn't matter where she hid. The Mrs Watson lady was angry that Chrissie had stolen her silver thing. She would tell her dad. After that nothing would matter.

She heard footsteps and shut her eyes as if by not seeing, she wouldn't be seen. *Bella!* When Chrissie dared look again, she saw that it wasn't Bella. She made no sense of who she saw.

Her dad was carrying a bag. He took out two things. Chrissie blinked. One thing was a fork for digging and the other thing was a bag like a tent. Chrissie's finger clutched at the door; it shifted and the crack widened.

Her dad was helping Mrs Watson into the bag. Chrissie expected Mrs Watson to mind, but she didn't. It couldn't be Mrs Watson because she would mind. Chrissie shut her eyes again, tightly this time. Her lips working soundlessly, she recited Run 82:

'Leave by left Gloucester Road, Right Elvaston Place, Left Queen's Gate, Right Kensington Gore…'

When she opened her eyes there was no one there. She clambered out of the cupboard and ran across the tiles. She flung herself at the doors and, tumbling out on to the veranda, she was instantly met by a bluff of heat.

Her dad read her *The Cat in the Hat* without turning the pages. She would try to stay awake because he got cross if she went to sleep while he was taking the trouble to read to her. In the waking dreams that followed she mixed her dad up with the cat. The Cat in the Hat drove a huge taxi, big enough for his tall hat. He drove too fast and didn't care what got in his way.

The lawns shimmered in the haze. There was no one there. Dazzled by sunlight and stupefied by the heat, Chrissie's mind worked fast to protect herself from the enormity of what she had seen. It wasn't Mrs Watson on the tiles in the house with no rooms. It wasn't her dad with the bag with Two Things. It was the Cat in the Hat whose tricks were *very* bad indeed.

She leapt down the steps on to the grass. She tore along a path, oblivious to stones lacerating the soles of her feet, until, crippled by a stitch, she skidded to a stop beneath a crumbling arch. A faint track went up a steep bank. Chrissie scrambled up and collapsed in scrub in the shade of a tree. In the bright sunshine she saw that the tree had a name. A notice was nailed to the bark: '*Eucalyptus gunnii*'.

She crawled deeper into the shadows and, exhausted by fright and dazed by the heat, she fell instantly to sleep.

It seemed to Chrissie that it was hours later that she was woken by a bell ringing. She rolled over and peered through the branches of a bush. Her dad was digging. The metal fork kept catching on stones. *Ting. Ting.* The hole must be deep because she could only see his middle. He vaulted back up to her level and began to drag a bag up to the hole. The bag was like a giant Christmas stocking. He shoved it in. Chrissie heard a thump. She covered her face with her hands and saw a fish bowl balanced on the tip of an umbrella. The fish was mouthing something at her through the glass.

Help!

There was no one there. Gingerly she crept out from behind the eucalyptus. There was no hole. She was lying to herself now. Bella said that her lies would catch up with her. Her dad was drawing dead plants. She rubbed at her temples. *Liar!* Her dad was driving his taxi. Snatching at the spectre of truth she intoned:

'Run Twenty-seven, Leave on left Addison Road, Right Kensington High Street, Forward Addison Bridge, Forward Hammersmith

Road…' She stumbled down the bank. Her dad didn't let anyone else call over the runs, not even Michelle. She was his Crystal. When he asked if she loved him more than anyone else in the world, she said that she did.

In the shadow of the arch, nestling in the grass, was a black thing. Chrissie stooped down. It was a black shoe with a buckle.

foan.' She marched down the bench. He lay for a few minutes all over his rant, not even Mathew. She was his. When he asked if she loved him more than anything else in the world, he said that she did.

In the shadow of the arch, Justin... watched Mrs Mac... ... Child, Childs stopped down it was a blackout. Nicholas had...

Chapter Sixty-One

November 2014

When he switched the engine off, Jack saw that the car in front of his van was a Toyota Yaris Verso. It was the same make and model as Terry's car, even the same blue. He got out. The Toyota had no dents; the paintwork was gleaming as if it had recently been valeted. It wasn't Terry's car, but Jack knew better than to ignore it. The blue Toyota was a sign.

Across Kew Green the bells of St Anne's Church struck seven. Lugging the equipment bag, he unlatched the gate to Kew Villa. The windows were dark. But as before when he had 'visited' there was a light at the top of the house. Watson was home.

Jack was on edge. He approved of Stella's tactic that he should arrive unexpectedly, but he had never done this before. He was used to entering the homes of True Hosts with what he liked to consider was tacit invitation and settling in. He was used to cleaning for Stella's clients. But he had never crashed in unannounced at a time when most households would be eating supper or watching television. Watson would be within his rights to ask him to come back at a more convenient time. Stella's brief was that Jack must gain entry and do the job come what may. At the time, he had done a hop and a skip to hear her talking this way. Now that he was on the doorstep, he felt less confident. Hugging the bag to his chest, he gave the door two taps with the knocker. The door shifted. He would have no trouble entering Kew Villa. The front door was already open.

Chapter Sixty-Two

November 2014

'I want you to catch a murderer!'

Tina hadn't told Stella that the murderer she wanted her to catch was her own father, the man whom Stella had understood Tina adored.

There was a click and the door-locking indicator went off. Stella flung herself out of the cab and straight into Cliff Banks. She smelled the rank odour of stale smoke, on his clothes and on his breath, and was hit by a wave of revulsion before fear kicked in.

'All right, Stell?' His laugh was high and fluty. He linked her arm through his and pulled her to him. He began to walk fast, forcing her along with him.

'Let go of me!' she shouted. Her voice was lost in the wind.

'Wouldn't dream of it, so far from home.' His breath hot on her ear, he gripped her more tightly.

The ground was uneven. Stella tripped, splashing into a puddle. In places the darkness was solid and she couldn't see her feet. It seemed they walked for hours when they stopped in front of towering iron gates.

With a shock Stella recognized where they were. They were outside the Brentford Gate to Kew Gardens. They must have passed the Estates Office, but there would be no one there. Stella pricked with fear. To her right was the River Thames, slick and black. Hidden behind the Herbarium, Ferry Lane was long and unlit. There were no houses nearby. If she called for help no one would hear.

Chapter Sixty-Three

November 2014

Jack lowered the equipment bag to the floor and pushed the door
to behind him. He didn't shut it. When he visited True Hosts he
made no changes as he moved about their homes. Tonight he had
the uneasy conviction that George Watson was expecting him.
It was nonsense of course.

The hall was chilled by the night air. By the door the longcase
clock was still stopped at 11.43. Its motionless face somehow accentuating the silence. When Stella had told him what rooms were
where, Jack had listened, unable to say that he knew the layout of
the entire house. Several times during her briefing, he had been
tempted to tell the truth, but since at last they were working as a
team again, he couldn't bear to threaten it.

There was the coat on the newel post. He caught a whiff
of mothballs.

'When did you last wear your coat, Rosamond?' he whispered,
his lips to the wool. He dipped his hand into the pocket and pulled
out a plastic wallet holding an Oyster card. Jack knew that if he
had online access to Mrs Watson's journey history he would find
that she had made trips up and down the District line. Mr Watson

was a botanical illustrator: the man had an eye for detail. He would take the actions of a life, of his dead wife's as well as his own.

He began to climb the stairs. He had fitted his ancient but immaculate Crockett and Jones brogues with rubber soles and they were soundless. He was careful to keep to the edge of the tread where a stair was least likely to creak. This area was beyond the Clean Slate remit, but when Watson appeared, he could say that he was looking for him.

I'm looking for your wife.

It was colder on the landing. He touched a tubular radiator outside the Watsons' bedroom and whipped back his hand. It was piping hot. The heating was on and yet the house was like a fridge.

He tapped on the bedroom door, a minute sound that Rosamond or George Watson would hear only if they were inside. Hearing nothing, Jack eased open the door and went in.

'Mrs Watson?' He blinked into spangled darkness. He swept his hand along the wall and found the light switch. The bedroom was unchanged from his last visit. The heavy curtains were drawn; the silk quilt draped over the bed had no creases. No indentation suggested that Mrs Watson had recently lain down for an afternoon nap or to recover from the headaches that her husband claimed she was prey to. Perhaps Watson wasn't quite as on it as Jack had supposed.

He searched through the drawers in the dressing table. There was the jewellery and make-up, but of course the newspaper cuttings weren't at the back of the drawer. He pulled the articles from his coat. Checking that the folds were correct, he snapped on a pair of plastic gloves and removed the drawer. He wedged the wad of newspaper into the back and replaced the drawer. A charade that restored the link between the house and the articles as if he had never broken it.

There *was* a difference. There was a framed photograph by the bed. Still wearing gloves, Jack held it to the light. Two boys stood outside a house, one of those Victorian terrace houses found across the country. The boys wore shirts and trousers with snake-buckle belts. The older one must have moved as the shutter went because his face was blurred. His companion – grinning for the photographer – had those elastically mobile features that denote charisma. Jack's heart chilled. The smile was too broad, too confident. Judging by the hairstyles – military-style short back and sides – the photo was taken in the fifties. The boy with the big smile was so vivid that Jack expected him to step from the frame. He turned the picture over and saw, written in precise and careful script, 'Cliff Banks with GW, 1955. 25 Rose Gardens. W6'.

The grinning boy was Tina's father. Although he had seen Watson only once, from behind, descending the stairs in Kew Villa, and the boy in the picture was out of focus, still Jack saw the older Watson in the fuzzy image. His head was bowed down as if to fit into the frame. Watson and Banks had known each other as boys. Jack shut his eyes and pictured the inventory of items stolen from the Ramsay house listed in Malcom Bennett's article.

Aside from the ring, they were a Rolex timepiece, a significant sum of money and a silver locket containing a photograph of Gerald Ramsay and his wife Anne. Judge Ramsay confirmed that the watch, an early Rolex, was purchased by his late father in 1921.

Bella had said that Watson wore an original Rolex. The shot had been taken before many of the houses in Rose Gardens were demolished for the Great West Road. Number 25 was the house that Stella had established was where the dead man found under the A4 in 1976 had been murdered. This picture placed Watson and Banks at the scene of a murder and it put them in the frame for the robbery. The article had said the window in the Ramsay house was too narrow for adults to have climbed though. Both boys looked small for their ages, Watson was skinny and wiry, Banks thick-set, shorter than his friend. Capable of entering through the narrow window. And the police were wrong – how many times had Jack insinuated himself through the tightest of apertures? Given that it implicated him in two crimes, why had George Watson put the photograph in such a prominent position?

He scrutinized Cliff Banks. The shape of his eyes, dipped at the outer corners, was like Tina's. But while the lawyer's eyes had glittered with a metallic flash that laid low her enemies and won cases, her father's were blank and without feeling. The boy had the eyes of a True Host.

Jack nearly dropped the photograph frame. Banks had asked Stella to clean Tina's flat. At the funeral, Stella said he had questioned her about what his daughter had left her. Her last words. Not the anxiety of a grieving father, the probing of a killer. Banks had wanted to know what his daughter knew and what she had told her best friend. Heedless of Watson hearing him, Jack fumbled with his phone and dialled Stella.

'This is Stella Darnell, I'm sorry I can't come to…' Jack drummed on the bedside table as he waited for the message to finish and then shouted as if Stella might hear him:

'Stell, it's *not* George Watson. Cliff Banks is the True Ho— is the murderer that Tina wanted us to catch. I'll explain. Call me as soon as you get this!' He tore up the stairs to George Watson's studio.

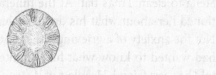

Chapter Sixty-Four

November 2014

By half past nine rush hour had abated and those out for the evening had yet to return. But for the occasional lorry or bus and a few cars leaving London, Kew Road was quiet. Mizzling rain made a watercolour wash of the lamplight. In Kew Gardens, beyond the high brick wall, a blustering wind shook the trees and the darkness was complete.

Inside the Marianne North Gallery a blue light cast a bleak glow over the paintings and across the tiles. No light penetrated from the windows in the roof. The doorways to the two ante-chambers were ghostly rectangles.

'We shouldn't be here.' Stella's voice was weirdly disembodied as if nightfall made a difference to the acoustics. 'Security will see the tripped alarm.'

'No worries, Stella, I killed the alarm. Security can carry on sleeping. Funny, Jimmy Hailes said the same thing. But he was stupid and you are not. Pity you had to stick your nose in where it doesn't belong. I was getting to like you. He was dispensable, the money-grubbing little shit!'

Cliff Banks was strolling around the gallery, hands behind his back, as if admiring the paintings. He paused by one. Stella saw that it was the *Flame Tree*. He moved on. He had let go of her, but both the doors into the vestibule and out on to the veranda at the front of the gallery would be locked. If she tried to run, he would catch her.

No one knew she was here. When she didn't meet him at Kew Villa, Jack would go to Rose Gardens North. When he got no answer, he'd try her phone and, getting the voicemail, he would leave a message. He'd assume she was with Cashman. They didn't have a history of keeping in touch. They didn't have a history of being a proper team. When she didn't come to work tomorrow, Jackie would try her phone. She would worry, but by the time they found the van outside Tina's flat, it would be too late. Stella's limbs turned to water.

'I want you to catch a murderer!'

'George's got a thing about the lady who did this stuff.' Banks waved a hand at the paintings. 'Weird about her, he is.' The heels of his shoes clicked on the ceramic. The precise sound made Stella's skin crawl. 'A person can yell like a stuck pig and no one comes. Your dad would have called it returning to the scene of the crime.' He giggled girlishly. 'Or he would of if he'd got close to proving there was a crime! Poor sod. You miss him?' He contemplated her with apparent concern.

'You killed Rosamond Watson and her brother James Hailes.' Too late Stella remembered Terry's advice:

Safety first: avoid being trapped with a person you suspect of murder and if you are, don't say anything likely to inflame.

'Shame you didn't work that out till now. Like Detective Darnell, one step behind!' He rubbed his hands together. 'You did your homework down the library good as gold. Got to admit, you had balls to con your way into poor old George's place. Gave him a right turn! You lied to me, Stella. I don't like liars. Michelle said Tina did leave you keepsakes. Mitch never could keep a secret. I brought up my girls to tell the truth.' He made a sucking sound through his teeth.

The paintings closed in on her like a giant grid. She was chilled.

They had been after the wrong man. George Watson wasn't the murderer. They had found the clues, but come to the wrong conclusion. Terry had said keep an open mind, test each clue against other possibilities. Blinded by Tina's death, Stella had seen a grieving father. Not a murderer. They had followed one theory at the expense of others.

'Rosamond Watson married George to polish up the rough diamond. George could do lovely flower pictures, but she wanted him to be Darwin. She backed the wrong horse. Me and George go back a long way. I told her, I'm not going anywhere. When it comes to George, I keep him on track. I'm in charge.' He giggled. 'She *loved* that!'

'Why did you kill her?' Stella stuffed her hands in her anorak to avoid Banks seeing them trembling. It was a cliché to keep him talking – he would know the tactic – but she must buy time, however futile any delay might be.

'When they found that soldier under the road in 1976, George goes and panics. He tells the lovely Rosamond about our little robbery when we was kids. Tears and all, stupid git. Says he killed the bloke. Best thing he ever did: the vermin was dossing in my mum's parlour. She only decides they'll go down the nick and tell them it was me that stuck the knife in. Their word against me. Money and class speak loudest. Men like your dad would lick her arse. She was going to *lie*!' Banks was outraged. 'I finished the bloke to put him out of his misery. All my life I've tidied up after George. Call me the Cleaner!' He gave a high-pitched whinny.

My mum's parlour. 'You're the boy in the photograph!' The boy grinning on the wall. She should stick to cleaning.

'What photograph?' For the first time Banks looked worried.

'It's in the Hammersmith Archives.' She played her faint advantage. 'I gave it to the police. You're Ivy Collins's son. You're sitting outside her house. The picture links you to the site of the murder.' She spoke rapidly.

'I said we shouldn't of let that bloke take our picture, but my mum made us.'

Banks wandered into the antechamber where Stella had found the body. She edged towards the other chamber. If she could get to the yard and shout, someone beyond the wall, or even in the houses on the other side of Kew Road, might hear. Banks was back. 'It don't prove nothing.'

He was right. The photograph proved that he had been outside a house that had stood on a spot where a body was found. Even when it was established he had lived there, it didn't link him to the soldier's murder.

'A signet ring on the body was traced to a burglary in St Peter's Square. The thief was a boy. They know a boy lived at twenty-five,' she lied. Then she remembered a nugget of truth: 'They have a fingerprint.'

'Stella, you can do better than that, sweetheart!' Banks was at the doorway to the rear gallery, where Tina must have seen him putting the body of Rosamond Watson into a sack. 'I was wearing gloves. George left his at home. It'll be his print.'

She could do better. Fear had paralysed her thinking. 'You stole a silver locket from the Ramsay house engraved with Gerald Ramsay's initials with a picture of Ramsay and his wife inside. George Watson gave it to his wife. She would have assumed that the letters stood for George and Rosamond.' Stella was gabbling. *She should have given the locket to Cashman; he would have listened to her.* 'I gave the bag of things that Tina left me to the police.' She heard how unconvincing she sounded. 'If anything happens to me, they'll connect it to you.' If the police knew, Banks had nothing to lose: he might as well kill her.

'Your copper boyfriend has only just worked out that old Jimmy Hailes isn't Hooker! I collect stuff that's left behind in my taxi. I planted the licence and the fags on him. Like lambs the police went for it.' Another giggle. 'George lost that locket years ago.'

He knew about her and Cashman. A taxi had driven away the last time Cashman had visited. Banks had been watching her.

'Even after I sorted Rosamond, George didn't learn his lesson. It took a visit from your daddy to make him see sense.'

'What do you mean?' Stella hadn't meant to ask anything. It was vital that she appeared to know.

He grinned and dimples appeared in his cheeks. 'I called the police from a box near George's work. I suggested they ask George about his wife.'

'They could have arrested you. Watson could have told the truth to my dad.' Stella had let herself be drawn in.

'I knew George would clam up. It was Rosamond who had the bottle. The odds were stacked against him. He killed that soldier. He lured his wife here. She liked it here, she had been when she was a kid. He's not so smart, it never occurred to him that this place would risk putting him in the frame. He was shitting himself when, after you found Jimmy's body, the cops interviewed every-one working at Kew. If I go down, he goes down. Then he won't have some plant named after him. That's a laugh – should be a weed by rights!' He whinnied again. 'No, our George knew to keep his mouth shut. Lucky for him it was your dad that showed up. Wasn't much of a detective, was he!' He snuffled into his hand as if the joke was rude. 'My daughter lied to him and he swallowed it.' He stopped smiling. 'Don't know why she did that.'

Fear had made Stella lose the thread of her argument. 'The police will work out who killed James Hailes.'

'You're scaring me, Stella.' He wandered into the rear chamber. In the low light, the cupboard that she and Jack had looked into earlier that day was a hulking shape. With no other escape route, Stella had to follow him.

'Like I said, George isn't so clever. He gets to university and nabs himself some rich girl, but he'll never win the Nobel Prize. Drawing flowers isn't like the law, or cabbing. He's a lackey for those odd-bods in Kew Gardens. I'm my own boss.' He whistled a snatch of 'Three Blind Mice'. The notes carried around the gallery, rising up towards the roof. 'Fickle bitch! Afterwards Rosamond acted like I was something off of her shoe.' Fury twisted his grin. 'As for her whining brother… Hippy Jimmy came back from India finding that having a few quid comes in handy after all. He'd come back to get his share from his sister. She and George had done the dirty on him. After his dad had caught him pawning the family silver. "Borrowing" was what he called it.' His shoulders shook with suppressed laughter. 'Georgie was all for telling him his sister was pushing up daisies in Kew Gardens! I told him, "Come with me, Uncle Clifford'll sort it."' He swivelled on a heel. 'This new to you, Stell? Maybe stick to washing floors!'

Although his comment chimed with her earlier conclusion, Stella was angry. Fury cleared her mental fog. 'Watson didn't lose the silver locket that you stole.'

'What?'

'Tina – your Crystal – stole it when she was there for a drawing lesson. She gave it to me one morning in her office and told me where she found it.' Not true, but he didn't know that.

'My Chrissie wouldn't... steal,' he faltered. Bullseye.

'Not ordinarily, but you sent her to an expensive school and instructed her to lie about her background to fit in. She claimed to her friends that George and Rosamond Watson were her parents. She stole the locket to back up her story. When he found out, Watson told her to keep it. It was his insurance policy. She would never tell on him.' The truth was unfolding. 'He had to protect his career so he co-opted your daughter to bolster up the fiction that his wife was alive. Each had something on the other. In the end though, Tina played you both.' Stella didn't believe in ghosts or she would have supposed that Tina was in the gallery, feeding her lines.

'The morning she was admitted into the hospice, Watson rang her from that phone box outside the Herbarium. I was with her when she took the call.' Stella opened her mouth and the words flowed: 'Tina told Watson she was going to tell the truth. He would be arrested for murder, and so would her dad. Matthew Ayrton had asked Watson to draw a plant that he claimed to have discovered in the Herbarium. It would be a new species. Watson implored Tina to think again. She said she told him that, and these were her actual words, "time is not a luxury at our disposal".' Stella paused. When she had heard Tina say that, she hadn't supposed she meant it literally. 'Tina was a diligent lawyer. She had gathered hard evidence. Her last words to me were in a text. The police have it.'

'What text?' He glared at her.

Stella sniffed advantage. *'Police never said throat was slit, how did he know?* It was never reported that the soldier found in the crater in the Great West Road had been stabbed. The police said that he was crushed by falling masonry during the demolition. They embargoed the truth to give them advantage over the murderer. The "he" in Tina's text was you. You had mentioned it to Chrissie when she was a child.' Stella was making it up as she went along, but knew it was the truth.

'You're losing me, Stella.' But she could see he had registered his mistake.

Safety first: avoid being trapped with a person you suspect of murder. Don't ask questions likely to inflame. 'Inflammatory' was her only option.

'The day you murdered Rosamond Watson, you had a witness.' Like a magician she flung open the cupboard doors. She almost expected to find Tina – Chrissie – crouched inside. 'Your daughter watched you put Rosamond Watson in a bag and then bury her.' She had hit home. Banks was rigid with shock. Not smiling now.

'She told her friend Emily that the murderer was the Cat in the Hat, a cat in a bedtime book that you read to her when she was little. When she told me that, I was envious. My dad was never home before I went to sleep; we didn't live in the same house. When she saw you, she couldn't compute that her dad was a killer so she made up her own story. She lied to herself. You were the Cat in the Hat who calls at a house and causes chaos and stuffs people in bags.' If Stella was going to be Banks's next victim, the third he had murdered in the Marianne North Gallery, she would go down fighting.

'Finished?' Banks's eyes were as blank as Harry Roberts's.

'When my dad came to Kew Villa, Tina told him she had seen Rosamond Watson because her tea had been left out as usual. She had convinced herself that she had just missed her. When she found her flip-flops in your taxi, you said she'd left them at the Watsons'. But Chrissie had taken them off outside the Marianne North Gallery. Had you lied? By then she was lying so much to keep her end up at school that she didn't know what was true or whom to trust. When she was diagnosed with cancer Tina interpreted it as punishment for colluding with Watson, for turning her back on a crime. As she neared death, the scene here in the gallery came back to her. She tried to make a deal with death. If she handed over the murderer, she would live. The last time I saw her in the office, Tina asked me to help her.' Stella stopped as she took on the full force of her lie. She had been preoccupied by Tina's appearing to question her cleaning and hadn't seen that something was wrong. When Tina had asked to see her, she had left it too late. Her voice thick, she ploughed on, 'Only at the very end could Tina admit that her own father was a killer.'

This knowledge seemed to have galvanized him. Banks snatched the cupboard door from her grasp. 'Time to go.' Again Stella was shocked by his strength. Any hope of overcoming him vanished as he pulled her out of the side entrance of the gallery into the cold night.

Above her the lights of an aeroplane blinked. Beyond the gates puddles glistened on Kew Road. A car shot by, tyres swishing, the driver's eyes fixed straight ahead.

'Keep up, Stell!' All pretence of friendliness gone, Banks frogmarched her along the path she and Jack had used that afternoon. The path that Banks had taken her along after Tina's funeral. Japonica bushes shrouded the boundary wall, closing in on them. Suddenly Stella knew that the area around the Ruined Arch had significance. Cliff Banks had been looking for something on the ground. She had thought he was looking through the grille in the ruined arch. She felt a coil of pure fear rise up like a snake. No one would hear, but she had nothing to lose.

'Help!' She yelled so hard it felt as if a scalpel cut into her throat. He clutched her around the waist like a vice.

'Shut up!' he hissed.

The bushes were thicker. Stella stumbled and Banks tightened his grasp. 'Steady.' He gave his odd giggle again.

Tina had tried to warn her. Confounded by the paraphernalia of illness and the profound change in Tina, Stella had ignored her. Worse, she had assumed that the illness had warped Tina's mind. She had seen one truth: Cliff Banks loved his daughter. Awed by his attachment to Tina and aware of what she didn't have with Terry, she hadn't seen that the love wasn't mutual.

They were under the Ruined Arch. Her face grazed against damp bricks. Clamping a meaty hand over her mouth, Banks hooked his thumb under her jaw to stop her biting him and jerked back her arm in a lock. Stella recognized the second action: the police used it as a restraint.

'Rosamond also thought she was smarter than me. You're nothing but a cleaner. My Chrissie was only nice to you to make sure you did a proper job of cleaning.' His breath was hot on her ear. 'You was no friend to her. Mitch said she asked for you and you took your bloody time coming. It was her old mates from her posh school that she turned to when she knew she was ill, not a bloody cleaner!' He pushed her through the arch and propelled her up the slope into the undergrowth above the arch.

He shone a torch, wheeling the beam around as if searching for something and Stella saw a notice pinned to a tree trunk.

'*Eucalyptus gunnii*'. 'EG'. She caught her breath. RW @ EG. This was Banks's burying ground. In the shadow of a eucalyptus tree. The torch swung down and Stella saw she had been right that Banks had a specific reason for coming here.

At her feet was a rectangular hole about two metres deep. *Six feet.* She teetered, but Banks stopped her from falling.

She was looking at her grave.

Chapter Sixty-Five

November 2014

A thin line of light spread under the studio door. Jack had believed that he was a match for someone in the grip of evil. He knew all the tricks of a True Host. He could handle dark streets of glistening cobblestones echoing with distant footsteps, empty houses, rooms flitting with shadows. In the dead of night he was at his happiest dawdling in subway tunnels humming nursery rhymes or taking short cuts down alleyways and across cemeteries. After his mother's death he was afraid of nothing. Only her favourite colour, green, could instil fear in him. And bright red when it was blood.

Encircled in the light of an anglepoise lamp George Watson might have been asleep on the floor, his cheek resting on a hand. Blood was flowing from a deep wound in his neck. It spread over the floor. In one hand he clasped a scalpel. An empty glass lay beside him. Jack took it all in. It was no cry for help: there was no coming back.

Heedless of the blood, Jack squatted down by Watson and placed a finger on his neck. The skin was pliant and warm. He felt a faint pulse. Watson looked at Jack, struggling to focus.

Jack pulled his phone from his pocket and stabbed the keys. 'Ambulance. Police.' He reeled off the address. He took Watson's hand in his and stroked it. 'George, stay awake.' Useless advice to a man intent on sleeping for ever.

Watson trapped him with a stare as if he was hanging over a cliff edge imploring Jack not to let go of his fingers. Urging him to sink with him into the darkness. Jack held his gaze, blotting out the sight of the pooling blood that threatened to engulf him.

'George, where is Banks?' He repeated urgently: '*Where* is he?'

'Eucalshsh... gun...'

'What? George!' Jack stopped himself from bellowing. A milky film descended over the man's eyes. His gaze shifted beyond Jack to the far distance.

Jack let go of Watson's hand and got to his feet. A bottle stood on the table: 'Kew Mix. Ingredients, Ethanol, Glycerine and Formaldehyde'. The last was toxic.

Next to the bottle was a botanical illustration. Jack knew not to compromise a crime scene but, by craning over Watson's body, he could look at it. The constituent dissected elements didn't depict the character of a plant. In fine black pen, Watson had drawn vignettes arranged clockwise, each one contributing to the whole picture, creating a sinister depiction of impending death enhanced by the dramatic use of shadow and sunlight. The raw and uncompromising drawings reminded Jack of the work of Victorian illustrator Gustav Doré. He understood what he was looking at. An artist to the end, the intricately drawn plate was Watson's 'suicide note'.

The police would be here any minute. He must see the drawing before they stopped him.

The first drawing showed the silhouette of a wrecking ball against a dark sky. A full moon cast eerie light over a half-demolished house numbered twenty-five.

Jack's heart beat so violently that he began to sweat. Wild-eyed creatures, executed with finesse, beckoned to him, luring him into the monochrome world. The dead man at his feet was less real than the man – his throat slashed open – who lay in a contorted heap amidst smashed masonry, lath, splintered wood and plaster. The jagged line of a missing staircase jigsawed the image in two. Jack felt himself sliding into hell.

Another drawing showed a road dug away to reveal strata: tarmac, soil, London clay and the same suited body. Jack shuddered. The face was a skull. He beckoned to Jack with a skeletal finger on which was a signet ring. His eyes were intact. Jack shut his eyes, but the ghastly image was burnt on to the inside of his lids. He felt the hairs rise on the back of his neck. His skin was clammy; he shivered. He rarely felt afraid, but he did now. The plate expressed an underworld that, like Orpheus, he courted in his search for True Hosts. Yet he was afraid of finding it. The drawing plunged him into the mind of a tortured soul.

A little girl and a man stood in bright sunshine; black shadows slanted down the path of a house that was Kew Villa. Another drawing replicated the octagonal floor tiles in the Marianne North Gallery. On these a woman's corpse lay sprawled, eyes bulging. The paintings crowded in on her. She was looking at Jack as if he was her killer.

He didn't hear the wail of sirens. Faint, but growing louder.

A cleaning sign showed a stick figure slipping on a wet floor. A tall thin woman, her face shrouded within the hood of an anorak, carried a mop. The handle rested on her shoulder like a scythe. Watson had drawn Stella as Death.

Another illustration swam into focus. A eucalyptus tree anchored one side of the plate. *Eucalyptus gunnii.* Beneath was a headstone engraved with the names: Rosamond Watson and James Hailes. Jack saw another name. Stella Darnell. The beam of light that revealed the stone came from the headlamps of a black taxi cab. Serial number: 34425.

Blue light flashed across the ceiling. The lurid pulsing added dimension to the drawing. The eucalyptus tree shifted with a dry rattle. Jack recoiled as the characters began a strange and terrible dance towards him.

He lunged towards the door, slipping on Watson's blood. The room was crowded. Jack yelled, 'Stella's in trouble!'

'So are you!' Cashman clamped handcuffs on to Jack's wrists. Obliquely Jack saw he still wore the plastic gloves. *'Jack Harmon, ... do not have to say anything. But it may harm your defence...'* His voice came as if from underwater: *'...if you do not mention when questioned something you later rely on in court. Anything you do say may be given in evidence...'*

The handcuffs cut into Jack's wrists. Cilla Black sang 'Something Tells Me (Something's Gonna Happen Tonight)'. Jack was past understanding that it was his phone ringing. The vibrating handset gyrated lazily on the floorboards moving closer to the blood.

Cashman answered it. 'Lucie! Sorry, Harmon can't talk. I've arrested him for murder.'

Chapter Sixty-Six

November 2014

Rain stung her cheeks. It caught Banks unawares: torch in one hand, he let go of Stella and dashed water from his face.

It was only a second, but Stella didn't waste it. She elbowed him with all her strength. Banks staggered backwards towards her 'grave'. She charged down the path. With no light, she had to rely on her sense of direction. It was usually good, but darkness and fear had bewildered her. She cast about for her bearings. *She couldn't afford to hesitate*. Behind her she heard Banks smashing through the foliage. Crazy shadows swung about her as he searched her out with the powerful beam of his torch.

Stella tried to tread lightly, but this slowed her progress. She was deafened by the drumming of blood in her ears. She left the path and was impeded by snarled undergrowth. Thorns tore at her trousers. He would hear the snapping twigs and crushing brushwood. She tripped and pitched forward on to the ground, grazing her palms. The pain was remote. She rolled over and, clambering up, tumbled on to short springy grass. She was in the open. Lit by silver moonlight was a ghostly palace, curving glass merging with the moonlight. The Palm House.

Stella sped off across the grass, skirting the lake, keeping low as if dodging bullets. However fast she ran, the Palm House got no closer. Like a mirage, it shifted and shimmered, the glass incandescent in the sweeping beam of Banks's torch. Bright darts like fireworks danced across the curving roof.

He was gaining on her. He ran with no attempt at stealth, his steps plodding like a robot, a measured tread that ensured he would inevitably catch his prey. Sick with fright, Stella was exactly where he wanted her. Like a beater at a shoot, he had driven her from her cover.

The Queen's Beasts, strange creatures ranged along the front of the Palm House, took on an awful reality. She flattened herself against the plinth of the giant dog on its haunches. Light raked the lawn. It stopped by the dog and moved up, then down. It took Stella too long to grasp that the rhythmic movement was because Cliff Banks was strolling over the grass towards her.

She raced on past the Beasts; horns and wings seemed to surround her. Limbs leaden, she powered around the lake. A stupid decision: Banks could cut her off from the other side. Her muscles and lungs burned and the cold rain smacked at her like tin tacks.

She was in a blaze of white. Her shadow was elongated on the path before her. Caught in the torch beam as if between the crosshairs of a sniper's gun.

Stella cut through bushes on her right, or on her left. She had no sense of where she was. She should be at the Victoria Gate by now. She had gone the wrong way. Finally spent, she rolled under a tree and hunched in a ball against the trunk. The bark was smooth.

Jack had said that in a chase fantasy, it was impossible to imagine a scenario in which you died. Stella supposed that it was the survival instinct. But Jack was wrong. She *could* imagine that she wouldn't be around to see how this chase ended.

'My dad has the Knowledge; he's a living compass. He never gets lost. Leave on left King Street, Right Weltje Road, Left Great West Road, Right Hammersmith Bridge Road, Forward Hammersmith Bridge...'

Tina hadn't been boasting about her dad, she had been trying to tell Stella the truth about him. Or to come to terms with the truth herself.

Pale orange clouds bundled across the sky; it had stopped raining. She was leaning against a eucalyptus tree. *The* eucalyptus. She had run in a circle and was back at the Ruined Arch near the Marianne North Gallery. Metres from her was her burial hole.

She scrambled around the tree. Beyond the plastic cordon were two people. The torchlight swung wildly about. It must be George Watson. Stella gazed in bewilderment. Like Cliff Banks, the other person was wearing a green polo shirt. She made out a logo on the shoulder. George Watson was wearing a Clean Slate uniform.

Abruptly Cliff Banks appeared to rise into the air and drop to the ground. The other person loomed over him. Stella heard a clink and a snap and with a thump Banks fell into the hole and disappeared. The torch beam cut the sky and her hiding place was flooded with light.

'He won't be pointing Percy at the porcelain for a while.' A corncrake laugh. 'I rather took out my feelings for my ex-hubby on him. Hope I didn't dazzle you, Stell.'

Dazzled, Stella stumbled to her feet. If she was in one of Jack's escape fantasies, she had conjured up the wildest of happy endings.

Lucie May was prancing around the hole, waving the torch like Rumpelstiltskin. She wore a Clean Slate uniform and looped around her neck was a Kew Gardens access card on a lanyard. As she capered, it swung back and forth like a pendulum. 'Talking of those whose genitals we might damage...' She was cheery. 'Cashman and his merry men are on their way. Once I persuaded him that Jackanory isn't London's latest serial killer. Are you up to seeing Cash-for-Questions?' Now she sounded concerned, as if she would prevent Cashman coming if Stella wasn't up to it.

All Stella could think was that she wasn't going to die. Not today anyway. She stumbled to the edge of the hole and looked down. Banks lay still at the bottom. His hands were cuffed behind his back.

'Is he … ?' Lucie May had never made a secret of her philosophy of an eye for an eye.

'Much as I'd like to see him swinging from Kew's Unluckiest Tree, I've spared him for the justice system. Not smiling now, are we, Smiler!' Lucie aimed a kick and sent loose soil and stones down into the hole. 'Let's bury you with Rosamond Watson. What happened, did she reject you after you and she did it?' She turned to Stella. 'It's always about the bedroom in the end.'

'I'll get you.' Banks spluttered soil from his mouth.

'Fighting talk, Cliffy-Whiff!' Lucie scoffed.

It had never occurred to Stella that Cliff Banks had had an affair with Rosamond. *'Afterwards Rosamond acted like I was something off of her shoe.'* Some detective. 'Look!' She directed Lucie's torch towards the hole. Poking out of the impacted earth was a shoe. A silver square buckle glinted dully. 'It's Rosamond Watson's.'

'You and Rosamond together again!' Lucie's expression had grown serious, her eyes cold.

Cliff Banks tried to struggle to the other side of the cavity. More soil fell as he kicked and scuffed.

'C'mon, I need a pavement.' Lucie May scrambled down the slope to the Ruined Arch.

'How did you know it was Banks?' Stella asked when they were on the path.

'You're not the only one with files in the attic.' Lucie May was referring to the Rokesmith murder, Stella and Jack's first case, which Stella had found in her dad's attic after his death. 'I've spent all day amongst cobwebs, excavating the treasures of my past work. I found stuff on that soldier in the Great West Road in 1976. Your hunch about the boy living at 25 Rose Gardens was spot on. Ivy Collins née Banks had a son, Clifford, "out of wedlock". I couldn't find a trace of a Mr Collins. Ivy and Clifford were rehoused in Westcroft Square, where she died in 1971. By then Banks was married with two kids.'

Stella wouldn't tarnish Lucie's glory by admitting that she had worked some of this out. Lucie had filled in many gaps. She stopped under the Ruined Arch to get her breath.

'I'd done roadside interviews with some rubberneckers sniffing about the crater for more corpses. One was a Mr Clifford Banks. Bingo!' Lucie shone the torch at Stella. 'Feel free to say it, "Lucille May, you are bloody brilliant!"'

Stella had been thinking something like this. But her throat was raw so she couldn't speak. However, apparently Lucie didn't expect her to.

'Banks was aerated that the man had been in his mum's house. "Made me sick how he was dossing down in her parlour like he owned the place." Question: how did he know the man was in the parlour?'

'It's the obvious room?' From Tina's text, Stella knew that Banks had made another slip – about the victim's throat being slit – to her.

'I write what people say verbatim.' Lucie's voice boomed in the alcove. 'He said "*Made* me sick". He had known the man was there *before* 1976. And how did he know he was acting like he "owned the place".' Her voice dropped. 'I missed that. Then, pissed off that my idiot editor took me off the story, I dropped it. Mistake.'

'How did you know it was Banks who killed Rosamond Watson and not George Watson? Or James Hailes?' Or Matthew Ayrton. Stella was astonished to hear Lucie admit to an error. She was faintly gratified too.

'After you and I talked, I decided to pay a call on Watson. I told him that Banks had pointed the finger at him.'

'Had he?' Lucie had taken over the case. Stella told herself it didn't matter if they revealed the truth.

'It's the oldest trick in the book – tell one villain that the other one has dobbed them in. I doubted Watson'd bite, but it might scare him. Seems you went there yesterday. You suggested that you'd been in touch with his wife. Since Banks had killed her, Watson knew you couldn't have. So when I said Banks had done for him, he went as white as bleached knickers!' She cackled happily.

'I realized I'd said that.' She had put Jack in danger. Lucie May too.

'It's all on here.' Lucie pulled out her mobile phone from the Clean Slate trousers.

Stella breathed in damp moss mixed with earth and stone. Moonlight trickled down from the grille in the arch's roof. Ivy leaves, black as pitch, curled around the bars. On the day of Tina's funeral Banks had brought her to Rosamond Watson's unmarked grave.

'Posh school, law degree, down-payment on an office lease. Banks wanted his daughter to scale the social ladder to dizzy heights. George told me he stabbed the soldier. That put him in Banks's clutches. Banks made him finance his daughter through her career. At some point Tina Banks found out. Seems like she didn't stop him. As a lawyer she must have been shitting bricks. Her past was an axe waiting to fall. It's like *Great Expectations*!'

'She didn't know.' Stella was firm. 'She buried the knowledge and it only returned to her when she got cancer.' Stella's tiredness after running was compounded by confusion.

'She forgot that her dad had murdered his best friend's wife? Easily done, I suppose.' Lucie pulled a carrot out of her Clean Slate trousers.

'We forget important things.' After her parents separated, she had blotted out much of her life with her dad. Had Tina known that her success was founded on a lie? Stella would never prove it.

'If I was dying guess I wouldn't think straight,' Lucie conceded to her carrot.

Stella ducked out of the arch on to the path. 'She didn't have time on her side.' She paraphrased Tina's words.

'It seems Banks and Watson's murders all went tickety-boo until Rosamond's brother flew in from Madras in October.'

'He was living in a Buddhist commune.' Stella told Lucie what Cliff Banks had said about Banks being a hippy.

'Om!' Lucie rolled her eyes. Fiddling with her phone, she held it up to Stella.

416

'I should have told Jimmy about Rosamond. I should have gone to the police and told the truth. But there was watsonii. I wouldn't let Cliff ruin that too. Cliff said he would just have a word with Jimmy and send him back to India. We went to the gallery. Cliff said he would warn him, rough him up a bit so he got the message. He sent me out to keep a watch for the cleaner, she was due soon. He chose Marianne's gallery to implicate me if it went wrong. I should have realized. The police questioned all the Kew Gardens staff. Cliff was my alibi, he said I'd been in his taxi at the time of the murder. I knew if they found out Jimmy's real name, they'd be back. I gave Christina the drawing of the tree where Rosamond's buried. I hoped that one day she'd realize it was a map. I suppose I wanted her to see the truth and stop the nightmare.' The voice subsided into a prolonged cough. Then he started speaking again. Stella thought Watson sounded different. Like a boy whose voice is breaking,

'Cliff didn't care if I went to prison. He said he'd do Borstal and walk free. He said I'd hang by the neck until…'

He gave a strangled sob. Lucie switched off the phone.

George Watson had let three people die to preserve his reputation and ensure his name would go down in botanical history. A soldier who had fought in the war, his wife and her brother. Like Tina's, Watson's life was a lie.

Ahead of them the Marianne North Gallery was again a *Psycho* house against the blustering sky. Clouds raced past the chimneys. The seven windows were black as eye sockets. Shuddering, Stella was glad to have Lucie there.

'I knew that Terry's handcuffs would come in handy one day!' Lucie remarked apropos of nothing.

'How come you have his handcuffs?' Surely her dad wouldn't have kept police-issue equipment. If Lucie replied, it was lost as an aeroplane flew low above them. Stella left it there. Sometimes a lot of knowledge was a dangerous thing.

There were police vehicles outside the Marianne North Gallery. Blue lights lit up the red brickwork. Figures were going in and out through the porch and around the back. She pictured a criss-cross of muddy footprints on the tiles.

'How did you know Banks was here, in Kew Gardens?' It was easy to dismiss Lucie as a door-stepping hack. Perhaps she was a better detective than either of them.

'You didn't answer your phone.' Lucie parted the branches of a japonica bush and headed towards the gallery.

'I left it in the van.'

'I called your office not expecting to get a live person and got Belinda. Is she real?'

'Beverly. She shouldn't have been there so late.'

'She'd diverted the office phone to her mobile. She said she had to practise talking to people. I thought I got the weird ones in my job!' Lucie bit the end off her carrot. 'Jackie Rottweiler Makepeace would have seen me off. But Beverly said you were cleaning your old flat. She said that she shouldn't have told me, but had done so since I sounded worried. Don't tick her off: the kid saved your life.'

Stella had no plans to tick Beverly off. Except for working outside office hours.

'When I got to the flat, there was your van with your phone on the dash. I leant on all the door buzzers. A bloke answered and said he'd seen you leave in a taxi. From then on it was two and two make four. The cabby had to be Banks. Watson had said that the Marianne North Gallery is his killing field. I dropped in on Mrs Rottweiler, she lent me this costume and here I am!'

'Uniform,' Stella muttered. 'That card wouldn't have got you in. Security know the hours that the cleaners do.'

'I always get in.' Lucie finished her carrot. 'No wall too high, no river too deep. All hunky dory until you started racing about the gardens, in and out of those horrible beasties. Lost you for a bit by the Palm House. My lungs are string bags!'

'Banks could run fast,' Stella marvelled. 'I've worked out, he's got to be over seventy.'

'Seventy's not old,' Lucie barked. 'You did the running. He

waved his torch about like a dick, giving the impression he was chasing you.'

'I heard his footsteps.' She remembered the mechanical plods closing in on her.

'That was me.'

'Why didn't you call out?'

'I didn't want Banks to know I was there.' Lucie produced another carrot from her trousers. 'I jumped him as he was about to clonk you with a spade.' She approached the steps to the gallery. 'The self-defence training worked a treat. Banks went down like a ninepin. I cuffed him and tossed the toad in his hole. Job done!' A hearty corncrake laugh.

'What self-defence training?' When Stella was seven and no longer living with her dad, he had taught her to fell a six-foot man in five seconds.

'Terry showed me how to overpower a six-foot man in five seconds.' Lucie looked dreamy. She roused herself: 'Oh and I forgot to tell you, Watson's dead!'

'Dead?' *Jack had killed George Watson.* Stella felt her world end. Lucie's voice came from a long way away.

'...seems our little chat tipped the artist over the edge. He topped himself with a scalpel and quaffed a noxious cocktail that botanists use to preserve specimens. His last bid for immortality!'

'You're sure it was suicide?' Stella managed to ask.

'Jack said Watson left a drawing that showed it all.'

'You OK, Stell?' Cashman was beside her.

'If she is, it's no thanks to you, Detective Chief Superman,' Lucie May snorted. 'You need to take your fairground along to the Ruined Arch, that's where the action is.' The corncrake laugh carried across the lawns.

Stella realized that she was all right. 'Cashman, you'll find the body of Rosamond Watson buried by the Ruined Arch.' She turned away from the gallery. 'Clifford Banks killed the man in the gallery, whose name is James Hailes. He's George Watson's brother-in-law.'

419

'I know about Hailes. We just retrieved the dental records. Hey, Lucie, stop!' Cashman broke into a run after Lucie May. The reporter had taken the opportunity to slip under the cordon and was making for the gallery, notebook at the ready.

As the chain of strobing lights moved towards the Ruined Arch, a man stepped from the shadow of a japonica bush. He was tall, dark and gaunt.

'There you are,' he said.

'Come back to mine. We need to take stock.' Stella linked arms with Jack. 'I bought fresh milk.'

Chapter Sixty-Seven

November 2014

Kew Killer Charged.

Stella read the headline on the *Evening Standard* vendor's box outside the mini-mart. A plastic carton of milk dangled from her fingers. She frowned. Although it had been Tina's dying wish that her father be caught, Stella was grateful that she couldn't see his face plastered all over the front page. Cashman had told her that Banks would get life.

'At his age, life really will mean life.'

Jack said that if Banks was alive when he came up for parole he'd be unlikely to get it. A psychopath with no care for others, he would show no remorse.

Passing fruit and vegetables displayed on the sloping fake grass, Stella pushed on the door to Clean Slate's office above the mini-mart. The insurance company had left it on the latch. Jackie had lined up three new office premises to look at. Tina would say, *Move on.*

There was a man on the landing.

'Fancy a coffee, Stell?' It was Cashman.

'No thanks.' She eased around him. 'Unless it's urgent.' But then she relented; his eyes were like Stanley's when she had to leave him at home.

'I wanted to tell you that me and Karen are giving it another go,' he said brightly. 'I saw her in Sainsbury's yesterday evening. Think she clocked the pizza and beer in my basket and took pity. One thing led to another.'

'Lucie said she saw you with Karen last *week*.' Stella couldn't help herself. Now Cashman would think it was why she had sent the text.

'Lucie May could make a story out of what I had for breakfast!' Cashman reddened. 'Mind you, have to hand it to her, she's been brilliant over this case. Terry rated her.' He wiped a hand down his face. 'I did see Karen last week, bumped into her in Kew. We saw Jack Harmon – surprised he didn't say.' He had stopped using product in his hair. Stella decided that he looked less attractive. She admitted that she was lying to herself. If anything he looked more attractive.

'When I got your text, I was gutted. But, like you said, it couldn't work. Maybe in a different—' He clenched his jaw.

'I'm pleased for you both,' Stella managed.

'I'd like it if we could get back to how it was.' Talking to a dent in the plaster on the wall, Cashman smoothed his tie against his shirt front.

Stella nodded. 'I would too.' This was true. Their paths would cross and she didn't need awkwardness between them.

'You were key to solving this case. We wouldn't have got Banks without you. Maybe sometimes I could pop round after work and chew the cud?'

Stella shook her head. 'Best not.'

'No. Best not.' He lingered on the stairs as Stella carried on up.

'Stella?' he called up to her as she reached the Clean Slate door. She looked over the banister. 'Would you give apologies to, um, to Harmon? He had blood on him and was trying to run out of Watson's room. It looked bad so I was a bit tough on him.' He raised his eyebrows. 'I'll be sending a formal apology, but you have a way with words…' He gave a tentative smile and seemed about to come up the stairs.

She knew from Lucie that Jack had been arrested and handcuffed. Jack hadn't told her. Nor had he said he'd seen Cashman with his wife.

'If it hadn't been for you and him, and for Lucie, Banks would be driving his taxi and getting away with murder.' Cashman cleared his throat. 'You and Jack, you're good together.' He took the rest of the stairs to the ground floor two at a time. Stella heard the outer door slam.

'You just missed Detective Chief Superintendent Cashman!' Beverly looked fit to explode with suppressed excitement.

'Bev, make us a nice cup of tea.' Jackie was leafing through the morning's post. 'Then I'm letting you loose on some follow-up calls with your new natural approach!'

'I'm on it!' Holding the kettle as if it were a precious object, Beverly glided out of the room.

'You OK?' Jackie picked up a reinforced envelope from the pile.

'Yes.' Stella *was* OK. She had a day at Clean Slate, drawing up contracts, writing letters and reading her mum's 'Customer Report' just in from Sydney. Later she and Jackie would view office space. Definitely business as usual.

'Got an Instagram picture from Suzie this morning. She says she's back next week.' Jackie slit the reinforced envelope open with a letter opener and withdrew a gilded card. She nodded at a colour print on the heap of post. Stella looked at it. It was a picture of her mum sitting in an armchair with a cat on her lap. The caption read, *Home on Wednesday, can't wait to see you all. Sx.*

'This is normal,' Stella said.

'Normal? What do you mean?' Jackie asked absently. She was reading the card in her hand.

'Mum's not in some weird costume or wearing a silly hat. In the pictures she sends me, I hardly recognize her. It's like she's someone else,' Stella grumbled. 'She sent me a photo of herself dressed as a frog this morning saying, *Hopping to see you next week love Me xx*.'

Jackie laughed and flapped the card. It flashed gold. 'Thing is, Stella, your mum lets herself be adventurous with you. She dares to try out other selves because she trusts that you'll get her,' she said peaceably. 'Seems she lets her hair down with you and Dale.'

'I *don't* get what's adventurous about wearing a deerstalker.' But Jackie's explanation had mollified her.

'I take it you won't be going to this.' Jackie handed Stella the gold-edged card. 'We ought to have a presence. I could twist Graham's arm again.'

Stella read the card. In a by-the-way voice, she said, 'I'll go.'

Chapter Sixty-Eight

November 2014

The first thing Jack noticed when he walked into Stella's living room were the pictures on the wall.

'Those are the Marianne North prints!' He couldn't disguise his astonishment.

'Tina left them to me in her will.' Stella sat in her armchair with Stanley on her lap.

'You don't like art.' Jack was grateful that Jackie wasn't there to hear his lack of tact. He sat on the sofa and took a sip of his hot milk with honey.

'I like these.' Stella's gaze rested on the *Flame Tree*. 'I was reading Mum's client report this morning. The Royal Botanic Gardens is our 764th commercial customer.'

'Right.' Jack gripped his mug. Stella had put art on her wall and now she was waxing about numbers.

'And 764 is the number of North's *Flame Tree* painting.' Stella was patient, although she had clearly expected him to get it immediately.

'So it is!' Jack felt a flood of happiness. Sometimes signs revealed their meaning in retrospect. This one signified a return to order.

In the bright centre light – Stella wasn't a fan of mood lighting – the orange flowers were vibrant. 'What is client 766, the number of the *Flowers of the Flame Tree*?'

'No idea.' Stella shrugged as if his question was peculiar.

Jack wouldn't test her limits of fanciful thinking further. 'I'm having botanical-illustration lessons!' he said. 'With Tina's friend Bella.'

'I'm not sure they were ever friends,' Stella remarked.

'Bella regrets being unkind to Tina. I told her, "Don't be hard on yourself." At any age we knock corners off each other and Tina Banks was tough. She thinks it's Karma that she's working for a botanist with the mind of a killer!' If one day Matthew Ayrton strayed beyond taxonomy to take an actual life, Jack would make sure that it wasn't Bella's. He didn't give all the credit for George Watson's suicide to Lucie May's visit. The 'extinction' of *watsonii* had killed him.

'Bella was the least of Tina's problems.' Stella was still looking at the North prints. 'Michelle Banks says she and Tina used to humour their dad to stop him being in a bad mood. When Tina was nine, he got worse.' She pulled a face. 'I thought that she worshipped him.'

'That's why she buried her feelings. You're not supposed to hate your dad. Rosamond Watson was last sighted in June 1976. The year Tina – and you – turned ten. He had murdered her and dug a grave for her body. In that heat the soil would have been impacted. No wonder he was in a bad mood.'

'It must have scared Banks when they found the body in the Great West Road. He was careful to cover his tracks with the Watson murder, but Watson and Banks killed the soldier on impulse. The ring on his finger was a crude diversion: the police weren't fooled.' Tweaking at Stanley's moustache, Stella sipped her tea. 'Someone could have told the police that Cliff Banks had lived at number twenty-five. When he visited the crater in the road, and talked to Lucie, he narrowly missed arousing her suspicion. Lucie's cross with herself for missing his comment about the man dossing in his mum's parlour,' Stella said.

'This case is full of minor errors with major consequences. I mistook Matthew Ayrton for George Watson. If I had confirmed Ayrton's identity before running with it, think what time we would have saved. It was just that he was a True ... he was strange.'

'You can't suspect every strange person you come across.' Stella was firm, evidently guessing that he did just that. 'I was distracted by Banks's grief for Tina. I now think that when he took me to the Ruined Arch that first time, he was checking on his "deposition site".'

'I'd bet he was obsessed with Rosamond Watson. I wouldn't be surprised if he often went to the Ruined Arch to "visit" her,' Jack said.

Stella threaded Stanley's ears between her fingers. 'In some ways Lucie solved this case. We gave her the evidence and she did the brainwork.'

'Lucie played her part, but we were a team,' Jack said. 'With practice we'll become better detectives. Actually Stella, I was going to tell you, those cuttings—'

Stella was following her train of thought. 'Dad always said keep an open mind. We constructed the case to fit Watson instead of letting the evidence speak for itself. If we had, it would have led us to Banks sooner.'

'Perhaps. Banks was arrogant: he couldn't keep away from the crater in the road and he would have been disappointed that his interview with Lucie wasn't in the newspaper, even if it risked discovery. True Hosts are like that.'

'Who?'

'True Hosts are psychopaths with no sense of "other". Banks fitted that profile.' Stanley was looking at him, but Jack avoided the dog's gimlet gaze. He attributed superhuman powers to the diminutive woolly poodle. With his pert ears, Stanley knew more than either of them.

'What are you starting with?' Stella asked.

'Sorry?' His mind on True Hosts, Jack was thrown.

'What plant will you draw?'

'A daisy. Bella was reluctant, she says that it looks a simple flower, but is complicated. I've loved daisies since I was a boy. They're in the

Compositae family, a core species in Kew Gardens. It's defined in Bentham and Hooker's *British Flora*. That was written in the nineteenth century, but it still holds true. The yellow centre is hundreds of small flowers; the white petals aren't petals, but ray florets with teeth. Daisies have no dispersal mechanism, the florets fall off…'

Stanley gave a vast yawn and, flexing his paws, flung himself on to his side, his back to Jack. 'Dandelions are in the Compositae family too – and lettuce! Plants are like us, different but sharing qualities. A cleaner and a train driver who solve crimes. You and me, Tina, Bella and Emily, none of us fit into an order.'

'Are you drawing from "dead material"?' Stella asked.

She'd paid no heed to his ruminations on taxonomy, but Jack felt absurd pleasure that Stella had recalled the term for specimens in Kew's Herbarium. 'I insisted. Bella says that reconstructing a dried plant is difficult for a beginner,' he said happily.

'Are your lessons one to one?'

'My driving shifts mean I can't get to her classes.' Despite himself, Jack wanted Stella to mind him spending time with Bella as much as he had minded her being with Cashman.

'Much better: you'll learn quicker.' Stella put her empty mug on the glass-topped coffee table. 'Once you've mastered the basics, would you do a drawing for here?' She waved a hand at the wall.

'They won't be like Marianne North's paintings. I'm using pen and ink as if they were for a botanist.' Stella constantly surprised him. 'It's for science rather than art.' He bit his tongue at the pomposity. 'They won't be as good as Bella's or Watson's.'

'I'd like it to show the sepals, petals, stigma lobes and how they're arranged in relation to each other. And the ray florets you mentioned, if there are any.' Stella was definite. 'It must tell the truth about the plant.' She lowered Stanley to the floor where, shaking himself, he stood looking bewildered by the gas fire.

'Wonder what Harry Roberts is doing now,' Stella said. 'Enjoying his freedom?'

'He might miss the routine of prison.' Jack was pleased that Stella seemed to be able to put Roberts's release behind her.

She got up. Jack drained his mug. Evidently time to go. He had hoped to stay longer.

Stella was keying her pass code into her mobile phone, her mind already elsewhere. He wondered if, despite what Jackie had told him, it was back on with Cashman. But instead of making a call, Stella picked up a black cylindrical object on a shelf in the alcove and pressed a button on its base. Jack was incredulous: Stella had a Bluetooth speaker.

'Tina left me this.' She pushed the coffee table to the wall and shoved back the armchair. She dragged the sofa to the window; too late, Jack tried to help. 'You might want to take off your coat in case you get hot.'

Jack kept his coat on regardless of temperature, but was unequal to Stella's decisive tone. He draped it over the back of the sofa.

'Here goes.' Stella stabbed at her phone. Jack jumped out of his skin as the guitar riff for David Bowie's 'Rebel Rebel' bounced off the walls.

'We're doing the foxtrot,' Stella shouted and grabbed his hands.

Keeping perfect time, Jack and Stella foxtrotted. In flowing movements, like Fred and Ginger, they glided round and around the living room. As he had weeks before when Stella had danced with Tina, Stanley pranced gleefully in their wake, uttering sharp barks in four-four time.

After half an hour during which the track – set on repeat – played many times, Stella stopped the music. She let go of Jack and returned to the armchair.

Jack flung himself on to the sofa and Stanley came and settled on his lap.

'We'll be the *best* there,' Stella announced.

'Best where?'

Stella replied as if the answer was obvious: 'When we dance together at the British Cleaning Council Ball.'

Acknowledgements

I had lots of support and advice in the writing of this novel.

Stephen Cassidy, retired Detective Chief Superintendent with the Metropolitan Police, was, as ever, helpful and committed. (Not least, Stephen demonstrated that it was possible for Martin Cashman to take the role of Senior Investigating Officer when promotion should have precluded him from heading a murder case.)

Frank Pacifico, Test Train Operator for the London Underground, has once again given me advice and information.

Any errors regarding police detection or driving on the London Underground are mine.

My thanks to Andrew Luck-Baker, Producer for the BBC Radio Science Unit, for putting me in touch with Adrian Washbourne, his colleague in the unit. Adrian produced the wonderful *Plants: Roots to Riches* broadcast on BBC Radio 4 in 2014, a key inspiration for this novel. His suggestions as to whom to talk with at Kew Gardens and his 'botanical gems' were invaluable.

Staff at the Royal Botanic Gardens at Kew were extremely generous with their time and knowledge.

Lucy Smith, Botanical Artist at Kew Gardens, talked to me in depth; she showed me specimens, the equipment she uses during the process and answered my many questions. My meetings with Lucy were inspiring and exciting. Examples of her skilled, informative and downright exquisite drawings feature in this book.

Thank you to Dr William Baker, Assistant Head of Comparative Plant and Fungal Biology; Richard H. Barley, Director of Horticulture, Learning and Operations; Tony Cave, Facilities Manager; and Gina Fullerlove, Head of Publications, for making time to answer my questions.

Twice, while having tea in the Herbarium's staffroom, Lucy Smith found other botanists to solve my fictional (but very real) issues. I was privileged to be treated to mini-botanical seminars by Dr Nicholas Hind, Research Leader, Identification & Naming (Americas); Dr Gwilym Lewis, Research Leader, Integrated Monography; and Dr Tim Utteridge, Head of Identification & Naming and Senior Research Leader (Asia).

Again, any botanical or cleaning errors are my responsibility.

I set this novel in Kew Gardens because I have spent special times there, as a child and as an adult. The Marianne North Gallery is a treat; North's paintings are rich and absorbing. I acknowledge a debt to that redoubtable artist and explorer.

The public spending cuts have hit the Hammersmith Archives; the resource is open fewer hours and has lost a dedicated space, although I enjoyed visiting it in the tiled splendour of Hammersmith Library. It does, however, have dedicated staff. My thanks to Anne-Marie Purcell for her guidance and research help.

I'm grateful to Emeritus Professor Jenny Bourne Taylor for her reading suggestions on Victorian London.

I have benefited from the unstinting support and advice of my partner, Melanie Lockett. Thanks also to Sandra Baker, Tasmin Barnett, Melissa Benn, Domenica de Rosa, Juliet Eve, Kay Heather, Nigel Heather, Lisa Holloway and Alysoun Tomkins.

A fulsome thank you to all at my agents, Georgina Capel Associates Ltd. Especially, as ever, to Philippa Brewster.

My editor Laura Palmer brings perception and sensitivity to a role already demanding skill. Huge thanks to everyone at Head of Zeus for their hard work and encouragement.

Turn the page for a preview of The Dog Walker, *the fifth in the Detective's Daughter series.*

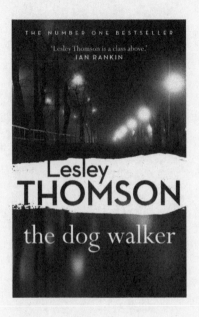

*A haunted house, a broken family
and a body that has never been found...*

January, 1987: Helen Honeysett, a young newlywed, sets off
for an evening run from her Thames-side cottage.
She never comes home.

January, 2016: Twenty-nine years later, Helen's body has never
been found. Her husband asks private detective Stella Darnell
to find out what happened all those years ago. But how can you
hunt a killer whose trail has long gone cold?

Prologue

January 1987

On a hot summer's day the Thames towpath between Kew Bridge and Mortlake Crematorium is stippled with sunlight spilling through willow fronds and shading oaks. Birdsong twitters above the rumble of a District line train crossing Kew Railway Bridge. Although in London, the leafy towpath resembles a pastoral idyll. Cyclists weave around strolling couples and families straggling with scooters and pushchairs.

In deepest darkest winter, lamplight from the north bank is absorbed in the black waters and only joggers and dog walkers brave the towpath.

On this night, a figure walked briskly beside the Thames. The sweeping arc of a torch picked out puddles in the mud. A dog nosing along the bank cocked its ears. The person – a man or a woman in baggy waterproofs – paused. There was the thud of footsteps. Emerging out of the gloom came a jogger accompanied by a dog. The dog walker moved to the river's edge to make way.

'Good evening!' the dog walker hailed the receding figure. No reply. The jogger's dog was circling on the path; he pooed and, kicking his back legs in triumph or relief, raced away.

Clear of trees, the path was stained by the orange of the light-polluted sky. The dog walker strode on along the path, seemingly unfazed by the slap of the river against the bank and rustling in bushes that might suggest a creeping assailant.

The arch of Chiswick Bridge was a tomb in which ice cracking beneath the dog walker's step was amplified.

It's the dog walker with their inquisitive pet straying off the beaten track who's likely to come upon the body of a murder victim. Bent on their daily routine, rarely does it occur to them that they themselves could be a victim.

'Oh, it's you!' The words hung in the wintry air.